IN JUPITER'S ATMOSPHERE

Their probe ship was in deep, the pressure about the same as two-hundred meters deep in Earth's waters, but with heavy radiation and a magnetic field that could unscrew the ratchets in a socket wrench. Faraday lifted his cup to his lips—

And something slammed into the side of the probe.

"Sheester's mother," his partner, Chippewa, swore.

"What was that?" Faraday managed. His cup went flying as he grabbed his controls and checked the emergency board. No hull breach; no oxygen tank leak or fuel-cell rupture. He looked up—

And caught his breath. Floating outside the thick Quad-plexi window, squarely in the center of the probe's external lights, was a two-kilometer-long solid object. It looked something like a cross between a dolphin and a very large, very fat manta ray with a pair of long tails trailing behind it.

And it wasn't alone . . .

BOOKS BY TIMOTHY ZAHN

*Denotes a Tor Book

MANTA'S GIFT

TIMOTHY ZAHN

TOR®

A TOM DOHERTY ASSOCIATES BOOK
NEW YORK

This is a work of fiction. All the characters and events portrayed in this book are either products of the author's imagination or are used fictitiously.

MANTA'S GIFT

Copyright © 2002 by Timothy Zahn

Edited by James Frenkel

A Tor Book
Published by Tom Doherty Associates, LLC
175 Fifth Avenue
New York, NY 10010

www.tor.com

Tor® is a registered trademark of Tom Doherty Associates, LLC.

ISBN: 0-812-58032-X
Library of Congress Catalog Card Number: 2002020467

First edition: September 2002
First mass market edition: August 2003

Printed in the United States of America

0 9 8 7 6 5 4 3 2 1

For my agent, Russell Galen,
who picked Achilles' other choice.

The *Skydiver* 7 had been filled with the soft sounds of beeping instruments and the ominous rumbling of the windstorm outside when Jakob Faraday had finally drifted off to sleep. Now, seven hours later, the storm was still raging against the probe's thick hull. But a new sound had also been added to the mix; a low but pervasive humming.

"Welcome back to the edge of the envelope," Scotto Chippawa greeted him as Faraday eased through the narrow doorway into the cramped control cabin. "Up a little early, aren't we?"

"Couldn't sleep," Faraday said, sliding into his chair beside the older man, listening to the faint whirring from his power-assist exoskeleton as he awkwardly strapped himself in. The gravity suit was a supreme nuisance, he'd long ago decided, and not nearly as user-friendly as its designers probably thought. But moving around down here in Jupiter's two and a half gees would be well-nigh impossible without it. "How are things going?"

"About the same as when you left," Chippawa said. "The wind's eased up a little, and the temperature's passed three hundred Kelvin on its way up again. Coffee?"

"Sure," Faraday said. "Double latte, easy on the cinnamon, with double cream."

"Right," Chippawa commented dryly. "Nearest latte's currently—" he peered at one of the displays "—a hundred thirty klicks straight up. Help yourself."

"Don't think I'm not tempted," Faraday grunted, swiveling his chair around to the zero-gee coffee pot in its heat-ing niche behind him. So they'd descended another forty kilometers since he'd toddled off to bed. That put them well into Jupiter's troposphere, not to mention within striking range of the record depth Keefer and O'Reilly had made it to last year. "I missed the rest of the cloud layers?"

"Slept right through them," Chippawa said cheerfully. "Don't worry, you'll get to see them again on the way up."

"Right," Faraday muttered, trying not to think about the hairline cracks the techs had found in Keefer and O'Reilly's probe after their dive. "I'll look forward to it."

He went through the unnecessarily complicated routine of drawing a cup of coffee from the zero-gee pot into his zero-gee mug. Another supreme nuisance, but one they also had no choice but to put up with. The Jovian atmosphere was about as calm and peaceful as one of the Five Hundred's budgeting sessions, and the pixel-pickers on Jupiter Prime got very upset when their glorified baby-sitters spilled coffee on expensive electronics.

Especially given the current funding battles the Jupiter Sector was having back on Earth. The Five Hundred, that oligarchy of the rich and powerful who effectively ran the Solar System, were constantly pushing humanity's boundaries outward, pressing on to new frontiers almost before the homesteading stakes had been driven into the ground of the last hard-fought conquest. With their attention now turned to new colonization efforts on Saturn's moons, Jupiter's interests and struggles were starting to get lost in the shuffle.

"By the way, Prime won't like it if they find out you shaved an hour off your sleep period," Chippawa commented. "They're very strict about the eight-hour rule."

"What was I supposed to do?" Faraday countered, sipping carefully at the brew. Fortunately, there wasn't a lot even Chippawa could do to ruin instant coffee. "Just lie there and stare at the ceiling?"

"Sure," Chippawa said with a power-assisted shrug. "That's what the rest of us do."

Faraday sniffed. "I guess I'm just too young and idealistic to sluff off that way when there's work to be done."

"Of course," Chippawa said. "I keep forgetting."

"It's that old-age thing," Faraday added soothingly. Chippawa was, after all, nearly fifty. "Memory always goes first."

"Yes, but at least I sleep well," Chippawa said pointedly.

Faraday grimaced. "It always feels like there's a sumo wrestler sitting on my chest whenever I lie down," he said. "I just can't sleep on these things."

"You'll get used to it," Chippawa assured him. "Somewhere around your fifth or sixth tether ride."

"If I last that long," Faraday said. "When did we pick up that humming noise?"

"About two hours ago," Chippawa said. "Prime thinks it's the wind hitting some sort of resonance with the tether."

Involuntarily, Faraday glanced up at the cabin ceiling. "Terrific," he said. "You ever hear of the Tacoma-Narrows Bridge?"

"I took the same physics courses you did," Chippawa reminded him. "Saw the same old vids, too. But this isn't that same kind of resonance."

"You hope," Faraday said, tapping a fingernail surreptitiously on the polished myrtlewood finger ring his mother had given him when he graduated from high school. Not that he was superstitious or anything; but the image of that bridge twisting and swinging in the breeze as the wind caught it just right, and eventually coming completely apart, had haunted him ever since he saw it. "They *will* keep an eye on it, I presume?"

"What, with two hundred million dollars' worth of equipment on the line?" Chippawa asked, waving around. "Not to mention you and me?"

"Right." Taking another sip, Faraday gave the status board a quick check. Outside temperature was still climbing, wind speed was manageable, atmospheric composition was still mostly hydrogen with a pinch each of helium and methane mixed in. Hull pressure . . .

He winced and looked away. They were already at

twenty bars, the equivalent of nearly two hundred meters below sea level on Earth.

Two hundred meters was nothing to an Earthbound bathyscaph, of course. But then, an Earthbound bathyscaph didn't also have to put up with heavy radiation and a magnetic field that could unscrew the ratchets on a socket wrench.

He'd seen the specs on the *Skydiver*'s design, fine-tuned somewhat since Keefer and O'Reilly had taken their plunge, and he knew how much pressure it could handle. Even so, the actual raw numbers still left his stomach feeling a little queasy. He lifted his cup to his lips—

And at that precise second, something slammed into the side of the probe.

"Sheester's Mother," Chippawa swore, grabbing for the stabilizer controls.

"What was that?" Faraday managed as his coffee tried to go down the wrong tube. Trained reflexes set in, sending his cup flying as he grabbed at his own controls and checked the emergency board. No hull breach; no oxygen tank or fuel-cell rupture; no hint of any other equipment malfunction.

"Sheester's Mother," Chippawa repeated, almost reverently this time. Faraday looked up—

And caught his breath. There, floating outside the thick Quadplexi window, squarely in the center of the probe's external lights, was a two-meter-long solid object. It looked something like a cross between a dolphin and a very large, very fat manta ray with a pair of long tails trailing behind it.

And as he watched, it rolled over and flapped away through the roiling atmosphere, its twin tails beating rhythmically at the air. A second later, two more of them swam into view around the sides of the probe and charged off after the first.

Slowly, Faraday turned to look at Chippawa. Chippawa was looking back at him.

Chippawa said it first. "I guess Keefer *wasn't* imagining things," he said, his voice studiously casual.

Faraday nodded, all the data from all of the manned and unmanned probes for all of the past twenty years flashing through his mind. There was no life on Jupiter. None. Zip, zero, nada. All the books, all the studies, all the experts agreed on that.

And all of them had ridiculed Keefer for what he'd claimed to have seen at the edge of his probe's lights . . .

"No," Faraday said. "I guess he wasn't."

Chippawa hunched his shoulders. The familiar whine of the servos in the suit seemed to get him back on track. "Well," he said briskly, keying for the radar section of their full-spectrum emscan sensors. "You'd better give Prime a full tie-in. I'll see what kind of track I can get on the things."

"Right," Faraday said, forcing his fingers to function. Whatever had swum past them had had the courtesy, or else the sheer clumsiness, to announce its presence with a loud knock on the hull.

Which could potentially be a very serious problem. The *Skydiver*'s hull was designed to handle immense but steady pressures, not the sharp impact of something solid ramming into it.

He keyed the tie-in first as Chippawa had instructed, giving the tether ship flying far above them full audio and visual access to what was happening inside the probe as well as the usual telemetry feed. Then, trying to ignore the feeling in the pit of his stomach, he activated the outside cameras and started a systematic examination of the hull.

Chippawa got to his finish line first. "Got 'em," he announced. "Four blips, moving off to starboard."

"I thought there were three of them," Faraday said absently, his own fingers pausing as the cameras located the impact point. It wasn't much, as impact points went; the dent was hardly even noticeable. But it *was* a dent.

And as he stared at the image he could swear he could see the marks of teeth . . .

"There must have been another one we didn't see," Chippawa said. "Wait a second. There are *five* of them out there. No; six. Sheester's Mother."

He shook his head. "It's a school of them," he said. "A whole double-clove-latte *school*. Like a pod of whales."

"Or piranha," Faraday said. "Take a look at this."

Chippawa glanced at the image on Faraday's display. "One of them bumped us," he said. "We knew that."

"Look closer," Faraday insisted. "I may be imagining things, but those look like teeth marks."

"You're imagining things," Chippawa declared. "Come on. Anything bigger than a puppy knows better than to chew on metal."

"Unless it's what they eat," Faraday countered crossly. Chippawa didn't have to dismiss his concerns quite so cavalierly.

"What, in the Jovian atmosphere?" Chippawa scoffed. "You think floating metal grows on trees around . . . oh, my God."

"What?" Faraday demanded, spinning around to his own emscan display.

And felt his skin prickling. There was a school of the fat mantas out there, all right. Maybe two dozen of them.

All of them clustered around two very large blips. Blips, if the radar could be believed, that were each the size of a nice little starter house in the suburbs.

Chippawa's comment on this development would undoubtedly have been a very interesting one. But he never got the chance to make it. Even as Faraday's brain registered the size of the newcomers, the probe lurched, the background humming hiccupping into a sudden twang. "What—?" Faraday yelped.

"Something hit the tether," Chippawa said. "There—look."

Faraday craned his neck. Another of the fat mantas was scooting along across the edge of the *Skydiver*'s light cone. Unlike the others, this one seemed to be trailing an expanding mist of bright yellow. "He didn't just hit the tether," he said, the bad feeling in his stomach getting suddenly worse. "He cut himself on it."

"Sure looks like it," Chippawa agreed as the manta vanished outside the range of their lights. "Better check it out." He reached for the camera control—

And suddenly the probe was slammed violently sideways.

Faraday grabbed at his board as his chair bounced down out from under him and then slammed hard up against his tailbone again. A stray thought caught oddly at the back of his mind; what had happened to his coffee cup and was it leaking on anything. There was a second jolt, this one from the other side, then a third that seemed to come from above. Something that looked like a gray wall studded with randomly placed dimples slid past bare centimeters from the Quadplexi. There was another slam from above, the worst one yet—

And with a horrible twisting of Faraday's stomach, his chair fell away from beneath him and didn't come back up. The tether to the ship above had been broken, and the probe was in free fall.

"Floats!" Chippawa snapped.

Faraday already had the safety cover wrenched up and out of the way. "Floats," he repeated, and pressed the button.

There was the *crack* of explosive bolts, and the moaning of the wind outside was joined by a violent hiss as the tanks of compressed helium began dumping their contents into the probe's rubber-raft pontoons. Faraday held his breath . . .

And then, with another horrible twisting of his stomach, the *Skydiver* rolled over onto its right side.

"Malfunction!" he barked, eyes darting to the error display as all his weight slammed down onto his ribs and his right armrest. The words flashed onto the screen in bright red—"Starboard tank's blocked," he reported tightly. A support slide unfurled from the right collar of his suit, moving into position along the side of his head to relieve the strain the change in attitude had put on his neck. "No helium's getting into the float."

"Must be water in the valve," Chippawa said grimly from his seat, now hanging directly above Faraday. "Firing secondary."

Faraday held his breath, straining his ears for the sound of hissing helium. But there was nothing.

And the error message was still glaring red at him.

"Secondary also malfunctioning," Chippawa reported. "Damn water must be in the line, not the valves. The expanding helium's frozen it into a solid plug."

And they were still going down. "Any way to get to it?" Faraday asked.

Chippawa shook his head, an abbreviated wobbling around his own suit's neck support. "Not from inside. It's bound to fix itself sooner or later—it's over three hundred Kelvin out there."

He clucked his teeth thoughtfully. "Question is, will it unfreeze in time to do us any good?"

Faraday's stomach felt ill, and not just from the deadly gravity. Already they were too deep for any chance of rescue from the tether ship. Now, they were drifting still deeper.

And as they did so, the rising atmospheric pressure would begin to compress their one working float, reducing its already inadequate buoyancy and making them fall still faster. After that, even if the other float fixed itself, the pressure of its helium tank wouldn't be enough to deploy it.

That was the physics of it. The cold reality of it was that he and Chippawa were dead.

They would be crushed to death. That would be the final end of it. The fragile walls of their capsule would shatter under the pressure from outside, shatter into a million pieces that would drive inward into their bodies like shrapnel.

And behind that shrapnel would come the full weight of Jupiter's atmosphere, squeezing in on them. Their blood vessels would explode; their bones would break; their skulls would shatter like empty eggshells. Crushed to death.

Crushed to death . . .

He looked up at his partner, expecting to see his same fear in the other's face.

But there was no fear there. Chippawa was concentrating on his board, apparently oblivious to the fate that was moving like a runaway monorail toward them.

And in that stretched-out instant of time, Faraday hated him. Hated the man's courage and professional calm. Hated his ability to ignore the fear and the danger.

Hated the twenty extra years of life Chippawa had experienced that Faraday would never have a chance to taste.

"Getting a reading," Chippawa called out over the wind. "Incoming. About eight meters long—roughly torpedo-shaped—"

"We're falling," Faraday all but screamed at him. So much for the luck of his wooden ring. He was about to die. They were both about to die. "What the hell does it matter—"

The sentence was choked off as his armrest again slammed hard into the side of his exoskeleton, the impact jarring his ribs. "What happened?" he demanded, eyes flickering over his instruments. No new error messages were showing.

"I don't know," Chippawa said. "It's—oh, boy."

Faraday looked up. And stopped breathing.

The slab of gray had returned. Only this time it had shifted around until an eye was visible.

Gazing steadily through the window at them.

Faraday stared back, the wind and the pressure and even the fact that he was a dead man suddenly fading into the background. The eye was big and very black, either with no pupil at all or else with all pupil. The kind of eye that would suck in every bit of radiation across a wide range of the electromagnetic spectrum, he realized, using every bit of light available to see in the gloom of Jupiter's deep atmosphere. There was a hint of polygonal faceting around the eye's edge, though it didn't seem to be an insect-type compound eye.

And like a textbook optical illusion that shifted from duck to rabbit and back to duck again, he couldn't decide whether the expression in the eye was one of interest, sympathy, or malevolence.

Or maybe that was just his imagination. Or his hopes.

Or his fears.

With an effort, he found his voice. "Should we wave?" he said.

"Unless you'd rather ask it to take us to their leader," Chippawa said. "Emscan's running . . . man, this thing's got one complicated internal structure."

"How complicated?" Faraday asked, starting to become interested in spite of himself.

"At least as complex as ours," Chippawa said. "I'd love to see the biochemistry of something that swims around in hydrogen and methane all day. You hear that?"

"Yes," Faraday said, frowning. It was a scraping sound, coming from somewhere beneath them.

"It's checking us out," Chippawa said. "Running a flipper or something along the hull."

"Is that why we've stopped falling?" Faraday asked. "It's holding us up?"

"Yes and no," Chippawa said, peering at the displays. "We *are* still going down, only not as fast."

"But it *is* intelligent," Faraday said, staring back at that unblinking eye. "And it's figured out that we are, too."

"Well, maybe," Chippawa said cautiously. "I'd definitely say it's curious. But then, so is a kitten."

"It *is* intelligent," Faraday insisted. "Something that big *has* to be."

"Yeah, well, as the cliché says, size doesn't really matter," Chippawa said with a grunt. "The last rhino I saw wasn't giving lectures on quark theory. Anyway, it may all be academic."

"What do you mean?" Faraday demanded. If the creature was intelligent, surely it realized they didn't belong here.

It could just carry them back up to the top of the atmosphere—

"One, we're still falling," Chippawa said. "That implies even with one float working we're too heavy for him to hold up. And two—"

He gestured to the emscan display. "We've got more company."

Faraday felt his mouth drop open. At eight meters long, the creature staring in at them was already pretty big. The suburban starter houses that the little guys had been clustering around had been even bigger.

But the two radar blips now moving up from below and to their right were another order of magnitude entirely. Like a pair of incoming grocery warehouses . . .

Abruptly, the armrest dropped out from under him again. He looked up, catching just a glimpse of their Peeping Tom as he scooted upward into the swirling air.

And the *Skydiver* was again falling free.

The seconds ticked by. A new set of creaks joined the howl of the wind outside, and a glance at the depth indicator showed they had officially beaten Keefer and O'Reilly's record.

They were also nearly to the theoretical pressure limit of their own hull. Not only were they about to die, he thought bitterly, but they were going to get to watch the countdown to that death.

Something flashed past the window, illuminated briefly by their exterior lights. "What was that?"

"One of our thirty-meter wonders," Chippawa said. "Got some pictures as he went past."

Lost in his own last thoughts, Faraday had forgotten all about the grocery-warehouse creatures that had chased off Dark Eye. "Anything good?" he asked, trying to force some interest.

"I'd say we've found the top of the food chain," Chippawa said. "Look at this—it's got a bunch of those mantaray things hanging onto its underside."

Like remoras on a shark, Faraday thought with a shiver.

Waiting to pick up the scraps from the big boy's kill. "So the smaller ones who ran past us were scouts or something?"

"Could be," Chippawa said. Something moved up into their lights from below—

And Faraday was slammed violently against his armrest as the *Skydiver* came to a sudden halt. For a few seconds he lay helplessly there, gazing at an incredibly lumpy brownish-gray surface outside the window. Then, with a sort of ponderous inevitability, the *Skydiver* rolled over into an upright position again.

"Have we hit bottom?" Faraday asked, knowing even before the words were out of his mouth that it was a stupid question. There was little if anything that could be called "bottom" on a gas-giant world like Jupiter. Somewhere below them there might be a rocky center or a supercompressed core of solid hydrogen, but the *Skydiver* would never survive long enough to get anywhere near that.

What had happened was obvious. Obvious, and frightening.

They had landed on top of Predator Number Two.

"We're still going down," Chippawa grunted. "These things must really be delicate. We're not *that* heavy, especially with one of the floats deployed."

"I guess we're heavy enough," Faraday said, rubbing the side of his neck as he gazed out the window.

His first impression, just before they'd hit, had been that the predator's skin was lumpy. Only now, as he had time to study it, did he realize just how incredibly lumpy it actually was.

The skin was covered with dozens of ridges and protrusions of various sizes and shapes, like a snowfield that had been whipped by the wind into odd drifts. Some of the lumps were low and flat, others long and narrow, sticking as far as eight or nine meters out from the surface. Like tree trunks, perhaps, whose branches had been stripped off.

No, he decided. Not like tree trunks. More like torpedoes or rockets pointed the wrong way on their launching pads.

Abruptly, he caught his breath. Like *torpedoes*? "Scotto . . ."

"What?" Chippawa asked.

"That lump out there," Faraday said slowly. "The tall one, dead center. What does it look like to you?"

"Like a lump," Chippawa said, a hint of impatience in his voice. "Give me a hint."

"Remember the fellow with the big eye?" Faraday said. "Wasn't he shaped like that?"

"Yes, but—" Chippawa broke off, leaning closer to the window. "But that's the same skin that's on everything else," he said. "The predator's skin. Isn't it?"

"Sure looks like it," Faraday agreed, his throat feeling raw. "As if the skin just grew up around one of them . . ."

For a long second he and Chippawa stared at each other. Then, in unison, they both turned back to their boards.

"Underside cameras have gone dark," Faraday announced tightly, his eyes flicking across those displays. "Forward ones . . . maybe the connections were knocked loose in the crash."

"Damn," Chippawa said. "Look at the window."

Faraday looked up. On the lower edge of the window, a brownish-gray sheet was slowly working its way up the Quadplexi.

"It's growing over us," Chippawa said, very quietly. "The skin is growing straight over us."

Faraday licked at dry lips. Tearing his eyes away from the window, he searched out the pressure sensors.

At least the news there wasn't any worse. "Underside pressure's holding steady," he said. "The skin isn't squeezing us any harder than the atmosphere is."

"Pretty small comfort, if you ask me," Chippawa said grimly. "Probably growing all the way up the hull. Whoops—main drive just shut back to standby. The whole ring, too. The skin must have rolled over all the proximity sensors at the same time."

Faraday grimaced. That was standard deep-atmosphere probe design: If there was something sitting right next to you, the computer wouldn't let you move that direction. Now, with something around all of them, the whole bank of drive engines had simply shut down. "Damn safety interlocks," he muttered.

"Well, it's not like we'd be able to go anywhere right now anyway," Chippawa pointed out, his voice far too reasonable for Faraday's taste. "Firing up the turboprops now would just snarl the blades. Wait a sec."

He bent suddenly over the controls. "Something?" Faraday asked hopefully.

"Just a thought," the other said. "If I can fine-tune the emscan a little, maybe we can see how thick the skin is over the other shipwrecks out there."

"Oh," Faraday said, feeling the flicker of hope fade away.

Still, now that Chippawa mentioned it, the view outside *did* rather look like a shipwreck scene. A dozen ships lying at the bottom of a murky ocean, with strange underwater seaweed growing up over all of them. "What do you want me to do?"

"Check the manual and see if there's any way you can boost power to the radio," Chippawa said. "If we can find a way to punch a signal through this soup, we can at least let Prime know about all this."

He smiled tightly. "I mean, we should at least let them know we're due some posthumous citations."

"Got it," Faraday said. He didn't smile back.

They worked in silence for what seemed like a long time. The only sounds in the cabin were the beeping of the instruments, the howling of the wind outside, and—at least for Faraday—the thudding of his own heart.

The window was almost completely covered by the time he finally gave up. "We're not going to get through," he said. "The atmosphere's just too thick. I can't even pick up their carrier; and if I can't hear them, they sure as hell can't hear us. Any luck there?"

"Possibly," Chippawa said. "The creature's skin in general is pretty thick, up to thirty centimeters in places. Definitely the same as the wrapping around the mummies out there, though that stuff's not nearly as thick. But *this* batch—"

"Wait a sec," Faraday interrupted him. *"Mummies?"*

"That's what the emscan shows," Chippawa said. "The big one, anyway. It has the same basic internal structure as the fellow who buzzed us."

"And that structure's intact? Faraday asked. "Not decayed or digested or anything?"

"Not that I can tell," Chippawa said. "That's point one for the good guys: At least we're not about to be eaten or absorbed alive. Point two is that the batch growing up around the *Skydiver* isn't nearly as thick or strong as the rest of it."

He nodded toward the window. "Which means that if the starboard helium line clears up soon enough, and if we're not too deep for the float to deploy, there's a chance we'll be able to punch our way out of here."

"Lot of ifs in that," Faraday pointed out doubtfully. An image floated to mind: a Golden Movie Age vid he and his brothers used to watch called *Pinocchio*, where the heroes had been trapped in the stomach of a giant whale. How had they gotten out of that? He couldn't remember. "Assuming all the rest of it, how do you propose we do that?"

The last remaining sliver of outside view vanished beneath the sheet of brown-gray. "I don't know," Chippawa admitted. "Maybe an electric discharge, if we can boost the voltage high enough and figure out how to deliver it. Or maybe some acid from one of our fuel cells will do something."

"Or maybe a fire," Faraday said. That was it; they'd made a fire in the whale's stomach. "Don't forget, most of that soup out there is pure hydrogen. If we can supply enough oxygen from our own air supply, we should be able to get a nice little fire going."

Chippawa whistled softly. "And maybe fry ourselves in the process," he pointed out. "But it's better than doing nothing. Let's figure out how much we can spare—"

He broke off as, once again, the chairs dropped out from

under them. "We're heading down again," Faraday said tightly, looking over at the depth indicator.

The indicator, contrary to what his stomach and inner ear were telling him, was holding perfectly steady. "What the—? Oh. Right."

"It's the pressure of the skin around us," Chippawa said. "Fouls up the readings. Still, at least that means we're not going to get flattened like roadkill."

"It also means that if we wait too long to punch our way out, we won't be able to do so," Faraday countered. "Not much point in breaking free if you're only going to get squashed a millisecond later."

Chippawa made a face. "Yeah. Point."

"And of course, with the depth meter off-track, we won't even know when we've passed that no-chance depth," Faraday added. "We don't even know how deep we are right now."

"Maybe I can do something with the emscan," Chippawa said. "You get busy and figure out how much oxygen we can spare."

Once again silence descended on the probe. This time, muffled in their freshly grown cocoon, there wasn't even the wailing of the wind outside to keep them company.

Wrapped up in his work and his thoughts, Faraday only gradually became aware of the new sound rumbling beneath his feet.

He paused, listening. In some ways it reminded him of the howling of a restless wind, rising and falling with no discernible pattern. But the tone was deeper and more varied than simple wind.

And as he listened, he could swear he could hear words in it . . .

"Scotto?" he murmured.

"Yeah," the other said quietly. "I'm not sure, but I think they're talking to each other."

Something with lots of cold feet began to run up and down Faraday's back. *"They?"*

Chippawa gestured toward the emscan display. "They."

The image was vague and indistinct, like looking through a thick layer of gelatin. But it was clear enough. There were at least twenty more of the lumpy creatures out there, some of them swimming around, others more or less floating in place. Straining his ears, Faraday discovered he could hear more of the windlike rumbles coming from outside, at least when the one they were attached to wasn't making any noise of its own.

It was like a damn roundtable discussion. And judging from the direction all of them out there seemed to be facing, he could guess the topic of conversation.

The *Skydiver*.

With an effort, he found his voice. "So *these* are the intelligent ones? Not the torpedoes?"

"Maybe they're all intelligent," Chippawa said. "Maybe none of them are. Maybe we've just stumbled on some kind of group mating dance or something."

There was a whisper of feeling in Faraday's inner ear. "We're moving," he said tightly, trying to sort out the sensations. On the emscan, the other images were dropping below them. "Moving . . . *up*?"

"I think so," Chippawa said, studying the instruments. "Yes, confirm that. We're moving up."

"What about the starboard float?"

Chippawa gestured helplessly. "No way to tell with the float held in the way it is. We won't know until we punch through whether it'll deploy or not."

"I was afraid of that," Faraday said. "It looks like we've got enough spare oxygen to make about a two-minute burn if we can dole it out slowly enough."

"And if we can't?"

Faraday felt his lip twitch. "Then we get a pretty decent explosion."

"I hate these either-ors," Chippawa grumbled. "Well, we're still going up."

"What do you think?" Faraday asked cautiously, not daring to jinx this by putting his hopes into words. "Act Two of your group mating dance?"

"He's not taking us up just to eat us," Chippawa said thoughtfully. "He could have done that down below. He's presumably now shown us to all the rest of his buddies, unless he's planning to go on tour around the whole planet. If we're still going up in ten minutes, I'd have to say he's trying to return us to the upper atmosphere."

And there it was, out in the open for everyone to see. Surreptitiously, Faraday tapped on his wooden ring. "I wonder how we'll go down in their history," he murmured. "The strange beings in the shining sphere who fell from the sky?"

Chippawa snorted. "I'd settle for being the pet frog his mother made him put back in the creek," he said. "Forget the dignity and just cross your fingers."

Ten minutes later, they were still going up. Fifteen minutes after that, Faraday had the oxygen tanks rigged for a slow leak. Or so he hoped, anyway.

And after that, it was just a matter of sitting back and waiting.

"Looks like more of the torpedo-shapes out there," Faraday suggested, peering at the emscan display. "We must be back up to where we ran into Dark Eye."

"You couldn't prove it by these pressure readings," Chippawa said, shaking his head. "You know, it occurs to me that if that skin layer out there is keeping up this kind of pressure, we may be completely enclosed. I mean, *completely* enclosed."

"Makes sense," Faraday agreed. "That would be why we weren't crushed while he was showing us off to his buddies."

"You miss my point," Chippawa said. "I'm wondering if we're even going to be able to get to the hydrogen outside."

Faraday opened his mouth, closed it again. "Oh, boy," he muttered.

"Maybe we can poke a hole with something," Chippawa went on. "We've got a couple of sampling probes we haven't extended, though they probably aren't strong enough. The pulse transmitter laser might do the job."

"Except that it's nowhere near the oxygen valve," Faraday pointed out. "Unless we can inflate the starboard float enough to push the skin back—"

He broke off as a muffled *thud* came from somewhere above them. "What was that?" he demanded, trying to penetrate the haze on the emscan display. "Another of those little guys?"

"Looks like it," Chippawa said. "Don't they *ever* watch where they're going?"

An instant later they were thrown against their restraints as the *Skydiver* was rocked violently by a quick one-two-three set of jolts. "Incoming!" Chippawa snapped. "Three of the big torpedoes."

The probe was slammed again to the side. "Depth gauge just twitched," Faraday called as the sudden change of reading caught his eye. "Settling down . . ."

"They've broken through the skin," Chippawa said. "They're tearing through the skin around us."

There was another thud, and this time Faraday could hear a distinct tearing noise along with it. "Tearing, nothing," he said. "They're *eating* their way through!"

"So what were you expecting, a can opener?" Chippawa retorted. "This is going to work, Jake."

"Like hell it is," Faraday bit out, grabbing for the lever he'd rigged up for the oxygen release. "Let's give 'em a hotfoot."

"No, wait," Chippawa said. "Don't you understand? They're eating the skin right off us. All we have to do is wait and we'll be free."

"Until they try taking a bite out of the *Skydiver*," Faraday shot back. "We're open to the hydrogen. I say we go for it."

"And I say we wait," Chippawa said firmly. "Come on—they can't bite through the hull."

"The mantas left tooth marks on it," Faraday countered. "These things are four times bigger. You think they'll have any trouble biting straight through?"

"We have to risk it," Chippawa insisted. "Just calm down—"

"Like hell," Faraday snarled. Setting his teeth together, he pushed the lever.

A wave of blue-green fire rolled across the window. The *Skydiver* shuddered violently, and a bone-chilling roar seemed to fill the cabin. "Jake!" Chippawa shouted. "What the *hell*—?"

"It worked," Faraday cut him off, jabbing a finger at the window. "Look—it worked!"

Chippawa inhaled sharply as the brown-gray skin seemed to melt away from the window, accompanied by a multiple splash of yellow liquid.

And a second later, accompanied by the sound of hissing helium, the probe jerked free from its prison. "Float deployed," Faraday shouted. "We're heading up."

"I've got the tether ship's carrier signal," Chippawa said. "They're on their way."

Something bumped Faraday's foot. He looked down, to find that his zero-gee coffee mug had come out of hiding and had rolled up against it.

He took a deep breath, let it out in a long, shuddering sigh. For the first time since the tether broke, he realized he was soaked with sweat. "It's over," he said quietly. "It's finally over."

But it wasn't over. In fact, it had just begun.

ONE

The doctors had been and gone, the neurologists had been and gone, and the biotron people had been and gone. For the first time in days, it seemed, Matthew Raimey was alone.

All alone.

He lay on his back and stared up at the ceiling. That was about all he could do, really, lie there and stare at the ceiling. The clean, soothing, pastel blue–colored damned hospital ceiling.

Like the ceilings he would now be staring at for the rest of his life.

It was quiet at this end of the hospital. The kind of quiet that made it easy to think. To think, and to remember.

Mostly, he found himself remembering the accident.

It replayed itself over and over against the pastel blue background, in exquisite and painful detail. The little squeaks and crunches of his skis as they slid lightly over the packed snow. The icy wind whipping at his ears and forehead and freezing the edges of his nostrils. The sharp aroma of the pine trees, mixed with a hint of drifting smoke from the lodge below. The familiar tension in his bent knees as he rode the crests and smoothed out the bumps of the mountain. Brianna's clear soprano voice behind him as she laughed and chattered and threatened to zoom past him. The tiny mound of snow that had caught the tip of his left ski and spun him a few degrees off course.

The giant Douglas fir that had loomed suddenly in his path.

He'd tried very hard to dodge that tree. Used every bit of his skill and the precious quarter-second of time he had to make sure he didn't slam into it. And to his rather smug satisfaction at the time, he had succeeded.

He shouldn't have tried. He wished desperately now that he hadn't. He should have just hit the tree, accepted whatever broken ribs it would have cost him, and been done with it.

But he had been too clever for that. Too clever and too skillful and too arrogant. Besides, Brianna had been right there behind him, with Alan and Bobbi somewhere behind her. He would have looked like an idiot, running into a tree like an amateur. Especially after having bragged about how close he could ski to the edge of the run without getting into trouble.

He'd avoided the tree just fine. But he hadn't managed to avoid the edge of the small bush beside it.

He could still feel the exhilarating sensation of spinning through the air. It had been like a carnival ride, exciting and mind-spinning, with that faint tinge of fear that gave zest to all the best carnival rides. After all, he was twenty-two years and seven months old, poised to graduate from college with his whole life stretching out like infinity in front of him. He was invincible, and invulnerable, and alive.

He could remember hearing Brianna afterward trying frantically to describe to the paramedics what had happened. She'd done a pretty poor job of it, too. She couldn't even tell them how many times he'd spun around in the air.

He could have told them. He knew. One and a half times. Exactly.

The ride had come to an end with the suddenness of a coaster braking. Oddly enough, there hadn't been any pain. Just that single muffled *crack* from somewhere behind his ear.

And then he'd been lying on his back in the snow, cold air on his cheeks and the unpleasant sensation of icy water seeping through his scarf onto his neck. Staring up at the overcast sky, just like he was staring now at the pastel blue ceiling.

Unable to move his arms and legs. Unable to even feel them.

For a while Brianna's face had blocked out some of the sky. He could visualize her face in front of him now, wisps of her brown hair twitching restlessly in the wind around the edge of her bright red ski cap, the smooth skin of her forehead stressed and wrinkled. Her wide, sensuous mouth had been twisted into something ugly by her fear, her deep brown eyes squinting in agony of her own as tears ran down her cheeks and dripped onto his. She'd cried and gasped and pleaded with him over and over to be all right.

As if he'd had any choice in the matter.

And then the paramedics had come. None of them had cried or gasped or pleaded. But their foreheads had been wrinkled, too, as they eased him onto the rescue sled.

Alan and Bobbi had been in twice to see him since his arrival at the hospital. Mostly they'd smiled their false smiles, talked loudly with false cheer, and muttered platitudes with false hope. Each time they'd made their escape as quickly as they could.

He hadn't seen Brianna at all. He'd thought about her a lot during the long, silent hours; pictured her smiling face, her easy laughter and spontaneity, her quick and unjudgmental acceptance of everyone and everything that came her way. He'd wished desperately that she would come by and brighten his darkening existence, at least for a little while.

But she hadn't, and he doubted now that she ever would. Brianna was the outdoors type, heavily into sports and hiking and fresh air and sunshine.

A girl like that had no time for a cripple.

There was a tap on his open door. "Mr. Raimey?"

It was a man's voice, unfamiliar to him. Raimey's neck still worked; he could have turned his head to see who it was. He didn't bother. "Doctor, biotron whiz, or chaplain?" he asked shortly.

Not that it mattered. None of them could help him anyway. All that mattered was that it wasn't Brianna.

The voice didn't answer. He heard soft footsteps, and then a face loomed over him, interfering with his view of the ceiling. An older face, he saw from the wrinkles and the gray salting in the man's otherwise dark hair. Somewhere around fifty, probably.

Fifty years old, and walking casually around without a care in the universe. Raimey would have hated him if he'd had any emotional energy left to hate with.

"Mr. Raimey, my name is Jakob Faraday," the man said. "I'm with SkyLight International."

SkyLight International: the private company that effectively ran the bulk of the Solar System's space travel under contract to the Five Hundred. He could vaguely remember studying the setup briefly in one of his political economics courses. "Is that supposed to impress me?" he asked.

"I'm not here to be impressive," Faraday said mildly. "I'm here to talk to you about an opportunity."

Raimey snorted. "Forget it."

"Forget what?" Faraday asked.

"Your so-called opportunity," Raimey shot back. "I read the newsnets. You want me for that—what's it called—that alpha-link stuff you're playing with. Forget it. I'm not going to spend the rest of my life wired up in a lab somewhere seeing if you can run a space barge off my brain."

"Ah," Faraday said, nodding. "You have other plans, then?"

The flash of anger vanished like dust scattered on a pond. "Go away," he muttered. "Just get lost. Okay?"

"I had a word with your doctors," Faraday said, as casually as if he were discussing the weather. He showed no signs of getting lost. "They seem reasonably optimistic about your chances."

"Oh, really?" Raimey bit out. "Which doctors were *you* talking to? *Mine* say I'm a cripple." It was the first time since the accident he'd spoken the word aloud. The sound of it was terrifying. "I'm paralyzed from the neck down. They can't repair it, they can't transplant into it, and there's too much damage for forced regrowth."

"There are always neural prosthetics," Faraday pointed out. "They're pretty good these days."

Raimey turned his head away. Neural prosthetics. Lumpy protuberances sticking out of his neck that would let him lurch around like Frankenstein's monster and manage to grip a spoon after a few months of practice. Even then, there was no guarantee he'd be able to hit his mouth with it.

And just enough of a sense of touch to let him know if he was walking on broken glass or sticking his hand in boiling water. Like being wrapped all over in a centimeter of velvet.

All over. Those special nights he'd had with Brianna, and Tiffany before her, and Jane before her, had been the last of that sort he would ever have.

Ever.

"Actually, I didn't come here to offer you test-dummy work," Faraday said. "I came to see if you'd like a chance for a life again."

"Really," Raimey growled. "And what'll this miracle cost? My immortal soul?"

"No," Faraday said. "Just your very mortal body."

Raimey turned his head back around, prepared to say something truly withering.

But Faraday wasn't smiling, or grinning, or leering. The man was deadly serious.

Or else he was just plain flat-out insane. "What are you talking about?" Raimey demanded cautiously.

The other didn't move a muscle, but Raimey had the sudden impression of a man settling in for the long run. Whatever angle he was working here, he figured he'd found his pigeon. And a captive audience, to boot.

And as curiosity and annoyance began to replace some of his self-pity, Raimey realized suddenly there was something familiar about Faraday's face. Something very familiar . . .

"Tell me, Mr. Raimey," Faraday said, "what did you plan to do after college?"

Automatically, Raimey tried to shrug. The muscles didn't even twitch. "What every other twenty-two-year-old plans to do," he said, hearing the bitterness in his voice. "Make a life for myself."

"And a name, too?" Faraday suggested. "To excel in your chosen field? To be the best, or the brightest, or the most respected?" He paused, just slightly. "Or perhaps even the first?"

Raimey felt his forehead wrinkle. "Let's cut through the donut glaze, all right? What's this all about?"

"As I said, an opportunity," Faraday said, resting his hand on the edge of the sensor railing. A polished wooden ring glinted subtly on his finger, Raimey noticed. Unusual jewelry. "Tell me, what do you know about the Qanska?"

The Qanska? "They're giant manta ray–shaped things that swim around in Jupiter's atmosphere," Raimey said, frowning. "We made contact with them about twenty years ago and have been talking ever since. There've been a couple of tries at trade agreements, but no one's ever figured out anything they could have that we might want. . . ."

He trailed off as Faraday's face suddenly clicked. The chapter on the Qanska, and Balrushka's mule-headed but failed attempts to work out a trade deal. "You're Jakob Faraday," he breathed. "*The* Jakob Faraday."

"Of the tether-probe team of Chippawa and Faraday," Faraday agreed, a slight smile briefly touching the corners of his mouth. "First men ever to make contact with the Qanska."

The smile turned into an ironic twitch of the lip. "Such as it was."

"They cut your tether," Raimey said, trying hard to remember the details. Balrushka and his trade negotiations had been the real point of that chapter, with Chippawa and Faraday more a sidebar than anything else. "One of the

Qanskan young ran into it, and one of the predators—"

"A Vuuka."

"Right—a Vuuka chewed through it," Raimey said. "Then one of the older Qanska caught you or something. They held a meeting, and decided to send you back up."

"Not bad," Faraday said. "You remember all the essentials, anyway. Now, let's try a real test. Do you remember the name of the man who finally cracked the Qanskan language code? Or the name of the two women who compiled the first English/Qanska tonal dictionary?"

Raimey made a face. "You must be joking. Of course not."

"Which is exactly my point," Faraday said. "No one remembers them, at least no one in the general public. But they were obviously highly important to history."

He smiled again, self-deprecatingly this time. "Far more important than Scotto and I were, to be perfectly honest. Just as the men who translated the First Immigrants' languages were more important to the history of the Americas than Christopher Columbus was. But everyone remembers Columbus and not them. Why? Because he was the first."

"Fine," Raimey said. "I agree; first is good. Now tell me the rest of it."

Faraday pursed his lips. "The Qanska have made us an offer," he said. "We believe it would be possible for a human to . . . well, to put it bluntly, to become a Qanska."

Raimey played the words over again in his mind, just to see if he'd actually heard them right. "And how exactly would this miracle of rebirth happen?" he asked.

"Actually, in exactly that way," Faraday said. "The human volunteer would be inserted into the womb of a pregnant female Qanska, where he would be partially absorbed into the fetus and then 'born' into a Qanskan body."

"What about physiology conflicts?" Raimey asked, the very outrageousness of the idea somehow allowing him to discuss it calmly. Surely Faraday wasn't serious about this. "Qanskan biochemistry can't possibly be compatible with ours."

"It's not," Faraday conceded. "The volunteer would start out as something of a hybrid: a human brain and mostly artificial spinal cord melded into a Qanskan body. There would also be a custom-made system of bioengineered organs that would synthesize nutrients from the Jovian atmosphere to support that part. Over time, the human elements would be replaced atom by atom, cell by cell, with the Qanskan equivalents, much the same way as wood petrification occurs. At that point the nutrient organs would atrophy, and the volunteer would be a true Qanska, only with his original human personality and memories."

"And how long exactly do they expect this petrification to take?" Raimey asked with a touch of sarcasm. "A thousand years? Ten thousand? Most of the bioengineered organs I've ever heard of have about the shelf life of fresh fruit."

"Oh, they're a bit better than that," Faraday assured him. "Especially state-of-the-art military versions."

Raimey frowned. "Are you saying this would be a Sol/Guard project?"

"Not at all," Faraday assured him. "It would be supported by both Sol/Guard and SkyLight, of course, but it would be under the direct control of the Five Hundred."

"So rich politicians instead of soldiers," Raimey said. "Big improvement. You haven't answered my question."

"How long the complete transformation would take?" Faraday shrugged. "We don't have a precise number yet, of course. But from the tissue and animal experiments we've run, our best guess is between eight and twenty months. Sometime during the Qanskan childhood stage, and well within the shelf life of your life-support system."

Raimey stared at him, a sudden tightness squeezing at his throat. "You're serious about this," he said.

"Deadly serious," Faraday assured him, his eyes glittering. "We have a chance—*you* have a chance—to do something no one else has ever done before. You can step into a brand-new culture, an alien culture, in a way no human being has ever done before. You'll be able to join with a new race, and learn about it from the inside. Think of what they might be able to teach us about philosophy, or social interaction, or biochemistry. The knowledge you gain and send back could influence mankind's perceptions and behavior for generations to come."

He gave Raimey a tight smile. "And as for *you*, your name would be set alongside those of Marco Polo and Columbus and Neil Armstrong. Forever."

"Yeah," Raimey said. "And all it'll cost is everything I've ever had or known or been."

Faraday shrugged fractionally. "How much of that do you have left now?"

"I have a lot left," Raimey snarled. "I still have a career, you know. Or I will, once I graduate. All you need for a job in business structuring is a computer, an office, and a brain."

"Is that what you want?" Faraday asked quietly. "To work all day, alone, in an office? And then to go home to an empty apartment with nothing but caretaker machines to keep you company?"

"Who says I won't get married?" Raimey countered.

Faraday lifted his eyebrows. Just slightly, but enough.

"And maybe they'll find a cure," Raimey muttered. "Maybe they'll be able to . . ."

"Give you back your life?" Faraday asked.

Raimey closed his eyes, feeling tears welling up in them. The last thing he wanted was for this man to see him crying. But there was no way for him to wipe back the tears.

"This is a rare gift the Qanska are offering you, Matthew," Faraday's voice said, soft and earnest. "On Jupiter you'll be able to swim and play and be with others. Yes, they're aliens; but in many ways their personalities are very similar to ours. You'll have friends, and companions, maybe even a family. All the things you'll miss out on here."

"What makes you think I won't be crippled in that body, too?" Raimey murmured.

"You won't," Faraday assured him. "For starters, you'll

have that artificial spinal cord, with no tissue-rejection problems like you have with your current body. On top of that, Qanskan physiology has a remarkable capability for regeneration, which should complete the healing process. The data you collect on that alone may help hundreds of people who find themselves in the same situation you're in right now."

Raimey stared up at the ceiling. "And what's my profit in this?"

He looked back at Faraday in time to see the other frown. "What do you mean, profit?"

"I mean profit," Raimey said. "I'm a business student, remember? Profit, loss; inflow, outflow; pluses, minuses—"

"Yes, I remember," Faraday cut him off. "And I just said you could have a real life again. Isn't that enough profit for you?"

"All deals sound good when they're pitched," Raimey countered. "Let's hear some specifics. You can start with Qanskan life expectancy."

For a moment Faraday just gazed down at him. Possibly, Raimey thought, reevaluating his choice of who to make this offer to. "Assuming you survive childhood," he said, almost grudgingly, "you'll have about another eight years. Maybe nine."

Raimey felt his breath catch in his throat. "Eight years? That's all?"

"That's all." Faraday paused. "Eight *Jovian* years, of course. Earth equivalent would be ninety-six."

Raimey smiled sardonically. "Cute," he said. "Standard salesman's tactic: Make it sound bad, then move in with the soother. Hoping I won't even notice that my life expectancy right now is ten years longer than that. *Earth* years, that is."

Faraday shook his head. "Read the stats," he advised quietly. "You're a quadriplegic now, with heightened susceptibility to all sorts of diseases and accidents. Your life expectancy from this moment on is another thirty years, max. Probably less. Become a Qanska, and you can triple it."

He lifted his eyebrows again. "Put *that* in your profit column."

Raimey turned his head away again. It was tempting. God help him, this whole insane idea was actually tempting. To be able to move again, even if it *was* in an alien body

To be able to live again.

"I'll think about it," he told Faraday, not looking back at the other.

"Take your time," Faraday said. There was the sound of footsteps, and the beep of a business card being swiped across Raimey's hospital room phone. "My number's in the phone," he added. "Call me any time."

"Don't hold your breath."

"Good-bye, Mr. Raimey," Faraday said.

More footsteps, out the door and fading down the corridor, and he was gone.

"Yeah," Raimey murmured to himself. "Good-bye."

That was the crux of the whole thing, wasn't it? *Good-bye.* Good-bye to everything he'd ever known.

But then, to be brutally honest, how much of it was actually left anyway?

It was three-thirty in the morning, with the silence of a nighttime hospital room pressing in around him, when he finally gave up.

TWO

The Contact Room, as it had been dubbed, seemed very quiet as Faraday passed through the security door and stepped inside. Quiet, but with the sense of a coiled spring about it.

Or maybe the coiled spring feeling was just him.

For a minute he stood at the doorway, running an eye over the semicircle of equipment consoles and the backs of the four young people currently manning them. As far as he could tell from here, it all matched the design schematics they'd shown him back on Earth.

Which, if true, would be nice for a change. SkyLight had always had a bad tendency to change perfectly good plans for no better reason than what seemed to be the unscheduled whims of the people at boardroom level.

But then, this operation was hardly SkyLight's exclusive baby. Not with what was at stake. This was squarely in the hands of the Five Hundred, all the way.

And though it hadn't been stated in so many words, Faraday had no doubt that, sooner or later, someone from the Five Hundred would come to Jupiter to watch over his shoulder.

Or that someone was possibly already here, he amended his musings as he looked at the command chair and console to his left. A tall, incredibly blond young man was sitting there, peering intently at the row of displays rising up over the heads of the seated techs.

Delicately, Faraday cleared his throat. The man looked over, and instantly bounded up out of his seat. "Colonel

Faraday," he all but gasped. "I'm sorry, sir—I wasn't expecting you so soon."

"That's all right," Faraday assured him. "And you are . . . ?"

"Albrecht Hesse, Colonel," Hesse said, offering his hand. "Council representative on Project Changeling. Welcome back to Jupiter Prime."

"Thank you," Faraday said, squeezing the proffered hand once and then releasing it. Not merely from the General Chamber of the Five Hundred, which held the public debates and made the official media pronouncements, but from the Supreme Mediation Council itself, where the *real* horse-trading and power decisions were made. Earth was taking Changeling very seriously indeed. "It's good to be back."

"I understand this is your first trip here since retiring from active duty," Hesse went on. "I think you'll find quite a bit has changed."

"Most of this wing is new, certainly," Faraday commented, nodding around him. "We only had the one rotating section when I left."

"That's right," Hesse said. "I think you'll find that having the second wing in counterrotation to the first has added tremendously to the station's stability. A word of warning, though: You'll need to watch yourself the first time you make the transition between them. If you don't pause long enough in the connecting mid-corridor, your inner ear can get very confused when you start turning it the opposite direction."

"I'll keep that in mind," Faraday said. It was marginally insulting advice, certainly considering how much of Faraday's life had been spent in space. Either Hesse was trying to establish the proper pecking order—with himself at the top—or else he was simply rambling as he desperately tried to find something to say to a living legend.

There might be an easy way to tell which it was. "You seem to have your people well on top of things," he commented, gesturing at the control board.

"*Your* people, sir," Hesse corrected hastily and firmly. "I'm strictly an observer here. And yes, they're ready."

"Good," Faraday said. So it was indeed number two: the Living Legend Syndrome. Slightly embarrassing, but after two decades he'd learned how to deal with that. Time and familiarity, he knew, should quietly put it to rest.

Time they would certainly have plenty of. And given the cramped quarters, familiarity wasn't likely to be a problem, either.

"Let me introduce you to the Alpha Shift team," Hesse went on, gesturing to the large, dark-haired man on the far left. "This is Everette Beach, communications specialist. He'll handle all the mechanics of our contacts with Mr. Raimey. He's also our expert on understanding Qanskan tonals."

"Colonel," Beach said, glancing away from his console long enough to give Faraday an abbreviated wave.

Hesse shifted his pointing finger to a short woman who looked as if she might come up to Beach's shoulder if he was willing to slouch a little. "Jen McCollum is our biology and xenobiology expert. Anything you want to know about Qanskan physiology, she can tell you."

"Or at least I can tell you what we *know* about Qanskan physiology," McCollum added over her shoulder. "There are a lot of blank spots that still need to be filled in."

"But you *can* extrapolate?" Faraday asked.

"You mean make stuff up on the fly?" McCollum asked blandly. "Sure. No problem."

Faraday smiled to himself. Young tech and science types, their heads still mostly in academia's clouds and thus mostly immune to Living Legend Syndrome. That would be nice for a change.

"That one's Tom Milligan," Hesse continued with the next in line, a man slightly shorter and less bulky than Beach, with stringy hair and a rather half-hearted goatee. "He'll be handling the sensors and the various deep-atmosphere probes we'll be using to keep track of him.

He's also our resident expert in physics, should we need something esoteric from that field."

He gestured to the fourth tech. "And finally, this is Hans Sprenkle, our psychologist."

Faraday frowned. No one had said anything to him about a psychologist. "Is the Council expecting us to go crazy out here?"

"Past tense, with this group," Sprenkle said cheerfully. He was built to the same scale as the other two men, though with a neatly trimmed moustache instead of Milligan's goatee. "My humble opinion, of course."

"I didn't know shrinks' opinions were *ever* humble," Beach commented from the other end of the control semi-circle.

"You haven't read any of the retractions in the professional journals," Sprenkle countered dryly. "It's amazing how low some people can grovel while still keeping their noses in the air."

"Dr. Sprenkle's also in charge of keeping track of the weather on Jupiter," Hesse jumped back in, sounding slightly embarrassed. "There are a lot of atmospheric storms—"

"Mr. Hesse?" Milligan spoke up.

"Yes?" Hesse asked, frowning at the interruption.

"I'll bet the colonel probably remembers that," Milligan offered.

Hesse reddened. "Yes, of course," he murmured. "Thank you, Mr. Milligan."

"Any time," Milligan said, turning back to his board. Not only was this group not impressed by living legends, Faraday decided, but they weren't overly impressed by authority of any kind. "Interesting combination of credentials, Dr. Sprenkle," he said. "Psychology and meteorology don't seem an obvious pairing."

"Actually, the meteorology started as a hobby," Sprenkle said. "But it sure came in handy when I was applying for this position."

"As you see, we don't have a lot of room in here," Hesse

pointed out. "Even with the second wing, floor space on Prime is hard to come by. We thought it would be useful if our people could double up on their areas of expertise wherever possible."

"Sounds reasonable enough," Faraday said. "Are Beta and Gamma Shifts equally talented?"

"Ha," Milligan said under his breath. "Rank amateurs, all of them."

"Hardly more than kids, either," McCollum put in.

"All right, that's enough," Hesse said tartly, sounding even more embarrassed. "I have to apologize for this behavior, Colonel. Somehow, Alpha Shift seems to have gotten the impression they're the cream of this particular crop."

"That's all right, Mr. Hesse," Faraday said. It was more than all right, actually. In his experience, this kind of casual camaraderie was the mark of a well-functioning team. Whether the group had picked it up in training or had simply clicked together on a personal level, it was a good sign. "So *are* Beta and Gamma Shifts composed of rank amateurs?"

"Hardly," Hesse said, glaring at the back of Milligan's head. "As a bonus, they've also managed to maintain a certain degree of professionalism. If you'd like, we can shuffle the shifts around so that a different group is on duty when you want to be here."

"No, no, this group will be fine," Faraday said soothingly. "I can always send them to their rooms if it gets too bad. So if it's too late to keep this shift from going crazy, Dr. Sprenkle, why *are* you here?"

"Mostly, to monitor Raimey's mental and emotional state," Sprenkle explained. "The Council is concerned about psychological conflicts as he melds into his Qanskan body."

"Or to be more precise," Hesse added bluntly, "they're worried that he might forget who he is. It's vital that he not forget where his ultimate loyalties lie."

Faraday looked up at the main display, currently showing

the roiling clouds of Jupiter some ninety thousand kilometers below them. "No, I suppose not," he said quietly.

"Colonel?" Beach called, half turning around. "The surgeons downstairs say they're ready to go."

"Thank you," Faraday said as he stepped past Hesse and sat down in the command chair. Time to say good-bye to Matthew Raimey.

Or at least, to say good-bye to what Matthew Raimey had been.

It was, Raimey thought, rather like being in a coffin. A thick, form-fitting coffin, lined on every wall with conduits and pipes and tubing of every thickness imaginable. The kind of coffin that would be specially designed for the funeral of a master plumber.

The probe passed one of the corridor lights as it rolled along, and he got a quick glimpse of the particular group of tubes and jars sitting directly in front of his face. His brand-new digestive system, the techs had identified it: an external stomach and set of intestines, hanging out there in front of him where he could keep an eye on it.

What in the *world* was he doing?

From somewhere at the back of his head came a brief, feedbacklike squeal. "Mr. Raimey?" Faraday's voice came. "Can you hear me?"

"Just fine," Raimey growled. "I thought you were going to do something about that squeal."

"We're working on it," Faraday assured him. "It should be fixed before you reach the rendezvous point. I just wanted to wish you luck, and to thank you again for your willingness to—"

"Save it," Raimey cut him off. "There isn't any room in here to wave flags."

"Mr. Raimey, this is Dr. Sprenkle," a new voice came in. "Just try to relax. It's natural for you to be feeling a little nervous about this."

"Oh, well, thank you so very much," Raimey shot back,

trying hard to be angry. He hated condescension almost as much as he hated pity, and this Sprenkle character was managing both at the same time.

But the anger wouldn't come. The best he could do, in fact, was a sort of vague annoyance. They'd probably already shut down all the glands that were necessary to drive a good, solid anger.

Still ninety thousand kilometers away from the nearest Qanska, and already they'd started stripping his humanity away from him.

A gift, Faraday had called it back in that pastel blue hospital room. Some gift.

What in the world was he *doing*?

"It's not too late to change your mind, Mr. Raimey," Faraday said quietly.

Raimey snorted, or at least gave as much of a snort as he could in the tight quarters. "Oh, right," he bit out. "Forget all the time and effort and the public pronouncements and the millions of dollars. Let's just call the media and say, sorry, I've changed my mind. I'll bet the Five Hundred would love that."

"It doesn't matter what the Five Hundred think," Faraday said. "Only what seems right to you."

"Even now?"

"Even now," Faraday said firmly. "Nothing we've done yet is irreversible."

The almost-anger faded into an almost-depression. "No," Raimey said. "Nothing's irreversible. Except my accident."

"Matthew—"

"Oh, shut up," Raimey cut him off. "Let's get on with it."

"It's going to be all right, Matthew," Faraday said. "Everything's going to work out just fine." If he was offended by Raimey's tone, it didn't show in his voice.

Too bad. It would have been nice to offend the man, at least a little. Being able to offend people was another part of being human.

The rolling cart carrying the probe continued down the

corridor. It hadn't, Raimey noted cynically, even slowed down during the conversation. So much for him having the final say on what happened with his life.

But then, what life?

The probe rolled to a stop. There was a moment of tense anticipation; and then, suddenly, there was the stomach-wrenching return to free fall as it was drop-launched from the station. A moment later came the vibrating roar of the drive and pressure against his feet. After that came silence, punctuated every few minutes by the quieter hissing of the maneuvering jets. Faraday had left the various microphones open in the Contact Room, and in the silence he was able to hear snatches of low conversation from the techs controlling his flight.

It was actually rather peaceful out here, he decided. Rather like how he'd always expected death to be. Idly, he wondered what Faraday would say if he told them to call off the project and just let him drift along this way.

But the peaceful drifting didn't last very long. All too soon, he began to feel the faint vibration as his capsule started to skim into the Jovian atmosphere. The vibration became a gentle shaking, then a rougher shaking, and finally a very serious buffeting. "Faraday!" he shouted over the screeching of the wind around the plastic walls of his flying coffin. "You guys asleep up there?"

"Is something wrong?" Faraday's voice shouted back.

"Yeah, there's something wrong," Raimey snapped. "I'm being bounced around like a preppie at a bar. They didn't say anything about shaking my teeth out."

"It's all right," Faraday said. It was impossible to tell for sure over the wind, but it sounded to Raimey like there was a new rigidness in the other's voice. "You're in sort of a holding pattern right now."

"Holding? For what?"

"For whom," a new, rather Germanic voice put in. "The Qanska who are supposed to meet you don't seem to have arrived yet."

"Terrific," Raimey growled. "What the hell do we do *now*?"

"Just sit tight," Faraday said. "Maybe they went to the wrong place. We're looking for them."

"Yes, but . . ." Raimey broke off, frowning. There was an odd pressure against his skin. "Faraday?" he called. "Faraday!"

"Yes, Mr. Raimey, I'm here."

"There's something happening," Raimey told him tightly. "What are you doing?"

"Just stay calm," the Germanic voice said; and there was definitely a tightness in *his* tone. "It's under control."

A strange tingling joined the strange pressure sensation. "What do you mean, it's under control? What exactly—?"

And then, like the ground on that Aspen ski slope, it suddenly hit him. "You've started it!" he gasped. "My skin—you've started dissolving my skin!"

"Take it easy," the German said.

"Take it *easy*?" Raimey snarled. "What the *hell* are you doing? You said the Qanska aren't even here yet!"

"We thought they were," Faraday said. "We saw a group of them swimming upward in your direction—"

"You jumped the gun!" Raimey cut him off. His body—his helpless, paralyzed body—was being disintegrated all around him. "*Damn* you, anyway."

"Mr. Raimey, pull yourself together," the German said. "I mean—"

"Oh, that's funny," Raimey shouted. "That's real funny."

"He didn't mean it that way," Faraday said. "Look, there's a good wide timing margin built into the operation—"

"What operation?" Raimey countered. The tingling was getting stronger, and he could visualize his skin vaporizing away, layer by layer. Next would be his muscles, then his organs, then his bones—

"There they are!" another voice shouted suddenly. "Twenty-two by fourteen. Coming up fast."

"Maneuvering to intercept," someone else said.

"You hear that?" Faraday called. "They're here. It's going to be all right."

The pitch and direction of the noise outside changed as the pod shifted direction.

And as it did so, the tingling sensation faded away. Was his skin all gone? "Hurry," Raimey pleaded. His voice sounded strange. Was his larynx going, too? "Please. Hurry."

"Deploying remote surgical pod," another voice called.

"Intercepting," the first voice said. "Birth canal insertion . . ."

There was a sudden thump, a fresh sensation of pressure, and the sound of the wind faded away. "You're in," Faraday said. "It won't be long now."

"It's too late," Raimey called, his voice a bare whisper now. The last gasp of a dissolving throat.

"Mr. Raimey, hang on," the German insisted.

"Go to hell," Raimey murmured. "All of you, go to hell."

He closed his eyes, and the universe went black.

THREE

There was an odd buzzing in the back of his brain as Raimey drifted back toward consciousness. An odd buzzing, and an even odder sensation tingling through his arms and legs.

It was another minute, and a couple more levels up toward fully awake, before it occurred to him that he hadn't felt anything in those limbs for the past eight months.

He tried to blink his eyes open. He couldn't tell if it worked. His eyes felt funny, too.

And open or closed, there was nothing to see but darkness. Had he gone blind? "Hello?" he called tentatively.

There was a slight pause. The buzzing sound in his head cut off, to be replaced by a softer humming. The hum cut off in turn—"Mr. Raimey?" an unfamiliar voice said. "Oh, wow. Hang on—just a second."

The humming came back. Idly, Raimey started counting off the seconds, trying to keep track of them on his fingers. Strangely, though, he didn't seem to have any fingers. Trying to blink his eyes again—he still couldn't see anything— he gave up on the count and instead tried to take inventory of his situation.

There was precious little for him to work with. He could still feel the pressure of the capsule around him, and there was a deep rumbling sound that seemed to come from nowhere in particular. Aside from that, there was only that sensation of having arms and legs again.

Phantom limb syndrome, perhaps? But that would mean that the limbs were actually gone. He'd only been uncon-

scious for a few minutes; surely the destruction of his body
couldn't be that far along already.

Unless that was also why he couldn't see anything.
Maybe his eyes were gone, too.

A disembodied brain, floating in a tangle of nutrient
pipes. It was like something from a bad medical drama.

Only it was reality. *His* reality.

What in the world was he *doing*?

The hum vanished again. "Mr. Raimey, this is Colonel
Faraday," a voice said. It didn't sound very much like Faraday. Or at least not the way he'd sounded when Raimey
had had ears. Were his ears gone too? "How do you feel?"

"Well, nothing hurts, anyway," Raimey said. "That's one
hell of an anesthetic you're using. Are we going to get on
with this soon?"

Faraday cleared his throat. "Actually, it's all over."

Raimey tried to blink his sightless eyes. "That's impossible," he protested. "I can still feel the capsule. There's
pressure all around me."

"What you feel is the womb of your Qanskan mother,"
Faraday said. "Is the pressure more or less uniform around
you? Are there any gaps, or places where it feels stronger?"

Raimey concentrated on the sensation. "Neither, I don't
think," he said. "It all seems pretty even."

"Good," Faraday said. "That means the connections to
your sensory nerves were all done correctly. I should warn
you that your skin will probably feel a little odd until you
get used to it. Actually, everything's going to feel a little
odd, especially your vision and hearing."

"What vision?" Raimey said tightly. "I can't see anyth—
oh."

"That's because you're still inside—"

"Yeah, yeah, I got it," Raimey said crossly, feeling stupid. "How did the operation go, anyway?"

"As far as everyone could tell from here, it went fine,"
Faraday said. "The remotes worked perfectly, and all the
relevant Qanskan physiology was where the surgeons expected it to be. Of course, there's no way to know how

they did on the motor-nerve connections until you're out."

Raimey tried flexing his muscles. "Well, for what it's worth, it *feels* like I can move my arms and legs. Though I guess I can't call them that anymore, can I?"

"The proper terms are fins and tails," Faraday said. "Fortunately, with the Qanska swallow-type split tail you at least get two legs' worth of movement and feeling. That should be easier to adjust to than a single, fish-type tail would have been."

"I guess we'll find out." Raimey said. "The rest of me feels okay, I guess. How long did the operation take, anyway? I thought it was supposed to last a whole bunch of hours."

"Try seventy-three of them," Faraday said. "We started with the surgeons working in three-hour shifts, then backed it off to two."

"Seventy-three hours?" Raimey echoed. He would have sworn he'd only been unconscious a few minutes. "I was out for three *days*?"

"Six, actually," Faraday said. "You slept another three after it was over."

A sudden ripple of heightened pressure ran along Raimey's body, starting at his feet—his tails, rather—and moving up past his head. "Sounds impressive," he commented. "Kind of sorry I missed it."

"You may eventually end up being the only person in the Solar System who did," Faraday said dryly. "I understand that The Stars Our Destination Society and the Solar Medical Association are having a bidding war for rights to the video."

"Great," Raimey said. "Maybe you can put a TV and permchip player on a rope and lower them down to me. Once I've got eyes again, that is."

He frowned as a sudden thought struck him. "Wait a second. If I don't have a human larynx anymore, how am I talking to you?"

"You're subvocalizing," Faraday said, sounding puzzled. "We've got a throatless mike wired into your speech center, with a connection to the antenna paralleling your artificial spinal cord. I thought they went through all that with you."

Another wave of pressure ran up along Raimey's body. "I guess I missed that lesson," he said. "What's this Qanska been eating, anyway? Chili and beans?"

"What do you mean?"

"I mean I'm getting waves of pressure," Raimey told him. "Like she's passing gas or something."

"Sounds like it's time," a woman's voice said faintly in the background. "Time for what?" Raimey demanded.

"What do you mean, time for what?" Faraday said. "Time for you to be born."

"She's started moving upward," Milligan reported, peering at the sensor displays. "We've got a couple of Nurturers standing by in case she needs help."

Faraday nodded, wondering yet again how an arrangement like this could ever have gotten started. Qanskan females about to give birth were often too heavy and weak to make their way up to the more rarefied regions of the upper atmosphere, the layer the Qanska called Level One. At the same time, though, newborn Qanska were too small and fragile for the denser atmosphere and pressure of Level Two, where those same expectant mothers tended to sink to just before the critical moment.

The solution was for one or two of the older females, called Nurturers, to stand by ready to help. If necessary, the Nurturer would swim beneath the mother and lift her up to Level One where she could have her baby.

The technique was clearly a common one among the Qanska. A variant of it had saved his and Chippawa's lives, in fact, back at that first momentous contact with the aliens. What Chippawa had taken to be remoras hanging onto the underside of a shark had actually been a group of younger Qanska lifting the older one up to meet and protect the *Skydiver* before it fell deep enough to be crushed.

It made sense, certainly. The question was how such an

arrangement could have started in the first place, back before the Qanska developed this particular social structure. Was it pure instinct? That was the general consensus at human think tanks.

Except that the Qanska claimed not to have such things as instincts. Were they lying? Or were they just so naturally helpful to each other that the birth assistance could predate their social structure?

Or was the species so old that they'd simply forgotten what it was like before civilization?

There was a movement at the corner of his eye, and he turned to see Hesse step through the doorway. "You're just in time," Faraday greeted him. "Mr. Raimey's about to be born."

"We got him loaded just in time, I see," Hesse said. "I don't suppose anyone had a chance to run through his Qanska language lessons with him."

Faraday frowned at him. There was something edgy in the man's voice. "Hardly. He only woke up a few minutes ago. We barely had time to bring him up to date when the contractions started."

"That may be what finally woke him up, actually," McCollum commented, swiveling around to face them. "What's left of the pod sensors registered a couple of small contractions before he came around."

"Thank you, Ms. McCollum," Hesse said tartly. "I *was* watching the system monitors." He wiggled his fingers back over her shoulder. "As I believe you should be?"

The corner of McCollum's mouth twitched, and she turned back to her station without another word. "Take it easy, Mr. Hesse," Faraday said quietly. "These people haven't gotten much sleep in the past couple of weeks."

"Then they should learn to pace themselves." Hesse waved a hand. "Sorry. I'm just . . . I'm a little worried about whether he's going to be able to talk to them. They're going to want to ask him all kinds of questions as soon as he's born."

"I think they'll be willing to cut him a little slack," Faraday soothed. "After all, they don't know what to expect any more than we do."

"Or maybe they do," Hesse countered. "They know a lot more than they're letting on. And we know hardly anything about them."

"That's why Raimey's there," Faraday reminded him. "Now, you want to tell me what's *really* bothering you?"

Hesse's lips compressed briefly. "I'm sorry. It's just . . ." He sighed in resignation. "The Council has instructed me to reprimand you for your behavior during pre-insertion activities," he said, the words coming out in the monotone of direct quotation. "Specifically, for suggesting to Mr. Raimey that he could still call everything off."

"I see," Faraday said, nodding. So that was why Hesse had come in here acting like he had a bad taste in his mouth.

A taste that was rapidly transferring itself to Faraday's own tongue. "Did they happen to notice that he *didn't* back out?"

"I'm just the messenger boy, Colonel," Hesse said. "I'm sure they noticed that. They notice everything."

"Do they also micromanage everything?" Faraday asked. "Because if that's what they're planning, they might as well move up here to Prime for the duration and do it properly. Housing shouldn't be a problem—my quarters will be empty, for a start." ·

Hesse grimaced. "Try to understand how they feel, Colonel. The Five Hundred have put a lot of time and money into Project Changeling. They're naturally a little nervous."

"And I've put my name and prestige into it," Faraday countered with precisely measured force. "And I didn't come out here to be a figurehead or puppet. You tell them that. Either I'm running this show, or I'm not. There's no middle ground."

Hesse sighed again. "Yes, sir. I'll tell them."

"Good," Faraday said, turning back to the monitors. Generally speaking, his Living Legend status was a pain in the neck, hanging around his shoulders like a set of runner's weights.

But occasionally, when wielded just right, those weights could become a reasonably effective weapon.

It wouldn't hold them for long, of course. Not politicians; certainly not politicians at the very upper level of System government. But it should hold them long enough for him to get this project up and running, and to set Raimey on a steady course. Faraday hadn't expected to be here much longer than that, anyway.

He looked up at the monitor, his throat feeling suddenly tight. Jupiter. Heat, and twisting magnetic fields, and pressure.

Lots of pressure. Tons and tons of impersonal, inexorable pressure. Pressure that had almost killed him once.

And Raimey was about to slide right out into it.

Surreptitiously, Faraday rubbed his myrtlewood ring, and with an effort shoved the memories back under the mental sod where he'd tried to bury them. He didn't consider himself particularly claustrophobic, but Jupiter was a special case. A hand that had been once burned, after all, was forever afterward sensitive to heat.

No, he wouldn't be here long. Not long at all.

"Whoa," McCollum spoke up suddenly from her station. "Colonel; Mr. Hesse? I do believe we've started."

Raimey could remember, as a child, listening to his grandmother talk about the birth process, or the "miracle of childbirth," as she'd called it. He couldn't speak for the human equivalent; but from his current point of view, at least, the Qanskan version of the miracle left a lot to be desired.

At first it was just the pressure waves, getting stronger and more frequent until Raimey began to feel like the last glob of toothpaste in a tube from which the owner was determined to get his full money's worth. But as the minutes ticked by, he noticed he was starting to feel hotter, as well. In fact, he was starting to feel uncomfortably warm. . . .

"Mr. Raimey?"

Raimey tried to blink his eyes. Had he actually dozed off there? "I'm here," he said, trying to shift his shoulders around to help him wake up.

That was a mistake. Somehow, for some inexplicable reason, the movement sent a ripple of nausea flooding through him. He could feel his eyes bulging as the mists began to rise across his brain—

"Hold still, Mr. Raimey," Faraday said urgently. "Don't move at all. Just hold perfectly still."

"What is it?" Raimey demanded, relaxing his muscles and letting his body float.

"It's your umbilical cord," Faraday said. "It seems to be shutting down."

Involuntarily, Raimey's muscles tightened again. His reward was a fresh wave of nausea. "It can't be," he insisted. "I'm not out yet. I can't even see the outside."

"We know," Faraday said. "We don't know if this is something normal or whether we've got a problem. Your life-support system has a small oxygen reserve; we're feeding you a trickle from that to keep you from blacking out. But your best bet is to stay as still as you can, conserve your oxygen, and hang on."

"Terrific," Raimey muttered. "I was better off paralyzed."

"Colonel?" the woman's voice he'd heard earlier came dimly from the background. "We've got something happening, big time. I think she's ready."

"Mr. Raimey?" Faraday called. "Get ready. We think this is it."

"I'm glad *you* think so," Raimey bit out. "I hate to break it to you—" He broke off as a fresh wave of pressure hit him.

But this wave wasn't like any of the previous ones. Instead of a rippling movement along his body, this one was all around him, squeezing down hard as if his surrogate mother was trying to crush him. Not even a chance of muscle movement now. He could feel his eyes bug out further as the taste of claustrophobia bubbled in his throat—

And then, without warning, the pressure around his head and shoulders abruptly vanished.

And like a mustard-slick sausage being squeezed at one end of its wraparound, he slid forward through the birth canal and shot out into the open air.

The open air, and a virtual explosion of light and color.

It was dazzling. Far above him, the undersides of the Jovian clouds were a violent swirl of color, with hues stretching across a spectrum he'd never seen in any picture or video of Jupiter. Jupiter, hell—he couldn't recall seeing such a range and variety of colors even amid the lush landscape of Earth. The other Qanska gathered around him, far from being the drab brown-gray of the *Skydiver*'s records, were patterned in brilliant stripes and spots of red, green, yellow, and blue that reminded him of exotic tropical fish. Even the wind flowing around him showed subtle colors, like the fluid sculptures he'd played with as a child.

It would have been impressive enough just dropping into it from a probe or shuttle. Coming out of the total darkness and isolation of a Qanskan womb, it literally took his breath away.

"Mr. Raimey? What's happening?"

Raimey took a cautious breath. Then another, and another. His alien lungs and artificial life-support system both seemed to working just fine now. "I'm clear," he called back, stretching out with his arms and legs.

A stretch that instantly became an awkward flailing. His arms weren't arms at all, he remembered belatedly, but the pectoral, mantalike fins of a Qanska. What he'd been thinking of as his shoulders were the leading edges of those fins; and what he'd thought of as his legs were twitching around haphazardly as the long flukes of his split tail.

He'd known all this going in. He'd studied Qanskan physiology and Qanskan structure, and he'd endured endless and usually boring speculations on what it might be like to become a Qanska.

Not a single minute of it had prepared him for this.

"Hell in buckets," he growled under his breath, trying to bring his body under control. He'd done a lot of swimming as a kid, but none of those movements were of the least bit of use here. For a moment his flailing turned him sideways to the prevailing westerly wind, and he winced at the sudden roar and pressure in his left ear. His momentum continued him on through the turn, and the roaring dropped to acceptable levels as he ended up facing into the wind.

Spreading his fins wide, he tried to hold position, but succeeded only in overcompensating and spinning around the other way. He winced again as the wind roared into his right ear this time, and changed his goal to completing the turn and putting the wind at his back. But again, his unfamiliarity with his own muscles and joints betrayed him, and he wound up snout-down, belly-first to the wind like an upside-down kite. From somewhere nearby he heard a rolling rumbling sound, like punctuated thunder.

And suddenly, a brightly colored object came out of nowhere to slam hard into his left side, spinning him off course like a wayward billiard ball.

"Hey!" he yelled, fighting hard to regain his balance. The momentum of the impact had rolled him partially over onto his side, and he twisted his whole body as he tried to get a look at whoever this idiot was who was playing games with him—

And as he did so, something big and dark and torpedo-shaped shot through the space he'd just vacated. There was another roll of punctuated thunder—

"Raimey, get out of there!" Faraday snapped. "You've got a Vuuka on your tail!

"Move it, or be lunch!"

FOUR

"A Vuuka?" Raimey gasped, twisting back around to look at the torpedo shape that had overshot him.

It was a Vuuka, all right. A relatively small one, a detached part of his brain pointed out, no more than five meters long.

Five meters' worth of predator, compared to about a meter's worth of Raimey. A single bite on the fly, like he'd been coming in for, and Raimey would have been ripped in half. Belatedly, he realized that the Qanska who had slammed into him so annoyingly had in fact saved his life.

But that daring move wasn't going to be of any use whatsoever if Raimey didn't get his tail moving. Already the Vuuka was kicking up a small whirlpool of colored air as he braked and circled around for another try.

Unfortunately, as Raimey had already noted, moving his tail was a hell of a lot easier said than done. Frantically, he began flailing his arms and legs again, trying to visualize and duplicate the smooth and effortless movements he'd seen on the vids they'd shown him.

He *was* getting the hang of it—that much was clear. But he wasn't getting it fast enough. Not nearly fast enough. He didn't dare look around, but he could practically feel the Vuuka's eyes locking onto his back.

Getting ready to charge, with nothing but distance between him and his prey . . .

"Mr. Raimey, are you listening?" Faraday cut into his thoughts.

"Listening to what?" Raimey demanded.

"The other Qanska," Faraday said. "They're talking to you. Your Qanskan language lessons, remember?"

Raimey frowned. They were talking to him?

Then, suddenly, he got it. The punctuated thunder sounds he'd been hearing were Qanskan speech.

Only one small problem. Like his vision, his hearing was also all screwed up. The rolling thunder didn't sound the least bit like the tonal dictionary and grammar they'd drilled him on back on Earth. It was richer and fuller, with nuances and shadings that either the human microphones or his own formerly human ears hadn't been able to pick up. All that memorization, all that sweat and toil, was going to be good for exactly nothing.

But that was more explanation than he had time for right now. "I can't swim and translate at the same time," he snapped instead. "What do they want?"

"They're telling you to dive," Faraday said. "As fast as you can, as deep as you can."

"And how the hell do they suggest I do that?" he bit back, trying to bend forward for the sort of surface dive he could have done in a swimming pool at home.

Here, it didn't work nearly so well. But even as he struggled with it, he accidentally rolled onto his side again; and this time he found himself slipping into a sharp downward angle.

"Never mind, I've got it," he said, putting some muscle into it. This, at least, was a familiar sensation from his childhood: the effort to push himself deeper than natural buoyancy would normally allow him to go. Pushing hard with fins and tails, he forced his way downward.

It was a good ten seconds before the utter stupidity of this maneuver suddenly struck him. A five-meter-long Vuuka was considerably heavier than a Qanskan newborn. It had to be paddling like crazy just to stay up this high. Diving into deeper and denser atmosphere, into the levels where a predator that size would normally live, was playing straight into its hands.

Or rather, into its *mouth*.

"Faraday, this is nuts," he called.

"Just keep going," Faraday said tersely. "You're doing okay right now. Some of the Qanska are harassing him, trying to slow him down."

Raimey's new head wasn't really built for turning, but as he tried to look over his back he discovered his eyes could do an amazing amount of swiveling. Another of those half-rolls, and the Vuuka was in sight again.

There were several Qanska swarming around it, all right, slamming into its sides with the bony protrusions of their foreheads. Even as he watched, one of them darted straight past the predator's snout.

"That's the one who shoved you out of the way," Faraday identified the daredevil. "I swear he's going to get his tails bitten off if he's not careful."

"Never mind that," Raimey snarled, rolling back forward again. The last thing he cared about right now was someone else's tails. "Where the hell are the—" he searched for the word "—the Protectors? Aren't they supposed to be up here guarding the babies?"

"They're coming," Faraday assured him. "If you can just—What?"

He broke off. There was some low conversation in the background, but with the blood pounding through his brain Raimey couldn't make it out. "What's the trouble?" he shouted. "Faraday?"

"No trouble," Faraday said. "Cut to your left. The Qanska have arranged a surprise."

Swearing to himself, Raimey waddled his body into a leftward curve. He could see nothing there: no Protectors, no Breeders, nothing. He continued his curve a few more degrees—

And caught his breath. Rising ponderously through the swirling air beneath and beside him was another Qanska.

But not the ten-meter-long Protector he'd been hoping desperately to see. Not the young adult, strong and fast, that he needed to take on the Vuuka and get him out of this mess. This thing was more the size of a small neighborhood convenience store, its pectoral fins spanning at least twenty meters. Its colors were faded, like the paint on an old house, its entire surface distorted by lumps and bulges until it was almost unrecognizable as a Qanska.

"You wanted a Protector," Faraday said, his voice sounding relieved nearly to the point of smugness. "How about a full-fledged Counselor instead?"

Terrific, Raimey thought bitterly. Yes, the newcomer was big, all right. Much bigger than the attacking Vuuka, and impressive as hell.

But size was hardly the important ledger entry here. The predator was young, fast, and aggressive; and there was something distinctly decrepit about the way the Counselor tentatively flapped its huge fins. *Just terrific. I need a Wall Street wizard. So what do they send me? A Trade Commission bureaucrat.*

Still, maybe he could at least hide behind it. Leaning into the thickening air, he pushed his fins for all they were worth. The big Qanska was coming up fast—

"Duck!" Faraday snapped.

Startled, Raimey momentarily faltered. But the result was basically the one desired. The sudden loss of motive power combined with the overly dense air around him sent him popping upward like a cork. Ducking, sort of, only in reverse.

And once again, the sudden change in direction was just in time. The Vuuka shot past beneath him, coming close enough for its fins to scratch briefly across his underside.

And continued on to slam full-tilt into the upper left fin of the rising Counselor.

The predator gave a sort of elephantine howl as it bounced off the Qanska, staggering in midair like a bird that had flown into a window. It started to sink, and for a moment Raimey thought it was simply going to disappear into the depths where it had come from. On the Qanska, at the point of the predator's impact, he could see bright yellow-orange blood beginning to seep out onto the faded color scheme.

But then the Vuuka's flukes twitched and began to beat the air again. The howl cut off, and the Vuuka drove back up toward the Counselor like a Doberman charging a rhino. It opened its mouth wide as it curved around, giving Raimey a glimpse of several rows of awesomely intimidating teeth.

And zeroing in on the yellow blood, it slammed teeth-first into the Counselor's fin.

Raimey winced in sympathetic pain. The initial trickle of blood became a wide mustard-colored stream running down the Qanska's side as the Vuuka began to chew its way into the skin. Some of the blood spattered into the air around the Vuuka's head in the fury of its attack, like a paint sprayer gone mad.

"Mr. Raimey?" Faraday called anxiously. "Are you all right?"

"*I* am, yeah," Raimey called back. The Counselor was still rising, and he could see now that it was being lifted on the backs of a half dozen smaller Qanska. Maybe that was why there hadn't been any Protectors around to defend him, he thought with a flash of bitterness. Maybe everyone in the area had been pressed into luggage-cart duty.

If so, the Counselor was certainly paying for that decision. The Vuuka was going at his prey like a boring machine, with no sign of slowing down. Already his head had nearly vanished from sight below the level of the skin. "This big lumpy help the Qanska sent is in big trouble, though," he added to Faraday. "The Vuuka's going at him like a worm into a rotten tomato. . . ."

He paused, frowning. Something was wrong here. The Vuuka was still eating into the Counselor's side, but it was digging in far too fast. Even as Raimey had been speaking its head had disappeared entirely from sight, and it was moving almost visibly into its self-dug tunnel.

No. The Vuuka wasn't digging down. The Qanska's skin was moving *up*. Moving up along the predator's body like multicolored tar, oozing up as it enveloped the Vuuka's body.

What the *hell*?

And then he remembered. The dark and extremely muddy vid Chippawa and Faraday had taken from their *Skydiver* bathyscaph . . .

"You were saying?" Faraday asked.

"Never mind," Raimey murmured. "I think the Counselor's got it under control."

The punctuated thunder had come back. "They're talking to me again," he told Faraday.

"What are they saying?"

Raimey tried to shrug. The movement merely threatened to flip him over on his side again. "How should *I* know?"

"You've had the same language lessons I have," Faraday reminded him.

"Yeah, but I don't have a computer down here to help me," Raimey retorted. "Besides, nothing sounds the way it did in the lessons."

"Well, you'd better get used to it," Faraday said. "That's what you're going to be listening to the rest of your life."

You bastard, Raimey thought up at him, clenching his teeth. At least he still had teeth he could clench with.

But the Counselor was still rumbling; and for the moment, hating Faraday wasn't going to do him any good. Forcing back his anger, Raimey concentrated on the sounds.

It wasn't as bad as he'd first thought. As he'd already noted, the tonal pattern sounded more varied to Qanskan ears than to the human equivalent. But now that he could focus his full attention on them, he was able to hear the core sounds that he'd been taught. He still had no idea what all the extra harmonics and other stuff meant, but for now he should be able to get by.

Greetings to you, child of the humans, the Counselor was saying. *I am Latranesto, Counselor of the Qanska. In the name of the Counselors, and the Leaders, and the Wise, I welcome you to our world.*

Okay, Raimey thought to himself. Step one completed: He'd understood what they were saying. Now came the

tricky part: trying to talk back. The words he was supposed
to say had been pre-chosen by his instructors back on Earth.
It was up to him, though, to hear the alien tonal words in
his head and then try to recreate them. "I greet—"

He broke off, startled by the sounds that had emanated
from somewhere in his throat and chest.

Yes? Latranesto said. *Please continue.*

Raimey took a deep breath, feeling the strange sensation
of cool hydrogen gas whistling in along his new body's
twin throats as he did so. Clearly, talking Qanskan was
going to be a lot easier than anyone had expected, now that
he had a set of genuine Qanskan vocal cords to work with.
A hell of a lot easier, apparently, than relearning how to
swim. "I greet you and your people, Counselor Latranesto,"
he started over. "I am honored in turn to be here."

There was a ripple of a new sound, something like fin-
gernails scratching on a piece of flat slate. A sound of respect or greeting? A ritual noise of greeting that they hadn't
thought to mention to their human contacts up in Jupiter
Prime?

Or were they just laughing at his accent?

You are welcome among us, Latranesto said. *If I may
remember in your presence, it has been a long time since
my first meeting with your kind.*

Raimey frowned. Could this possibly be . . . ?

No, he realized. Latranesto couldn't possibly be the Qanska who had rescued Chippawa and Faraday and their crippled bathyscaph. That one had looked at least twice this
size in the *Skydiver*'s vid, probably even bigger. Besides,
that had been twenty years ago. "I do not understand," he
said, trying to match the other's tone and to pick up some
of the nuances he was hearing. It would be nice if he was
getting some of the words right, too. "When before have
you met other humans?"

*When before have you met other humans, you mean to
say*, the big Qanska said.

A correction, obviously. Only Raimey had no idea how
the Counselor's version differed from his. So much for this

communication stuff being easy. Salesman's cockiness, they'd called this in business school, and warned against it. *The encounter was long ago, and very brief,* Latranesto went on. *I was the Baby who foolishly collided with the machine's cord.*

Ah—so that was it. He'd been the baby Qanska who had bounced off the *Skydiver*'s tether line. "I see," he said.

It was my fault that those humans inside neared death. Latranesto said. *I left a taste of my blood on the cord, which was what drew the Vuuka to attack.*

Raimey looked over at Latranesto's fin. Only the Vuuka's tail flukes remained uncovered by the Qanska's spreading skin, and they had long since ceased to beat at the air.

And Latranesto had a new surface lump for his already impressive collection. "So that was why it attacked you," he said. "A Qanska four times its size. It was attracted by your blood."

By blood, and by movement, Latranesto said. *That was what drew it to you. By movement and blood do Vuuka hunt.*

Raimey grimaced, remembering all that flailing around as he tried to get his new muscles to cooperate. "You could have said something," he said accusingly.

Your words have no clear meaning.

"I mean you should have warned us there would be a predator on my tail the minute I was born," Raimey said. "You should have had a Protector waiting, too."

From one of the Qanska under Latranesto's wide belly came a noise that sounded suspiciously like a harrumph. *There is normally no need for a Protector,* Latranesto rumbled. *Qanskan babies are born still and quiet, and do not attract the Vuuka.*

"Damn and a half," Faraday's voice murmured in the back of Raimey's brain.

Raimey felt his whole body twitch. To hear a human voice suddenly interjected into the rumbles of Qanskan conversation was startling. It felt very . . . alien. "What?" Raimey demanded.

"The atrophying umbilical cord," Faraday said. "That makes Qanskan babies slightly air-starved before birth so that they'll go to sleep."

Another voice, female-sounding, said something unintelligible in the background. "What was that?" Raimey demanded.

There was a click of another microphone opening up. "I said, and then they're shot like a torpedo out of the birth canal," the voice repeated. Probably McCollum, the Qanskan expert, Raimey guessed. "That gets it far enough away from the mother that any predators zeroing in on her movement or any blood from her afterbirth probably won't even notice the kid. Cool."

"We're glad you're impressed," Raimey growled. "Can everyone just shut up now? Okay?"

With an effort, he shifted his mind back to Qanskan tonals. "I understand that now," he rumbled to Latranesto. "I did not understand at the time." He hesitated for a moment, but he couldn't resist. "My people do not understand the Qanska as well as they think they do."

It is good that you learn, child of the humans, Latranesto said. *That is why you are here, is it not?*

Raimey felt himself frowning, or what would have been a frown if he'd had a human face to do it with. On the surface, the comment certainly seemed reasonable enough.

And yet, something about it struck him as being just a little bit odd. From the words alone, it could have been straight, sarcastic, indulgent, amused, or even offended. Again, he wished he had a better handle on the nuances that were clearly going over his head. "I am here to bring understanding and harmony between our two peoples," he improvised, hoping that would cover all the bases.

Of course you are, Latranesto said. *And it is time that that harmony should begin.*

"I'm ready," Raimey said. Distantly, he wished he'd had the foresight to take a few more Salesman's Technique classes back at school. The people-reading aspects taught there would have been a lot more useful here than all those stock market analysis labs he'd dripped the midnight sweat over. "What's the first step?"

Before all else, you must learn to survive, Latranesto said. *To that purpose, the Counselors, and the Leaders, and the Wise have chosen a companion for you.*

He made a sound like a foghorn with a cold, and from behind him came a much smaller adult Qanska. *This is Tigrallo, a Protector,* Latranesto identified him. *He and your mother, Mirasni, will look after you until you have learned all of what it means to be a Qanska.*

"Thank you," Raimey said sourly, feeling a reflexive flicker of embarrassment. Here he was, twenty-three years old, a full-grown adult human being, and they were saddling him with not just one but *two* baby-sitters.

He looked again at the fresh bulge on Latranesto's side, the bulge that had once been a Vuuka. On the other hand, there were worse things on Jupiter than a little embarrassment. "I thank you," he said again, and this time he meant it. "I am sure I will find their assistance of great value."

Then you will be a Qanska in truth, Latranesto said. *You must also become a Qanska in name.*

Raimey blinked. "I'm sorry?"

I do not understand sorrow for a name.

"No, that's not what I meant," Raimey said. "I meant—"

"Raimey," Faraday murmured in his ear.

"What?" Raimey snapped, annoyed at the interruption. Again, it was oddly difficult to switch back to English, even subvocalizing this way.

"I mean your name: Raimey," Faraday said. "It's a female Qanska's name. An I-sound ending. Male names end in an O-sound."

"That's nice to know," Raimey growled. "You suppose someone might have mentioned this to me a little sooner?"

"I'm sorry," Faraday said. "I just assumed the prep team would have told you that."

"Well, they didn't," Raimey said, disgusted with the

whole lot of them. "What else haven't you told me?"

"I said I was sorry," Faraday said, an edge to his voice this time. "What else do you want?"

Raimey snorted. But then, what else should he have expected from a huge, stable, terminally comfortable operation like SkyLight? His Corporate History classes had demonstrated how, over and over again, fat and sassy led directly to sloppy and lazy.

Throw the contentious politicians of the Five Hundred into the mix and it only got worse. He should probably count himself lucky that they'd gotten him to the right planet.

Do you speak to your former people instead of to the Counselor? Tigrallo demanded, swimming a corkscrew pattern around him. His voice was less deep than Latranesto's, but Raimey could hear the same range of subtleties there.

And if Tigrallo was getting impatient, Latranesto probably was, too. "My apologies," Raimey said, switching back to tonals and trying mightily to come up with something clever for a name. Clever, and easier to remember than these jawbreaker types the rest of the Qanska seemed to have.

Tigrallo flipped over on his back and started corkscrewing the other direction. Looking like a mad impressionist painter's idea of a cross between a dolphin and a manta ray . . .

Well, why not? "I have chosen a name, Counselor," Raimey said. "I wish to be called *Manta.*"

That is not a proper name, Latranesto said. *You are a male. You must choose a proper male's name.*

"But I am not only Qanska," Raimey reminded him. "I am also human. I contend it is proper that I have a name that is unique among the Qanska."

Latranesto rumbled something. Someone from the group of Qanska underneath him rumbled back, and the discussion was on. Raimey tried to follow along, but his efforts quickly ended in a dead end. The conversation seemed composed almost entirely of nuances, with none of the tonal words he recognized. Either this was a different dialect from the one he'd been taught, or else they'd been enunciating things very slowly and carefully up to now.

It seemed to go on forever, but eventually the rumblings began to die away. *Very well*, Latranesto said at last, switching back to something Raimey could understand. *From this day until the passing into the Deep, you shall be known as Manta.*

The passing into the Deep. That one definitely sounded ominous. The Qanskan version of *till death do us part*?

I must now leave you, Latranesto continued. *Once again, in the name of the Counselors, and the Leaders, and the Wise, I welcome you to our home. Use your time and abilities with courage and strength and wisdom.*

"I will do my best," Raimey said. "I hope we shall meet again."

Perhaps, Latranesto said. *Until that day, may you swim in peace and contentment.*

The Counselor gave an elaborate ripple of his fins, which was apparently the signal the lifting Qanska had been waiting for. In unison they ducked out from under him and swam clear of his bulk. Latranesto dropped like a stone, quickly sinking out of sight in the swirling mass of atmosphere below.

Come.

The voice had come from behind him. With an effort, Raimey managed to turn himself around.

Tigrallo was hovering there, his fins flapping rhythmically with smooth but powerful strokes. *Your first task is to learn how to find food*, the Protector said. *You do like to eat, do you not?*

Raimey was suddenly aware that whatever passed for a stomach in this new body of his was feeling extremely empty. "You bet," he said. "Let's go."

Faraday flipped off his microphone and stretched the tension out of his fingers. For the moment, at least, things seemed under control. "Well," he said to the room in general. "Evaluations?"

"Nothing like a good heart attack to get a project up and running." Hesse grunted. "That one was just too damn close."

"I seem to remember it was *your* idea to boost his oxygen flow," Milligan pointed out, an edge of scorn in his voice. "If we hadn't done that, he wouldn't have attracted that Vuuka in the first place."

"Excuse me, Mr. Milligan, but I thought it might be nice to keep him from suffocating before he was even born," Hesse shot back, his face reddening noticeably beneath his blond hair. "And as long as we're talking *ifs* here," he added, shifting his glare to McCollum, "*if* our vaunted xenobiologist had told me the umbilical contraction was natural—"

"Don't try to load this one on *me*," McCollum objected. "It's been twenty years of pulling teeth just to find out what we *do* know about Qanskan physiology. They never said a word about this."

"All right, that's enough," Faraday interrupted, putting some of that Living Legend authority into his voice. "All of you. I know it's been a tense few days, and I know that we're all tired. But let's be professionals here. Finger-pointing is for bureaucrats."

McCollum made a face, but obediently fell silent. Faraday looked at Hesse, who also said nothing, then around at the others. "All right," he said again. "Now. Evaluations?"

"He's adjusting very well to his transformation," Sprenkle offered. "Almost *too* well, in fact."

"Meaning?" Faraday asked.

"It's hard to pin down," Sprenkle said, fingering his moustache thoughtfully. "Did you notice how he seemed to hesitate every time he had to switch back to English?"

"Lots of people do that when they're going between two different languages," Beach pointed out.

"True," Sprenkle agreed. "But he also seemed rather annoyed about having to stop what he was doing to talk to us. Sometimes borderline hostile, in fact."

"Maybe because we almost got him killed," Milligan muttered.

Hesse turned a glare his direction. "No, I don't think so," Sprenkle said. "Remember that comment about us not knowing as much about Qanskan physiology as we thought we did?"

"No kidding," McCollum muttered.

"The point is that he seems to be already picking up an us-versus-them way of thinking," Sprenkle said. "Identifying with his new body, and his new people."

"But that's what we want to happen," Faraday said. "Isn't it?"

"Certainly, at least to some extent," Sprenkle said. "He'll be miserable the rest of his life if he never considers himself a part of Qanskan society. All I'm saying is that we didn't expect it to start this soon."

"Maybe there's something else going on," Hesse said. "I've seen parts of Raimey's file. The man has a lot of resentment and anger still festering over his accident. Maybe that dig was part of that anger."

"Who exactly is he angry at?" Beach asked.

"The universe in general," Sprenkle said. "Humanity in particular. Raimey is definitely the sort to hold and nurture a grudge."

"So hold a grudge at the universe," Beach said, frowning. "But why drag humanity into it? No one planted that tree in front of him."

"No, but he *was* showing off for his girlfriend," Sprenkle said. "For someone like Raimey, that might be all it takes to start assigning blame."

McCollum snorted under her breath. "This guy wasn't exactly a prize before his accident either, was he?"

"Let's not concentrate on his psychological flaws, people," Faraday said mildly. "I'm sure Dr. Sprenkle could write up an equally flattering file on each of us, too. Besides, if Raimey hadn't been mad enough at humanity to turn his back on us, he might not be swimming around down there right now."

"I was just thinking about a cartoon I saw once," Milligan said slowly. "An Old West, cowboys-and-First-Immigrants strip. The commander of the fort has called his scout into his office to report. The scout says, 'I did what you told me, Colonel—I made friends with the natives, learned their ways, studied their culture.' The colonel says, 'And what do you have to tell me?' The scout says, 'Get off our land.' "

"Boy, wouldn't *that* be a kicker," Beach murmured. "If he went completely native and told us to go take a collective hike."

"I don't think that'll happen," Sprenkle said. "Jen, you said the cellular substitution had already started?"

"Pretty much as soon as the surgeons finished," Mc-Collum confirmed. "That was a little faster than anyone expected, too."

"Right," Sprenkle said. "And yet he's still apparently the same lovable Matthew Raimey that he always was, resentments and grudges and all. I don't think he's going to lose all connection to humanity."

"Unless it's waiting until the transformation reaches his cerebral cortex," Milligan said. "This could still blow up in our faces."

"Nothing's blowing up in anyone's face," Faraday said firmly. "We'll just have to keep an eye on him. Was there anything else?"

The others glanced around at each other, but no one spoke. "All right, then," Faraday said. "When your duty shifts are over, I'll expect each of you to do a complete analysis of your data and write it up."

"In the meantime," Hesse added, glancing at his watch, "the Five Hundred are waiting for word of the blessed event."

"You want me to go ahead and forward the conversation?" Beach asked.

"No, this one Mr. Hesse and I should probably do ourselves," Faraday said, getting to his feet. "Historic significance, and all that. We'll be in the transmission room if you need us. Stay sharp, and let us know immediately if there are any problems."

"He'll be fine," McCollum said, gesturing toward the sensor board. "No one's going to bother him with his own personal Protector on call."

"At least not for the ten minutes it'll take you to send a message to Earth," Beach added dryly. "Take your time."

"Thank you," Faraday said, matching his tone and trying not to let his own private fears show through. It wasn't the next ten minutes he was worried about. Or the next ten days, or even the next ten months.

Because Sprenkle was right: Raimey was indeed the type to hold a grudge. What would he say when he finally learned that no one on Earth cared a stale cracker about whether he got his life back, or even about his place in the history books?

What else haven't you told me? Raimey had asked a few minutes ago. The question had been half rhetorical, and Faraday had managed to sidetrack the half that wasn't. *What else haven't you told me?*

Faraday grimaced. If he only knew.

FIVE

A wispy strand of bright purple vine rolled swiftly past Raimey to his right, apparently caught in some particularly brisk breeze. Abandoning the more subtle blue-green leaves he'd been munching on, he flipped over onto his side, did a swooping turn, and gave chase.

Kachtis, he vaguely recalled the purple foodstuff's name. Or maybe it was *chinster*, and *kachtis* was the other, lighter purple one, the one with the leaves and cone-shaped berries. After eighty-three ninedays on Jupiter, he still didn't have all these floating plants and near-microscopic groups of sporelike things completely sorted out.

But he *had* sampled all of them, or at least all those that grew on Level One. And the purple ones were definitely the tastiest.

Which was why they usually didn't last long up here among all the hungry Qanskan children and mothers. This time, though, he was determined to beat out the competition.

He was just closing in on the trailing end of the purple when another Qanskan child dropped in from above and neatly scooped it into his mouth.

"Hey!" Raimey snapped. "That was mine."

"Oh?" the other asked, rolling over on his side to look back at Raimey. "This your private ocean or something?"

Great, Raimey groused to himself. Not only a blatant food poacher, but a smart-mouth on top of it. "You saw me going after that tendril," he said. "You should have let me have it."

"Why?" the other said, rippling his fins in complete un-concern as he flipped his tails over to gesture behind Rai-mey. "Just because you've got your own personal Protector?"

Raimey rolled onto his side, too, and looked back. Ti-grallo was treading air a couple of dozen meters away, standing his usual stoic guard. "What about it?" he growled, flipping back upright.

"So what did you do?" the poacher asked, dropping his voice conspiratorially. "Get someone's tails in a twist or something?"

"Maybe he just likes watching over me," Raimey said stiffly. "Or maybe I'm special."

"Yeah, right," the other child said with a sniff.

The *other* child. Raimey grimaced. The *other* child; and *that* thought still rankled. Raimey was an adult human be-ing, with more knowledge and sheer life experience than anyone from here all the way to Jupiter's core could ever hope to have. Hell's bells—a *Counselor* had dragged his tails all the way up to Level One just to welcome him to the planet. That ought to count for *something*.

But he might as well forget about that, because the rest of the Qanska sure had. As far as everyone up here was concerned, he was just another normal, everyday child.

"Come *on*," the other persisted, lowering his voice still farther. "What did you *do*?"

"Pranlo?" a distant female voice called. "Pranlo? Where are you?"

"I'm over here, Mom," the child called back. "Here with—" He broke off. "What's your name?"

"Manta," Raimey said.

"I'm here with Manto," Pranlo called.

"Not Manto," Raimey corrected him irritably. "Mant*a*."

"Mant*a*?" Pranlo repeated. "What kind of name is that?"

"A special name," Raimey said. "You got a problem with that?"

"Well—" Pranlo floundered for a moment. "No, I guess not."

"Pranlo, come back over here with the rest of the children," the female called again, swimming toward them. "It's not safe way over there."

"Oh, crosswinds," Pranlo muttered. "Mothers never let you have any fun."

Suddenly, he flipped his fins. "*Wait* a second. Mom?" he called. "It's okay. There's a Protector right here. See?"

"He won't be there very long," the female warned. "The rest of the children are over here."

"Well, can I stay until the Protector comes back?" Pranlo cajoled. "I promise to come back when he does."

"It's all right, Cintusti," Tigrallo called. "I'll watch him."

"Well . . . all right," the female said reluctantly. "But you come straight back when he does, Pranlo. Understand."

"Sure."

Reluctantly, Raimey thought, the female turned back to the herd. "Whee!" Pranlo said softly, doing an excited back flip. "This is great. Our own private Protector. Hey, let's get some other kids and play tagabuck, okay?"

"Well . . ." Raimey hesitated. He was an adult, damn it, even if he was trapped in a alien child's body. To play some stupid children's game would be far beneath his dignity. Especially with all those people up there in the station undoubtedly watching his every move from one of their spy probes.

And yet, even as he opened his mouth to make some excuse, it suddenly occurred to him why he'd been so surly lately.

He was lonely.

The realization came like a slap in the teeth. Yes, he swam with the general herd of children, parents, Protectors, and Nurturers. And yes, he wasn't unpleasant or unfriendly toward any of them.

But at the same time, most of his conversations were brief and casual. And ninety-plus percent of the time he stayed at the edge of the herd, or even ranged beyond it like he was doing now.

Mostly, it was just him and Tigrallo. And Tigrallo wasn't very good company.

"It might be good for you," Tigrallo suggested, just loud enough for Raimey to hear. "Tagabuck's a useful game for learning how to run and dodge. Things you need to know."

Raimey blinked. Tigrallo had never offered a suggestion like that before. He'd hardly even spoken to Raimey, for that matter, except to offer brief tips about how to do something Raimey was struggling with. Mostly he'd just hung around in the background, chased away or killed the occasional small predator, and otherwise left Raimey to his own devices.

Was this just another tip to help Raimey learn how to become a Qanska? Or had he noticed Raimey's mood, understood the cause for it, and was giving him an excuse to get some badly needed socialization?

He'd heard a lot of speculation during his training as to what kind of intellectual and emotional makeup the Qanska had, and whether human beings would ever be able to understand them. The lectures had been one hundred percent bull-manufactured guesswork, because in twenty years of talking with the Qanska no one had a clue about what went on behind those dark eyes.

Yet, here was at least a hint that the Qanska had picked up a lot more understanding of human nature than they'd let slip about themselves. And it didn't take a marketing genius to realize what kind of potential bargaining advantage that put them in.

Was that what this whole project was ultimately about? Humanity's attempt to even those odds?

Maybe. In which case, who the hell cared how silly he might look back on Prime? He had a job to do.

"Why not?" he said. "Sure, Pranlo, let's get a group together. I don't know how to play, though."

"We'll teach you," Pranlo said, doing another excited flip. "Come on, let's go meet everyone."

The Contact Room was quiet as Faraday walked through the security door, its lights lowered to the same "nighttime" level as the rest of the station. The four people on evening duty were being quiet, too, lounging comfortably at their stations as they kept watch on Raimey and his Qanskan friends.

Faraday peered around the room, floundering a little as he tried to put names to the faces. He'd been introduced to all three shifts when he'd first come aboard the station, of course. But in the ten and a half months since then their paths had seldom crossed, and he'd never been good with names and faces anyway. Two of the faces were complete blanks; the third he had a vague recollection of.

The fourth, in contrast, was almost painfully familiar.

"Mr. Milligan," he greeted the young man, stepping over to the sensor tech's chair. "You're up late."

"Pandre called in sick this evening," Milligan said. "I volunteered to sit Beta Shift for him."

"Um," Faraday said, pulling his chair over from his usual place by the command board and sitting down beside him. "Did Mr. Hesse approve?"

Milligan shrugged slightly. "Mr. Hesse mostly watches things with an eye toward politics. How Earth and the Five Hundred are affected. I didn't think this qualified."

"Mr. Hesse has a good eye for detail," Faraday pointed out, casting around for some way to stick up for the man. Hesse was Milligan's boss, after all. He deserved at least a surface layer of respect. "That's very valuable in a manager. He also brings a strong enthusiasm for the project."

"He brings a strong enthusiasm for you, you mean," Milligan countered. "The project I'm not so sure about."

Faraday grimaced. He'd hoped it wasn't quite that obvious to everyone else. "One and the same, really."

"It is now," Milligan countered. "But what happens to us when you leave? More to the point, what happens to Raimey?"

Faraday had wondered about that himself. Often. "So what's the big secret?" he asked, running an eye across the sensor displays. "Things seem quiet enough."

"They're in sleep cycle," Milligan said. "Things were hopping pretty good an hour ago."

Faraday nodded. The Qanskan pattern seemed to be just under seven hours of wakefulness followed by just under three hours of sleep as they drifted along with the winds. It all synched perfectly with Jupiter's nine-point-eight-hour rotation.

Though why anyone down there should care about the planet's rotation in the first place was a mystery. Below the clouds, where all the Qanska lived, they got more heat and radiation from Jupiter's core than they did from the distant sun.

Still, experiments with Raimey had demonstrated that Qanskan eyes could easily pick out the sun's location, even through all that muck above them. Perhaps it was built into all living creatures to match their rhythms to their local star, no matter how great or minor its influence on their environment. "More reindeer games?" he asked.

Milligan blinked. "More what?"

" 'They never let poor Rudolph join in any reindeer games,' " Faraday quoted. "Didn't you ever watch the classics?"

"I liked taking TV sets apart more than I did watching them," Milligan said. "But, yeah, they were playing for a while. Raimey's definitely getting his act together, swimming-wise. Oh, and Tigrallo also had to chase away some more troublemakers."

"Vuuka?"

"No, those smaller ones. The whatcha-call-'em—"

"Sivra?" Faraday asked, frowning. Sivra usually weren't strong enough to swim their way up to Level One.

"No, the other ones," Milligan said. "Pakra. The scavengers who sometimes get delusions of predatorhood."

"Ah," Faraday said. "He didn't have any trouble with them, I presume?"

Milligan shook his head. "Not a bit."

"Good," Faraday said. "So I repeat: Why am I here?"

"I was playing around with the sensor data this afternoon," Milligan said, swiveling half around to tap some keys on his board. "Found something I wanted to show you."

One of the displays showing sleeping Qanska shifted to an overall view of the equatorial region of Jupiter the station was currently flying over. "Here's Raimey's herd, sitting smack dab on Jupiter's equator," Milligan said. "Here's the group of Protectors, running a little deeper but staying basically right below them. Here's the herd ahead of them; here's the herd behind them. Almost every Qanska we've ever seen has been running within a couple thousand kilometers of the equator."

"Right," Faraday said, cultivating his patience. They knew all this. "So?"

"So why?" Milligan asked. "They've got the whole creaking Jovian atmosphere to play around in. Why do they all hug the equator that way?"

"Maybe they're just gregarious," Faraday said. "Or maybe it's more comfortable for them. They get more sunlight there than they would closer to the poles."

"Negligible," Milligan said flatly.

"Negligible to us," Faraday countered. "Maybe not to them."

"But a thousand kilometers?" Milligan said. "That's an incredibly narrow band, especially considering Jupiter's size. We sure went out and populated *our* whole world, and the sunlight makes a lot more difference to us than to them."

Faraday rubbed his eyes. "Mr. Milligan, why are we having this conversation right now?"

"Because I think this is something worth checking out," Milligan said. "I think we ought to send a couple of our deep probes into the higher latitudes to see what's out there."

Faraday glanced around the control board. None of the other three techs were looking at them, but they were obviously listening closely to the quiet conversation. "Why don't you bring this up tomorrow morning?" he suggested. "That way Mr. Hesse and I could hear it together."

Milligan's lips tightened. "Mr. Hesse has already made it clear that he wants to save as many probes as possible for when Raimey gets bigger and starts going deeper in the atmosphere."

Faraday nodded cynically. "In other words, you've already tried this pitch on him," he said. "And having struck out, you naturally came to me."

"Well, no, not really," Milligan hedged. "I haven't exactly *suggested* it. But from things he's said, its clear he's hell-bent on sticking to whatever grand scheme the Five Hundred have hatched. According to him, we're not in the pure-research business."

"He's right, we're not," Faraday murmured. "And those deep-probes cost nearly half a billion dollars each."

"Yeah, he's mentioned that, too," Milligan said sourly. "But this isn't just pure research, and it sure isn't just for the fun of it. We don't have any idea what's out there, except that the Qanska seem to be avoiding those areas. There could be masses of predators or other dangers, things that could directly impact the whole project."

"Nice speech," Faraday complimented him. "You've been practicing."

"It's something we need to know," Milligan insisted. He paused, just for a second—"Besides," he added, dropping his voice still lower, "it could be that the Qanska are hiding *it* out there."

Faraday looked up at the display. *It.* The Holy Grail, as Hesse liked to refer to it. The whole point of Project Changeling. "Or it could be that the Qanska simply cluster their young together for protection," he said. "Maybe once they're older and larger, they spread out more evenly over the planet."

"Maybe," Milligan said. "But we won't know until we take a look, will we?"

"Or until we let Raimey take a look," Faraday pointed out. "Let's give it a little longer, shall we?"

Milligan made a face. "In other words, no."

"In other words, not yet," Faraday corrected. "We can always take another look at our options after Raimey reaches adulthood and is out on his own."

"Which is at least two years away," Milligan muttered. "Longer if he gets picked for Protector duty."

"That's all right," Faraday soothed him. "We've got time. This is why Raimey's here, after all. Give him time, and he'll be able to do a far more efficient search than we ever can. Even with all this expensive hardware."

"Or at least he will once you tell him about it." Milligan looked sideways up at him. "When *are* you planning to tell him, by the way?"

"When the time is right," Faraday said. "And it'll be my problem, not yours. Was there anything else?"

Milligan glowered at his board. "No. Sir."

"I'll see you in the morning, then," Faraday said, standing up and returning his chair to its usual place. "And keep a sharp eye out for that Vuukan hunting pack Chang spotted last night. They may not have given up."

"I'll watch for them," Milligan promised. "After all, we can't risk losing our secret agent, can we?"

"Exactly," Faraday said, glancing around the room. "Good night, all."

And that was precisely the point, he thought darkly to himself as he walked down the dimly lit corridor toward his quarters. If Milligan was allowed to launch his probes—if by some miracle he was actually able to find Hesse's precious Holy Grail—then what use would the Five Hundred have anymore for Project Changeling?

The answer was as cold as an accountant's bottom line: none. And Faraday had had more than enough experience with government to know that when the interest dried up, so did the money. An hour after Raimey lost his value to Earth, Faraday and the rest of the Changeling team would be packed and on their way back to civilization.

And there was no way in hell he would do that to Raimey. Not after he'd been the one to talk the boy into this in the first place.

So Milligan wouldn't get his survey probes. Not yet. Not until Raimey was old enough to take care of himself.

They owed him that much.

SIX

"Hey, Manta! Wait up, will you?"

Raimey rolled over onto his side and looked back. Pranlo was swimming rapidly up behind him, with that slightly wavering stroke that meant he was getting tired. "Vuuk-mook, but you're fast. What's the hurry?"

"Hurry?" Raimey countered innocently. "What hurry? And by the way, what are you lazing around for?"

"Funny," Pranlo grunted. "What are we doing out here, anyway?"

"I want to show you something," Raimey said, doing a slow spin to look around them. No one was nearby, with the usual exception of Tigrallo treading air watchfully below them.

Always there. Except when it really mattered.

He shook the thoughts away. "Come on," he said, turning his back on Tigrallo.

"Where?" Pranlo asked.

"Straight down." Rolling over and flipping himself up to vertical, Raimey started down.

He had come a long way, he thought distantly, since his arrival on Jupiter and that first botched attempt at a swim. He could vividly remember his terrified awkwardness as he'd tried frantically to elude that Vuuka that had been zeroing in on him.

Now, in contrast, his movements were smooth and fluid. His fin muscles pushed effortlessly against the swirling wind, his stomach and buttock muscles contracted his internal buoyancy sacs instinctively, without need of conscious thought or effort.

How long had it been since then, anyway? He didn't know, exactly. Somewhere around two hundred ninedays, he guessed; just over two of the ninety nineday groupings that the Qanska quaintly called dayherds. He could always ask if he were really curious about it; there were Qanska back in the herd whose job was to keep track of the days.

But time didn't matter that much to him here. Besides, he didn't interact with the rest of the herd very much any more. At least not with the adults. Not since that terrible day . . .

"Pranlo?" a girl's voice called faintly from above him. "Hey, Manta. Wait up, you guys."

"Manta?" Pranlo called. "Wait up, huh? It's Drusni."

"I know it's Drusni," Raimey called back, snapping out of his hovering depression into full-swimming annoyance. Of course it was Drusni. Every time he turned around, it seemed, there was Drusni. Floating around chattering about nothing, or pushing her way uninvited into the run of food he was going for, or bugging him with questions even a newborn should know the answers to. She was like his kid sister, plus all his kid sister's friends, all rolled into a single bubble-pack.

"Oh, come on, Manta," Pranlo cajoled. "She's okay."

"So are Pakra when they keep their mouths shut," Raimey muttered. Still, reluctantly, he eased back on his dive.

"Whew!" Drusni said as she caught up. "Where are you guys going?"

"It's a secret," Pranlo said. "Okay, Manta, we're ready. Let's go."

"And I mean *secret*," Raimey warned. "*Really* secret."

"Yeah, I know," Pranlo assured him.

"I wasn't talking to you," Raimey said, flipping sideways to pin Drusni with a glare.

"Oh, sure," she said with an annoying combination of innocence and earnestness. "You can count on me."

"Yeah," Raimey muttered, rolling over onto his back again. "Okay, come on."

They headed down together, Pranlo and Drusni chatting cheerfully together as they swam. A couple of kids, Raimey thought sourly, without a single care in the world.

But then, why shouldn't they be cheerful? Why shouldn't they both be cheerful?

After all, *they* still had mothers.

An extra-fast layer of wind brushed across his stomach. Almost there. "Okay, we're coming up on it," he told the others. "Get ready." The wind eased off . . .

And there it was, directly below them: a thick run of green *prupsis* and red-speckled *morchay*, with more of the deliciously purple *kachtis* mixed in with it than Raimey had ever seen before in his life.

Obviously more than Pranlo and Drusni had seen before, either. "Wow!" Pranlo gasped.

Drusni, for her part, let out an excited squeak. "How in the world did you find this?"

"Native talent, of course," Raimey said modestly. Which wasn't entirely true, of course. Faraday and his helpers far above had done some kind of emscan analysis through one of the probes and suggested he might find a concentration of food plants trapped between layers of extra-fast wind.

Raimey could remember one of the techs going on and on with very learned-sounding stuff about laminar flow and turbulence layers and such. But he hadn't paid much attention to that part. Faraday had said food, and he'd been right, and that was all that mattered.

And for right now, at least, it was all theirs. Enough *kachtis*, he guessed, to fill even Drusni's big mouth.

It was quickly clear that she intended to put that theory to the test. With another happy squeak, she dove in, scattering food around her like the water of a pool she was splashing in. Pranlo was right behind her.

Midlings, Raimey thought with a condescending sniff as he carefully maneuvered through the slipstream to one edge of the floating smorgasbord. No sense splashing any of this good stuff out into the winds and letting the herd ahead of them get it. Flicking out his tongue, he began to delicately pull the slender purple vines into range of his teeth.

There was a subtle change in the pattern of wind across his back, and he looked over to see Tigrallo sidle up beside him. "This is not wise, Manta," the big Protector warned. "Vuuka and Sivra know about these clusters, too. They often lurk nearby, waiting for unwary Qanska to appear." He flipped his tails emphatically. "And this one in particular is far too deep for Midlings of your age and size."

"We're hardly Midlings anymore," Raimey countered. "We're nearly Youths, you know. Anyway, isn't that why you Protectors are here? To keep us all nice and safe?"

For a moment Tigrallo was silent. "You blame me for Mirasni's death," he said at last.

"It doesn't matter," Raimey muttered, turning back to the food. "Anyway, pointing heads doesn't do anyone any good."

"It *does* matter," Tigrallo said. "It's been three ninedays now, and you still haven't spoken of it. Yet I know it's still a problem that lies undigested inside you."

"What good would talking do?" Raimey demanded. "She's dead because you were too busy chasing off a couple of incompetent Vuuka to go help her. End of story."

"Those incompetent Vuuka, as you call them, might have killed you," Tigrallo said.

"Oh, come on," Raimey growled. "I was swimming tail loops around them. They were biting air the whole time, and that's all they would have bitten. I wasn't in any danger, and you know it."

"No, I *don't* know it," Tigrallo said stiffly. "But whether you were or not doesn't matter. What matters is that you are the one the Counselors and the Leaders and the Wise have ordered me to protect. That's my responsibility, and I will fulfill it to the last of my ability."

"Great," Raimey said contemptuously. "Turn off your brain and concentrate on following orders. You'd have made a terrific bureaucrat."

"I don't know that word."

Raimey flipped his tails. "Forget it."

He turned back to the floating food, trying to block the image of his mother's torn body out of his mind, awash in the sickening yellow of her own blood as the Nurturers tried futilely to save her life. But he couldn't.

And even the *kachtis* had lost its taste.

"Hey, Manta," Pranlo called from somewhere below him. "Come here."

Taking a deep breath, Raimey flipped over and started down, spinning around as he did so to locate his friend. There he was, flapping against the slipstream wind at the bottom of the food clump. "What is it?" he asked as he pulled out of his dive beside him.

"Grab yourself one of these things," Pranlo said. He flicked out his tongue and snagged an unfamiliar-looking blue-green cluster. "Come on, taste it."

Frowning, Raimey located one and took a cautious bite. It was better even than *kachtis*. "What are they?" he asked.

"Fin-bit if I know," Pranlo said. "Hey, Tigrallo. What are these things?"

"They are called *drokmur*," Tigrallo said, drifting down to join them. "They aren't usually found this high up."

"Oh, so this is the stuff you adults keep for yourselves," Pranlo said. "Can't say I blame you."

"It's not a matter of keeping anything for anyone," Tigrallo said, sounding annoyed. "Midlings your age are simply not heavy enough to reach the areas where it usually grows."

"Well, I suppose it's nice to have something to look forward to when we grow up," Pranlo said around a mouthful.

Tigrallo made a chuckling sound in the back of his throat. "Among other things, yes."

"Hey, guys," Drusni's voice wafted in from ahead of them. "You try these blue-green things yet?"

"Yes," Raimey and Pranlo called back in unison.

"Matter of fact, we saw them first," Pranlo added. "That means we've got first rights to them."

"You go right ahead and try," Drusni called back.

"Raimey?" a voice murmured in the back of Raimey's head.

Raimey started, nearly biting his own tongue. "What?" he asked

It wasn't until the word was out of his mouth that he realized he'd answered in Qanskan tonals instead of English. He tried to switch languages—

And to his rather startled chagrin, he found he couldn't. His brain, immersed so deeply for so long in Qanskan, was simply refusing to wrap itself around the proper words.

For a moment he struggled, trying stubbornly to make his brain go there anyway. Then, abruptly, he changed his mind. Interrupting his meal had been their idea, not his. Why should he get his tails in a knot just to accommodate them?

To the Deep with it. If they wanted to talk to him, they could jolly well translate for themselves.

"Ask him how far down these *drokmur* usually grow," Faraday said.

Raimey flicked his tails in annoyance. What was he, anyway, their private messenger boy?

He grimaced. Actually, that was exactly what he was. Finding out about all these things was the reason he was here in the first place.

"You said these things don't usually get up here," he said to Tigrallo "Where *do* they usually grow?"

"They are usually found at Levels Three, Four, and Five," the Protector told him.

"Levels Three, Four, and Five," Raimey repeated for the benefit of the eavesdroppers upstairs. "So usually only Youths, Breeders, and Protectors get to eat them?"

"Yes," Tigrallo said. "Manta, I strongly urge you to leave this level and rejoin the rest of the herd. The Vuuka could appear at any time."

"We'll go up when we're ready," Raimey said shortly, turning back to his meal. "You get that?" he added quietly.

"Yes," Faraday said. "Thank you."

"That's why I'm here," Raimey said with a touch of irony in his voice. Though whether Faraday and his buddies could even pick up such subtleties with their totally inadequate tonal recording equipment he didn't know. Probably not. Even full-blown sarcasm would probably be lost on them.

He was savoring another bite of *drokmur* when the rest of it suddenly caught up with him.

Faraday had asked what levels the *drokmur* grew on. But Raimey had never mentioned levels up till then.

For that matter, he hadn't even mentioned the word *drokmur*.

Which meant that Jupiter Prime wasn't just listening in on what *he* said right now. They were listening in on what everyone else around him was saying, too.

He did another slow spin, searching the area carefully. It was one of their probes, of course. It had to be. But if there was one lurking around, he couldn't spot it.

Which left only one other possibility.

Like the *kachtis* before it, the *drokmur* suddenly lost its taste. What *had* Faraday said about this subvocalizer gadget they'd built into him, anyway? Raimey couldn't remember, exactly, but he knew he'd gotten the distinct impression that they could only pick up what he himself was saying.

But had Faraday actually *said* that?

He couldn't remember. And if he couldn't remember a specific statement, chances were suspiciously high that Faraday hadn't made one.

So in other words, Raimey wasn't just their messenger boy. He was also their self-mobile espionage probe.

And if they had audio capability, what else did they have?

He slid his tongue across the rough insides of his teeth in frustration and annoyance. Still, he had to admit that it made sense. There were probably things their instruments could pick up and analyze that he himself couldn't.

Though what those things might be he didn't know. Certainly Qanskan sight and hearing were a lot sharper than any human had guessed. But of course, no one had known that when they'd designed this experiment.

Or had they?

"Manta?" a voice said softly from his right.

He rolled over and looked that direction. Drusni had come up beside him, and was gazing at him with an oddly anxious expression on her face. "It's okay," she said quietly. "I know it hurts. We've all lost family and friends. It's just the way things are."

She stroked her fin across his. "But we're your friends. We'll help you get through it."

Raimey took a deep breath. Clearly, she'd completely misinterpreted the reason for his sudden silence. Typical Drusni, really.

Still, even amidst his annoyance at her, he had to admit that the unexpected expression of sympathy felt kind of good against the rawness of his anger and pain. "Thank you," he said quietly. "I'm—look, I know I pick on you a lot. But you and Pranlo—"

"I know," she said, some of her normal cheer peeking through her seriousness. "But friends do that."

She touched his fin again, only this time it was more like a playful slap than a stroke. "Come on," she said, flipping away from him. "Tigrallo's right—we've got to get out of here."

"Okay," Raimey said. "But not until I clear out this *drokmur* first."

"Not if I get there first," she called over her back. "Race you for it."

Raimey rolled over and headed after her. And wondered at the odd tingling in his skin where her fin had touched his.

"Well?" Faraday asked.

Beach lifted his hands helplessly. "Near as I can tell, everything's working just fine," he said. "If there's a glitch in the subvocalizer, it's not showing up on any of the diagnostics. Maybe there's some interference from the life-support equipment."

"Not a chance," McCollum insisted, peering closely at her own board. "Besides, it's geared down to barely a tenth its original output. What could it be doing *now* that it wouldn't have done before?"

At the other end of the board, Sprenkle cleared his throat. "You're all assuming there's a technical problem with the equipment," he said. "Maybe there isn't."

"Then why isn't he talking to us?" Beach demanded.

"He *is* talking to us," Sprenkle pointed out. "He's just talking in Qanskan, not English."

"That's right," Beach said in a tone of strained patience. "Which means he's having trouble with his subvocalizer."

"Why does it mean that?" Sprenkle asked. "Maybe he's just more comfortable speaking in Qanskan now." He paused. "Or maybe he's forgotten how to speak English, even on a subvocalizer."

Beach threw an odd look over his shoulder at Faraday. "Am I the only one in here who doesn't like the sound of that?" he asked.

"Let's not panic just yet," Faraday advised. But he could feel the skin starting to crawl at the back of his neck, too. "Dr. Sprenkle, how could he *forget* how to speak English? I thought you said his memory and personality profile were holding steady through the cell replacement process."

"They are," Sprenkle said. "Or at least, they were at the last check six weeks ago. But things do change, you know. Sometimes without much warning."

There was a sound of footsteps from outside the door. Faraday turned to look—

"Good morning," Hesse said, striding into the Contact Room and glancing around at each of them. "How are things going?"

"Raimey can't or won't talk English to us," Beach said. "Hans thinks he may be going native."

Hesse's jaw dropped a couple of millimeters. "Really," he said.

"And welcome back," Faraday added. "How was Earth?"

"Just fine, thank you," Hesse said absently, crossing over to stand behind Sprenkle. "What exactly does 'going native' mean here?"

"Everette is exaggerating a bit," Sprenkle said, sending a slightly vexed look across at Beach. "It could just be that Raimey didn't feel like changing verbal gears in the middle of a conversation. He's never been the type to go out of his way to be helpful to others, after all, and he knows we can translate Qanskan tonals."

"Or it could be the equipment," Hesse said, rubbing his cheek. "Where is he now?"

"Down at the bottom of Level Two," Milligan said, looking over at the image from one of the spy probes. "He's feeding on some stuff we haven't seen before."

"Interesting about that, too," McCollum added. "You'd think that as you move farther away from sunlight you'd get less variety in the vegetation, not more. But this is plant life that doesn't exist farther up."

"Maybe it doesn't need sunlight," Hesse suggested, leaving Sprenkle and walking over to look at her board. "Maybe it lives on the equivalent of those hot sulfur vents in Earth's deep oceans."

"Possibly," McCollum said. "The obvious candidate for that role being the radiation from Jupiter's core. Or the plants could have the kind of life cycle where their main growth occurs at the top of the atmosphere, after which they go dormant and sink farther down."

"Well, stay on it," Hesse said, turning to Milligan. "What about the McCarthy setup? That's still functional, I presume?"

Beach and McCollum exchanged a quick glance. "No way of knowing," Beach said. "There's no way to test it apart from a full activation."

"Which I'd advise against doing right now," Sprenkle put in quickly. "There's no indication he knows anything yet."

"I'm aware of that, thank you," Hesse said. "On the other

hand, I also notice there's a lot more static than usual on the audio feed."

"That's just because of the depth he's at," McCollum said.

"Which is exactly my point," Hesse said tartly. "If we're starting to lose him before he's even at Level Three, there's a damn good chance he'll be out of reach well before he *does* know anything."

He turned a glare on Faraday. "And if in the process he 'goes native,' whatever that means, we could have a serious problem on our hands."

"So what are you suggesting?" Faraday asked calmly. "That we go ahead and tell him the real reason he's there?"

Hesse looked back at Sprenkle. "You're the psychologist," he said, making the sentence an accusation. "You think he's in danger of forgetting he's human?"

Sprenkle's lips puckered. "The problem is, of course, that he *isn't* human," he reminded Hesse. "At least, not physically."

"But he still has his human memories and personality, right?" Hesse persisted.

"So it appears," Sprenkle said. "But the physical body does affect mental and emotional states. How profound that effect is, or how profound it's going to become, there's simply no way of knowing."

"If you want my vote, I say we tell him," Beach offered. "And the sooner the better. This lie's gone on long enough."

"When Changeling becomes a democracy, I'll let you know," Hesse said icily. He hissed gently through his teeth, then shook his head. "No, we'll hold off a little longer. Let him get bigger, give him the kind of swimming range he'll need for the job. He'll still have access to Level One for quite a while—surely he'll bounce up there at least occasionally."

He made an attempt at a smile. "So. Thank you all for your input."

He turned and headed for the back corner where the cof-

fee pot and tea samovar were simmering softly to themselves. Glancing at the techs to make sure their attention
was back where it belonged, Faraday strolled over to join
him.

Hesse got in the first word. "Sorry," he muttered as he
drew a mug of coffee. "I shouldn't have snapped at them
like that."

"No need to apologize," Faraday said. "At least, not to
me. I take it things didn't go well on Earth?"

Hesse's cheek muscles tightened visibly. "The under-
statement of the decade," he said. "The Five Hundred are
becoming impatient with Changeling, Colonel, particularly
the faction that pushed through the scheme in the first place.
And I get the impression that impatience extends to the two
of us personally."

"It's been barely two years," Faraday pointed out, irri-
tated in spite of himself. As far as he was concerned, the
Five Hundred's veiled impatience had started midway
through Day Two. It was pure political power-jockeying,
and he for one was getting pretty tired of it. "Raimey's
hardly past the Midling stage, for heaven's sake. If they
couldn't figure out this was a long-term project, they
shouldn't be allowed to cross the street by themselves."

Hesse sighed. "I think it's more a matter of overall political pressure," he said. "There've been a lot of minor
crises of confidence over the past few months, and I get
the feeling there's been serious slippage in the Five Hundred's support. And not only on Mars and Luna, either."

"And of course, the novelty of Changeling has long since
worn off as far as the general public is concerned," Faraday
pointed out.

"As the novelty of such things always does," Hesse
agreed sourly. "Especially when you've got something as
exciting as Martian riots going on a few channels over."

Faraday grimaced. "The whole station was following that
one," he said. "Plenty of arguments going back and forth,
too. I understand you were actually there?"

Hesse shrugged. "I rode part of the way back here with

Councilor Yakamura and got to sit in on a couple of sessions with his mediation team. I didn't do any of the talking, of course."

"I was rather surprised that Yakamura didn't reveal Changeling's real purpose during the talks," Faraday said. "Or did he, and they simply suppressed it from the newsnets?"

"No, he didn't say a word," Hesse said. "No point to it, really."

"No point?" Faraday echoed, frowning.

"Changeling is a long shot," Hesse said grimly. "Long shots are risky things to hang negotiations on."

"Even so, I'd have thought it would help defuse the situation," Faraday insisted. "I mean, we *are* talking about the ultimate solution to the whole overcrowding problem. Presumably a lot cheaper than developing Titan and Janus, too."

Hesse shook his head. "You're thinking long-term," he said. "The Martians aren't. All they can see is the immediate issue of the Council wanting to pour a ton of money into grinding out a few foothold bases on Saturn's moons instead of upgrading facilities on the colonies we already have."

"I can't say as I entirely disagree with them, either," Faraday said. "Saturn's a mighty long way out."

"So was Jupiter a generation ago," Hesse reminded him. "I dare say that the idea of putting colonies and stations here wasn't all that popular when it was first proposed."

"It wasn't," Faraday had to concede. "I can remember when they first started building Jupiter Prime. From the way Mars and Ceres howled, you'd have thought they were being left to wither on the vine. Especially since all the surveys proved that no one with half a functioning brain would want to live this far from Earth."

"And now there are nearly half a million people living in the Jovian Sector," Hesse said wryly. "And in that same period Mars's population has more than tripled. So much for withering on the vine."

"The Martians still have a point," Faraday said. "The farther out we go, the more expensive the real estate is to develop. The Five Hundred might well do better to expand the facilities we already have instead of pushing for new ones. Certainly the Jovian Sector has lots of room for expansion."

"True," Hesse said. "But the living space itself is only part of the story. Human beings need frontiers, Colonel. We need places where the restless and ambitious can go."

"And where the troublemakers can be dumped?" Faraday suggested pointedly.

Under his brand-new Earth tan, Hesse reddened slightly. "There's some of that, too, I suppose," he conceded. "The bottom line, though, is that the Solar System stops at Pluto, and that's not all that far away anymore. If Raimey doesn't come through . . ." He shook his head.

"He'll come through," Faraday assured him. "If there's any way to do it, he will."

"I hope you're right," Hesse said.

Faraday looked back at the fuzzy monitors. *Yes*, he added silently to himself. *So do I.*

SEVEN

The pressures at the bottom of Level Three were stiffer than anything Raimey had yet encountered. But the temperature was pleasantly warm and there were interesting new foodstuffs to sample.

And best of all, for the moment at least, he was alone. Or at least, as alone as he ever got.

"It's not wise to be down here alone," Tigrallo warned from his perpetual spot at the edge of Raimey's vision. "And of all days, this one would be more properly spent with the others of the herd."

"They won't even miss me," Raimey told him shortly, straining to dive still deeper. To get away from the herd, and the Babies, the Midlings, and the other Youths.

And, most of all, to get away from Drusni.

"They'll be singing the Song of Change in less than a ninth-part," Tigrallo reminded him.

As if Raimey needed reminding. "I've already heard it," he said. "Twice."

"But you've never heard it sung for you," Tigrallo said.

"I'll become an adult whether they sing it or not," Raimey said. "Besides, I don't have a mother to sing it to me. I'd just be hearing it from strangers."

"They're hardly strangers," Tigrallo said with mild reproof. "Or at least, they shouldn't be."

"I know, I know," Raimey growled. Tigrallo had been on his tails forever about spending more time with the herd instead of off by himself.

"That's not what I meant," the Protector said gently. "I

was simply trying to point out that there are many who will gladly sing the Song to you. To you, as well as to the other Youths who are without family."

Raimey flipped his tails. "Willingly, maybe, but not gladly. At least, not in my case."

"You know that's not true," Tigrallo said severely. With a flip of his tails, he moved closer to Raimey's side. "The Song isn't the real problem, is it, Manta? It's something else."

Raimey turned away from him, a dozen conflicting emotions and frustrations tearing through his stomach like baby Pakra fighting each other for the scraps of a kill. "It's nothing," he said. "I'm just not feeling like company today, that's all."

He tried to swim away, but Tigrallo stayed right with him. "Is it Drusni?" he asked.

Drusni. Raimey slashed viciously at the air with his tails. Drusni. Sweet, clumsy, caring, flippant, vibrant, maddening, radiant Drusni. Half the time she drove him crazy, the other half he couldn't stand to be away from her.

And try as hard as he could, he couldn't get her out of his mind.

"She's okay," he said, trying hard to sound casual. "Mostly, she's a pain in the throats."

For a moment Tigrallo was silent, but Raimey could feel the air currents as the Protector swished his tail back and forth. He kept his back to the other, not daring to look and see what kind of expression that tail-swishing might be taking. The last thing he needed right now was to have his personal Protector laughing at him.

"Perhaps," Tigrallo said at last. There was no amusement or condescension in his voice that Raimey could detect, not even in his hypersensitive state. "Perhaps not."

"Are you calling me a liar?"

"Not at all," Tigrallo said, deflecting the challenge calmly. "There may simply be more to it than even you realize."

He swished his tail again. "It's not so many dayherds since I was a Breeder myself, you know."

"I'm not a Breeder," Raimey insisted. "Not yet."

Tigrallo gave a shrug. "The Song of Change is merely a formality. Physically, you're certainly no longer a Youth."

Raimey grimaced. No, he certainly wasn't. He could feel the hormones swirling inside him, playing a mass game of tagabuck with his thoughts and emotions. It was very much like being fifteen again.

There was only one problem. These were *alien* hormones, driving him toward *alien* females. That alone was enough to make his skin crawl, in an eerily tingly sort of way.

All right; there were two problems, actually. He didn't *want* to be fifteen again.

"But ceremony or not, we should leave this place," Tigrallo went on. "Or, if you still insist on staying this deep, we should find a group of Breeders to swim with. It would be safer."

"I already told you I didn't want company," Raimey bit out. He turned back to the drifting food—

"Manta?" a clear voice called from somewhere above him. "Manta?"

It was, of course, Drusni.

Raimey's heart sank and leaped at the same time, an amazingly good trick. "Great," he muttered. "Just what I needed."

"Manta?" she called again.

"Are you going to answer her?" Tigrallo prompted quietly.

For a long moment Raimey was tempted to say no. The atmosphere seemed especially murky today, and if he kept his mouth shut Drusni could search for a long time without finding him.

But then she might miss the ceremony, too. And everyone would blame him.

He shook his fins with frustration. No matter what he

did, he wasn't going to win this one. "Over here," he called with a sigh.

"*There* you are," Drusni said, pushing her way into sight from above and settling in beside him. "What are you doing down here?"

"Hunting for Pakra eggs," Raimey growled. "How did you find me?"

"Pranlo told me you'd been spending a lot of time down here lately," she said, flipping her tails. "You okay?"

"I'm fine," he said. "What do you want?"

"I want you to come up, of course," she said, sounding surprised. "The Song of Change, remember? It's going to be starting soon."

"I hadn't forgotten," Raimey said. "I just thought I'd give it a pass, that's all." He gestured upward. "You'd better get back, though."

"Not without you," she said firmly. "This is our last big bite before adulthood. The Three Musketta, remember?"

"Musketeers," Raimey corrected her for about the ninetieth time since he'd introduced her and Pranlo to the term. "The Three Muske*teers*."

"Whatever," she said, not taking offense. "Come on, Manta, it'll be fun. I mean, adults honoring us and children looking up to us with awe? Think of the possibilities. We can play this one for all it's worth."

"You go play it," Raimey said stiffly. "I'm not interested."

"Oh, come on," she cajoled. "Don't you want to grow up to be one of the Wise someday? And get to go live on Level Eight?"

Raimey snorted. "Right. Level Eight. Where only the Wise can go, where there aren't any predators or scavengers, and where a Qanska can live as long as he can swim."

"Oh, good," Drusni said cheerfully. "You *do* pay attention during story circle. I've always wondered about that."

Raimey flipped his tails in a shrug. "Hey, I *like* the stories," he said. "Even the ones that sound like wishful thinking."

"Level Eight isn't wishful thinking," Drusni insisted. "Ask any Protector or Nurturer. They'll tell you about someone they know personally who lives down there."

"Or at least that they personally know a Counselor who claims to have talked to a Leader, who says he's seen a Wise," Raimey countered. "Sounds pretty bogus, if you ask me."

Drusni wiggled her fins. "If you think you can chase me off the subject by starting a different conversation, you're mistaken," she said primly. "Now, what about the Song of Change? Please?"

"I hate ceremonies," Raimey growled. But he could feel himself weakening in the glow of her gaze. "Especially this kind. They're always so overpuffed."

"Why don't you try thinking of it like it's another story?" she suggested. "Just like story circle, only this one's set to music."

"But I don't *like* ceremonies."

"Please?" she asked again. "For me?"

Raimey ground his teeth together, trying hard not to look at her. But she was impossible not to look at. So radiant . . . "Drusni, look. I just—"

"Go!" Tigrallo barked, practically in Raimey's ear. "As fast as you can!"

The Protector flipped around so suddenly that the tip of one of his tails slapped across Raimey's back. Raimey rolled over to glare at him, opening his mouth to say something nasty.

The words jammed sideways in his throats. Swimming straight at them, coming into view through the haze like avenging ghosts, wiggled a whole group of small, eel-like creatures.

A pack of hunting Sivra.

"Go!" Tigrallo snarled again over his back. Flapping his fins defiantly, he threw himself straight into the center of the pack.

"You heard him," Raimey snapped at Drusni, righting

himself and slapping at her side with the tip of his fin. "Get moving!"

She swam a couple of strokes away, then seemed to falter. "What about you?" she asked.

Raimey swore under his breath, his own fins locked in place with indecision. Rolling half over, he looked back at Tigrallo.

The sight froze his blood. The Protector could barely be seen through the cloud of Sivra now swarming madly around him. Raimey caught a glimpse of one of Tigrallo's fins as it flapped violently, the colorful pattern of stripes almost completely obscured by the predators clinging to it. And bright yellow Qanskan blood was everywhere.

What do I do? the frantic thought raced through Raimey's mind. Should he run? Or should he try to help Tigrallo? The Song of Change they were preparing up above would presumably contain instructions for his new societal duties. But that Song hadn't been sung to him yet, and he hadn't paid very good attention the times he'd heard it sung to others of the herd.

He stiffened his fins. No. He wasn't just a simple-minded Qanska, who needed some ancient Song to tell him how to behave. He was human, too; and humans always knew the right thing to do. A Protector's job was to guard Qanskan children, whether Babies, Midlings, or Youths.

But Raimey was no longer in any of those categories except in name. He was effectively an adult now . . . and being an adult didn't mean running like a coward when someone was in trouble. "Hold on, Tigrallo," he called, diving toward the mob scene below. "I'm coming."

"No!" Tigrallo bellowed. But it was a weak and hoarse bellow, full of pain and grim hopelessness. "Go. Run."

"I'm coming," Raimey repeated. He leaned hard into the heavy air—

"Manta!" Drusni gasped from behind him. "Help!"

Raimey rolled over and looked back. Drusni, still lingering behind him instead of swimming for the herd like she'd been told, had been overtaken by two of the Sivra.

Even as he flipped around and charged toward her, one of them got a grip on the trailing edge of her left fin.

She screamed; and as she did, Raimey felt fear and rage flood through him like twin waves of superheated air, giving him a strength he would never have guessed he could have. "I'm coming," he called, driving up toward her. "Hold on, I'm coming."

"Hurry!" Drusni pleaded, corkscrewing madly through the air as she tried to shake off the little predator hanging from her fin like a drab holiday streamer. The second Sivra was darting around her, trying to get a grip of his own.

He was still trying when Raimey ducked his snout and slammed forehead-first into him.

There was a sound like wet leather slapping onto rock, and with a forlorn little whistling moan the Sivra fell away into the gloom. Twisting around, Raimey caught the tail end of the other Sivra in his mouth and bit down as hard as he could.

Qanskan jaw muscles weren't designed for such things, and the bite wasn't nearly as hard as Raimey would have liked. But apparently it was hard enough. The Sivra let go of Drusni's fin and spun around toward this new assailant, screaming in rage and pain. For a stretched-out pulse of time they glared at each other: the five-meter Qanska almost-adult, and the half-meter hunting Sivra.

And then the pulse passed, and with a flip of his flat-snake body the Sivra attacked.

Raimey dodged, but he wasn't nearly as maneuverable as the smaller predator. Teeth raked across his back, drawing blood; and then, as he tried to twist away, the Sivra sank his teeth firmly into the front edge of his right fin.

A shiver of pain shot through him. But with the fury still flooding his blood, he hardly even noticed. He continued his twist, rocking violently back and forth, trying to break the Sivra's grip. But the predator hung on doggedly.

And then something flashed past his eyes: Drusni's tails, slashing against the Sivra's body. "Manta!" he heard her gasp.

"Get away," he snarled at her. "Go."

"No!" she said, slashing at the Sivra again. "Not without you."

Raimey twisted again, harder this time. But the predator's grip didn't loosen. He came to a jerking halt, twisted back the other direction—

And then, through the pain, he suddenly felt something give. The Sivra wasn't letting go, exactly, but something about its grip felt different. Pausing in his thrashing, Raimey peered down along the edge of his fin.

The Sivra was still there. But at the point where it had grabbed Raimey's fin, its drab brownish body had taken on a new color scheme: blue, with edges of a dark red.

The same color scheme, in fact, as Raimey's own skin.

Raimey stared, so fascinated that for a moment he forgot the pain, the danger he was in, and even Drusni. He'd seen Qanskan skin growing up around attacking predators before; in fact, he'd seen it happen his very first day on this planet. But he'd never seen it happen with his own body.

It was the strangest thing to watch, and an even stranger thing to feel. Rather like a scab starting to itch, he decided, but with a strange sort of stretching sensation added to it as well. The skin had crept nearly halfway up the Sivra's length now, and the creature had stopped struggling. Dead, Raimey decided, though still managing to maintain a death-grip on his fin.

Of course, snugged into Raimey's self-growing cocoon, the Sivra's teeth didn't really have any choice but to stay where they were. No wonder older Qanska were so lumpy.

A slap on his other fin jolted him out of his fascinated reverie. "Manta, come on," Drusni panted. "We've got to get out of here."

Raimey twisted over and looked behind him, suddenly remembering the deadly danger they were both in. If the other Sivra were still on the hunt—

But no. This particular pack of Sivra weren't going to be bothering him and Drusni. At least, not any time soon. They already had their meal well in hand.

He looked away from the predators' feast, sickened to his core. "Yes," he told Drusni quietly as he started swimming upward. "Let's go."

"What's happening?" Hesse demanded, hovering behind Beach with all the nervous anxiety of a mother hen watching her latest batch of eggs being readied for Sunday brunch. From the speaker, the gasps and panting and clipped instructions continued to flow, all of it overlaid with a thick layer of static. "Damn it all, what's *happening*?"

"I'm working on it, I'm working on it," Beach said, his fingers bouncing across his keyboard like twin kittens on a serious catnip high as he tried yet another sound-scrubbing program. "The relay probe's on its way down, but until it clears the cloud-layer turbulence I can't risk deploying the antennas. We're looking at ten more minutes, tops."

"He could be dead in ten minutes," Hesse shot back. "*Damn* it all. What did he think he was doing down there, anyway?"

"Avoiding the rest of the herd, probably," Sprenkle said. "If you think about it, he's been doing a lot of that since his mother's death."

"What are you talking about?" McCollum asked. "He and his friends have been practically joined at the fin for the past eight months."

"Agreed," Sprenkle said. "And all three have been pushing outward from the herd, with Raimey as the driving force. He's still running away; he's just taking a little company along with him."

"But isn't that normal?" McCollum argued. "They're nearly adults, preparing to go off on their own. In a lot of Earth species, they'd have been kicked out of the herd already."

"And don't forget that Raimey's been an adult stuck in a kid's body ever since Day One," Milligan added. Like Beach, he was typing busily at his console, working the controls of the relay probe. "He's going to be straining at the leash even harder."

"Pig drippings," Hesse said sourly. "If he was so anxious to be officially declared an adult, he'd be in the front row right now at that Song of Change ceremony. He's hotdogging, that's all. Seeing how deep he can go, and to hell with the consequences. The same idiot stunt he was pulling when he broke his stupid neck in the first place."

McCollum turned halfway around in her seat. "You're being very quiet, Colonel," she commented.

"Am I?" Faraday asked, gazing at the thrashing snow on the displays. "I was just thinking about Mirasni. Wondering if Raimey has ever really understood what she gave up so that he could be born in her son's body."

"I doubt it," Sprenkle murmured. "It's not the sort of question that's likely to even cross his mind. Raimey's a fairly shallow character, when you come right down to it. His number-one focus in life has always been himself."

"Well, he sure picks odd ways to demonstrate it," Hesse said with a snort. "He goes charging off maverick from the herd, and thereby runs square into whatever the hell is going on down there. Doesn't sound like self-preservation to me."

"True," Sprenkle agreed. "But self-absorption and self-preservation don't always go together."

Hesse frowned at him. "Are you suggesting he's become suicidal?"

"Not necessarily," Sprenkle said. "But that doesn't mean he might not give up without a fight if death came staring him in the face."

"Hell," Hesse muttered, looking back at the displays.

"Here we go," Milligan announced suddenly. "Probe's in range."

Faraday's eyes flicked across the displays. But there were only Raimey and Drusni, swimming hard, with no predators anywhere in sight. Whatever had happened, it looked like it was all over, and they'd made it through all right.

And then, a sudden cold thought squeezed at his throat, and he took a second look at the displays.

Raimey and Drusni were there. But Tigrallo was nowhere to be seen.

"Looks like they're heading up," Beach said.

"Is he all right?" Hesse demanded anxiously. "Ms. McCollum?"

"He's swimming smoothly, and I don't see any blood," McCollum reported, gazing at the images. "Looks like there's something hanging off his fin now, but it seems to be covered with his own skin. Probably a Sivra."

"They're still heading up," Milligan reported. "Looks like they're going all the way to Level One."

"I've got him on emscan now," Milligan added. "Heading for the herd, all right. Score one for the good guys."

"Better make that score two-thirds," Faraday corrected quietly. "Tigrallo's not with them."

There was a long, dark silence. "Oh, no," McCollum murmured.

"Maybe he's hanging back as rear guard," Beach suggested hesitantly.

"No." Milligan said. "I've got him on emscan from the probe. Or at least, what's left of him."

"Sivra," Beach muttered. "Damn little bastards."

"Any of them pursuing?" Hesse asked. Even he, Faraday noted, sounded subdued.

"No," Milligan said. "Everything looks clear."

"For now," McCollum said under her breath.

Milligan's lip twisted. "Yeah."

Hesse looked at Faraday. "That was close," he muttered. "Too close. We nearly lost everything."

"That was always the risk we took," Faraday reminded him, a small back corner of his mind noticing the irony in that statement. The risk *they* took? "The Five Hundred know that."

"Maybe they did once," Hesse said tightly. "I'm not so sure they do anymore."

Faraday frowned at him. The younger man's face had an

expression of pinched intensity on it, a look Faraday had never seen there before. "What do you know that you're not telling us?" he asked.

Hesse threw him a sideways look, as if suddenly realizing what he was giving away. "I don't *know* anything," he said, the intensity smoothing out like someone was going over his face with a cement trowel. "I just know how to read politicians. Do you know offhand when the next Qanskan sleep cycle is?"

Faraday glanced at the clock, did a quick calculation. "About three hours. Why?"

Hesse nodded at the displays. "I think maybe we should go ahead and let Raimey in on what he's really doing down there."

About time, too. "You think it's best to do it when he's supposed to be sleeping?" Faraday asked.

"He speaks exclusively in tonals these days," Hesse reminded him. "I said it's time to let *him* in on the secret, not every Qanska who can eavesdrop on his half of the conversation."

"I suppose." Faraday pursed his lips. "Though maybe we ought to hold off a few more days now. Tigrallo's been his closest companion for the past three years, probably some of the toughest and most challenging years Raimey's ever had to live through. Watching him die like that has to have been pretty traumatic."

"In that case, we'll be doing him a favor," Hesse growled. "Get his mind off his own troubles for a while."

"I was thinking more along the lines that he's probably feeling very Qanskan right now," Faraday said, trying hard to be diplomatic. "Dragging his thoughts back off Jupiter might be taken as something of an intrusion."

"All the more reason to do it now," Hesse said shortly. "It'll remind him that underneath all that alien skin, he's still a human being."

Faraday threw a glance at the back of Sprenkle's head. But it was clear the psychologist was going to keep whatever opinions he had to himself. "It's your call," Faraday said, turning back to Hesse. "Just make sure he's really alone. He's going to be called on the carpet for sure on this one, and the Leaders may want to hold him over past the sleep cycle for more questioning."

Hesse frowned. "What makes you think he's going to be in trouble?"

"You may know how to read politicians." Faraday looked up at the displays. "Me, I know how to read Qanska."

EIGHT

The Song of Change had been sung, the newly graduated Breeders had been congratulated by the parents, children, Protectors, and Nurturers, and the herd had split back up into individual family groups for perhaps their last private time together before the Breeders struck off on their own. Drusni and Pranlo had each invited Raimey back to join their families; he had politely but firmly refused them both.

He was swimming alone at the edge of the herd, wondering what in the world he was doing here, when one of the Protectors brought him a message.

Counselor Latranesto wanted to see him on Level Four. Now.

Latranesto and a small group of Protectors were waiting when Raimey and the messenger arrived. "Greetings to you, Counselor Latranesto of the Qanska," Raimey said, trying to flip his fins in the pattern of respect he'd been taught.

He didn't do a very good job of it. The air at this level was awkwardly dense, and he needed all his strength and fin-work to keep himself from popping back up to Level Three like a newborn without any buoyancy sac control. "I'm honored by your presence and attention," he said, hoping that quoting the proper words would help cover up the lack of postural respect.

"And greetings to you, Breeder Manta of the Qanska," Latranesto replied. His fins were also beating hard against the air as he struggled to hold position in what was—for him—very rarefied air indeed. If he was offended by Raimey's lack of a complete greeting, he didn't comment on it. "I greet you in the name of the Counselors, and the Leaders, and the Wise."

Raimey grimaced to himself. So this was indeed going to be an official meeting and conversation. The messenger's attitude had implied it would be, but Raimey had still privately hoped that Latranesto merely wanted to congratulate him on his passage to adulthood. "I'm honored in turn by their attention," he said. "What gift of service may I perform for you?"

"We are disturbed by the events that took place just prior to your herd's Song of Change," Latranesto said, his voice controlled and emotionless. "The events which ended in the death of Protector Tigrallo. We would like your explanation."

"I'm not sure what there is to explain," Raimey said cautiously. "He and I were feeding on Level Three and ran into a Sivra hunting pack. Tigrallo ordered me to leave, then stayed behind to fight them."

Latranesto's eyes turned pointedly to the fresh protuberance on Raimey's right fin. "And did you obey him?"

"I left as quickly as I could," Raimey said. "One of my companions had joined us by that time, and she was also attacked. It took me a few ninepulses to break up that attack and save her."

"You are a Breeder," Latranesto said, a hint of severity peeking through the flat official tone. "You are to protect yourself, not others."

"Not even when they're friends?"

"Not even then," Latranesto said. "Defense of others is the task of Protectors. You will have time enough to exercise such courage and concern when you are ready for it. Now. Continue."

It took Raimey a moment to find his tongue. What kind of people, he wondered darkly, forbade the protection of friends? "I drove away or killed the two Sivra who had attacked us," he went on. "Then she and I swam back to Level One. That's all."

"That is not all," Latranesto retorted. "Tell me why you were on Level Three hunting for food instead of preparing for the Song of Change with your herd."

I was hungry, was Raimey's first reactive answer. But somehow he didn't think flippancy was going to digest well with Latranesto today. "I didn't think any preparation was needed," he said instead. "The ceremony wasn't going to start for at least a ninth part."

"You *did* intend to join your herd for the ceremony, then?"

Raimey hesitated, smelling a verbal trap. Did Latranesto suspect that he'd been planning to skip the thing entirely? Could he even have spoken to Drusni already, or else had someone else question her about the incident? "I had felt uncomfortable at the thought of the ceremony," he said carefully, trying hard to read Latranesto's expression. But the big Counselor wasn't giving anything away. He would have made a great executive sales manager. "As you may know, my mother was killed when I was a Youth. Ever since then, herd activities that center on families and family life have been painful for me."

"All Qanska have experienced pain," Latranesto countered. "It's a part of all life, here or anywhere else. You cannot permit it to control your actions or define your decisions."

"No, of course not," Raimey agreed, trying to decide whether or not he was hearing a note of sympathy in the Counselor's voice. If so, it might be something he could capitalize on. If not—if this was a straight lecture—he would have to play it differently. "I'm not excusing my thoughts, but merely explaining them."

"I understand," Latranesto said, sounding a bit mollified. "You *did* intend to join your herd for the ceremony, then?"

"As I said, I had thought of not attending," Raimey said, choosing his words carefully. "But after further consideration, I realized it was both right and proper for me to do so. And so I did."

For a long minute Latranesto just hovered there, flapping

away and gazing intently at him. Raimey tried to hold the gaze without flinching, and mostly succeeded. What he had said was the truth, he told himself firmly, at least in a way. In any case, Latranesto certainly couldn't prove otherwise.

At last, the old Qanska gave an unreadable flip of his tails. "You are a thought puzzle, young Manta," he said. "It was part of our agreement with your people that you would be brought here to become one of the Qanska. Yet, while you have certainly done so in body, your heart and spirit are still those of a human."

"Does that displease you?" Raimey asked, wondering what in the world he was going to do about it if it did.

Latranesto seemed to sigh. "Pleasure and displeasure are also parts of life," he said. "We will continue with the experiment. But you are an adult now, and you must behave like one."

Raimey grimaced again. "I'll try," he said. "But there's so much I still don't understand."

"I know that," Latranesto said. "And we'll help you as best we can."

He gave a rumble of summons, and one of the Protectors floating around him flapped his way forward. "This is Protector Virtamco," the Counselor identified him. "He will be your guardian now."

"I thought I was an adult," Raimey pointed out, frowning at Virtamco. For all the subtleties that he still couldn't read in Qanskan expressions, he was having no trouble at all with this one. Virtamco wasn't at all happy with his new assignment. "What do I need a Protector for?"

"As you yourself said, there is still much you don't know," Latranesto reminded him. "Protector Virtamco will teach you."

"And protect me, too, I suppose?"

"You object to being protected?"

"I don't want any special treatment," Raimey said firmly.

"You don't have a choice," Latranesto said, just as firmly. "By your very nature you're a special person, with a special reason for your life among us. Everything about you must necessarily be special." He flipped his tails with finality. "You will have a Protector. The Counselors and the Leaders and the Wise have decided."

And with that, Raimey realized sourly, the discussion was over. "I obey the Counselors and the Leaders and the Wise," he said with as much grace as he could muster.

"Go, then," Latranesto said. He hesitated—"And may you swim in peace and contentment all the days of your life," he added.

"May you also," Raimey said, suddenly seeing the Counselor's heavy swimming in a new light. Level Four, he knew, was typically as high as a Counselor could reach without assistance. But from the way Latranesto was struggling to stay afloat, the big Qanska must be getting close to Leader age by now, not to mention sheer Leader size. At the same time, though, Level Four was typically as deep as even a full-grown Breeder could reach.

Which meant that this could be the last meeting the two of them would ever have.

With an effort, Raimey shook off that oddly depressing thought. There would be other opportunities, he told himself firmly, certainly once he himself was large and heavy enough to make his way down to Level Five.

Assuming, of course, he and Latranesto both survived that long.

"Farewell, Breeder Manta," Latranesto said; and in his voice, Raimey could hear the same note of finality that he himself was feeling. Perhaps Latranesto knew this was their last meeting, too.

Slowing his fins, the big Qanska began to sink downward. The rest of his Protector escort followed, keeping their formation around him.

"Farewell, Counselor Latranesto," Raimey murmured as he watched the other depart. A moment later, the group had faded from sight into the mists.

Leaving Raimey and Virtamco alone.

Raimey eyed Virtamco. The Protector eyed him back. "Fine," Raimey said with a sigh. "Now what?"

"We return to your herd," Virtamco said.

No *hellos* or *how-are-yous* or *it's-an-honor-to-be-of-service-to-yous*. Just a simple, straightforward instruction.

Or an order.

"Why?" Raimey asked, more as a test than anything else. Certainly he had no desire to hang around down here. Not after what had happened to Tigrallo.

"As Counselor Latranesto said, you've got a lot to learn about being a Qanska," Virtamco said. "You'll say good-bye to the Protectors and Nurturers of your herd, and pay the respect that's due them. Then you'll leave Level One and not return."

Raimey frowned. "Wait a minute. What do you mean, I won't return?"

"Is there something complicated about the words?" Virtamco asked sarcastically. "Young unmated adults aren't permitted in the breeding and birth grounds."

"Fine. Whatever," Raimey said, stretching out his buoyancy sacs and increasing his speed upward. Jupiter was a big place, and if he didn't get back before Drusni said her own good-byes and left, he might never find her again. "So let's go."

"And as we travel," Virtamco added, flapping his fins to rise alongside Raimey, "you can decide how you're going to change your name."

Raimey had just about had it with comments and complaints and misunderstandings about his name. "What about my name needs to be changed?" he demanded.

"You're a Breeder now," Virtamco said with an air of strained patience. "Breeders may add an extra syllable to their names."

Raimey snorted under his breath. "Thanks, but 'Manta' will do just fine."

Virtamco turned sideways to look at him. "It's not an option," he said. "You *will* add a syllable to your name."

"No, I *will* not," Raimey told him firmly. "Apparently, you weren't listening to Counselor Latranesto closely enough. Everything about me is special, remember? I don't have to follow rules like that if I don't want to."

"You wish to always be thought of as a child?" Virtamco countered. "Because that's what will happen."

"Oh, really?" Raimey said. "All the Qanska I meet from now on are going to mistake a six-size Breeder for a one-size Baby? I guess I'll have to reevaluate my assessment of your species' eyesight. Or maybe their intelligence."

For a moment Virtamco just glowered at him. Then, with a contemptuous flip of his fins, he rolled over and headed for the surface. "Have it your way," he called over his back. "Come back to your herd. *Manta.*"

As it turned out, this particular set of worries had been for nothing. Drusni and Pranlo were still there, waiting for him just beneath the herd as he arrived at Level One. "What happened?" Pranlo asked anxiously. "We heard you'd been hauled down to Level Four for a tail-whipping from a Counselor."

"It's okay," Raimey assured them. "Counselor Latranesto just wanted to know what happened with Tigrallo."

"Two Protectors came and talked to me about that, too," Drusni put in. "They kept asking why we almost missed the Song of Change."

Raimey frowned. So they *had* talked to her, and apparently at some length. And assuming she'd been honest, Latranesto must have known that Raimey had never really changed his mind about the ceremony.

So why had he let him off the hook?

"But it's all okay now?" Pranlo asked.

"It's all okay," Raimey said, wondering if it really was. "I was just heading up to pay my respects to the Protectors and Nurturers."

"We've already done that," Pranlo said. "They told us we had to leave Level One, but we've been stalling down here. We wanted to make sure we didn't disappear before you came back."

"Thanks," Raimey said. "I didn't want to lose you, either. So where do we go next?"

Pranlo flipped his tails in a shrug. "We wander around Levels Two or Three, I suppose. Eating and getting bigger and eventually—" He broke off. "Well, you know. All they said was that we had to stay off Level One."

"You'll come with us, won't you?" Drusni asked. "At least for now. That way, we can figure out this whole adult thing together."

"I'd like that," Raimey said. "Did they say anything to you about changing your names?"

"Oh, yes, that was the other thing," Pranlo said. "We're all supposed to add a syllable. I'm changing mine to Prantrulo."

"I'm going to be Druskani," Drusni said. "They said we get to add another one when we become Counselors."

"Prantrulo and Druskani." Raimey flipped his tails. "Sorry, but that's going to take some getting used to."

"Actually, you don't have to," Drusni said with a smile. "They said family and close friends are allowed to use the old names."

She flipped her tails. "And the three of us are both family *and* friends, right?"

"I've always thought so," Raimey said, feeling warm all over. Sweet, radiant Drusni . . .

"What's *your* new name going to be?" Pranlo asked.

"I'm keeping it just plain Manta," Raimey told him.

"They'll let you do that?" Drusni asked, frowning.

"Of course," Raimey said loftily. "I'm a special case."

"I guess so," Drusni said. "Well, I'm hungry. You wouldn't happen to have noticed any *kachtis* on your way to and from your big meeting, would you?"

"As a matter of fact, I spotted a few runs down on Level Three," Raimey said. "Come on, I'll take you there."

"Great," Pranlo said with a grin. "The Three Musketta, together again."

"Forever," Drusni added.

"Yes," Raimey said, strange feelings seeping through him as he gazed at her. "Forever."

"Raimey!" Faraday called yet again. "Raimey! Can you hear me?"

"No use, Colonel," Beach said, shaking his head as he peered at his board. "We're just not getting through."

"That's impossible," Hesse objected angrily. "I can hear the sounds of the wind. If we can hear him, why can't he hear us?"

"Because we've got computers up here to scrub out the static," Milligan told him. "He doesn't. Even with the relay probe, the signal getting to him is pretty weak."

"He'd probably be able to hear us if he was awake," McCollum added helpfully. "But your voice is just too buried in static for him to notice while he's sleeping."

Faraday nodded, his mind flashing back to that barely controlled fall so many years ago. He'd learned firsthand how hungrily the ionization in Jupiter's atmosphere could swallow radio signals. "We'll just have to wait for him to wake up, then," he said.

"No," Hesse said.

Faraday frowned. "No?"

"I told you before, I don't want to have this conversation with other Qanska wandering around," Hesse said, glaring at the displays. "What if he were higher up? Could we get his attention then?"

Beach threw a sideways look at Faraday. "Probably," he said cautiously. "Are you suggesting . . . ?"

"What else is it there for?" Hesse countered. "Bring him up."

Beach looked again at Faraday. "Colonel?"

"I gave you an order, Mr. Beach," Hesse said before Faraday could respond.

"Go ahead, Mr. Beach," Faraday confirmed.

Beach took a deep breath and turned to the panel between him and McCollum. The one they'd never used before . . . "Yes, sir."

"I hope this is a good idea," Faraday warned Hesse quietly. "The McCarthy setup was only supposed to be used in emergencies. We don't even know if the thing will work."

"I have full confidence in the Five Hundred's techs," Hesse said. "Mr. Beach, you'd better bring him all the way up to Level One."

"He's not supposed to be that high," Sprenkle put in.

"Just keep him away from the herds and there shouldn't be a problem," Hesse said.

"I'm not so sure," Sprenkle persisted. "The Qanska have shown a strong propensity for strict letter-of-the-law thinking."

"Raimey's a special case, remember?" Hesse countered. "It'll be all right."

He looked back at Faraday. "It has to be done," he insisted. "You said yourself he's started thinking of himself as a Qanska. We need to realign any loyalties that might have drifted off-beam."

"And what if we can't?" Faraday asked. "What are you going to do, fire him?"

"I'm prepared to do whatever it takes," Hesse said, his voice grim. "But I don't anticipate any serious trouble. After all, he got into this in order to carve himself a big fat historical legacy. This is made to order."

"He's moving," Beach announced, his voice oddly strained. "Heading upward."

"Good," Hesse said. "I *am* curious, though, Colonel. Why did you name this thing after an old United States senator?"

"What are you talking about?" Faraday asked, frowning.

"The McCarthy setup," Hesse said. "It *is* named after Senator Joe McCarthy of the 1950s communist witch hunts, isn't it?"

"No," Faraday said, shaking his head. "It's named after Charlie McCarthy."

Hesse frowned. "Who was he?"

"An associate of Edgar Bergen's," Faraday said. "A wooden-head."

Hesse frowned even harder. "A *what?*"

Faraday looked at the displays, thinking back to the Golden Age vids he'd loved as a child. When life had been so much simpler.

And you never had to worry about whether you were betraying someone who had trusted you. "He was a ventriloquist's dummy," he told Hesse. "In other words . . . a puppet."

"Mr. Raimey?"

Raimey awoke with a start. Had someone actually called him by his old Earth name? Or had he just dreamed it?

"Mr. Raimey?"

He flicked his tails in annoyance. It was real, all right. It was *them.* "I'm here," he growled. "What do you want?"

There was a short pause, no doubt as their computers worked busily to decipher the tonals. Shaking the sleep out of his eyes, wondering why no one up there had bothered to learn the language, he looked around him.

And with a jolt came fully awake. This wasn't Level Three, where he'd gone to sleep. This was Level One.

Level *One?*

"Mr. Raimey, this is Hesse," Hesse's voice spoke up in the back of his brain. "Sorry to have wakened you, but we needed to talk to you privately."

"You could have called when I was already awake," Raimey growled, still trying to figure this out. Had he been sleepwalking or something? He'd never done it before, not as a Qanska or even back when he was a human.

Unless the adults or the Protectors of his herd had always just nudged him back to the rest of the group before.

"We didn't want anyone else to even know we'd been in contact," Hesse said. "Do you remember when Colonel Faraday first recruited you for this job? He told you you'd go down in history as the first man to live in and study an alien culture."

"Of course I remember," Raimey said tartly. If this was one of Dr. Sprenkle's stupid memory tests, he was going to have some choice words to say to all of them.

"Good," Hesse said. "As it turns out, the truth is even more exciting than that. The Qanska—"

"Wait a ninepulse," Raimey cut him off. "What do you mean, 'the truth'? What was the rest of it, a lie?"

"No, no, not at all," Hesse said hastily. "It's just that there's *more* truth than we first told you."

"Oh, good—bonus truth," Raimey said sarcastically. "How nice. Why haven't I heard about this before?"

"It was a decision made at the highest levels," Hesse said. He was starting to sound a little rattled now. "I promise you, there was no intent to—what I mean—"

"It was decided we couldn't afford the risk of it leaking out to the Qanska," Colonel Faraday's calmer voice put in. "I'm sorry for the deception. You'll understand when you hear."

"I'm listening," Raimey said, keeping his voice neutral. Off to his left he could hear the distant squeaking of hungry babies beginning to awaken, along with the much deeper rumblings of Protectors telling them to be patient. There must be a herd that direction.

And he'd been told to stay away from herds. He'd better get this over with and drop back down where he belonged.

"We've been exploring Jupiter by telescope since Galileo, and by space probes since the late twentieth century," Faraday said. "In all that time, right up to the point where Chippawa and I literally ran into them, we never spotted even a hint that the Qanska existed."

"They live underneath the clouds," Raimey reminded him patiently. They'd dragged him out of a good sleep for *this*? "Of course you didn't see them."

"*And* we'd been using deep probes and tethered capsules for twenty years before we ran into them," Faraday went on as if Raimey hadn't spoken. "I've seen the data, and we had the planet pretty well bracketed."

"Which is a big help, considering that they keep mostly to the equatorial regions," Raimey pointed out.

"Well, we know that now," Faraday conceded. "We also know there are only a few million of them, far fewer than our first estimates."

"Which is maybe why you kept missing them?"

"Perhaps," Faraday said. "But perhaps not."

Raimey sighed. "I assume there's a point buried in here somewhere?"

"An extremely important point," Faraday assured him. "Even taking all the rest of it into account, those who have reviewed the data have come to the conclusion that the Qanska are not native to Jupiter."

Raimey frowned. "What do you mean, not native? Then where in hell did they—?"

He broke off as it suddenly struck him. "No," he murmured. "That's crazy."

"It's not crazy," Faraday said quietly. "There is a very strong probability that your Qanskan friends came here from somewhere outside our Solar System. Which means that they have a stardrive.

"And I'm afraid we want it."

NINE

"Wait a ninepulse," Raimey said, his head spinning like an eddy vortex. "This is crazy."

"I know it sounds that way," Faraday said. "But that's the inescapable conclusion. The Qanska weren't there when we started looking at Jupiter. They didn't arrive by huge colony or sleeper ships or anything else slower-than-light—"

"How do we know that?" Raimey cut him off. "They could have sneaked in when no one was looking. Astronomers don't spend *all* their time staring at the Outer System."

"No, *they* don't," Faraday acknowledged. "But there are thousands of amateur comet-hunters who do. If the Qanska had come here through normal space, someone would surely have spotted their ships."

Raimey flicked his tails in a grimace. "Maybe you're just wrong about them being imports, then. Maybe your fancy probes aren't as good as you think they are."

"Why are you fighting this so hard?" Hesse asked. "What, does it bother your worldview or something? You act like we're asking you to believe something completely outrageous."

"I don't know why it bothers me," Raimey said. "But since you bring up the subject, what exactly *are* you asking me to do?"

"We need that stardrive, Matthew," Faraday said, his voice quiet and sincere. Excruciatingly sincere. "We've looked now into every corner of the Solar System, and there's nothing there but cold rock or half-liquid gas. We've worked at developing every plot of ground that was economically feasible, and quite a few that weren't. The end of the road is ahead of us, and it's not all that far off. Without a stardrive, humanity will soon be without a frontier for the adventurous to cut their teeth on. And without a frontier, the whole race will stagnate and eventually die."

"Great speech," Raimey said sardonically. "Noble sentiments, well-practiced phrasing, and it even sounded sincere. So let me guess. You want me to find and steal this alleged stardrive of theirs. Right? Or did you have a more noble way of putting it?"

"We're not going to steal it," Faraday said firmly. "At least, not permanently."

"Besides, who says they've only got one?" Hesse put in. "They could have dozens or even hundreds of them for all we know."

"All we want is the chance to get one of them on a lab table and learn how it works," Faraday added. "Once we know how to build one of our own, we'll return it."

"Really," Raimey said. "And what happens if there *is* only one, and you *can't* figure it out? You think that after going to all that trouble the Five Hundred will just meekly hand it back?"

"They've given their word that they will," Faraday said.

"Whose word?" Raimey countered. "The group running the show at this particular ninepulse? Come on, Faraday— they try to give it back, and they'd spark the biggest floor fight since the Leyster Seating. Even I know enough about politics to figure *that* one out. And you've got three guesses as to which side would win."

"It won't come to that," Hesse said firmly. "Anything the Qanska can create, we can duplicate."

"In that case, what do you need the Qanska for?" Raimey shot back. "Go build one of your own if you're so smart."

"Are you saying you won't help us?" Hesse asked, his voice tight.

"Matthew, your people need you," Faraday said before Raimey could answer.

"That's nice to hear," Raimey said. "Okay, fine—let's assume for a ninepulse that you and the Five Hundred are as pure as the air in a Baby's buoyancy sac. What happens if all that careful study ends up destroying it? *Then* what? Apologies all around, and we go our separate ways?"

"You keep assuming there's only one of them," Hesse said, starting to sound annoyed. "There are probably—"

"Yes, I know," Raimey cut him off. "Hundreds and hundreds of them, as far as the eye can see. So how many have you ever actually seen? Or detected with probes, or picked up with deep radar?"

"If we knew where they were—"

"Then you wouldn't need me," Raimey concluded. "Right. So you go ahead and assume whatever you want. *I'm* not even ready to concede there's even one, let alone whole clouds of them. And you haven't answered my question."

"Mr. Raimey, what do you expect us to say?" Hesse demanded. "Of course we'll be as careful as humanly possible. And Colonel Faraday's right; one way or another we *will* give it back. What more can we tell you?"

"How about telling me that this is all a bad joke?" Raimey suggested. "Or something Dr. Sprenkle dreamed up, which is basically the same thing? How about telling me that you're not really asking me to betray my friends and my people this way."

"Your *people*?" Hesse asked, an odd note in his voice. "Mr. Raimey, your *people* are here."

"Are they?" Raimey countered. "Are you sure?"

"Aren't you?" Faraday asked. "No matter what you look like on the outside, on the inside you're still Matthew Raimey."

Raimey flapped his fins restlessly. "I don't even know that anymore," he muttered.

"Look—" Faraday began.

"No, that's enough," Raimey cut him off. "You've had your say. I'll think about it."

He heard someone hiss a sigh. "All right," Faraday said reluctantly. "But don't think too long. We need to get moving on this."

"Push too hard, and you'll come to a flapping stop right here," Raimey warned. "And the next time you want to talk, do it when I'm awake, okay?"

He flipped over and headed down, his thoughts a tangled swirl—

And pulled up sharply as he nearly slammed headlong into Drusni.

"Drusni!" he gasped. "What are you doing here?"

"That was *my* question," she said, peering closely at him. "I was following you. Are you all right?"

"Following me?" he asked stupidly.

"I woke up, and you were leaving," she explained. "I think you must have brushed against me or something."

"Sorry," Raimey said. "I don't know what happened. Maybe I was sleepwalking."

"Sleepwalking?"

"Well, sleep-swimming, I guess you'd have to call it," he corrected himself. "We sometimes get that among— well, it happens to humans sometimes. Have you ever heard of anything like this with Qanska?"

"No," Drusni said. "But we can ask around. Were you sleep-*talking*, too?"

Raimey felt something cold grip his throats. How much of the conversation had she heard? "The humans were talking to me," he said, the words coming out stiffly. "They wanted me to do something for them."

"So I gathered," she said. "Sounded like you weren't very interested, either. You want to tell me about it?"

"Well . . ."

"But on the way down," she added, rolling over and flipping herself vertical. "We're not supposed to be up here."

"I know," Raimey said, glad of an excuse to change the subject. He flipped vertical himself—

And suddenly flattened out again, flapping his fins to hold himself steady. There was something in the air . . .

"Come *on*," Drusni called, reversing her own plunge and rising up beneath him. "You want a Protector to catch us here?"

"No, wait," Raimey said, sniffing the air. Where had he smelled this particular scent before?

And then, abruptly, he had it. The smell that had flooded over him as he watched Tigrallo fighting for his life. "Sivra!" he hissed. "There's a pack of Sivra nearby!"

"Sivra?" Drusni echoed, spinning in a tight curve as she looked around them. "What in the Deep are you talking about?"

"Trust me," Raimey said grimly, trying to get a direction for the odor. "I know what they smell like."

"But they never come up to Level One," Drusni protested, still peering around. "They're too heavy, and they don't have enough fin size to let them swim this high."

"Well, someone must have figured out a way to do it," Raimey said. There it was; off to his left.

The same direction as the herd he'd noticed earlier.

He looked around, suddenly remembering Virtamco. But the other was nowhere to be seen. Apparently, Raimey's little sleep-swimming trick had given his private Protector the slip.

Which meant it was up to him and Drusni. "Come on," he said, curving around and pushing hard against the air. "We've got to warn them."

"But—"

Raimey didn't wait to listen, driving off through the dim sunlight as fast as he could swim. The sounds of those innocent newborns were growing louder in his ears, as was the faint aroma of hunting Sivra.

And laid over all of it like a ghostly transparency was that horrible mental image of Tigrallo's torn body.

Ahead, a shape was beginning to emerge from the gloom. A female Breeder, a couple of meters bigger than he was, and very pregnant. She was drifting away from the herd at an angle as she methodically scooped up mouthfuls along a run of *chinster*. The smell was getting stronger . . .

And then, suddenly, there they were: a whole pack of the eel-like predators, hanging by their teeth to a small Vuuka pumping his way laboriously upward. Even as Raimey tried desperately for more speed, the Vuuka and his entourage reached the oblivious female.

And as the Vuuka swam over her, the Sivra shook themselves free from him and dropped down toward her.

"Look out!" Raimey shouted. Startled, the female spun to look at him—

And wailed a scream as the first of the Sivra bit hard into her back.

"Damn!" Raimey snarled, driving toward her. "Drusni, go get the Protectors."

"Right," she called from somewhere behind him.

But they wouldn't get there in time, Raimey knew. Even as the pregnant female thrashed around in a desperate attempt to shake them off, the rest of the pack landed on her back and fins, their long teeth slicing through the thick skin as they started to bore their way inside. The Qanskan skin-growth defense mechanism could only handle so many of them at once, Raimey knew; and as soon as the rest were able to eat through to vital organs, it would be all over.

And there was no one close enough to stop them. No one except Raimey.

The Breeder was still thrashing around as he shot low across her back. Keeping his fins rigid, he sliced across the rows of chewing Sivra like a mowing machine cutting through a wheat field.

The results were decidedly unimpressive. The impact managed to dislodge one or two of the predators, but the others had enough of a grip to stay attached.

The female screamed again. "Don't do that," she gasped. "It hurts!"

Raimey ignored the plea, braking hard and swinging around for a second pass. Yes, pulling at entrenched Sivra was going to hurt like the Deep. But it beat all the alternatives. He swung over her again, slower this time, grabbing at the Sivra with his mouth as he passed and biting down on each as hard as he could.

The results this time were a little better. He was able to dislodge two or three of the latecomers, but the rest either ignored him or were so deeply dug in that they couldn't have let go even if they'd wanted to. Again he flapped to a quick halt and swung around; but this time, the female's thrashing fin caught him squarely in the belly, knocking some of the breath out of his lungs.

Not only his lungs, but also his buoyancy sacs. Even as he gasped for air, he found himself dropping down away from the battle. Clenching his jaws tightly, he flapped hard with his fins, forcing himself back up into the thinner air. The female was also starting to sink as her attempts to shake off the Sivra grew weaker. Raimey charged up toward her—

And was suddenly bowled over by the turbulence as four big Qanska roared past him.

The Protectors had arrived.

"Stay back," the last one in line snapped, flashing a glare at Raimey as he passed. A second later they were grouped around the female, biting and flapping and slashing with their tails at the remaining Sivra, knocking them loose or crushing them against the Breeder's skin.

There was a whisper of air at Raimey's side. "You all right?" Drusni panted.

Raimey flipped an affirmative with his tail, still too winded to talk.

"That was really brave," Drusni said, her voice sounding awed as she gave his fin a quick stroke. "I hope she'll be okay. Come on, let's get out of here."

"Right," Raimey managed. Rolling themselves vertical, they headed downward.

Raimey had thought the previous day's conversation with Latranesto would be the last he would ever have with the big Counselor.

He was wrong.

"Breeder Manta, you have broken one of the most important laws of the Qanska," Latranesto rumbled, his fins churning at the Level Four air like he was trying to make butter out of it. The other two Counselors hovering at his sides were flapping even harder.

Most of that was the need to keep afloat, of course. But somehow, Raimey had the feeling that that wasn't the whole story. All three Counselors were furious, even if they were trying with varying degrees of success not to show it.

And the worst part was that Raimey didn't know why they were so mad. What was there about this particular law that made it so important?

"If you have an explanation for your actions, you will speak it now," Latranesto went on. "After that, judgment will be decided on and pronounced."

Think fast, kid, Raimey told himself, glancing to his right. Because this time it wasn't just him in the hot draft. Beating rhythmically at the air as she hovered beside him, Drusni was looking tense and tired and vulnerable, and more than a little scared. He needed to pull this out as much for her as for himself.

"I apologize deeply for my intrusion into Level One," he said, keeping his voice and demeanor as humble as he could manage while still flapping madly at the dense air. "I have no explanation to offer, for the simple reason that I don't understand myself how it happened. The traveling occurred while I was asleep, and I was completely surprised when I woke to find myself there."

"Then why did you not immediately leave?" one of the other Counselors demanded, the broad red stripes across his fins glinting as he flapped.

"I was communicating with the humans up above," Raimey told him. "They wished to talk, and it's easier to do so at the higher levels."

"Is your life to be made easier at the cost of Qanskan law?" the other Counselor challenged. His skin, in contrast to the other, was mostly a pattern of blue stripes with some shorter green and purple ones mixed in. "What other laws, may I ask, do you intend to break with that excuse?"

"I did not intend to break any laws," Raimey insisted, starting to feel annoyed despite himself. "And may I also point out that if I hadn't been there, that female and her baby would certainly have been killed."

"We have already discussed this principle, Breeder Manta," Latranesto said in a severe tone. "You are a Breeder. Your role in life is not yet the defense of others."

"I'm sorry," Raimey said. "I know that's the Qanskan way. But it's not the human way. We protect and defend each other, wherever and whenever we need to. Sometimes that instinct comes through, despite my efforts to suppress it."

He looked at Blue Stripes. "And I don't mean that as an excuse," he added, "but as an explanation."

"Our laws were not invented solely for your inconvenience," Blue Stripes shot back. "There are good and proper reasons why young Breeders are not allowed in the birthing grounds. Particularly *male* breeders."

"The mating urges are strong in Breeders your age," Latranesto said. "Sometimes to the point of violating females who are already bonded."

Ah-ha. So that was it. They were worried about young adults getting carried away by lust. "Even those females who are pregnant?" he asked.

"Especially those who are pregnant," Latranesto confirmed. "Those nearing birth often give off false aroma signals of receptiveness. But mating during that time will almost certainly kill the unborn young."

"We also don't want Breeders mating in view of Level One herds," Red Stripes put in. "It's upsetting to the children."

Raimey glanced sideways at Drusni. This line of conversation was definitely becoming uncomfortable. "I understand," he told the Counselor, "though I had not heard this explanation until now. But again, I didn't go to Level One with any such thought or intention in mind."

"No, you went to talk to your people," Red Stripes said darkly. "Tell me, what was so urgent that they needed to speak with you at that particular ninepulse?"

Raimey hesitated. What in the world could he tell them? Not the truth, obviously; but he needed to say *something*. What could he come up with that would satisfy them?

But even as he tried to think, Drusni slid smoothly into the gap. "The humans had seen the approaching Vuuka and the Sivra attached to him," she said. "They called to warn Manta of danger."

"I was not talking to you, Breeder Drusni," Red Stripes snapped. "The time for your hearing will come later."

"Why?" Raimey asked, jumping to her support. "She did nothing wrong except follow me to see if I was all right, and then to obey me when I sent her to call the Protectors. If she's to be judged and punished, it should be in connection with my hearing."

Red Stripes bristled. "You dare speak to a Counselor in that tone of voice?"

"Do you punish honest ignorance and bravery?" Raimey shot back.

"Enough," Latranesto said firmly. "All of you. Breeder Drusni, you heard Breeder Manta's conversation with his people?"

"I did," Drusni said. "But only his side of it. I couldn't hear the humans."

"Then how do you know what it was they told him?"

"I saw the result of their conversation," Drusni said, twitching her tails defiantly. "And Manta is right. The female and her baby would have died if he hadn't come to her defense."

"The law does not look at final results," Blue Stripes said. "To do so would move in the direction of whim and self-interested interpretation and chaos."

"Yet at the same time, Manta is by necessity a special case," Latranesto said reluctantly.

He looked at Drusni. "And by extension, those he deals with must be allowed extra space to swim," he continued.

"There will therefore be no punishment. *This* time."

He fixed Raimey with a dark look. "But you are both on notice that this will not be permitted to occur again," he warned. "If either of you is found improperly on Level One again, there *will* be punishment."

"I understand, Counselor Latranesto," Raimey said, flipping his fins in respect.

"As do I," Drusni added. "Thank you for your understanding and compassion."

"Yes." Latranesto paused. "And despite the laws that were broken, we in turn also thank you for your assistance in saving two Qanskan lives. Farewell; and do not require us to hold such a hearing again."

With that, the three Counselors and their Protector escort sank downward. "Whew!" Drusni said under her breath, turning to face Raimey as the two of them started floating the opposite direction, upward toward Level Three. "Well, that was fun, wasn't it?"

"Oh, I could do this every day," Raimey said with a snort. "Sorry I dragged you into it. And thanks for the assist. I wasn't at all sure how I was going to get out of that one."

"No problem." She eyed him quizzically. "So what *did* you and they talk about?"

Raimey threw a furtive glance off to the side. Virtamco was floating up alongside them, away at the edge of his vision. Probably within eavesdropping range, unfortunately.

And his expression was not exactly a pleasant one. Had he been given a lecture of his own for losing track of his charge? Probably. Preoccupied with his own trouble, that thought hadn't even occurred to him.

"I can't tell you just now," he told Drusni. "Maybe later, okay?"

"Sure." Drusni flipped her tails. "Hey, we're friends, right? What's friendship if you can't trust each other?"

Raimey grimaced. *Trust.* If she'd worked long and hard, and spent a couple of ninedays at the task, she still couldn't have come up with a word that would have twisted harder into his belly than that one.

Trust. The Qanska had trusted the motives of the Five Hundred in allowing Raimey to come here in the first place. They'd invested time and energy and more trust in nurturing him to adulthood. And now Latranesto had renewed that trust by not punishing him, as he surely would have done to any other young Breeder who had invaded forbidden territory that way.

And in repayment of that trust, all Faraday and Hesse wanted him to do was steal possibly the most valuable thing the Qanska possessed. Terrific.

Raimey frowned suddenly to himself. *The most valuable thing . . .* A stardrive was a thing, all right. A thing; an artifact; a mechanical device.

How could the Qanska possibly build something like that? For that matter, how could they build *anything*? They had no hands; no gripping appendages of any sort. Certainly nothing that would be suitable for delicate work. Besides, floating here in the middle of the Jovian atmosphere, what was there for them to build anything *with*?

Could it be the Qanska weren't the highest form of life on Jupiter? Could there be something farther down, some more intelligent and dexterous species that was actually in control? Could *they* be the ones with the stardrive, and the Qanska merely part of the ecology the masters had brought with them?

Certainly that was possible. But unless those tool-building beings lived right down at the mushy solid hydrogen core, that still left the question of what they were using to build their tools out of. Something biological, perhaps? Again, that was possible, though the thought of a stardrive knitted out of *chinster* and *kachtis* vines was about as lunatic an idea as he'd ever come up with.

He wondered if Hesse and Faraday had thought this part through before they'd dragged him out of Level Three in the middle of the sundark. If they hadn't, he was going to be very annoyed with them.

If they had, he would love to hear the answers they'd come up with.

"Hello?"

Raimey started out of his thoughts. "Yes?" he said, focusing on Drusni again.

"Nothing," she said, sounding rather amused. "You just looked like you were halfway around the planet, that's all. I didn't want you to miss Level Three and go floating up to Level One again."

"Thanks," Raimey said dryly.

"Sure you don't want to talk about it?" she asked, going serious again. "Sometimes sharing a problem with friends is the best way to solve it, you know."

"So I've heard," Raimey said. "But this isn't exactly a problem. At least, not yet."

"Okay," she said. "But if it gets to be one, you be sure and let me know."

"You'll be the first," he promised.

"I'll hold you to that," she warned, mock-threateningly. "Hey, there's Pranlo."

Sure enough, there he was, swimming toward them in the distance. "Hey, guys!" he called as he approached. "So what happened?"

"We've been exiled, of course," Raimey called back. "Just stopped by to pick up a snack."

"Not funny," Pranlo grunted as he braked to a halt beside them. "People *do* get exiled, you know."

"No, I didn't," Raimey said soberly, annoyed with himself. "Sorry. It was supposed to be a joke."

"Don't worry about it," Drusni soothed him. "But that snack idea sounded really good. Don't just float there, Pranlo—take us to the good stuff."

"As you command," Pranlo said, flipping over and heading off. "This way."

TEN

It took a few ninedays for them to settle into their new routine. They had considerably more freedom as Breeders than they had had as children, and Pranlo and Drusni in particular seemed to relish the opportunity to go wherever they wanted, whenever they wanted to. The Three Musketta, as Pranlo persisted in calling them, ranged far and wide, laughing and talking and eating their way through the Jovian skies. They flitted up and down between Level Two and the upper parts of Level Four, crisscrossed back and forth across the equator a dozen times, and sometimes even skipped part of their normal sleep cycle in their excitement.

Raimey, who had grown up in the shadow of a personal Protector, didn't notice nearly as much of a change in his freedom as the others did. But their spirit was both contagious and fun to watch, and he jumped into the new activities right alongside them. Besides, even he found a certain relief in not having to always know where the herd was so that he could get back to it before sundark.

Still, as always, there was also a debit side to the freedom ledger. None of them, including Raimey, had ever realized quite how much work their leaders had put into locating food sources and guiding the rest of the herd to them. Now, as the Three Musketta moved about on their own, they discovered that the delicate tendrils and swirls of tasty color weren't nearly as plentiful as they'd always thought. Some days they had to hunt for ninth-parts on end before they found anything at all to eat.

Especially as they were now competing for that food

with all the other Breeders who had recently left their herds, not to mention all those who had graduated to adulthood before them. At first it had been fun to meet Qanska from other herds, to exchange names and stories and find out what life was like swimming in different winds. But the excitement began a distinctly downward curve the first time they tried to swim with a group of others, only to learn that they'd already cleaned out every bit of food in the vicinity.

And by the time a different group forcibly ordered them to go away, even the gregarious Drusni had had enough. From that point on, they swam alone.

There were other dangers besides hunger, too. Larger Vuuka prowled these lower levels than had generally been able to reach the nurseries on Level One, and from the lower parts of Level Two downward there were packs of Sivra to deal with, as well.

Again, the Three Musketta didn't have nearly as much trouble with predators as the typical Breeder, not with Virtamco plying his silently watchful path off to the side. Just the same, in those first few ninedays they had to beat off three Vuuka attacks and outrun a pack of Sivra. And it was always a darkly sobering experience to come upon the remains of a Vuukan or Sivran meal and wonder if the Qanska had been anyone they'd known.

So the thrill of new adulthood quickly and quietly faded away, winding down to a matter of survival. Survival with good friends and occasional laughter and enjoyment, certainly, but survival nonetheless.

And then, as if the universe were conspiring to complicate matters as much as possible, Raimey began feeling strange and discomfiting changes taking place inside him.

Latranesto had spoken of mating urges at that last hearing he and Drusni had gone through, warning of the possible uncontrolled consequences if those urges occurred in the wrong place. But as near as Raimey could remember, he hadn't felt anything of the sort when he'd been defending that pregnant female from the Sivra. There had been determination and anger, even fear, but nothing that could possibly qualify as an urge. For a long time afterward he had worried about that, wondering whether there was something wrong with him. Something in his human psychology, perhaps, that could override even the basic biochemistry of his Qanskan body.

But now, in a way that was somehow both sudden and subtle, the urges and feelings were beginning to come over him. He couldn't tell whether it was the new freedom that was triggering the changes, or the different and more varied diet they were being exposed to, or even simply the fact that he was getting older.

Or perhaps it was Drusni.

Drusni. Sweet, caring, vibrant, radiant Drusni. He found himself watching her every move, listening to her every word, hanging eagerly onto her every thought. He couldn't get enough of her. Her image danced through his mind, her voice sang in his dreams. Drusni.

And eventually, one sundark as the three of them were winding down toward sleep, he finally had to admit to himself that he was in love with her.

It was a startling discovery, all the more so coming from someone who could still remember what it was like to be human. There had been many women he'd known back then . . . but somehow, all of them paled in comparison to Drusni.

That was startling, too. Startling, and sobering. Had he become so much a Qanska that even his memories of human friends and lovers paled against the Qanskan equivalents? Or was it simply that, in his shallow youthfulness, he'd chosen his lovers solely on the basis of superficial attractiveness of face and body?

Because Drusni was more that just that. Far more.

He lay awake for a long time after sundark, gazing into the darkness and trying to sort it all out in his mind. He and Drusni . . . but it wasn't as ridiculous as it sounded. Was it?

But even if it wasn't ridiculous, it wasn't going to be nearly as simple as it had been on Earth. He'd caught glimpses of other Breeder couples in the distance over the past few ninedays; had seen the complicated half-dance, half–synchronous swim ritual they'd done as they prepared for their bonding.

Trouble was, it was a ritual he had never learned. Either it had been taught back in the herd while he was off on one of his extended wanderings, or else it drew on some basic Qanskan instinct that his human mind simply didn't have.

But he couldn't approach her without it. *Wouldn't* approach her without it. When it was time to ask her, he wanted everything to be perfect.

And there was only one person to whom he could turn to for help and advice. Only one.

He suffered secretly through the long ninth-parts of the next day, striving for patience as he and Drusni and Pranlo swam and talked and ate together. But finally the gloom of sundark descended on them.

And as the other two fell silent and motionless, drifting to sleep on the winds, Raimey stole quietly off into the darkness.

Virtamco was also just settling down to sleep. "Yes?" he said, in that same gruffly neutral voice he always seemed to use when speaking to Raimey. "Do you want something?"

"I need a favor," Raimey said, trying to keep his voice steady. It was odd, he thought distantly, how little he'd truly appreciated Tigrallo when he was alive. He'd always thought of him as aloof and critical, more like a glorified nursemaid than anything else.

But now, with Virtamco to compare him against, Raimey realized that Tigrallo had been far more than just a keeper saddled with unpleasant duty. He'd been an adviser, and a guardian, and a companion.

And a friend.

"Yes?" Virtamco prompted impatiently. "Speak up, Breeder Manta."

"Counselor Latranesto said you would teach me those

aspects of being a Qanska that I don't yet know," Raimey
reminded him. "Well, there's something I need to know."

"Now?" Virtamco said, looking pointedly around at the
gathering gloom. "Can't it wait until sunlight?"

"I don't think so," Raimey said. "I mean, no, it can't."
He braced himself. "I need you to teach me the courtship
ritual."

For a long moment Virtamco just stared at him. "You
want what?" he asked at last, his tonals practically vibrating
the sky with disbelief.

"I need you to teach me the courtship ritual," Raimey
repeated, an uncomfortable feeling beginning to chew its
way into his hopes and dreams. Virtamco's expression . . . ,
"Counselor Latranesto said you would teach me—"

"Are you making a bad joke?" Virtamco demanded.

Raimey jerked back. "No," he said. "No. But Latranesto
said—"

"Why, you arrogant, foul-minded, little profaner," Virtamco bit out. "How *dare* you even *think* such a thing?"

Raimey had to fight hard to keep from flipping over and
swimming away as fast as he possibly could. The sheer
weight of the other's disapproval was like being hit in the
face by a slashing wind swirl. "I—I—" he stammered.

"Get out of my sight," Virtamco roared, slapping his tails
across his fins like he was trying to sweep something disgusting off of them. "Get away, you—you *half-breed*." He
lunged at Raimey, his jaws snapping—

And with his soul wailing inside him, Raimey turned and
fled.

He didn't know how long he swam, or even in what
direction. All he could see was Virtamco's scandalized
face; all he could hear was that horrible, condemning word.

Half-breed.

He would have cried if Qanska had been capable of tears.
Half-breed. Because the Protector was right; that was exactly what he was. A half-Qanska, half-human mongrel. A
scientifically created perversion of nature.

A monster.

And he'd dared to think Drusni would actually bond with him? Not only was he a monster, he was also a fool.

"Manta!" a voice called from somewhere behind him.

He tensed, his headlong rush suddenly faltering. That voice. Could it really be . . . ?

No. His ears, and his mind, were playing tricks on him.

"Manta, wait up."

He turned around . . . and if his ears and mind were playing tricks, so were his eyes.

It was Drusni.

"Crosswinds, but you're fast," she panted as she came up to him. "What's going on? Another message from the people in the clouds?"

"No, I—" Raimey broke off, swallowing hard. This was it. He didn't know the proper methods, or the proper words, or the proper anything. But this was his chance. Maybe his only chance. "Drusni . . . look, I don't know how to say this. I wish . . . but I don't. Maybe it doesn't matter."

She had gone very still. "Yes?" she asked softly.

Raimey braced himself. "Drusni . . . will you . . . will you bond with me?"

For a long moment she hovered motionlessly, only her fin tips undulating slowly to hold her position in the air. "Wow," she murmured at last. "I don't know what to . . ."

She took a deep breath. Raimey, for his part, held his. "I'm flattered, Manta," she said softly. "I really am. You're a wonderful person, and a good friend. We've been together a long time, and I love you a lot. If things were different . . ."

She stopped. "It's all right," Raimey said, feeling a hundred razor-edged Sivran teeth poised at the edges of his heart. "Go ahead."

She moved closer, resting her fin gently on top of his. "But the truth of it is," she said, the words coming out in a rush, "I've already agreed to bond with Pranlo."

Raimey turned away from her. Turned away from that earnest look; eased his skin away from that agonizingly warm touch. "Of course," he managed. "I should have guessed. Congratulations. Or whatever it is you say here."

"I'm sorry, Manta," Drusni said gently, and he could hear some of his own pain echoed in her voice. "Really." She moved up close behind him and again laid her fin across his.

And as all those phantom Sivran teeth chewed their path of destruction across his heart, something inside him snapped. "Don't *touch* me," he snarled, slapping her fin violently away from his. "You're happy. Wonderful. Be happy. But be happy somewhere else."

"Please, Manta, don't do this," she pleaded. "If there was any other way—"

"But there isn't, is there?" he snarled. The pain in her voice was twisting though his heart, doubling the agony there. But he no longer cared about pain, or her, or himself. "So go. Go and be happy with Pranlo."

"Manta—"

"I said *go!*" he thundered, spinning around to glare at her. "I don't ever want to see you again. Ever!"

For a single heartpulse their eyes locked. The last view of those lovely eyes, Raimey knew, that he would ever have.

And then, with a choking sob, she flipped around and drove blindly away into the sundark.

He stared for a long time in the direction she had gone. Perhaps she would return, one last tendril of hope whispered to him. Perhaps after a time she would decide that he was the one she loved the most, and she would say goodbye to Pranlo.

But she didn't come back. As he'd known she wouldn't.

Eventually, he shook himself back to reality. The ninthparts of the sundark were passing quickly, and soon all those in this part of Jupiter's sky would awaken and begin the day's activities.

He intended to be long gone before that happened.

He dove deep, not leveling off until he was nearly to the bottom of Level Four, as deep as he could force his body to go. Then, turning his left ear into the winds, he headed northward. Most of the Qanska, he knew, kept to the equatorial region of the planet, riding with the winds. Away from that relatively narrow band, there was a lot of unknown and presumably unexplored territory. Plenty of room to lose himself in.

And the sundark hadn't been a total waste. At least now he knew exactly what he was, and how he was perceived. And with that revelation, he also knew what his priorities had to be.

Hesse and Faraday had better get their lab tables cleared off and ready to go. Because one way or another, he was going to get them that stardrive.

And to the Deep with the Qanska. All of them.

ELEVEN

The Protector was a big one, nearly twice as long as Raimey, with a skin that was so lumpy and scarred he was almost unrecognizable as a Qanska. Clearly, he'd been in a lot of fights throughout his lifetime.

And unless Raimey did something quick, he was going to be in one more.

"I asked you a question, Breeder," the Protector rumbled warningly. "What in Pakra worms do you think you're doing in my *drokmur* patch?"

"I'm sorry, Protector," Raimey said, fighting to control the trembling in his voice. The shaking wasn't so much fear—though there was some of that, too—but simple hunger. He hadn't found anything to eat in the past four days, and his whole body was starting to shake in reaction.

And of course, now that he *had* finally found food, he'd also found a crazed Protector who seemed to think he owned it.

Which was blatantly unlawful, of course. But here, several ninedays' journey north of the equator and the center of Qanskan culture and authority, laws were apparently only followed when it was convenient.

"Well?" the Protector demanded. "What are you waiting for?"

"I'm very hungry, sir," Raimey said, the trembling even worse now. Simple hunger; but of course, the Protector would assume it was fear.

And why on Jupiter should he bother to give away any

of his precious *drokmur* to a Breeder who was obviously scared to death of him?

Apparently, the Protector couldn't think of a reason, either. "Then go find yourself some food," the other growled. "But do it somewhere else. Now go away, or I'll give you more than just your belly to worry about."

Raimey thought longingly of the days with Tigrallo, or even those with Virtamco. If he'd had a Protector of his own here to back him up . . .

But he didn't. And there was no point in arguing the point any further. With a sigh, he flipped over and swam slowly away. *Okay*, he told himself firmly. *Just a little setback. That's all. Just a little setback.*

But the pep talk didn't help. Mainly because lately, it seemed, life had become nothing *but* a continuing series of setbacks.

It hadn't always been so. The first dayherd had been decent enough, once he'd gotten used to the solitude. He'd had to outfight or outrun quite a few predators along the way, and had turned a small Vuuka and two more Sivra into distended lumps on various parts of his body and fins. But the food supplies had been plentiful enough, and there had been other Qanska swimming around to talk to when the loneliness became too much to bear. That potential for companionship, even of such a brief and superficial sort, was the main reason he'd abandoned his original plan of leaving Qanskan territory entirely.

But now, midway through his second dayherd, things seemed to be on a downward dive. The food supplies had been slowly but steadily dwindling, at least the ones he could find, with more and more Qanska nudging or bullying or flat-out chasing him away from it. As his body grew heavier, and he ranged lower and lower into the atmosphere, the resident Qanska seemed to grow less and less friendly and hospitable, particularly to strangers. It was almost as if, once the breeding stage was passed, the Qanska out here had gathered into informal herds again.

Or maybe it was like that everywhere, even back at the

equator. There was so much he still didn't know.

But for this particular ninepulse, academic curiosity was definitely somewhere way back in the slipstream. Food was the top priority, and he wasn't finding any. Perhaps, as his old business school buddies used to say, it was time for Option B.

Trouble was, there *was* no Option B.

True, he could continue on northward as he'd originally planned and try to leave Qanskan territory behind. But that would require him to become a complete hermit, and he'd already discovered he wasn't wired for that kind of life.

Or he could head up to Level One, avoiding the herds and their Protectors, and try to contact Jupiter Prime. But they'd want to know why he'd been silent for so long, and he absolutely didn't want to talk to them about what had happened. Anyway, there wasn't a whole lot of anything they could do for him.

Or he could go back, cross the equator the other direction, and see if life in the southern areas was any better than it was here in the north. But that would mean passing through the center of Qanskan activity, and Latranesto probably had every Breeder and Protector and Counselor down there on the lookout for him. If he wasn't ready for a lecture from Hesse and Faraday, he sure as the Deep wasn't ready for one from Latranesto.

Besides, somewhere back there in the equatorial region Pranlo and Drusni were swimming along together. And seeing them right now would very likely kill him.

He sighed again, the dull ache within him throbbing to life again. Drusni. A hundred forty ninedays later, and he still hadn't gotten over her.

He probably never would. He would hold her image next to his heart, wrapped in his quiet pain, until his death.

Death. Maybe that was the only real Option B left to him. There didn't seem any real point to his life now. Better for everyone if he was just gone. Maybe the next time the Sivra attacked, he would just let them have him. Better for him. Better for everyone.

Back in that shadowy former life, back when he'd been a paralyzed human being, Faraday had talked about this being a glorious gift he and the Qanska were offering him.

Some gift.

"Falkaro giving you a hard time?" a voice asked from behind him.

Raimey spun around, startled. A large female was hovering there, bigger even than the Protector who'd chased him away from his private *drokmur* patch. Probably a Counselor, he guessed. Like the grouchy Protector, her skin was also studded with the lumps and distortions of past battles. "I'm sorry?" he asked. "Who is . . . ?"

"Falkaro," she repeated, flipping her tails back in the direction Raimey had just come from. "That grouch of a Protector back there. I asked if he gave you a hard time."

"Not really, I suppose," Raimey said. "I mean, he didn't hurt me, but he wouldn't let me eat anything. Seems to think he owns all the food within swimming distance."

"Yes, you get that around here sometimes," she said with a shrug. "It's probably a lot less civilized than what you're used to."

Raimey frowned. "How do you know what I'm used to?"

"Oh, come on," she said with a smile. "Your accent gives you away. You're from the Centerline. What are you doing this far across the winds?"

"Just sort of exploring," Raimey said cautiously. Could Latranesto's all-points bulletin have reached all the way out here?

"Right," she said, her tone making it clear that she didn't believe that for a ninepulse. "But mostly, you're going hungry? Hmm? Tell me I'm wrong."

"No, you're not wrong," he admitted. "I don't suppose you'd happen to know if there's any food nearby?" He flipped a tail back toward Falkaro's private kingdom. "Unclaimed food, that is?"

"Mm," she said, looking him up and down. "I might. Tell me, how are you with pressures?"

Raimey frowned. "I can usually handle them okay. Why?"

"Well, I just happen to know where there's a very good run down on Level Five."

He grimaced. Level Five. It might as well have been on Europa. "I don't think I can get that far down."

"Yes, I figured that," she said. "But if you *could* get there, do you think you could handle the pressures?"

"I don't know," Raimey said, starting to feel a little annoyed. What point was there to discussing pressures if he couldn't get down there in the first place? "Probably."

"Good," she said. "Then hold still."

She swam up over his back, as if she was leaving, then stopped directly above him. "What are you doing?" he said, frowning up at her.

"I said hold still," she said, her fins rippling almost delicately as she adjusted her position. "Here we go."

And with an audible *whoosh* of collapsing buoyancy sacs, she began to sink.

With Raimey, held firmly in place beneath her massive fin, sinking right along with her.

"My name's Beltrenini," she said, her voice sounding oddly muffled in this position. "What's yours?"

"Uh—Raimo," Raimey improvised. Even out here, the Qanska might have heard of the strange half-human, half-Qanskan monster named Manta.

"What was that?" she asked.

"Raimilo," he corrected, remembering this time to add the extra Breeder syllable.

"Ah," she said. "Interesting name. Don't think I've ever heard it before. How come you're out here alone?"

"What do you mean?"

"I mean without a mate," she said. "You're a Breeder, right? Why aren't you busy breeding?"

Raimey grimaced. "It's not something I want to talk about."

"Oh, come on," she cajoled. "I'm a Counselor, right?"

"That's purely an age thing," Raimey reminded her

tartly. "It doesn't necessarily mean you've got any actual skill at counseling people."

"A little respect, there, Breeder Raimilo," she warned testily. "Maybe all I've got is age and experience; but that's already more than *you* have. Hmm? Tell me I'm wrong."

For a moment, Raimey was sorely tempted to rattle off a list of *his* achievements and knowledge, from the business and organizational classes he'd taken right up to the experience of skiing down a snowy mountain with solid ground beneath his feet. *That* might shut her up.

He resisted the temptation. "You're right," he said humbly. "I apologize."

"That's better," she said. "So let's hear your story. Starting with why you're not swimming with some nice female Breeder."

"I appreciate your concern," Raimey hedged, coming to a decision. Wherever she was taking him, food or no food, it wasn't worth having to float through an interrogation. He didn't even want to think about Drusni, let alone talk about her to some nosy-snouted stranger. Flexing his fins, he tried to wiggle his way free.

And to his shock, discovered that he couldn't.

He tried again, putting all his strength into it. But it was no use. He was nestled solidly into the slightly concave area where Beltrenini's fin joined her body, and they were already deep enough that his own natural buoyancy was pinning him there. And with her three-to-one size advantage, there was no way he was going to physically shove her aside.

Which meant he was helpless. Beltrenini could basically take him anywhere she wanted, however she wanted, whenever she wanted. Back to the equatorial regions, maybe, or directly to Latranesto for punishment.

Or even to his death.

His muscles tensed uselessly against the massive bulk as a horrible suspicion suddenly struck him. Beltrenini had as good as admitted that the usual Qanskan rules didn't apply out here. And it also occurred to him that he hadn't seen too many Vuuka prowling around lately.

Could she have possibly have made some sort of devil's bargain with them? After all, Earth predators were typically more intelligent than their prey. He'd never heard a hint about Vuukan intelligence; but then there was a lot the Qanska hadn't told him. Maybe they could be talked to, even bargained with.

And the simplest bargain a prey could make a predator would be to deliver food in exchange for not becoming food herself.

Could he, Raimey, be Beltrenini's latest sacrifice to them?

He wiggled again, with the same nonresults. "Hold still," Beltrenini ordered, giving a little wiggle of her own in emphasis. Raimey had a quick flash of boyhood memory: his uncle shaking him by the shoulders to get his attention when he'd been misbehaving. "This is hard enough without you flailing around like a newborn."

"Where are you taking me?" he asked tightly.

"Where do you think?" she retorted. "To get food."

Or to be food? Still, unless she wanted to risk getting bit herself, she would have to release him before the Vuuka attacked. That would give him one last chance . . .

Something brushed past his fins. He tensed, focusing his attention on the air.

To discover a stream of delicate reddish-silver leaves flowing past them.

"Here we are," Beltrenini announced, settling them into the middle of the fast-moving river. "Food for two. Wait a pulse—let me turn around into the flow. Makes it easier."

She swiveled a hundred eighty degrees around, turning them to face the winds that were sweeping the silvery plants along. Raimey opened his mouth, and let them flow in.

Even with four days of hunger to add spice to the menu, he quickly decided that the stuff looked better than it tasted. Still, it wasn't bad, and it was definitely filling. Best of all, there weren't any big ugly Protectors around to chase him away from it.

"How's the *feemis*?" Beltrenini called down around a mouthful of food.

" 'sgood," Raimey said, his own mouth almost too stuffed to get the words out.

"Take it easy," she warned. "Don't choke yourself. There's plenty to go around."

"You sound like my mother," Raimey muttered, swallowing that bite and looking around as he opened his mouth wide for the next. Just because there were no Protectors around, of course, didn't mean they had the silver stream all to themselves. There were two more of the big Counselors ahead and a little bit below them, grazing along at the bottom edge of the run. And in the distance off to the left he could see what appeared to be a group of Qanskan children feeding in the middle like he and Beltrenini were.

He frowned suddenly in midbite. Qanskan *children*?

"Well, I *was* a mother myself once, you know," Beltrenini reminded him. "Your mother still alive?"

"No, she was killed by a Vuuka," Raimey said mechanically, peering hard off to the left. No mistake; there were at least a dozen small Qanska over there. Or at least they *looked* like Qanska. They certainly weren't Vuuka or Sivra or Pakra.

Trouble was, whatever they were, they were far too small to have made it this deep without the kind of elevator ride Beltrenini had given him. And there were no larger Qanska anywhere nearby.

Were his eyes playing tricks on him? Could the silvery glint of the plants be messing up his estimation of distance?

"I'm sorry," Beltrenini said. "When did it happen?"

"It was a long time ago," Raimey said. "Just before I switched from Midling to Youth."

She let out a low, vibrating rumble of surprise. "And you survived to adulthood? Whoa. You must have had a really supportive herd."

"One of the Protectors kind of looked after me," Raimey

told her. "Look over to the left. Are those *children* over there?"

"What?" she said, swiveling her whole body around. "Where?"

"Those small Qanska," Raimey said, trying to point. But his tails were squeezed up against Beltrenini's belly, and she wouldn't have been able to see the gesture anyway "Looks like twelve or fifteen of them."

"You mean those Brolka?" she said. "There are thirteen of them over there."

Brolka? "Yes, if that's what they are," Raimey said. "I've never seen one before."

"You're joking."

A cold chill ran through Raimey from snout to tailtips. In that single heartpulse, Beltrenini's voice had gone from casually chatty to something dark and ominous.

What had he said? Had admitting his ignorance about these Brolka somehow given away his true identity? "I— uh—" he stammered.

"There aren't any in Centerline?" she demanded harshly. "None at all?"

"I don't know," Raimey said. "All I said was I'd never seen one. Maybe our herd just didn't run into any."

For along ninepulse she was silent. Raimey held his breath, oblivious to the silvery *feemis* streaming past his snout. What in the name of Pakra droppings had he *said*?

"Maybe," she said at last. "I guess there's no point in worrying about it. Well, eat up."

The rest of the meal was eaten in silence. Raimey keep an eye on the Brolka, trying to figure out what was so important about them. They didn't move quite like regular Qanska, he decided, but that was about the only conclusion he was able to come to. They kept drifting farther away as they ate, eventually vanishing completely from his sight.

"How are you doing?" Beltrenini called. Her tone, Raimey noted, had regained most of its earlier good cheer. "About done filling that empty hole yet?"

"Sure, I could call it a day," Raimey agreed. "I'm ready

to leave. Unless you weren't planning to go back to Level Four?"

"No, no, we can go together," Beltrenini said. "It's getting late, and I like Level Four best for sleeping. Besides, you still haven't told me why you're out here alone."

"How about you?" Raimey countered as Beltrenini started easing them upward out of the *feemis* stream. "*You're* here alone, aren't you?"

"That's different," Beltrenini said quietly. "I *was* bonded, once. He died."

Raimey grimaced. "I'm sorry," he said. "I didn't mean to bring up a painful subject. When did it happen?"

"A long time ago, just like you," she said. "Back when he was a Protector and I was a Nurturer. He was killed defending our children's herd."

She waggled her fins in emphasis. "But we weren't talking about me. We were talking about *you*, and *your* lack of companionship."

"But I *have* companionship," Raimey protested smoothly. "I've got you, right?"

"Flattery won't grow the *drokmur*," she said, waggling again. Still, she sounded secretly pleased by his comment. "Come on, quit stalling. Or were you going to try and tell me all the female Breeders from your herd had already died? Along with all the female Breeders from the nine neighboring herds?"

Raimey sighed. "No, she's still alive. She just picked someone else to bond with, that's all."

"So why didn't you just pick someone else yourself?"

Raimey grimaced. "It's not that simple."

"Of course it's that simple," Beltrenini persisted. "Okay, so you liked this one better. Big deal. Weren't there any others you could have chosen? Besides, didn't the Nurturers insist? Oh," she interrupted herself. "So that's why you took off across the winds. They ordered you to bond with someone else, and you were too stubborn to do so."

"Actually, I left before anyone had a chance to give any

orders," Raimey admitted. "Though if they had . . . I probably would still have run."

She snorted. "You have got to be the strangest Qanska I've ever met, Raimilo," she said. "Okay, let's hear the story. The *whole* story."

TWELVE

Milligan shook his head. "Sorry, Colonel," he said. "Even with boosters, they're definitely out of range. We could try chasing the spy probe after them, but that's the best I can offer."

"But don't forget that we don't know anything about their senses," McCollum warned. "If you get the probe too close, you could spook them."

Faraday glared at the displays, making a supreme effort to hold on to his already strained patience. Typical. The first new creatures they'd spotted since Raimey's first couple of months on Jupiter; and now the damn things had wandered off before they could collect any real data on them.

And if that female Counselor's reaction was any indication, there was something important about these Brolka things. Maybe even something critically important.

But there were realities up here, too. And one of those realities was that there was only so much equipment to go around. "No, we'd better leave it on track," he said reluctantly. "If we move it, we might lose track of Raimey completely. The Five Hundred would have our heads if that happened."

"Don't know why," Beach grumbled. "If he's looking for their stardrive, he's doing a lousy job of it."

"At least he's trying," McCollum said.

"Is he?" Beach retorted. "You sure couldn't prove that by me. If this is all the territory he can cover in a year and a half of wandering, we're going to be here until the sun burns out."

"Somehow, I don't see the Five Hundred being patient enough for that," Sprenkle murmured.

"I'm surprised they've lasted this long," Milligan agreed with a snort. "Speaking of the Five Hundred, has anyone seen Mr. Hesse surface yet?"

"He's back, and he's been through Receiving," Faraday said. "Aside from that, I haven't seen him."

"When was that?" Milligan asked.

Faraday pulled up the station log on one of his displays. "About an hour ago."

"That doesn't sound good," McCollum muttered. "He's usually down here three minutes after they green-light him in."

"Sometimes faster than that," Sprenkle agreed. "Sounds like he's bringing bad news."

"What do you expect after that last profile you sent to Earth with him?" Beach growled.

Sprenkle spread his hands. "Hey, I have to write what I see," he protested. "If it's obvious Raimey's pining for a lost love, what am I supposed to say?"

"You didn't have to make it sound so much like he's gone over the edge," Beach said with a sniff.

"You want me to lie?" Sprenkle shot back. "If I'd wanted to do that, I'd have gone into politics."

"You ask me, we've *all* gone into politics," McCollum said.

"Amen, sister," Milligan said.

The budding argument subsided into a roomful of grumpy silence. It was amazing, Faraday thought blackly as he looked around, what a difference five short years could make. Back when Project Changeling had just been getting underway, the whole team had been excited and upbeat, ready to watch and learn and be part of the cutting edge of humanity's frontier.

Now, in stark contrast, they'd become tired, touchy, and about as burned out as he'd ever seen anyone get.

What had happened to them? Was it just the monotony of watching Raimey swim endlessly around the atmosphere, eating colorful plants and fending off predators? Was it the subtle pressure of the media and the less subtle pressure from the Five Hundred for Changeling to show some progress? Was it the fact that, as McCollum thought, the politics of the situation had seeped like polluted groundwater into the more noble and aloof science and technology they were used to?

Or was it something a little closer to home? A failure of leadership, perhaps?

A failure of *Faraday's* leadership?

There was the soft thud of footsteps on metal flooring. "Welcome back, Mr. Hesse," he said without turning around. "How was Earth?"

"I'm afraid Mr. Hesse won't be joining us just yet," a clear female voice said.

Faraday turned, blinking in surprise. The woman standing just inside the doorway was well past middle age, with pure white hair and a face lined with wrinkles so deep that they looked almost like scars.

And from the way those wrinkles had settled comfortably into a solid, no-nonsense look, it was clear that was her default expression. "Excuse me?" he said, standing up. "May I help you?"

"My name is Arbiter Liadof," she told him. Her eyes swept the room, pausing briefly on each of the startled faces turned back toward her. "I'm the new representative of the Five Hundred on Project Changeling."

"I see," Faraday said carefully, a hard knot forming in the pit of his stomach. He had never met Katrina Liadof, but he had heard furtive references to her during the long preparations back on Earth. She was one of the top movers and shakers of the entire Five Hundred, a woman who had never held a Council position for the simple reason that she preferred to do her work in the shadows behind the throne. "I wasn't aware there was a problem with our old representative."

Her quick-glance evaluation of the room completed, she turned those dark eyes onto Faraday. "Mr. Hesse has served adequately up until now," she said evenly. "But it appears that Project Changeling has glided itself into a rut. I'm here to pull it out."

"I see," Faraday said, fighting back the automatic surge of defensiveness. Changeling *was* in a rut, he had to admit, though hardly one of his or anyone else's making.

Besides, annoyance wouldn't buy him anything here. Diplomacy, clearly, was the order of the day. "At any rate, we welcome you to Jupiter Prime," he added. "We're honored by your presence."

"Actually, you're resentful of my presence," she corrected him, still watching his face. "Or else you're terrified of it. Those are the two more probable responses."

Faraday's first instinct was to drop into the old military pattern of duck-and-cover: keep your head down, shift blame in any and all directions, try to get the official sledgehammer to come down somewhere else.

But he resisted the impulse. *A failure of leadership*, the phrase whispered again through his mind. And part of leadership was to be the one standing under that sledgehammer. "Perhaps the more probable," he said evenly. "But not the only ones. Tell me, Arbiter Liadof, do I have anything personally to fear from you?"

The lines in her forehead deepened, just slightly. Maybe she'd been expecting a duck-and-cover, too. "No particular reason I know of," she said.

"Do any of my people?" he asked.

She didn't even bother to look at them. "I don't deal with routine hirings and firings," she said shortly.

"Well, then," Faraday said, inclining his head in a small bow. "In that case we aren't terrified by your presence, nor are we resentful. We are, however, still honored."

For a long moment she gazed at him, her expression a mixture of thoughtfulness and suspicion. Faraday held his breath, and then, to his relief, she smiled. A tight, knowing smile, but a smile just the same. "In that case, I thank you, Colonel Faraday."

She held his gaze another moment, then leisurely looked around the room again. "Now. I wish to learn about my new responsibilities. You will show me around."

"Certainly, Arbiter Liadof," Faraday said. It hadn't been a request; but then, he hadn't really expected one. It had probably been years since Katrina Liadof had done anything but give orders. "If you'll come this way . . ."

". . . and so she left," Raimey concluded. "And then I left. And I've been out here ever since."

Beltrenini flipped her tails. In amazement or disbelief; Raimey wasn't quite sure which. "That's quite a story," she said. "That's it? All of it?"

"That's it," Raimey assured her. It wasn't, of course, though there was no way Beltrenini could know that. He'd left out such minor details as who he was, and where he'd come from, and the fact that Drusni had refused to bond with him because he was a half-breed monster. But it was the whole story as far as Beltrenini was ever going to be concerned.

"Interesting," the Counselor commented. "It wouldn't win you any honors in the herd's story circles, but I can see how it could still hurt. What I *don't* see is why you don't just forget her and move on to someone else. I mean, you only get about four and a half dayherds of breeding time, and you've already squandered one and a half of them. The way you're going, you'll wake up some sunlight to find that you're a Protector, and that you've missed your chance to bond with anyone."

"So what?" Raimey said. "What's the point of bonding at all if I can't do it with the one I want? I'd be better off alone."

"Don't give me that," Beltrenini said severely, flipping her tails in annoyance. "This obsession of yours with getting exactly what you want or else not taking anything at all is as selfish and self-destructive as anything I've ever seen. It's also completely ludicrous. Who gave you the right to demand perfection every single time, anyway?"

"That's easy for *you* to say," Raimey snapped. "You *got* the mate you wanted."

"Who says?" she countered tartly. "As a matter of fact, Kydulfo was my third choice. *I* was *his* fifth."

Raimey winced, the taste of shame trickling into his mouth. "Oh," was all he could come up with to say.

" 'Oh,' " she mimicked. "And yet, we did well enough. We had five broods, you know. Six healthy young Qanska." She paused. "And in time," she went on quietly, "we came to care very deeply for each other. Even now, I miss him terribly."

"I'm sorry," Raimey said, feeling embarrassed and depressed, not to mention ashamed. She was right: Who *had* given him the right to demand perfection?

But this was Drusni he was talking about. *Drusni.* How could he possibly settle for second-best after her? How could Beltrenini even expect him to?

"Being sorry won't feed the Pakra," Beltrenini chided. "If you want this to mean anything, then you make sure you learn from it. My advice is that you go back, find yourself a nice female Breeder, and get on with your life."

"I don't have to go back for that," Raimey pointed out. "I could find someone here and save myself the trip."

"No," she said firmly. "You have to go back. If she cares about you as much as you said she did, even as just a friend, she's probably worried sick about you."

Raimey snorted. "I doubt it. Not with Pranlo there to keep her company."

"That's nice," Beltrenini rumbled. "You say you love her, and then go ahead and insult her in the same breath. I'll say it again: If she cares about you at all, she's going to be worried."

Raimey swished his tails restlessly. "I'll think about it."

"You do that," Beltrenini said. "Meanwhile, it's about that time. I'll see you at sunlight, right?"

"Uh . . . sure."

"Good," she said. "Sleep well." Her gently fanning fins fell still, and her breathing slowed and evened out. A ninepulse later, she was asleep.

Raimey gazed at her, feeling a surge of envy at her ability to fall asleep so easily. It had been ninedays and ninedays since he'd been able to do that. Maybe her conscience was less troubled than his.

Or maybe she was just old.

He peered into the gathering darkness. In the distance he could see other Qanska settling down to sleep: Protectors and their Nurturer mates, floating and twisting together in the eddy currents. There was a loose group of the larger Counselors, too, drifting in his and Beltrenini's direction. Some of them were settling down for the sundark in pairs; others, like Beltrenini, were alone.

I should go, he told himself. Beltrenini was right: A lone Breeder like him didn't belong here. Besides, if he waited until sunlight, she would just nag him some more about going back to face Drusni. That was something he didn't particularly want to hear.

On the other hand, if he left her, where would he go? Back to the equator? Not a chance. Just float around some more? What was the point of that?

Besides, his ostensible reason for being on Jupiter was to study the Qanska, and it was abundantly clear that the culture here in the northern latitudes was sharply different from the one he'd grown up in at the equator. He might as well learn what he could about this area; and who better to learn it from than someone who lived here?

Anyway, there was a comment she'd made that had piqued his curiosity. Five broods, she'd said she and her mate had had, and then had mentioned having six baby Qanska. The arithmetic implied she must have had twins somewhere along the line.

Problem was, he'd never heard of such a thing among the Qanska. Every birth in his herd had been single babies, and none of the stories in the herd circle had ever even mentioned twins.

Was that something else that was different out here? Or had Beltrenini simply gotten her memories crossed?

Either way, it would be worth a nineday or two to check it out. And it wasn't like he had somewhere else he wanted to be, anyway.

He let his fins go limp, letting the wind take him. The air out here seemed unusually warm, but pleasantly so. Maybe that was why Beltrenini could fall asleep so easily.

Eventually, so did he.

The tour Liadof had requested took over an hour. Faraday assumed it was at least somewhat enlightening for her, though she seemed to be quite familiar already with both Changeling's history and its current status.

It was, unfortunately, far less than enlightening for him. Every time he tried to delicately probe into the reason for her unexpected arrival, she either deflected the question or changed the subject entirely. By the end of the tour, about all he'd been able to glean from her comments was that she and the Five Hundred were rapidly running out of patience. But what that actually meant in terms of changes in policy or operation, he couldn't guess.

He'd also rather expected that when the tour was over Liadof would leave, either to return to her quarters or else to launch herself on an inspection of the rest of the station. Instead, she pulled a spare chair directly behind Beach and settled into it, listening silently to the computer give its slightly broken translation as Raimey told Beltrenini about his fiery breakup with Drusni.

It was another two hours before Faraday was finally able to make his excuses and ease his way out of the Contact Room. There was only one man on the station, he had already decided, who might be able to give him a clue to this new mystery.

He found Hesse on his first try. The younger man was

sitting at a back table in the smaller of the station's two bars, fingering a half-empty glass of dark beer and staring broodingly into the cheery glow of the faux fireplace in the corner. "Mr. Hesse," Faraday said, sitting down beside him. "Welcome back."

"Oh, thank you so very much," Hesse growled, throwing an almost furtive glance at Faraday and then shifting his gaze back to the fireplace. "It's so good to be back, too. Do you like the present I brought you?"

"You mean Arbiter Liadof?" Faraday shrugged. "Certainly an interesting choice of gifts."

Hesse snorted under his breath. "She's a barracuda with legs," he declared.

"It's not considered polite to talk about your boss that way," Faraday warned, glancing around the mostly empty room. This was *not* the way one talked about a member of the Five Hundred. Particularly not in public.

But Hesse merely gave another snort. "What do I care?" he countered. "She won't be my boss much longer."

He took a sip from his drink. "If you're lucky, she won't be *your* boss much longer, either," he added.

"You telling me you're quitting the project?" Faraday asked.

"No need," Hesse said. "Give her a few weeks, and the whole project will die out from under me on its own."

"Oh, come on," Faraday said, trying to ignore his own misgivings about Liadof. "She can't be *that* bad."

"She can, and she is," Hesse insisted. "She and the people she's fronting for are worse than you could ever imagine."

He shook his head. "I had such high hopes for Changeling, Colonel," he said quietly. "But she and her group are absolutely going to kill it."

"How many drinks have you had, anyway?" Faraday asked, peering closely at him.

"Just this one." Hesse smiled wanly. "Don't worry, Colonel, I'm not drunk. Unless you want to count self-pity and frustration. *Those* I might be drunk on."

Faraday sighed. "Look. If this is about being replaced—"

"This isn't about me at all," Hesse cut him off angrily. "Don't you understand?"

"No, I *don't* understand," Faraday said. "I can see how the Five Hundred might be getting impatient about our lack of progress. But they've also invested huge sums of money in Changeling. No one's going to cancel it simply out of pique or spite. Not Liadof or anyone else."

"I never said she was going to cancel it," Hesse said tartly. "I said she was going to kill it. Unintentionally, maybe, but it'll be just as dead." He pressed his lips tightly together. "And in the process, there's a fair chance they'll kill Raimey along with it."

Faraday stared at him. "I think," he said quietly, "that you'd better tell me what's going on. Starting with what exactly happened back on Earth."

THIRTEEN

Raimey was startled awake by a thin, wailing cry of fear and pain. He snapped himself to full alertness, twisting around to see what the trouble was.

That instinctive move probably saved his life. Even as he spun around, a sharp stab of pain scraped across his left fin; and suddenly he was face to face with a pair of unblinking black eyes.

Vuuka!

He rolled over in midtwist, angling away from the wide mouth already opening for another try. Again the chomping teeth snapped together, this time catching the very tip of his right tail and biting it off.

He spun around again as a second jolt of pain shot through him, turning a tight circle as he tried to assess the situation. It was still mostly dark, with the sunlight glow just starting to appear in the east. But it was bright enough for him to see that three more Vuuka were dodging in among the suddenly awakened Qanska, snapping at them like wolves in a sheep pen.

But even as he completed his circle, all three of the other Vuuka suddenly abandoned their pursuit of the fleeing Counselors and turned toward him.

And as he twisted around to point himself upward, he caught a glimpse of his now ragged tailtip, and the trail of yellow blood droplets dribbling away into the wind.

And he was now officially in big trouble.

He drove upward toward Level Three, twisting like a leaf in a hurricane as he swam. These Vuuka were as big as he was, and in a straight head-to-head race he knew they would eventually run him down.

But while their torpedo-shaped bodies might be faster in a straightaway, his was a lot more maneuverable. As long as he kept twisting and turning, he could hope to keep out of their reach.

Unfortunately, at this point that looked to be a very temporary hope. The Qanskan healing process was quick but not instantaneous; and until his tail healed over, the trail of leaking blood was going to draw them like magnets.

And at four-to-one odds, sooner or later he was going to run out of maneuvering space.

He spun around some more, still heading upward as fast as he could. Vuuka of this size, he knew, were most comfortable on Level Four or even Level Five. The higher he got, the harder it would be for them to keep up with him, let alone match his maneuvering. If he could keep them off him until his tail healed, they might give up and go after easier prey.

Easier prey. Like maybe one of the bigger but slower Counselors back behind him.

Like maybe even Beltreniul.

And somewhere deep inside him, a part of him that he'd thought was dead suddenly surged back to life.

Evasion and playing herd odds were the standard Qanskan approach to survival. They were the techniques he'd been taught when he was just a Baby, and the ones he'd employed countless times in the hundreds of ninedays since then.

But suddenly it wasn't good enough to just outdistance these predators and hope they picked on someone else. Inside this multicolored carcass, he was still a human being. That made him a predator, too.

More than that, he was a tool-using creature, even if no one this side of the Great Yellow Storm even knew what a tool was. There was a way to defeat a Vuuka; and he was sure as the Deep going to figure out what it was.

Sharp teeth slashed across the back of his right fin, again

just missing a solid hold. Raimey cut around in a three-quarter circle, shooting beneath the Vuuka's belly and heading off at right angles to him. The other three predators were coming up hard on the leader's flukes, one of them close enough to take a snap at Raimey as he passed practically in front of their snouts. Close; but now it would take a few seconds of frantic braking and turning for them to change direction after him.

He had that long to come up with a plan.

All right, he thought, forcing his mind back into the half-forgotten patterns of all those business logic classes he'd taken a lifetime ago. *Profit, loss; inflow, outflow; pluses, minuses.* What were a Vuuka's pluses? Sharp teeth, mainly, plus speed, strength, and stamina. What were its minuses? Lack of maneuverability and a densely packed body type that gave it less vertical range through the Jovian atmosphere than Raimey had. In his mind he laid out a spreadsheet of credits and debits, adding in everything he and that biologist McCollum up on Prime had been able to figure out about Vuukan physiology since his arrival here.

Behind him, he heard a bull-like snort as the four Vuuka got themselves lined up on him again. Another ninepulse, and they would be up to speed and gaining.

Speed, and stamina . . .

Raimey smiled tightly to himself. Okay. He had a plan. Now to see if it worked.

He kept going, wiggling and ducking to keep the Vuuka off-balance, until he felt the hot breath of the leader on his tailtips. Then, with a drop-and-flip maneuver he had to basically invent as he performed it, he did a half circle that brought him head-up beneath the Vuuka's lean body.

And ducking his snout, he slammed his bony forehead squarely into the Vuuka's lungs.

The predator's whole mouth seemed to explode outward with an agonized cough as the impact knocked all the wind out of him. A pulse later the other three shot past, snapping angrily at Raimey but going too fast for a quick stop. With lungs and buoyancy sacs both temporarily paralyzed, the winded Vuuka dropped like a rock; twisting around out of his way, Raimey continued his climb.

His tail, he noticed as he rose upward, had stopped bleeding. Theoretically, the loss of the brain-deadening blood trail should now allow the remaining Vuuka to think straight again and possibly reevaluate their chances of actually snagging this particular meal.

But either this group wasn't bright enough for such abstract thought, or else they figured they'd already put too much time and effort into the chase to abandon it now. Still snorting, possibly madder than ever, they charged up after him.

But that was okay. Raimey was feeling pretty righteously indignant himself just now. He'd already taught one Vuuka to be a little more leery about attacking Qanska with impunity. With luck, maybe he could double the class size for that particular lesson.

Again he dodged and ducked and maneuvered until he could feel the breath of the lead attacker on his tail. Then, cutting sharply into his new drop-and-flip maneuver, he swung around into a tight circle on course for the Vuuka's lungs.

But this particular predator had seen Raimey pull this trick already. Instead of continuing on in a headlong charge as his hapless predecessor had done, he braked hard, quickly cutting his forward speed down to nearly nothing.

So that as Raimey came out of his half circle, he was no longer on course for the Vuuka's lungs. Instead, his momentum was about to take him directly in front of the predator's gaping jaws.

But that was okay. What the Vuuka had forgotten was that Raimey *knew* he'd seen the trick already. This time, Raimey was deliberately not going fast enough to deliver the same kind of stunning blow to the lungs. He was, in fact, only moving fast enough that a midair flip was enough to kill his momentum on the spot before he could get in range of those razor teeth.

And in that position, poised directly above the Vuuka,

he slapped his tails with all his strength across the predator's eyes.

The Vuuka screamed in rage and pain, thrashing about madly in an attempt to nab his tormentor. But Raimey was already shooting away, a fresh throbbing of pain from his injured tailtip hardly dampening his grim satisfaction. Twice now he, the prey, had taken the battle back to the predator. It felt good. It felt *really* good.

Of course, in the process he'd also used up both Option A and Option B. Unfortunately, at the moment, he had no Option C.

Fortunately, an Option C turned out to be unnecessary. With two of their group out of action, the remaining Vuuka apparently decided they had had enough. Letting their massive flukes come to a halt, they let themselves coast to a stop behind Raimey. Then, rather sullenly, Raimey thought, they rolled over and slid back down toward the lower levels.

Raimey cruised along on Level Three for a while, just to make sure. Then, feeling better about himself than he had in a long time, he dropped to Level Four and headed back.

He found Beltrenini and the other Counselors still in the process of regrouping after their scattering by the Vuuka. "Raimilo!" Beltrenini gasped in surprise as he swam up to her. "Well, I'll be fin-bit. I thought for sure we'd seen the last of you. How did you get away from them?"

"I didn't, really," Raimey said modestly as he came alongside her. "I knocked two of them out of the chase, and the rest decided I wasn't worth the trouble."

"You did *what*?" one of the male Counselors demanded. "How in the Deep did you do *that*?"

"Well, the first one I slammed into just over his lungs," Raimey told him. "He wasn't much use after that. As for the other one, I was able to slash my tails across his eyes. Easy as grazing, really."

The male snorted. But it was an amazed, respectful sort of snort. "If you say so."

"You're hurt," a blue-and-green-spotted female said, moving close to examine his mutilated tailtip. "Bleeding's stopped, anyway."

"Yes, it only bled long enough for me to draw the Vuuka away," Raimey said. "It all worked out pretty well."

"Amazing," Beltrenini said. "I always thought there was more to you than met the eyes."

"And he's only a Breeder, too," Blue-green added, still examining his injured tail. "The clouds above only know what he'll be doing once he's a Protector."

"I've never even seen a Protector get past four Vuuka before," the male declared. "Certainly not by himself. You sure you didn't have any help out there, Raimilo?"

"None at all," Raimey assured him. "I will concede, though, that I *did* have more than my share of luck."

"Luck is a gift that comes to those who don't depend on it," Beltrenini said. "Qanska like you make their own luck."

"Thank you," Raimey said. "Does that mean you're not going to make me go back to Centerline?"

"You were going to *what*?" another female asked before Beltrenini could answer.

"I'd like to see you make him do *anything* he didn't want to do," the male rumbled.

"Hold on," Beltrenini protested. "I was never going to *make* you go back, Raimilo. I only said it would be good for you to face Drusni sometime."

She flipped her tails. "But there's certainly no reason you have to go right now."

"Absolutely not," Blue-green said firmly. "If you wanted to stick around, we'd certainly love to have you. As a matter of fact, I know some very nice female Breeders who travel nearby on Level Three I could introduce you to."

"Maybe later," Raimey said cautiously. "Right now, all I need is a little food."

"All he needs is a little food," someone else said with a laugh. "He just took out four Vuuka; and all he needs is a little food."

"That we can help with," Beltrenini said cheerfully.

"Come on, I know where there's a nice little run of *breekis*."

"Thanks," Raimey said, wondering what *breekis* was. Yet another food plant he'd never even heard of, apparently.

"As a matter of fact, why don't we all go?" Blue-green suggested.

"You mean, in case there are more Vuuka around?" another female asked slyly.

"Of course not," Blue-green said in a mock-hurt voice. "I just happen to like his company, that's all. My name's Nistreali, by the way. You can swim next to me."

A chuckle ran through the group as they headed off together, Beltrenini leading the way.

And as they swam, and as Raimey listened to the chatter of the Counselors around him, he wondered if he'd finally found what he'd been looking for ever since emerging from his Qanskan mother's womb in his brand-new body. Perhaps even since he'd accepted Faraday's offer to come here in the first place.

Not a release from his Earthly paralysis. Not a herd of children and adults who patronized him or treated him like a disgusting half-breed. Not alleged friends like Pranlo, who simply used him to get what they wanted. Especially not someone like Drusni, who would casually break his heart without a second thought.

No, what he'd finally found with Beltrenini and her more mature friends was something he hadn't had for a long time. Something he hadn't even realized he'd been missing.

He had found a home.

Faraday's quarters aboard Jupiter Prime were typical military issue: small and plain, with the minimum amount of space for a single human being to live in, plus the slight extra margin customarily granted to an officer of his rank.

Normally, he found them reasonably comfortable. But

then, normally he didn't have four extra people crammed inside along with him.

"I appreciate you all coming here tonight," he said as he sealed the door behind the last of them. "I apologize for the inconvenience, but I didn't want to risk using one of the conference rooms. Too much chance we might be overheard."

"Too late," Beach said as he sat down on the edge of Faraday's bed. "I listened to a couple of risqué jokes about the Five Hundred today. Liadof probably already has me wired for surveillance."

"Funny," Milligan growled, finding a bare section of wall to prop up with his shoulder, crossing his arms over his chest. "This better be important, Colonel. I have to take Grant's shift in six hours, and I'm behind on my sleep as it is."

"Don't blame the colonel for that," McCollum warned. Beach patted the bed beside him in invitation; pointedly, she stepped past him and sat down in Faraday's desk chair instead. "If you weren't always in engineering or the EVA ready room getting conned out of your paychit—"

"Hey, I work damn hard at my job," Milligan snapped back. "Poker's about the only way to unwind around here that doesn't involve rotting your brain, your teeth, or your liver."

"Come on, everyone, cool down," Sprenkle said tiredly, looking around the room and then sitting down on the bed beside Beach. "It's been a long day, and our nerves are all a little on edge."

"Nerves on edge," Beach echoed, shaking his head. "Man, I love psychiatric jargon."

"I'm sure you hear a lot of it, too," McCollum put in. "Can we knock it off and listen, so we can get out of here? No offense, Colonel," she added, looking at Faraday.

"None taken," Faraday assured her. "I'll try to make this quick. I had a long talk with Mr. Hesse this afternoon, and heard some things about Arbiter Liadof that I thought you should know."

"Like Hesse would be a good, unbiased source on that," Milligan growled. "She *is* his replacement, you know."

"Yes, I know," Faraday said. "And I took the possibility of bias into account. I don't think Mr. Hesse's feelings come into this at all, except in regards to how Project Changeling could be affected."

"In your *expert* psychiatric opinion, of course," Milligan muttered under his breath.

"I'd be happy to let Dr. Sprenkle talk to him later, if you'd like," Faraday offered, lifting his eyebrows at Sprenkle.

"If it seems useful or necessary," Sprenkle said. "What exactly did he have to say?"

"Let's start with Earth," Faraday said. "It seems there's been a coup inside the Five Hundred."

That one finally got their attention. Even Milligan, who had been glowering at the floor, turned narrowed eyes on Faraday. "A *coup*?" McCollum echoed disbelievingly. "But—"

"When?" Milligan demanded. "There wasn't a word on the newsnets."

"It happened a couple of weeks ago, before Hesse and Liadof headed out here," Faraday told him. "And there won't be any public news about it, at least not if they can help it. The whole thing was very quiet, very peaceful. Civilized, almost. They've kept the same Council, just to keep up appearances, but there's now an entirely different group in the background calling the shots."

"This isn't just because of the latest protests on Mars, is it?" McCollum asked, still sounding incredulous. "I mean, that would be like . . ." She waved her hands, groping for the word.

"Overreacting?" Milligan suggested.

"Try lunatic," Beach offered darkly.

"The protests may have been the trigger," Faraday told her. "But it sounds like this has been brewing for a long time."

"I heard this morning that Sol/Guard Marines have been

moved in against the protesters," Milligan said. "Sounds
like a serious policy change has been implemented."

"I heard that, too," Beach growled. "Most of the com-
mentators are saying the lockdown's just the beginning."

"You've got family on Mars, don't you, Ev?" McCollum
asked quietly.

Beach nodded. "Mother and two brothers."

"Things must have been pretty rough for them," Milligan
said.

Beach shrugged, too casually. "No rougher than for anyone else in the Solar System," he said. "Everyone's feeling
the budget cutbacks."

"Yeah, but at least on Earth they don't have to manu-
facture their own air and water," Milligan reminded him.
"Everywhere else, you crank down the support funding and
things can get critical pretty damn fast."

"If you ask me, the whole thing is crazy," McCollum
declared. "We're not even close to running out of room—
not even on Earth, let alone anywhere else."

"It's this whole frontier mentality they've gotten themselves locked into," Sprenkle said. "They're so afraid of
not having any distant place to send malcontents that everything except the current cutting-edge developments gets
shortchanged."

"Pop psychology at its best?" Milligan suggested, a note
of challenge in his voice as he looked at Sprenkle.

But the psychologist merely shrugged. "No argument
from me," he said.

"And so the only way people figure they can get Earth's
attention is to stage a riot," McCollum murmured.

"Something like that," Beach agreed. "Used to work
pretty well, too, as long as the riot was kept to just a very
loud protest. The Five Hundred came in long enough to fix
the most critical of the crises, and you went back to watching them spend the bulk of their money someplace else."

"Until this new bunch got in power, anyway," Milligan
said. "Sounds like they don't want to hear any noise, from
anyone."

"Trouble is, all a lockdown accomplishes is to bottle up the resentment," Sprenkle pointed out. "Sitting on them just makes it worse somewhere down the line."

"Why do I get the feeling that's where Changeling comes in?" McCollum asked, looking back at Faraday.

"Exactly," Faraday agreed soberly. "Apparently, the new leaders realize they're sitting on a tiger, and that the only long-term solution is to find a new source of meat to throw to it."

"In the form of new worlds to conquer," Sprenkle said.

"As you said, their frontier mentality," Faraday said, nodding to him. "They also seem to have concluded that the original Project Changeling plan is moving too slowly." He looked around the small room at each of them. "Arbiter Liadof has apparently been sent to move up the timetable."

"And how exactly does she expect to do that?" Beach asked contemptuously. "Launch an extensive search of all one point four quadrillion cubic kilometers of the atmosphere?"

"Mr. Hesse doesn't know the new plan," Faraday said. "But whatever it is, I doubt it involves anything as straightforward and unimaginative as a search." He hesitated. "And from what I've heard of Arbiter Liadof, I don't expect the approach to be a polite request to the Qanskan Leaders, either."

The other four exchanged glances. "And how exactly would Raimey fit into this new approach?" McCollum asked carefully.

Faraday frowned at her. There had definitely been something under the surface of that question. "Again, I don't know," he said. "Why do you ask?"

Another round of glances. "We weren't supposed to tell you this," Beach said. "But after you left, there was a Vuukan attack on Raimey and that group of Counselors he's been hanging out with."

Faraday felt something catch in his chest. "What happened? Is he all right?"

"Oh, he's fine," Beach hastened to assure him. "Got the tip of one of his tails bitten off, but that'll grow back. The point is that Liadof wouldn't let me warn him they were coming."

Faraday felt his mouth drop open. "Why the hell not?"

Beach lifted his hands helplessly. "All she said was that she was curious to see how he did against four predators. She hadn't seen firsthand how Qanska managed—"

"Wait a second," Faraday cut him off, his emotional balance teetering back and forth between stunned disbelief and black-edged outrage. "There were *four* Vuuka?"

"Four, count 'em, four," Milligan confirmed. "All about Raimey's size, too."

"Four full-grown Vuuka," Faraday repeated, trying to convince himself he'd really heard it correctly. For the moment, the stunned disbelief was definitely winning. "He managed to outrun *four* full-grown Vuuka?"

"Oh, it's better than that," Milligan said. "He didn't just outrun them; he actually took two of them out of the fight, right on the fly. After that, the other two gave up and went away."

"He hit the first one right over the lung sack," McCollum added. "Knocked all the wind out of him. I always wondered if he was paying attention during those physiology discussions we had way back when. I guess he was."

"Or else he's picked up a few new tricks along the way," Beach said.

"If he did, they're tricks we've never seen," McCollum pointed out.

"And neither have the rest of the Qanska," Milligan agreed. "Beltrenini and her group about split their stripes when he showed up in one undigested piece. Impressed as hell. They practically rode him out to breakfast on their shoulders."

"Really," Faraday said, looking at Sprenkle as a sudden thought struck him. "Do you think . . . ?"

Sprenkle shrugged. "Too soon to say," he said. "But it certainly looks promising."

"Yes," Faraday murmured. One of Raimey's biggest problems, Sprenkle had always said, was that in five years he still didn't really fit in with the rest of Qanskan society. Not even before his blowup with Drusni; certainly not afterward. Could this finally be the social breakthrough they'd been waiting for?

If it was, he would bet his pension that Liadof had missed the significance of the event entirely. She might know all of Changeling's facts and figures, but she had no feel for any of the more subtle stuff going on beneath the surface. "What did Liadof say afterward?" he asked. "Was she was suitably impressed?"

"Probably as impressed as her sort ever gets," Beach said sourly. "She basically just said 'interesting,' then made us promise not to tell anyone."

"Including me?"

"Especially you," Sprenkle said. "She said that if you weren't interested enough to stick around till the end of the shift, then you didn't deserve to know what was going on."

"Hmm," Faraday said, rubbing his chin. Insulting, but also revealing. So Liadof wasn't all that interested one way or the other in Raimey's survival. Less interested, apparently, than getting an entertaining live-nature show.

But at the same time, she didn't want to tip the cart over by letting Faraday get wind of it. Did that imply that Raimey was expendable, but that Faraday still had some influence on what went on here?

Or did she merely not want to bother with the kind of noise he could make with the Five Hundred? A Marine lockdown on Jupiter Prime, after all, would be rather counterproductive.

"So what's the next move?" McCollum asked.

Faraday shook his head. "I don't know," he said candidly. "Ideally, I'd like some idea what she's up to. Unfortunately, she's apparently the only one who knows."

"Does it have something to do with that eight-man tech group she's got working down in Bay Seven?" Milligan asked.

Faraday stared at him. "What tech group?"

"The one putting together a top-secret, high-end probe," Milligan said. "Rumor has it they've thrown all the station personnel out of the bay and support areas and taken the whole place over."

"You're kidding," Faraday said. He hadn't heard even a hint of this one. "Where did you hear this?"

"Where do you think?" Milligan threw a slightly smug, slightly injured look at McCollum. "Those poker games aren't just for the redistribution of wealth, you know. *Someone* has to keep tabs on what's happening around here."

"Consider us duly chastised," Faraday said dryly. "What else have you heard?"

Milligan grimaced. "Like I said, it's supposed to be top secret," he said. "The only reason I got anything is that the regular station guys are pretty sore at having been kicked out."

"Happens all the time on a space station," Beach grunted. "We must have kicked someone out of the Contact Room when we moved in, too."

"Yeah, but it was the *way* Liadof's people took over," Milligan said. "High-handed and stiff-nosed was the way one of the guys put it."

"Sounds like the sort of people she would hire," Sprenkle said.

"It does, doesn't it?" Faraday said, frowning. A new, high-tech probe. What could Liadof be doing with a new, high-tech probe?

"You don't suppose she really *does* intend to search the whole planet, do you?" Beach asked. "I *was* kidding about that."

"Never kid about politicians," Milligan advised him. "The more bizarre the joke, the more likely it'll come true."

"Still, I can't imagine them thinking anything *that* bizarre," Faraday said. "The range of current emscan technology . . . on the other hand, maybe someone's made a breakthrough they haven't told us about."

"Sounds like our first step is to find out more about this

probe," McCollum suggested. "Does anybody besides Tom have an in with this group?"

"Hey, *I* don't even have an in with the techs doing the actual work," Milligan warned. "I just know some of the station engineering guys, and they don't know any more than the rest of us do."

"Then let's get to know Liadof's people," Faraday said. "Try to make contact, befriend them—that sort of thing. They must be feeling a little isolated, working down there all by themselves. Any idea what their timetable is?"

"One of them said Liadof's got the bay reserved for the next two months," Milligan said. "For a crew of eight, that's probably about right for assembly and testing a deep-atmosphere probe."

"So we've got two months," Faraday said. "Fine. Let's see just how friendly we all can be. And we can start by trying to coax one of them outside Bay Seven for some kind of social visit. *Any* kind of social visit."

He looked at Milligan. "Including a poker game."

"Sounds good to me," Milligan said blandly. "They talk more when they're winning, though. You willing to subsidize me a little?"

"Within reason," Faraday said. "In fact, I'll go you one better. I'll offer a cash bonus to the first person who gets one of them out on a social visit."

Sprenkle half raised his hand. "Colonel, what about Beta and Gamma Shifts? Are you going to bring them into this, too?"

Faraday hesitated. "Not right now," he said. "I don't know any of them nearly as well as I know you four; and I *do* know there are a couple among them who are very big on blind obedience to governmental authority. They might not be comfortable with this."

"I know which ones you mean," Beach said, making a face. "You're right, we'd better keep it here."

"At least for now," Faraday said. "Well. Does anyone have anything else to add or ask?"

There was a moment of silence. "Then that's it," Faraday said. "Thank you all for coming."

With a rustle of cloth and a muttering of good-byes, they got up and filed out of the room.

All of them, that is, except Sprenkle.

"You have a question?" Faraday asked him as the door closed behind the others.

"More of a comment, really," Sprenkle said. His posture was studiously relaxed as he sat on the edge of Faraday's bed, the sort of pose that put people at their ease. An old psychologist's trick, no doubt. "I just wanted to make sure you realized just how far out your neck is stuck on this one."

"I have a pretty good idea," Faraday said. "My question for *you* is whether it's stuck out there all alone."

"Meaning?"

"Meaning that if push comes to crunch, are they going to stand with me?" Faraday said bluntly. "Or are they going to think only of themselves?"

"I would say that's partly up to you," Sprenkle said. "For whatever it's worth, I think you've taken a good first step here tonight."

"Which step was that?"

"Reinvigorating them," Sprenkle said. "You saw what they were like when they came in. Over the past couple of years this job's gotten breathtakingly boring. We know most of what there is to know about Qanskan society, and frankly Raimey isn't all that interesting to watch anymore."

"Is that why they've been picking at each other so much?"

"It's a common outlet," Sprenkle said. "But as I'm sure you saw, when they left here they left as a team again. You've given us something new to think about and work toward together."

He cocked his head. "Whether that's going to be enough for them to stand by you, I don't know. You have a name and a reputation that even the Five Hundred might hesitate to take on. None of the rest of us have that kind of armor plating."

"My name and reputation would be standing in the dock along with them," Faraday pointed out.

"True, but armor plating extends only so far," Sprenkle said. "It's easy to talk big and confident here in a private meeting. It's not nearly so easy to turn that talk into action. Especially not when you're facing the possible loss of your entire future."

"You think Liadof's got that kind of power?"

Sprenkle snorted. "I would say she could probably break any one of us with a five-minute phone call," he said bluntly.

"Even if we're following our legal duty and she isn't?"

Sprenkle's eyes narrowed. "I don't follow."

"Go back and reread Project Changeling's mission statement," Faraday said. "Paragraph four says explicitly that our legal duty is to protect Raimey's life, insofar as that's compatible with the objective of finding and gaining access to the Qanskan stardrive."

"Liadof isn't putting Raimey's life at risk," Sprenkle pointed out.

"She already has," Faraday countered. "She failed to warn him of a Vuukan attack. Endangerment through inaction is legally as damning as any other sort."

Sprenkle's lip twitched. "Perhaps paragraph four has been rescinded."

"Not in writing, it hasn't," Faraday said. "And until it is, the law says I have to assume it's still in force."

"Even if an Arbiter of the Five Hundred says otherwise?"

"There's no mention of verbal orders anywhere in the mission statement," Faraday said.

Sprenkle shook his head. "Technically, you may be right," he said. "But if it comes down to your push-and-crunch, with you against Liadof, I have to say my money would be on her. Sorry."

"No apology required," Faraday said dryly. "To be honest, so would mine."

He looked at the photo of Jupiter he'd set up over his desk. "But I was the one who talked Raimey into going down there in the first place. I can't abandon him just because the Five Hundred have decided he's unnecessary. Or inconvenient."

"No," Sprenkle said. "I suppose not."

There was a moment of silence. "You said whether the team stands together on this is partly up to me," Faraday reminded him. "What else does it depend on?"

Sprenkle smiled faintly. "Ironically, perhaps, Raimey himself."

Faraday frowned. "Raimey?"

"Yes," Sprenkle said. "You see, his socialization problems haven't just been with the Qanska. They've also been with us. Face it, Colonel; Raimey has hardly shown himself to be a very likable person."

Faraday grimaced. "He was a typical self-absorbed twenty-two-year-old who watched his grandiose plans for the future crash down around his ears. What did you expect?"

"I *expected* some of the bitterness to wear off after a while," Sprenkle countered. "I also expected a little more gratitude after we and the Qanska gave him back something resembling a real life. It's something called maturity."

"I know," Faraday had to agree. "And unfortunately, Drusni's rejection seems to have simply solidified that poor-me attitude of his."

"Unfortunately," Sprenkle said. "He also has a bad tendency to throw the blame for everything onto other people instead of accepting his fair share."

"So what are you saying?" Faraday asked. "That the more unlikable Raimey is when the crunch comes, the less likely the team will stick their necks out for him?"

"Do you blame them?"

"Not really," Faraday conceded. "Trouble is, it looks like we've only got two months before that crunch. Any chance at all he can get his act straightened out by then?"

"I suppose it's possible," Sprenkle said, getting to his

feet. "Back when he was a Midling, making friends with Drusni and Pranlo was what drew him out of himself and his self-pity, at least a little. If this Vuukan incident affects him the same way, he may end up as both a better Qanska and a better human being."

"Yes," Faraday murmured. "We can hope, anyway."

"Regardless, I wish you luck, Colonel," Sprenkle added. "For whatever it's worth, I admire your stand on this."

"Thank you," Faraday said. "I notice you're not also offering your unqualified support."

Sprenkle smiled tightly. "As I said, it's easy to be brave when the threat isn't actually looming over you. I'd like to believe I'll be noble when the time comes . . . but I also know better than to make a promise I don't know if I can keep."

"I understand," Faraday said. "If I can't have loyalty, at least give me honesty."

Sprenkle inclined his head in an ironic bow. "Nicely put, Colonel, and expertly manipulative. You should have been a psychologist."

He stepped to the door, then paused. "One other question, if I may," he said, turning around again. "I've studied everything we've got on Raimey—his family, schooling, psychological and social profiles, and all that. But I've never seen anything in his files that would have caught *my* eye if I'd been looking for a likely candidate for this job. May I ask how exactly you and the Five Hundred picked him out?"

Faraday sighed. "We didn't," he said. "We made the same offer to forty-seven other quadriplegics around the System. Raimey was the only one who took us up on it."

"Oh," Sprenkle said, sounding a little taken aback. "I see. Well . . . good night, Colonel."

"Good night."

He left. For a moment Faraday gazed at the door, trying to marshal his thoughts. Then, stepping over to his desk, he sat down and flipped on his computer. If Liadof had brought a group of men aboard, their travel files must be in the station's log somewhere.

After all, the first step to befriending someone was to learn his name.

FOURTEEN

"The brown ones are called *ranshay*," Beltrenini said, waggling her tails at the clumps floating past. "The silvery-blue ones are *jeptris*. Try them together."

Obediently, Raimey scooped up a half mouthful of each. "Whoa," he said, his eyes and mouth both tingling with the reaction. It was like some kind of food he vaguely remembered from his previous existence. Italian, maybe? Or was it Mexican? "That's . . .intense."

"Isn't it?" Beltrenini agreed, sounding rather pleased with herself. "Alone, they're not so terrific—the *jeptris* is a little too spicy, and the *ranshay* is disgustingly bland. But together, they're truly a taste to swim for."

"Sure are," Raimey said. "Ah, the joys of being a Breeder."

"What's this?" Nistreali put in, flapping over beside them. "Did you say the joys of being a Breeder? I thought you weren't interested in meeting my friends."

"I was referring to this *ranshay* and *jeptris* combination," Raimey said, wishing mightily that he'd picked a different way of phrasing it. Nistreali had been all over his fins for five ninedays now, nagging him to let her fix him up with some of those female Breeders she knew up on Level Three.

And for five ninedays now he'd been dodging and weaving like a Youth trying to avoid a particularly persistent Vuuka. He had no doubt that Nistreali's friends were nice young Breeders, but he wasn't interested in trying to replace his memories of Drusni just yet. If indeed he ever could.

"What do you mean?" Nistreali asked, clearly puzzled. "What does eating have to do with being a Breeder?"

"I just meant that being big enough to get down to Level Four has its advantages," he said. One of these days, he told himself firmly, he would have to stop making idle comments in Nistreali's earshot. The complications were never worth it. "I never had food like this when I was a Youth."

"What do size and age have to do with it?" Nistreali asked, sounding more puzzled than ever. "*Ranshay* and *jeptris* grow all the way from Level One to Level Five."

Raimey twisted around to stare at her. "What?" he demanded. "You're kidding, right?"

"Nistreali never kids about food, Raimilo," Beltrenini said dryly. "Or nice young female Breeders, either—"

"Wait a second," Raimey said. "You say this stuff grows on Level One? Then how come I've never seen it before?"

"Maybe you have another name for it back on Centerline," Nistreali suggested. "It looks a little bit different up there, too."

"How different?" Raimey asked.

"Well, it's in smaller clumps, for one thing," Nistreali said. "The air's thinner up there, after all."

"The *ranshay* is usually a lighter brown, too," Beltrenini added. There was suddenly something odd about her tone. "Though the *jeptris* looks pretty much the same as it does here."

Raimey flipped his tails in a negative. "No," he said. "There was nothing even remotely similar where I grew up."

Beltrenini gave a deep sigh. "It's true, then," she said quietly. "The Time of Valediction really is coming."

"You don't know that," Nistreali warned, her voice filled with dread. "I mean, we've only got the experiences of one Centerline Breeder here."

"But he didn't know about the Brolka, either," Beltrenini said heavily. "He'd never seen them before."

"Clouds above, I hope not," Nistreali murmured. Suddenly, she seemed uninterested in the food floating past her. "I hope not."

"What is this Time of Valediction?" Raimey asked, a shiver of darkness sweeping over him. The sudden somber mood was contagious. "I've never heard of that, either."

"You haven't heard of much of anything, have you?" Beltrenini said, sounding distracted. "Did you sleep through all your herd's story circles, or what?"

"I didn't sleep through any of them," Raimey insisted. "I listened as well as any child there; and I tell you, no one mentioned any Time of Valediction. I don't even know what it means."

"Valediction: leaving or farewell," Beltrenini said. "It's when our world begins to change, and those who are wise enough and worthy enough leave to seek a new home."

Raimey felt his breath freeze in his throats. *The Qanskan stardrive!* Faraday and Hesse had spun him that idea once, he remembered, just before Drusni had broken his heart.

But in the long, lonely days since then he'd concluded they were either delusional or simply biting wishful thoughts at the air. There was no way the Qanska could possibly have built themselves anything mechanical or electrical. Not here. No way at all.

But if Beltrenini was right, they had. Somehow, they had.

Unless, of course, the Time of Valediction was nothing but a myth. More biting at the air.

"I never heard of that," he said carefully. "How does all this happen?"

Nistreali flipped her fins in a shrug. "Well, obviously, we've never seen it ourselves," she said.

"Or ever known anyone who remembers, either," Beltrenini added. "The Wise who came here did so well before our time."

"But they *did* come here from somewhere else, right?" Raimey persisted. "I mean, somewhere *else*, not just another part of the planet."

"From outside the clouds, to within the clouds," Nistreali

said. "At least, that's how the story goes. You sure you never heard it?"

"Yes, I'm sure," Raimey said. "But how does it happen? Where do they go?"

"They go *here*," Beltrenini said. "Or places like here."

"Yes, but from where?" Raimey asked impatiently. "What I mean is, where do they go to *go* to places like here?"

Beltrenini gave him a perplexed look. "You use the strangest sentence constructions I've ever heard," she said. "Is that a Centerline thing?"

"No, just a Raimilo thing," Raimey said with a sigh. Clearly, this was getting him nowhere. Either they didn't want to talk about the stardrive's location, or they really didn't know where it was. Probably the latter.

But now he knew that Faraday's fever-dream speculations had been right after all. The Qanska really *were* visitors from somewhere else.

Five ninedays ago, facing down four Vuukan throats, he'd felt a stirring of the human spirit that he'd thought was buried too deeply to ever see again. Now, with this revelation, he felt an even stronger stirring of that same spirit. A stardrive. Mankind's dream ever since he began looking up at the sundark sky.

And it was here. *Here.*

Nistreali was saying something. "Sorry," Raimey said, dragging his attention back to her. "What did you say?"

"I asked if you wanted me to help you go down to Level Five and go hunt up some *feemis*," she said. "That's always good for clearing your mouth after a *ranshay/jeptris* experience."

Raimey frowned. "How can you think about eating at a time like this?" he asked.

"A time like what?" Nistreali asked.

"Nistreali can always think about eating," Beltrenini said.

"You said the Time of Valediction was coming," Raimey reminded them. "Don't we need to start getting ready or something?"

Both Qanska burst into laughter. "Oh, my, Raimilo," Nistreali chuckled when she could talk again. "You really *are* a flap-fin hurry-up sort, aren't you?"

"I just said the Time of Valediction was coming," Beltrenini pointed out. "I didn't say it was coming anytime soon. Certainly not in *our* lifetimes."

"Oh," Raimey said, feeling stupid.

"Though I suppose it *could* be in *your* lifetime," Beltrenini conceded, eying him. "You'll undoubtedly be one of the Wise someday, and you'll have a say in the whole thing."

Raimey grimaced. "If I live that long."

"A Breeder who can chase off four Vuuka?" Nistreali said with a sniff. "There's no doubt in *my* mind. And anyway, if you really want to get ready for the Time of Valediction, you ought to come down with me and scoop a few mouthfuls of *feemis*."

"Thanks." Raimey took a deep breath. "But I think it's time for me to go back to Centerline. At least for a while."

"You ready to heal matters between you and Drusni?" Beltrenini asked quietly.

"I—well, I'm willing to give it a try," Raimey hedged.

"I'm glad," Beltrenini said. "You know where she is?"

"I suppose she's still with the herd where we grew up," Raimey said, frowning. With the variable wind speeds at the different latitudes, he realized, getting back to their herd area was going to take some tricky navigation. "I just hope I can find it."

"You won't have any trouble," Beltrenini assured him. Sidling up alongside him, she stroked his fin gently with hers. "I've enjoyed having you around, Raimilo. If you decide you don't want to stay in Centerline after you talk with her, you'll always have a home with us."

"Thank you," Raimey said, his throats oddly tight at the thought of leaving. To have gotten so comfortable in so short a time was a new experience for him.

Especially here on this alien world.

"You'd better go, then," Beltrenini said, all brisk business now. "Come and see us again, all right?"

"I will," Raimey promised. "Good-bye. Good-bye, Nis-treall."

"Take care, Raimilo," she said, her own voice heavy with emotion. "Chase a Vuuka for me, okay?"

"Every chance I get," Raimey said, smiling.

With a flip of his tails, he turned and swam away. Back toward the equatorial regions, and the center of Qanskan civilization.

Because in reality, healing his relationship with Drusni was the last thing on his mind, even if such a thing was possible. What he *did* need to do was get in contact with Faraday and the rest of the humans; and back along Centerline was where they had always talked to him before.

Apparently the only place they could do so, too. There had been some talk about relay probes, he remembered, but nothing ever seemed to have come of it. Certainly they'd been silent since he and Drusni had had their big fight and he'd struck out on his own for the northern latitudes.

But now, after over five dayherds of living on Jupiter, he finally had proof that a Qanskan stardrive did indeed exist. Or if not proof, at least some strong anecdotal evidence.

He would love to see Faraday's face when he told them. But he would settle for hearing the sound of his voice.

"He's still heading southward," Milligan confirmed. "Looks like he really is heading back."

"Very good," Liadof said. Her voice and expression were calm and controlled, with even a hint of feigned indifference.

But in her eyes was a glint that sent a chill down Faraday's back. After years of quiet hope, heated argument, and rampant speculation, they finally had at least folklore-level proof that the Qanskan stardrive really did exist.

And Liadof wanted it. Wanted it very, very badly. "How long until he's back at the equator?" she asked.

"Hard to say," Milligan said. "It took him a couple of months to get that far north, but he wasn't in any hurry then. If he keeps up this pace, he could do it in a month. Possibly less."

"Or possibly more," McCollum put in. "The variety and concentration of food in the equatorial regions seems to be lower than at the latitudes where he is now. There also seem to be more Vuuka near the equator, or at least more Vuukan attacks. The extra grazing and dodging around is bound to cost him some time."

"Well, it doesn't really matter," Liadof said. "We know now that they definitely have a stardrive. It's just a matter of finding it."

"Which is not exactly a trivial problem," Faraday pointed out. "May I ask how you intend to accomplish that?"

"At the moment, that's still classified," Liadof said absently, studying the displays. "Ms. McCollum, do you know where Raimey's old herd is?"

"Yes," McCollum said. "They've drifted a little ahead of our position, but we still have a good track on them. There's obviously been some shuffling in the personnel, of course."

"And that female—Drusni—is she still with them?"

"Yes, Arbiter," McCollum confirmed. "And pregnant with her third child, too."

"Are you planning to wait until Raimey talks to Drusni before you contact him?" Faraday asked.

Liadof's answer was a surprise. "I'm not interested in contacting Raimey at all. If I wanted to talk to him, I could do it now."

Faraday frowned. "Then why is his destination important?"

"That herd is the one that knew Raimey the best," Liadof said, toying thoughtfully with the tooled ruby pendant she always wore. Faraday glanced at her fingers, feeling the same faint queasiness he always did in the pendant's presence. The bright red stone looked far too much like a trickling drop of blood for his comfort. Knowing Liadof, of course, it would undoubtedly be someone else's blood. "Since they were presumably hand-picked by the Qanskan chiefs, that implies the herd's leaders know a fair amount about humanity," Liadof went on. "That should make our upcoming conversation easier."

"Ah—so we're going to talk to the herd," Faraday said, nodding as if he actually understood where Liadof was going with this. "What are we going to talk to them about?"

Liadof glanced back at him. "Did anyone ever mention that you ask a lot of questions, Colonel?"

Did anyone ever mention that I'm still officially in charge of this project? the retort shot through Faraday's mind. "I'm concerned about Raimey's future," he said instead. "I'd like to know how he fits into your plans."

Liadof turned back to the displays. "What makes you think he fits in anywhere at all?"

"He's part of Project Changeling," Faraday reminded her. "Whatever else we do here, his well-being has to be taken into account."

"Especially since he'll be reaching the herd about the time your probe is ready to go," Beach added.

Liadof's head snapped toward him like a striking rattlesnake. "What do you know about the probe?" she demanded.

Beach's large form seemed to melt into his chair in the sudden heat of that gaze, his round face visibly paling. "I— well, your people have taken over a probe bay," he floundered. "I just assumed you had a probe you were getting ready."

"How did you know I'd taken over a bay?" Liadof persisted. "Who told you?"

"No one told him," Faraday jumped to his rescue. "No one had to. Station space allocations are a matter of public record."

Liadof spun back, and for a stretched-out pair of seconds she just glared at him. "Colonel, let's get something straight," she said, her voice quiet and controlled but with a quiver of compressed anger beneath it. "Your people run the equipment. You run your people. But *I* am Project Changeling now. Your people will do their jobs, and will keep their noses to themselves. Or they will get them broken."

She gave a little huff. "And that goes for you, too. Behave yourself, and you get to keep your name on this project. Otherwise, you'll find yourself locked away, waiting for the next transport back to Earth. Do I make myself clear?"

"Very clear, Arbiter," Faraday said stiffly, feeling his face reddening. Every rule of civilized behavior said you didn't speak to a person this way in front of his subordinates.

But then, rules like that probably didn't apply to the Five Hundred. And of course, she probably didn't consider them to be *his* subordinates, anyway.

"Good." Deliberately, she turned her back and resumed her study of the displays.

Faraday took a deep breath. Maybe she was used to instant cowering everywhere else she went. But not here. Not here. "You haven't answered my question, Arbiter," he said.

Liadof turned back, her eyes narrowed as they probed his face. Faraday forced himself to hold her gaze; and after another pair of seconds her lips twitched in a cold smile. "You don't flinch easily, do you, Colonel Faraday?" she asked, her tone almost conversational. The earlier anger was gone, or least buried away out of sight. "I can see how you wound up becoming a hero."

"Thank you," Faraday said, as if the compliment had been genuine. "What about Raimey?"

The smile vanished, the lines around her mouth settling into their more normal pattern. "Mr. Raimey is what he always was to this project," she said quietly. "A means to an end."

"Are you saying this new probe of yours renders him expendable?"

She turned back to the displays. "Let me put it this way,"

she said. "You should hope that Ms. McCollum is right, that he takes longer than expected to get back to his herd. He may not find it pleasant to be in the vicinity when the probe arrives there."

"That sounds rather disturbing," Faraday said cautiously. "We have agreements with these people—"

"We have nothing," Liadof cut him off. "No treaties, either signed or recorded. The only even marginally official agreement we've ever had was getting their permission for Raimey to enter their world as he did. That one has already been satisfied."

"So what you're saying is that the Qanska are fair game now?"

The lines around Liadof's mouth became even deeper. "We need that stardrive, Colonel," she said softly. "And we're going to have it. The Qanska can cooperate, or not."

She threw him a speculative look, then turned away again. "So can you."

Faraday looked over at the techs. All four were minding their boards now, studiously ignoring the conversation.

Carefully guarding their own careers, and their own futures.

And with a sinking feeling, Faraday realized that Sprenkle's warning had been right on the mark. Push had come to crunch; and Faraday's neck was stuck out here all alone.

So be it, he told himself firmly. If he was the only one who dared to stand up to Liadof and the Five Hundred, then that was how it would be. He owed Raimey that much.

And if it cost him his career, that was all right, too. After all, there wasn't that much left of it, anyway.

FIFTEEN

With one last bite, Raimey finished off the last trailing bit of *ranshay*. It was the first run of that particular plant he'd seen in a long time, and he guessed that it would likely be the last.

And Beltrenini was right. Without *jeptris* along to give it tang, the stuff was pretty bland.

He thought about that as he turned his right ear into the eddy winds again and continued his journey south. Why would plants like *ranshay* and *jeptris* be absent from the equatorial regions where he'd grown up? There was certainly a higher concentration of Qanska here than farther north; had they overgrazed the plants to extinction?

But that didn't make any sense. As he'd already seen, there was plenty of both types just a few ninedays' travel off the equator, plus at least five other species he'd never seen before. Was there simply not enough mixing of the atmosphere to bring them to the equator? That didn't seem likely. But then, he was hardly a meteorological expert.

For that matter, he was hardly an expert on anything, at least not anything that was of any use here. Why in the world had Faraday picked him for this mission in the first place?

He had no idea. But whatever the reason, the fact remained that he was the man on the spot. He was all they had; and when they found out that the stardrive really did exist, they would know he'd done his job.

At least, the first part of it. Now the real task would

begin: actually finding the thing, wherever in the Deep they had hidden it

In the gloom ahead, a dark shape moved. Raimey froze, letting the winds carry him as he peered at the figure. It was a Vuuka, probably about five-size long, laboriously working his way upward. Probably heading up toward some herd above on Level One, hoping to snatch a newborn or to take a few bites out of a careless Youth straying too far from the edge of the group.

He smiled to himself with bittersweet memory. It had been a Vuuka of just about that same size who had attacked him his first ninepulse out of his Qanskan mother's womb. His introduction to this wonderful world he'd volunteered to go to.

Of course, there wouldn't be anyone with Counselor Latrancsto's mass and bulk to trap and absorb this particular Vuuka. For a moment he considered taking the predator on himself, seeing if he could at least discourage it from raiding the nursery up above.

But no. There would be plenty of ten-size Protectors up there. The children would be safe enough.

Not that he really cared. He was a human, he reminded himself firmly, not a Qanska. He didn't care anymore what happened here, as long as it didn't happen to him.

Ahead, the Vuuka disappeared upward into the swirling air, and Raimey resumed his travel across the winds. He was seeing more Vuuka lurking around now, more than he'd run into while he was with Beltrenini and her Counselor friends. More Vuuka, while at the same time a smaller variety of food plants. Coincidence?

And fewer of those compact little Brolka things, too, come to think of it. In fact, he couldn't recall having seen any of them for the past nineday or so. He'd meant to ask Beltrenini about them, but somehow he'd never gotten around to it. Where did they fit into all this?

Impatiently, he shook the thoughts away. There was no point straining his brain on this one. McCollum was the xenobiology expert, and she'd probably already figured it out. As soon as he got within hailing range of the station, he'd simply ask her.

Until then, it was find food, avoid predators, and keep swimming. That was his life now. Probably all the life he'd ever have.

Still, it beat sitting paralyzed in a walking chair with voice-actuated robotics doing everything for him. Probably.

"Colonel?"

Faraday looked up from his tasteless eggplant parmigiana to find Jen McCollum standing across the table from him, holding a meal tray of her own. "Good evening, sir," she said with strained politeness. "May I join you?"

"Ms. McCollum," he nodded back, his immediate reflex being to politely tell her he wasn't interested in company. Last week's confrontation with Liadof was still fresh in his mind, as was the memory of those four turned backs as Liadof verbally took him off at the knees.

It was a confrontation whose echoes still reverberated through the entire project. A formal stiffness had replaced the more casual atmosphere that had once existed in the Contact Room. The techs were walking on duck eggs, afraid to make any comment outside the narrow range of their specific duties. Afraid of even challenging or arguing with each other.

Afraid of drawing Liadof's attention in their direction.

Bad enough that Liadof's presence had poisoned the Contact Room. Even worse was that the venom had also spilled over into off-duty relationships. Before her arrival, Faraday had had occasional meals with one or more of the techs, and had almost always paused to chat with them when they happened to bump into each other in corridor or meeting room. He'd never actually become friends with any of them, but he'd certainly considered them his colleagues.

Now, even when they were in the same room together, the others seemed completely unaware of his existence. The message had been sent and received: Colonel Faraday was on notice, and those who didn't wish to join him had better keep their distance.

And Jupiter Prime had become a very lonely place to be.

McCollum was still standing there, waiting for his reply. "Certainly," he said with a private sigh. Personal feelings aside, he could hardly hold this against any of them. In their place, at their age, he probably would have been equally reluctant to make an enemy of someone as powerful as Liadof.

"Thank you, sir," McCollum said, pulling out the chair across from him and setting her tray on the table as she sat down. "I'll just take a moment of your time."

"No rush," he assured her. She wasn't planning on spending an entire meal with him, anyway, he saw now. Her tray contained only the remains of her own dinner: empty plates, a mostly empty cup, and a standard-issue cloth napkin, carelessly folded.

She might be willing to risk being seen with him, but she wasn't willing to push it.

"I just wanted to apologize for not speaking up in your defense last week," she said. "It wasn't very brave of me. Not very loyal, either."

"Don't worry about it," Faraday assured her, his resentment abating somewhat. At least she recognized what she'd done and felt guilty about it. *If I can't have loyalty*, he'd told Sprenkle, *at least give me honesty*. "I'm less worried about myself than I am about Raimey," he added. "I can at least stand up and defend myself. Raimey can't."

"I know." McCollum pursed her lips, her gaze avoiding his eyes. She'd slowed down a lot these days, he'd noticed, her movements more deliberate, even leaden. A far cry from the early days, when Beach had with perfect seriousness dubbed her the station's FMSO: Fast Moving Singing Object. She didn't seem to be singing anymore, either, at least not in his presence.

"I see you got the parmigiana," she said. "How is it tonight?"

"Adequate," he said, cutting off another corner with his

fork. So that was it for Raimey, at least as far as tonight's conversation was concerned. Hardly surprising: If they weren't going to stand up with Faraday the Living Legend, they certainly weren't going to do so for Raimey the Expendable Sacrifice. "Not as good as mother used to make; and *she* was Scots-Irish, without a drop of Italian in her. But I've tasted worse."

"Possibly even on this very station?" she suggested.

"Very definitely on this very station," Faraday confirmed, eying her closely. She seemed to be running a mix of deference and restlessness tonight, a very odd combination for her. "It was back during the *Skydiver* program, well before your time. One of the cooks couldn't make Italian to save his life, but insisted on weekly attempts at it anyway. For a while, every Thursday night brought serious talk of mutiny."

"Pretty grim," McCollum said. Picking up her napkin, she dabbed delicately at her mouth with it. "Still, I'd be willing to bet the meat loaf tonight could have given him some competition."

"Still not getting the right proportion of spices?" Faraday hazarded, remembering her standard complaint about the cooking here.

"I don't think they even got the right *kind* of spices this time," she said, laying the folded napkin back down again.

Only instead of laying it down on her tray, she set it on the table beside the tray.

"Probably supply problems again," Faraday said, feeling his heartbeat pick up as he carefully avoided looking at the discarded napkin. In five years of the close observation that naturally came of living in such confined quarters with these people, he had long ago pegged McCollum as a neatness freak. Never in those five years had he ever seen her leave so much as a stray spoon behind her in the cafeteria.

If that napkin was still there on the table when she got up to leave, he might just owe her an apology.

"Probably," she conceded, glancing casually around. "I guess you can't blame the cooks for that."

"Not really," he agreed, forcing himself back onto this innocuous train of thought. "You could try blaming the security crackdown on the Inner System, though. That's probably what's slowing down the shipments."

"Or I could blame the protesters on Mars and Ceres," she suggested. "That's what inspired the crackdown."

"Or you could blame the overall System economy for not creating the unlimited wealth that would let us do anything we wanted to," Faraday said, getting into the game now. "With infinite money, we could develop Saturn's moons, colonize Pluto and Charon, *and* give every Martian their very own individual gold-plated dome home."

"Or I could blame God for only putting nine planets into the System to begin with," McCollum said.

Faraday made a face. "You win," he conceded. "Once you blame God, you've gone as far back as you can."

"And usually overshot the real target anyway," McCollum said.

"Indeed," Faraday said. "Well . . ."

"Maybe this scheme of Arbiter Liadof's will work," McCollum said. "If we can get a stardrive, the whole universe will be open to us."

"We can hope," Faraday said, nodding. "So. What have you got planned for the evening?"

"Not much," she said with a little shrug. "Probably read for a while and then go to bed. At some point soon, I'm guessing we're all going to be pretty busy. Might as well get caught up on my sleep before that happens."

"Sounds like a plan," Faraday said. "Maybe I'll do the same."

"Might be good for you." Picking up her cup, she drained the last sip. "Well. Good night, Colonel," she said, standing up. "See you in the morning."

"Good night, Ms. McCollum."

They exchanged nods, and she picked up her tray and headed toward the drop-off rack.

Leaving the folded napkin on the table.

Faraday returned to his meal, forcing himself to eat

slowly and casually. McCollum's abandoned napkin seemed as visible and obvious as a smoking assault rifle, and it seemed to him that every eye in the cafeteria must surely be locked on it. On it, and on him.

But the buzz of conversation never faltered, and no one strode up to his table and demanded to know what was going on. Either Liadof's agents were playing it very cool, or else there really wasn't anyone watching him.

Still, there was no point in taking chances. He finished his meal, gathered his dinnerware back onto his tray, and stood up. Then, almost as an afterthought, he casually picked up McCollum's napkin.

It was heavier than a simple square of linen had any right to be. Setting it on top of his own napkin, he headed off across the room.

And as he leaned over to place his tray on the drop-off rack, his body blocking the view from the rest of the cafeteria behind him, he slipped the folded napkin and its unknown contents inside his jacket.

No one leaped up, shouting in triumph. No one suddenly appeared in front of him, ready to slap a pair of cuffs across his wrists. No one even yelled at him for stealing a napkin.

Still, he could feel the sweat gathering across his forehead and the back of his neck the entire way to his quarters. There, behind a locked door, he pulled out the napkin and carefully unfolded it.

There were two items inside. One was a folded piece of paper. The second, the one that had provided most of the weight, was a piece of heavy metal mesh about fifteen centimeters square.

And he definitely owed McCollum an apology.

He started with the mesh. He had seen such things before, on the old experimental "open-skin" probes that allowed Jupiter's atmosphere to flow freely in and out of noncritical areas so as to equalize pressures during rapid descent and ascent. The wires of this mesh were thinner than those had been, though, no more than three centimeters in diameter, and with larger interstitial spaces between them. The mesh seemed more flexible than the open-skin version, too, though with a sample this size it was hard to say for sure. He couldn't identify the metal, but from the slight raggedness of the edges of his sample where it had been cut, it seemed to be pretty tough stuff.

Setting the mesh aside, he unfolded the paper. At the top were five lines of precise script he recognized as Mo Collum's handwriting:

> *I managed to finagle myself a short visit to Bay Seven. The probe looks something like this: I scrounged the mesh for you from a junk bin. Sorry I can't tell you more, but my new friend was pretty close-mouthed about his work and most of this tech stuff is way beyond me. Hope it helps.*

The rest of the sheet contained a rough sketch of a pair of connected ovoid shapes, the smaller one atop a much larger one, like a fat torpedo riding a dirigible. The upper ovoid had what looked like tether grab-rings fore and aft, a set of two large turboprop propellers inside protective ring-shaped cowlings, and a cluster of transmission and sensor antennae on its upper surface.

The lower ovoid, in contrast, had what looked like a hundred antennae dangling from its underside. The wrong place for antennae; but what else could they be? In addition, assuming he was interpreting McCollum's crosshatching correctly, it was the lower structure that was made out of the metal mesh.

He smoothed out the paper, frowning at it. A small probe, possibly a modified *Skydiver*, riding on top of a definitely nonstandard open-skin one. Was the upper one designed to push its way down to Level Three or Four, with the lower one then to jettison and go deeper, either flying free or tethered to the upper one?

Problem was, there was no tether shown between the two shapes. No tether rings, either. And while the upper probe had those massive free-flight turboprops, there was no indication of any engines at all on the lower ovoid. Nor did the lower one show any sign of floats, stabilizers, or airfoil surfaces.

On the other hand, as he studied the drawing more closely he realized it was amazingly short of details of any sort. Aside from the general shape of the external structure, there was basically nothing. There wasn't even a scale to give him an idea of the overall size of the thing.

McCollum hadn't been kidding when she said that tech stuff was beyond her, he realized with a flash of annoyance. Someone like Milligan or Beach could have gathered more data with a single glance than McCollum probably could have with a sketch book and half an hour to study the problem.

Which was, he had to concede, probably why her new friend had been willing to risk letting her see it in the first place. Briefly, he wondered what that glimpse had cost her, then put the question out of his mind. He probably didn't want to know.

Still, it was a start. Maybe there would be time for McCollum or one of the others to gather more data in the week and a half that remained before Liadof's current target date.

The door chime buzzed. "Colonel Faraday?" an unfamiliar voice called.

Reflexively, Faraday turned McCollum's paper over and laid it over the mesh, even as he recognized how unnecessary the move was. The door *was* locked, after all. "Yes?" he called.

And with a *snick*, the door popped and slid open.

"What the *hell*?" Faraday thundered, scrambling to his feet and putting his back to the desk as two men strode into the room. "What do you think—?"

"Save it, Colonel," the lead man cut him off. As his partner hung back by the doorway, he crossed purposely toward Faraday.

And only then did it register in Faraday's brain that the two men weren't wearing the light blue of Station Security. They were instead dressed in the dark violet uniforms and berets of the Five Hundred's own private Sanctum Police.

So Liadof had not only brought her own tech team to Prime with her, but had also imported her own police force. Dimly, Faraday wondered what Stationmaster Carerra thought of *that*. If in fact the man even knew about it.

The cop reached Faraday's desk and swept a hand across the top, sending the various neat stacks of paper and disks flying. McCollum's sketch went with the rest of them— "Here it is, Arbiter," the man called, scooping up the mesh.

And from out in the corridor, Liadof stepped into the doorway.

"Fine," Faraday said through suddenly dry lips. This was trouble, all right. Big, expansive, world-filling trouble. "I'll ask *you*, then, Arbiter Liadof. What in hell's name do you think you and your men are doing?"

"I'd watch your tone if I were you, Colonel," Liadof advised calmly, stepping inside and accepting the piece of mesh from the cop. "We're conducting a search; and *you* are in possession of stolen and highly classified material. You've got one minute to tell me where you got it."

Faraday took a deep breath. Resistance was useless, he knew that. But there was nothing to be gained by going all humble and conciliatory, either. Not with someone like Liadof.

And he was sure as hell's kittens not going to meekly hand McCollum over to them. "Or?" he demanded.

"Or I'll have you arrested for espionage," Liadof said. "As well as violation of the Universal Secrets Act, theft of government property, and conspiracies in all of the above. And your time is down to forty seconds."

Faraday shook his head. The mental gears, momentarily frozen by the suddenness of the invasion, were starting to churn again. "I don't think so, Arbiter," he said. "Nothing has been stolen. Even if it had been, I have every right to have that piece of mesh in my possession."

Liadof smiled coldly. "You have such authorization in writing, of course?"

"Of course," Faraday said. "It's called the Project Changeling Mission Statement."

"Really," Liadof said. "And who said this had anything to do with Project Changeling?"

Faraday inclined his head slightly. "You did."

The smile vanished. "What are you talking about?"

"This afternoon in the Contact Room," Faraday said, trying to keep his thoughts a step ahead of his mouth. "You said I was the one running the techs, but that you were Project Changeling now. Since you haven't shown me authorization for any different project—or even mentioned one, for that matter—the only reasonable assumption is that everything you've brought aboard the station comes under the Changeling aegis. And since the mission statement gives me full access to anything involved with the project . . . ?"

He lifted his eyebrows, letting that last sentence dangle in the air.

And Liadof was definitely not smiling anymore. "You must be joking, Colonel," she said in a low, dark voice. "You really think that bubble-wrap argument will hold acid for even a minute?"

"I don't know," Faraday said. "But I'm willing to try it if you are."

For a long moment she stared at him, the lines in her face deepening into small desert ravines. "Fine," she said at last. "I'll call that bluff. I'll call Earth tonight and have the reauthorization of Project Changeling here by morning. With myself as head, and with *you* completely off it."

"That is your prerogative, of course," Faraday said stiffly, wondering if she was bluffing in turn. Did she really have that kind of power with the Five Hundred? "But when you do, make it clear to them that I'm not going to be pressured or coerced into resigning. If they want me off Changeling, they'll have to fire me. That could be an interesting public relations challenge."

"The Five Hundred aren't nearly as interested in public

relations as you seem to think," Liadof countered. "Until then, consider yourself under house arrest."

Faraday shook his head. "I think not, Arbiter. As I've already explained, I have full authorization to know everything there is to know about Changeling."

"Only for the next few hours," Liadof retorted.

"Perhaps," Faraday said. "That still won't change the current situation. You can't make an ex post facto charge of espionage."

"We'll see what I can or cannot make," Liadof said. "Until then, as I say, you're confined to quarters."

"But you have no grounds to do that," Faraday insisted. Surely she couldn't simply rewrite the law.

"I don't need any grounds," Liadof said coolly. "The law says the legal authorities can order you held for twenty-four hours without charge."

"I'll appeal to Stationmaster Carerra," Faraday threatened.

"Go ahead," Liadof said, gesturing to her cops. "I've got twenty-four hours to respond to *him*, too. One way or another, Colonel, you're spending the next twenty-four hours in this room."

She stepped out into the corridor again. "And if I have my way," she added as the two uniformed men joined her, "it'll be the next five weeks." With that parting shot, she let the door slide shut.

Faraday gave them a count of sixty. Then, stepping to the door, he keyed the release. Even if Liadof had somehow managed to obtain a passcard, surely she hadn't also been able to talk Carerra out of a lockcard.

The door slid obediently open. So she *hadn't* gotten authorization to lock him in.

She hadn't had to. Standing stolidly across the corridor, glowering silently at him, was the larger of her two pet cops.

For a moment they eyed each other. Would the man really have the audacity, Faraday wondered, to use physical force to keep an uncharged man in his quarters? He was half inclined to try it and find out.

But it was already late in the evening, and he knew how much Stationmaster Carerra hated being dragged away from his scotch and soda after duty hours to deal with trouble. Better to let it go for now, get a good night's sleep, and get it straightened out in the morning.

Stepping back, he let the door close again. Out of simple habit, he locked it.

Besides, Liadof had already missed one trick. Retrieving the sketch McCollum had made, he sat down at his desk again and resumed his study of it.

He was still studying it ten days later when they finally came to get him.

SIXTEEN

In the eastern sky, the glow from the distant sun was just starting to drive the gloom away when Raimey came to the realization that he was finally home.

It was an odd feeling, especially considering the circumstances under which he'd fled this part of Jupiter. After nearly two dayherds, Drusni's rejection was still as fresh and painful as if a pack of Sivra were still chewing on him.

But even that ache couldn't dispel the excitement he could feel growing inside him as he continued to swim. He could smell the presence of his old herd; the subtle yet distinctive combination of odors that he'd grown up with. The same mixture, yet different, as the children he'd known had become Breeders, and as the original Breeders had become the Protectors and Nurturers leading the herd. The cycle continued as it had since the beginning, the old story-circle phrase whispered through his mind. The eternal cycle: always new, yet always the same.

Only now he knew that, wherever that cycle had started, it hadn't started on Jupiter.

The familiar scents were growing stronger. It might be interesting to take a look up there later, he decided, at least go up to Level Two where the male and nonpregnant female Breeders would be swimming, keeping watch for predators. He could pop in and renew acquaintances with some of the kids he'd hung out with, see which ones had bonded together. It might even be fun, provided he didn't run into Pranlo in the process.

Or, worse, Drusni.

But all that could wait. Somewhere up there, invisible above the upper clouds, were Faraday and Hesse. They'd clearly lost track of him since his departure from this region, but he knew that they would have kept monitoring the herd in the hope he would eventually make his way back there. If that transmitter they'd built into his brain was still working, they should be contacting him as soon as he got within range. He could hardly wait to tell them the news.

Speeding up a little, he swam toward the glowing sunlight.

The uniformed Sanctum cop escorted Faraday into the Contact Room and then stepped to one side, falling smartly into a parade rest beside the doorway. His partner, Faraday noticed, was already holding up the wall on the other side of the door. "Colonel Faraday," Liadof greeted him, half turning in the command station chair to face him. "Thank you for joining us."

"I'm sure I'm most welcome," Faraday murmured, looking around the room. There was Beach, hunched over his communications panel. Milligan was busy with his sensors; Sprenkle was looking over his weather reports or whatever stuff psychologists looked over at times like this. McCollum—

He felt his breath catch in his throat. McCollum's chair was empty.

"I suppose you're wondering why you're here," Liadof continued. "We're ready to launch the Omega Probe into Raimey's old herd; and, as we knew might happen, Raimey himself has just entered the area. I thought you should be on hand in case we decide to talk to him. Yours is the voice he knows best, after all."

"Of course," Faraday murmured, his eyes still on McCollum's empty chair. Could she be merely sick, or otherwise incapacitated? But then why hadn't Liadof tapped one of the other shifts for a replacement?

"I see you've noticed our lack of a Qanskan biology expert," Liadof commented.

"Yes," Faraday said, locking gazes with her. "Where is she?"

"In her quarters," Liadof said evenly. "Shortly after you were placed under house arrest, we discovered Ms. Mc-Collum was the one who had obtained that discarded section of mesh for you. She is therefore no longer with the project."

"She had every legal right to be in possession of that mesh," Faraday insisted. "Just as I did."

"The Five Hundred think otherwise," Liadof countered. "On both counts."

"I intend to appeal that decision," Faraday warned.

Liadof shrugged. "That's your right," she said. "But I doubt you'll find a negotiator willing to take the case."

Faraday clenched his hands into useless fists. So that was it. McCollum's future was officially dead now, her career prospects shunted off into the twilight oblivion reserved for people who had offended the Five Hundred.

And Faraday was the one who had done it to her.

Liadof might have been reading his mind. "Consider it an object lesson, Colonel," she said quietly. "You obviously don't care about your own career; but your people here are young and ambitious, with bright futures ahead of them." She considered. "Well, these last three are, anyway."

Faraday had never wanted to hit anyone as much as he wanted to hit Liadof. But he resisted the impulse. There were other ways to fight this. There had to be. Somehow, somewhere, he would find the right one.

And until he did, it would serve no purpose to get himself thrown back into his own quarters.

There was nothing he could do for McCollum right now. But maybe there was still something he could do for Raimey.

Stepping past Liadof, he went and stood behind Milligan. Liadof's top-secret probe was centered in one of the sensor displays, a three-dimensional version of the sketch he'd been studying and analyzing over the past few days.

A study which, he saw now, had been decidedly hit and miss. The top ovoid was indeed a modified *Skydiver* probe, as he'd concluded; but it appeared to be rigidly attached to the lower ovoid instead of being connected to it with a second-stage tether. The lower part was indeed composed of McCollum's mesh; but the mesh wasn't simply acting as a breathable outer skin. There was some kind of mechanism vaguely visible near where the two shapes joined, but most of the lower ovoid appeared to be completely empty.

And while the wands atop the upper probe were indeed control and sensor antennae, the ones stabbing downward from the lower ovoid were something else entirely. From all appearances, in fact, they seemed to be jagged-edged spikes.

"Omega Control to Contact Room," a voice announced from the ceiling speaker. "Omega Probe is ready to launch."

"Acknowledged," Liadof called back. "Launch Omega Probe."

On the display the double ovoid dropped away from its transport, descending rapidly toward the swirling clouds below. There were no tether lines visible, Faraday noted, which meant the thing was going to be free-flown. The grab rings must be simply for retrieving it later. "Which crew do you have aboard the tether ship?" he asked.

"My people are controlling it from Bay Seven, actually," Liadof said. "Omega's flight characteristics are outside the expertise of anyone on Prime."

"Then why are we even here?" he asked.

"You're here, as I've already said, in case we have to talk to Raimey," Liadof said. "The rest of Alpha Shift is here to handle the sensors and monitors and generally make themselves useful."

And to prove their loyalty in the face of McCollum's object lesson? Probably that, too.

Milligan was fiddling the telescope controls, keeping the

probe centered and in focus. "Rather confident designation, calling it Omega," Faraday commented. "Do the Five Hundred expect this to be the last probe design we're ever going to need?"

"As a matter of fact, we do," Liadof said calmly. "After Omega, the designation won't be 'probe' anymore."

Faraday frowned over his shoulder at her. "What's that supposed to mean?"

Liadof's lips compressed slightly. "If we're fortunate, you'll never have to find out."

"That's not much of an answer," Faraday said. "Is the next generation going to be bigger or faster or something?"

She shrugged. "No need for extra size. I hardly think the Qanska could build and control a stardrive bigger than that cage."

Faraday glanced at Milligan, got an equally blank look in return. "Are you telling me you know where the stardrive is?" he asked.

"Not yet," Liadof said. "But the Qanska will soon be giving us that information. After that—" She shrugged. "It'll simply be a matter of sending Omega to pick it up."

"Really," Faraday murmured, frowning at the displays. No. That couldn't possibly be the entire plan. Why on Earth would the Qanska just meekly hand over their stardrive?

He sent a sideways look over at Beach. His face was rigid, his lips compressed tightly together. He and McCollum had gotten along pretty well in the past, he knew. Could McCollum have picked up a few more pieces of this puzzle from her friend in Bay Seven before Liadof locked her away and passed them along to him?

Possibly. Easing away from Milligan's shoulder, he drifted in Beach's direction—

"You'd better come back here with me, Colonel," Liadof called, almost lazily. "We wouldn't want you distracting the techs with unnecessary questions, now, would we?"

Faraday gave Beach's profile one last look, then turned away. "No, of course not," he said.

"Right here, Colonel," Liadof ordered, indicating a chair

she'd set beside her. "You'll have a good view from here."

"And what is it I'll be looking at?" he asked as he sat down.

Liadof turned to the displays, her eyes shining again. "The end of an era," she said quietly. "And the beginning of the next."

Raimey had reached Level Two, and had leveled off from his climb, when he began to hear the first whispers of the distant Qanskan call.

He paused, letting himself drift with the wind as he listened. The voices were faint and indistinct, the tonals coming across as little more than mutterings. But if the words were still obscured, the tone of the call was clear as empty air.

Danger!

He resumed his swimming, putting a little more speed into it. He'd heard a thousand such warnings in his lifetime, most while he was a child, almost all of them signaling a Vuuka attack.

But he'd never heard a warning with such an edge of fear to it. What in crosswinds could be going on up there?

Whatever it was, it seemed to be getting worse. More Qanska were picking up the call now, echoing the original and adding to it. *Danger, attack, fear, terror.*

And there was something else different about it. Something that set it apart from all the other warnings he'd heard since birth. Something odd and chilling . . .

And then, with a jolt, he got it. All the voices in that call were female. *All* of them. The only ones who were calling for help were the Nurturers and the female Breeders. None of the Protectors were calling.

Which meant the Protectors were too busy fighting the attack to add their voices to the chorus.

Or else all of them were already dead.

Raimey leaned his muscles hard into his swimming, putting every bit of strength and speed he could into it. He had the direction now: straight ahead, definitely on Level One.

Somewhere near his old herd.

"You must be insane," Faraday said, tearing his eyes away from the displays and staring in disbelief at the woman beside him. "What are you trying to do, start a war?"

"Calm yourself, Colonel," Liadof said. Her own eyes, he noted, were still on the displays, her manner glacially calm. "And no, I'm not trying to start a war. I'm trying to end one."

"If you think a few Martian protests and riots constitute a war, you are sorely deficient in historical perspective," he bit out. "*This* is the sort of thing that starts *real* wars."

"Gently, Colonel," Liadof warned. "Proper respect and decorum, or I'll have you sent back to your quarters."

Faraday took a deep breath. *Calm down*, he ordered himself. She was right; and there would be absolutely nothing he could do to stop this madness if he was kicked out of here. He had to keep silent and control himself, to stay here and watch for something—anything—he could do.

And so he clamped his mouth tightly shut and let his eyes return to the displays. To the image of the Omega Probe, carrying out Liadof's grand scheme.

Carrying out her act of war.

A small group of Qanska shot past Raimey in the near distance, mothers and children of various ages, swimming as fast as they could. He thought of calling to them, but he didn't have the breath to spare right now for a conversation. Neither, he suspected, did they.

He kept going. More Qanska were visible now, most of them children with their mothers or other female Breeders, all of them swimming hard away from a point somewhere still ahead of him.

Something coming up from below caught his eye. *Vuuka*,

was his first, startled thought. But no, it was just a pair of Protectors, swimming upward toward the distress call. If they noticed him, they didn't say anything.

Ahead, now, he could see something moving through the atmosphere. Or maybe a pair of somethings, one of them attached to the back of the other. His mind flashed back to that Sivra attack so many dayherds ago, where the smaller predators had hitched a ride on a hijacked Vuuka.

But the shape ahead was all wrong for that. Besides, unless his eyes and distance perception were playing strange tricks on him, the thing up ahead was far too big for any Vuuka that could get up this high.

In fact, it was too big for a Vuuka of *any* sort, at least any Vuuka he'd ever heard of. That lower shape had to be at least a hundred-size across from nose to tail, bigger than anything but the oldest of the Wise. What in crosswinds . . . ?

And then, suddenly, it clicked. "Vuuk-mook," he muttered disgustedly to himself. This was no natural phenomenon threatening the lives and well-being of the herd. This was nothing but another of the humans' probes.

With an exasperated snort, he let himself glide to a halt, annoyed at himself and even more so with the Protectors and Nurturers of the herd. These were people who had seen Raimey delivered to them by this same sort of machine, after all. Had they forgotten all about that?

Apparently so. Ahead, he could still see Qanska fleeing from the probe's advance. Mostly they were the slower Babies and younger Midlings, all of them being herded frantically away by their mothers. Behind them, the Protectors were gathered around the probe, churning the air madly as they repeatedly rammed their bony foreheads into its sides.

Mentally, Raimey shook his head in contempt. Idiots.

Still, if they kept beating themselves against the probe that way, someone was going to get hurt. He'd better go over and patiently explain that this was nothing to be worried about.

He started forward again; and as he did so, the dull rumble of the probe's engines began to grow louder. The probe changed course, swiveling a few degrees into the wind and heading off toward Raimey's left.

Raimey frowned, altering his own course to compensate. What in turbulent air were the humans doing? Trying to get their probe away from the Protectors before they damaged it? Probably. He picked up his pace, noticing as he did so that the probe was likewise speeding up.

Still, if they wanted to get away, they were going to have to do better than that. Behind the probe, the Protectors had regrouped and were giving chase. Apparently, someone in charge over there was really determined to chase this intruder away.

The probe was still picking up speed, outpacing the pursuing Protectors, the sound of its propellers filling the sky. Already it was moving far faster than Raimey would have expected something that big could go. Clearly, the humans had decided their best bet was just to give up and go do their research somewhere else. It wasn't like the skies of Jupiter were that crowded, after all—

And then, abruptly, something seemed to catch in Raimey's throats. The probe wasn't running away, he suddenly realized. It was instead heading straight toward one of the straggler groups of Qanskan children and their mothers. Chasing them across the sky like a huge metal Vuuka.

And it was gaining.

"That's enough, Arbiter," Faraday said, the tightness of his throat making his voice sound strange in his ears. "Please. You already have more than enough. Just leave the others alone."

"Thank you for your advice," Liadof said coolly. "Mr. Boschwitz: those two on the left—the smaller ones. I want them both."

"Acknowledged, Arbiter," the voice replied from the ceiling speaker. "Commencing run."

Faraday took a deep breath. "Arbiter, this is completely

and thoroughly unconscionable," he said, fighting hard against the frustration boiling inside him.

"Again, your opinion is noted, Colonel," Liadof said coldly. "But the base rule of negotiation is that the more cards in your hand, the stronger that hand is." She nodded toward the display. "Two more will make a nice even ten. A good number to have when the Leaders finally arrive."

Faraday looked over at the techs. Sprenkle was staring back at him out of the corner of his eye, his face rigid. *Do something*, that look seemed to say.

But all Faraday could do was give him a small, helpless shrug in return.

The probe was closing fast on the fleeing Qanska. Raimey pushed hard against the air, trying to get there first, a sense of unreality swirling through his mind like a poisonous mist. For Faraday to be deliberately chasing down Qanskan children this way was utterly beyond comprehension.

But chasing them down he most certainly was. Raimey was close enough now to see that the hundred-size lower shape was made of a loosely woven mesh; and inside, pressed against the back wall by the probe's speed, he could see the figures of several more Qanskan children, flailing away in helplessness and fear.

An old, almost alien memory flicked into his mind: himself as a human child, spending lazy summer days hunting frogs in the creek that ran behind his house. But he'd always put the frogs back again afterward.

That couldn't be what was happening here. Could it? The humans had had over twenty dayherds to study the Qanska before Raimey had even come here. Surely they didn't need to swoop down now and take fresh samples.

But whatever they needed or thought they needed, the bitter-cold fact was that that was what they were doing. Even as he charged toward the probe, the front end of the mesh opened wide like a gaping mouth. Some kind of tentacle shot out the gap, snaking its way straight to one of the swimming Babies.

And as the tentacle reached its target, the tip exploded into a tangle of smaller threads, wrapping securely around the small form.

The Baby screeched in terror. Its mother braked hard, fins slapping against the air as she cut around in a tight circle to come to her child's aid.

But there was nothing she could do. The tentacle was reeling the Baby in now, pulling it into the gaping mouth of the humans' cage with the inevitability of a pack of Sivra chewing their way under the skin. And then, even as she bit and slapped uselessly at the tentacle, a second cable shot out through the opening, barely missing her. A ninepulse later, a second Baby was being pulled in with the first.

The first Baby vanished into the mesh cage. Its mother seemed to hesitate; then she, too, swam inside with her child. The second Baby was pulled in with them, and the mouth swung closed again. The deafening rumble of the engines faded, and the probe began to slow down, bouncing slightly in the buffeting of the winds.

"Manta!" a voice gasped from behind him.

An all-too-familiar voice. Raimey turned, his heart seizing up inside him.

And there she was, swimming up behind him like something from a dream, or a nightmare.

Drusni.

It was a moment he'd feared ever since making the decision to come back. He'd played the scenario over in his mind a thousand times, trying to anticipate every possible combination of emotion and conversation and conflict and outcome.

And now, in the midst of chaos, the moment had come. Here he floated, nose to nose with the female he realized now he still so desperately loved. Gazing at her, with the sounds of fear and panic raging behind him, he waited for the windstorm of emotion.

But it didn't come. The love he felt was still there, simmering deep within him. So was the pain that a portion of that love had decayed into.

But there was no anger, no recrimination, not even any awkwardness. For the moment, at least, the crisis swirling around them was driving everything else away.

"What's going on?" he demanded, swiveling around and coming alongside her so he could keep an eye on the probe.

"They're stealing our children," Drusni said, her voice trembling with fatigue and horror. "They said—I mean, a voice came and said—"

"Calm down," Raimey said, reaching over automatically to touch her fin with his.

She didn't recoil from his touch, as he'd half expected she would. Instead, to his surprise, she moved closer to him, pressing the side of her body against his as she huddled like a frightened child beneath his fin. "I'm sorry," she breathed. "I'm just—I'm so scared."

"I know," Raimey said. "Me, too. Now, what exactly did they say?"

"They want something from us, but I don't understand what," she said. "Something that takes us back and forth between the great lights. Do you know what that means?"

"Unfortunately, yes," Raimey said grimly, anger and contempt swirling together with the fear in his stomach. So that was how it was going to be. No requests; no bargaining; no negotiation or trading. Earth wanted that stardrive; and by the Deep, they were going to have it.

Even if they had to turn to kidnapping to get it. "And they said they would hold on to those children until we give it up?"

"Yes," Drusni said. "They said that someone was to deliver the message to the Counselors and the Leaders and the Wise, and call them here for a conversation."

Raimey lashed his tails furiously. What in the Deep was Faraday doing? Calling the Counselors *and* the Leaders *and* the Wise? He should know by now that only the Counselors could ever make it up to Level One, and they only with assistance. Had he lost his mind?

Or was Faraday even there anymore? Had he left the project, and someone else taken over?

Drusni shivered against him. "Why are they doing this?" she asked softly. "How many children are they going to take?"

"I don't know," Raimey said, pulling reluctantly away from her. Belatedly now, as he half turned to face her again, he noticed something he'd missed in their initial meeting: she was very pregnant. One of her children with Pranlo, no doubt. Distantly, he wondered how many others they'd had together.

And the humans up there were stealing children. No wonder she was on the edge of panic.

There was a sudden multiple thudding sound from the direction of the probe. Raimey turned again, to see that the pack of pursuing Protectors had caught up with it and resumed throwing themselves against the cage.

"But they're your own people," Drusni pleaded. "Can't you make them stop this?"

"I can try," Raimey said, searching his memory. It had been so long since he'd used that subvocalization trick. How had that worked again?

Ah. There—he had it. *Faraday?* he called silently. The English phonemes sounded starkly alien as they echoed through his mind, and he wondered if he was even getting them right. *Faraday, where are you? What are you doing?*

But there was no answer. Could he still be out of range?

Ridiculous. The probe was right *there*. If they could communicate with *it*, they could surely communicate with him.

Unless they simply didn't want to talk to him anymore.

His tails lashed viciously. So that was it. All they'd ever wanted in the first place was the Qanskan stardrive. Raimey had failed to get it for them; and so Raimey was no longer part of the plan.

"Manta?" Drusni asked anxiously.

"I'm sorry," Raimey said. "I can't get them to talk to me."

"Then you can't stop them?"

Raimey arched his fins, glancing again at her distended belly where her unborn child lay. Pranlo's child; and that too added a fresh layer to the ache inside him.

But if things had been different, it might have been *his* child she was carrying.

His child who was now in deadly danger.

"I don't know," he told her grimly. "Let's see."

And with that he leaped forward. One more Qanska battering himself against the metal cage, he knew, would probably not make a difference. But then again, it might.

One way or the other, he was going to find out.

SEVENTEEN

"**D**amage readings?" Liadof called. "Mr. Milligan?"

"Nothing major," Milligan said, his voice studiously neutral.

"Anything *minor?*"

Milligan shrugged. "Looks like we've got about a meter of partial link separation along the starboard edge of the probe/cage intersection."

"A *meter?*" Liadof demanded. "And you didn't think that was worth volunteering?"

"I assumed that because it's not a complete break, it wasn't something that required your attention," Milligan said stiffly.

"Or you hoped I wouldn't notice?" Liadof countered acidly. "That's the sort of attitude that borders on insubordination. That, or gross incompetence. Either one could have you joining Ms. McCollum under house arrest."

A muscle in Milligan's cheek twitched. Anger or surrender; Faraday couldn't tell which. "My apologies, Arbiter. I'll try to do better."

"Yes. You will." Liadof looked at Faraday. "Your Qanska are getting clever, Colonel. They've realized they can't do anything against the cage material itself, so they've shifted to attacking the more rigid interface."

"No, they're not stupid," Faraday agreed tightly. "And I remind you that we've never seen what they can do if they're pushed too far."

"Don't be absurd," she said contemptuously. "They're herbivores, without hands or any natural weapons except those bony foreheads of theirs. Trust me, Omega is perfectly safe."

"I wasn't necessarily talking about their physical strength," Faraday said. "Let me also remind you that our assumption is that they've built themselves a stardrive—"

"More likely inherited or stolen one built by someone else," Liadof interrupted. "They're certainly not capable of building anything themselves."

"Fine," Faraday said impatiently. "Whatever. My point is, if they've got a stardrive, who's to say they haven't got weapons to go along with it?"

"Arbiter!" Beach called sharply. "I'm getting a signal from Raimey."

"Put it on," Faraday ordered.

"I give the orders here, Colonel," Liadof said sharply. "What does he want, Mr. Beach?"

"So far, he's just hailing us," Beach said. "He's close enough to see the probe; I presume he wants to know what's going on."

"And he deserves to know," Faraday said, searching for a good reason to bring Raimey into the loop on this. "Besides, he needs the whole story in case you want him to help translate to the Counselors when they arrive."

"I thought we had computer programs capable of translating Qanskan tonals," Liadof said.

"To some degree, yes," Faraday told her. "But there are a lot of subtleties the translators still don't get."

"Subtleties aren't going to make or break this deal." Liadof lifted her eyebrows at him. "Besides, I thought you were the one who wanted to keep Raimey out of this as much as possible."

"I thought *you* were the one who didn't care how this affected his life," Faraday countered. "Besides, it's too late to keep him out."

Liadof shrugged fractionally and turned her attention back to the displays. "Situation, Mr. Milligan?"

"They still haven't broken through," Milligan reported.

"Of course not," Liadof said with an edge of sarcasm.

"That wouldn't be something you could pretend you hadn't seen, would it? Now tell me what they *have* done."

"They're still beating at the starboard intersection line," Milligan said. "Looks like they've battered, oh, two more links partially out of shape."

"How large is the gap they've made?" Liadof asked. "Big enough for the hostages to get out?"

"There isn't any actual gap," Milligan said. "The separation is only partial."

"I know that," Liadof snapped. "I meant that if they manage to work it all the way open, *then* will it be big enough?"

"Possibly," Milligan conceded. "But I doubt they'll get it open."

Liadof smiled thinly. "You doubt? Or you hope?"

"That's unfair, Arbiter," Faraday put in. "You've already made it clear—"

"Spare me, Colonel," Liadof said acidly. "Your people's token obedience hardly obscures true loyalties. Mr. Milligan, where is Raimey now?"

"He's headed for Omega." Milligan hesitated. "It looks like he's going to join the fight against the cage."

"Really," Liadof said, flashing a look at Faraday. "And so much for *his* loyalties. All right, Colonel, let's hear *your* opinion. Do *you* think they can break through the cage?"

"Ms. McCollum is our expert on Qanskan capabilities," Faraday said pointedly. "In her absence, I'd hesitate to even hazard a guess."

Liadof exhaled noisily. "Fine," she bit out. "Have it your way. If you and your people won't help, we'll just assume a worst-case scenario and take it from there. Mr. Beach, activate the McCarthy system."

She gave Faraday a tight, mocking smile. "You wanted Raimey involved, Colonel? Fine. Let's get him involved."

The smile vanished. "And let's see how well he can fight," she added. "On *our* side.

The major thrust of the attack seemed to be along the right-hand flank of the intruding machine, Raimey saw as he swam toward it, right at the seam where the probe itself joined the lower cage structure. The Protectors had an organized attack going, each one swimming toward it at top speed, ramming the target area, then circling around to wait his turn in line again. They were running four abreast, rhythmically hitting the intersection along a line probably fifteen sizes long. And of course, they had chosen to concentrate on the windward side of the cage, letting the wind give their attacks that much extra speed and impact.

It seemed a reasonable, well thought out strategy. Question was, was there a better one?

Raimey cut to his right, shifting into a wide circle around the intruder. He was by no means an expert on devices like this, but he would bet a nineday *chinster* feast that he was more familiar with human machines in general than anyone else on Jupiter. Maybe he could find a weakness that the others wouldn't be able to spot.

But if there was such a weakness, it was well hidden. A few of the Protectors were working themselves against the cage itself, but Raimey could see that the mesh was too flexible to be damaged that way. It merely absorbed the impact, dissipating it along its entire surface area, instead of bending or cracking.

The probe itself, in contrast, looked more promising, what with its turboprops and floats and various antennas. Other Protectors were swimming around up there, gingerly poking and prodding at it. For a moment Raimey wondered why they weren't attacking it more vigorously, until it occurred to him that disabling the probe would be instantly disastrous. Sinking it would also sink the cage, sending the helpless children inside to their deaths in the crushing pressure of the lower atmosphere.

Unless the Protectors could hold the cage up while others battered it open. Flipping over, Raimey headed around toward the underside to take a look. After all, enough Protectors working together had been able to lift Latranesto up to Level One the day of Raimey's birth. Surely this thing couldn't weigh more than a full-grown Counselor.

But the humans had anticipated that possibility. The underside of the cage was fitted with a forest of jagged spikes, clearly designed to gouge their way into any Qanska who tried to press up against it with his back.

Raimey couldn't tell if they were sharp enough to penetrate the tough Qanskan skin all the way to the vital organs. But then, it was hardly necessary to stab any of the supporting Protectors to death. At the first release of blood, every Vuuka in sniffing range would instantly be on its way. Enough Qanskan blood, enough Vuuka, and the winds would shake with the sounds of the slaughter. And the babies would sink to their deaths anyway.

It made him wonder why the humans hadn't simply put spikes around the whole cage. Were they that confident that it could stand up to anything the Qanska could do?

Well, maybe the Protectors could surprise them a little. Keeping well clear of the spikes, Raimey headed for the far side where the main attack was taking place. He could feel his heart pounding inside him as an odd sense of light-headedness seemed to glaze over his vision. An old phrase of his grandmother's—*so mad I couldn't see straight*—flashed through his mind. Maybe it wasn't simply the hyperbole that he'd always assumed.

He rounded the bottom of the probe and started upward toward the group of Protectors. One of the attack lines was shorter than the others, he noted, and he headed over to take his place at the back.

Technically, of course, he wasn't even supposed to be here on Level One. Under the circumstances, though, he didn't expect the Protectors would complain about being offered extra help—

Abruptly, a startled jolt ran though him. He had been heading up toward the back of the attack line, hadn't he? At least, that was what he'd intended to do.

So why was he instead skimming close in to the surface of the cage, heading directly toward the impact line?

He flipped his fins and tail, trying to change direction. But to his stunned disbelief, he found himself speeding up instead. He tried again, and again. But nothing he could do made the slightest bit of difference. Somehow, he had lost all control of his body.

He was still trying to figure it out when he swam directly into the path of one of the attacking Protectors.

The Protector hit him just in front of his tails, the impact spinning him around and sending a flash of pain through his side. "Look out, you fool Breeder!" the Protector snapped. His momentum dissipated by the collision, he skidded past Raimey and bumped harmlessly against the mesh. "Get out of the way!"

Raimey would have given anything to do just that. But to his horror, he instead found himself cutting a tight circle and moving directly into the path of the next Protector. This one managed to veer mostly out of the way, merely scraping against Raimey's belly as he shot past. But the dodging had ruined his aim, sending him bouncing off the more flexible part of the mesh.

"What are you doing?" someone shouted. "Get out of the *way*!"

"I can't," Raimey said, his voice shaking with the beginnings of panic. "I can't control—"

He gasped, the rest of the protest cut off as the wind was knocked out of him. His rogue body had leaped into the path of yet another Protector, with the same results as the first two times. His vision hazed over, the images of Protector and machine wavering. . . .

"—out!" someone shouted right into his ear.

Raimey started, snapping back to full consciousness as something began beating at his body. A group of Protectors had surrounded him and were nudging him none too gently away from the cage. "Come on, get out," the Protector ordered again.

"I'm trying," Raimey gasped. He was, too, as hard as he could. But it was no use. He could still feel his body; every touch, every ache and pain. But as far as muscle control was concerned, he might as well have been watching some one else entirely.

"What do you think you're doing?" the Protector snarled. They had shoved him away from the cage now, but Raimey's body was still perversely trying to force its way back. "You think this is a *game*?"

"No, of course not," Raimey panted, wishing desperately he could explain but knowing that the others wouldn't understand. They probably did think he was playing some game, that he was too stupid to see what was going on here.

He could hardly blame them. It was exactly as if he'd suddenly changed sides and become a blocker for the rival team.

Abruptly, he stiffened. *A blocker for the rival team . . .*

The humans.

And suddenly it all fell together. That sundark swim he'd taken in his sleep right after the Song of Change, when Faraday had first revealed what his true mission was on Jupiter. The Qanskan equivalent of sleepwalking, he'd assumed at the time.

But now he knew the truth. The subvocalization system wasn't the only thing the humans had built into his brain before sending him down here.

They'd also set up a remote control. And like a living puppet, they were using him against the Qanska.

The Contact Room had gone very quiet. The three techs sat stiffly at their stations, clearly hating the whole thing even as they carried out Liadof's orders. Liadof was silent, too, though hers was the silence of focus and anticipation.

And as for himself, Faraday was silent with the agony of fury and despair.

It was barbaric. That was the only word for it. To strip a person of his dignity and the use of his body this way was bad enough. But to then turn him against the people he'd lived with for nearly five years was utterly indefensible.

And it marked the end of any chance Raimey might ever have of fitting in with Qanskan society. However this ended, whether Liadof got what she wanted or not, Raimey was already as good as dead.

It was too high a price to pay. Too high for a stardrive; too high even if the Qanska had held the cure to some horrible plague. Nothing could justify what Liadof was doing.

What Faraday, by his silent acquiescence back when the McCarthy setup was first proposed, had helped give her the power to do.

"Where is he?" Liadof demanded. She was leaning forward in her chair, her eyes darting back and forth between the various displays. "He's gone off-camera. Where is he?"

"Don't worry, he's not doing anything," Milligan muttered. "The Protectors are just pushing him away. They've gotten him underneath and behind the cage where there aren't any cameras."

"I want to see him," Liadof said. "What about that other spy probe, the one that's been following him?"

"I thought the idea was to keep that one far enough away that he wouldn't know it was there," Milligan reminded her.

"That doesn't matter anymore," Liadof told him. "Bring it in. I want to see what's going on. And get him back in there. I want him blocking again."

"They're not going to let him," Faraday told her, fighting to keep his voice under control. What was she trying to do, goad the rest of the Qanska into beating Raimey to death right in front of her? "Can't you just leave him alone?"

"He'll be left alone when he's finished his job," Liadof told him tartly. "Right now, that job is to convince those Protectors that their attack is a waste of effort. That will facilitate our negotiating position when the Leaders get here."

"Why not just keep Omega moving instead?" Faraday asked. "You've got plenty of spare fuel. Keep it moving and the Protectors won't be able to mount a serious attack."

"I don't want to risk running out of fuel before we can get to wherever they've hidden their stardrive," Liadof said. "Mr. Beach, why isn't Raimey back in the firing line?"

"As Colonel Faraday said, the Protectors pushed him away," Beach said.

"Are they still on top of him?" Liadof demanded. "Well? Are they?"

"Not at the moment," Beach said grudgingly. "But I think Drusni is coming over to talk to him."

"Never mind her," Liadof growled. "Just get him moving."

Beach seemed to sigh. "Yes, Arbiter," he said, reaching again for the McCarthy panel.

"And put them on the speaker," she added. "I want to hear what they're talking about."

Finally, thankfully, the battering of the Protectors trailed off into silence. Raimey shook himself once, his whole body throbbing with pain at the movement, before turning carefully to look around him.

All that shoving had ended up pushing him well beneath the cage. Rolling onto his back, he looked up.

Directly above, the forest of spikes were pointed down at him. Beyond that, up along the side, he could see the Protectors continuing their attack. And between him and them he could see the group of Protectors who had driven him away, hurrying back to their places in line.

He rolled over onto his belly; and it was only then that his dazed mind caught on to the fact that he was back in control of his body again. Somehow, the humans' control over him had been broken.

That, or they'd simply decided he was of no further use and had tossed him aside.

Something bumped against his side, sending a ripple of pain through the already tender skin and muscle. He tensed, waiting for another round of Protector beatings—

"Manta, what were you *doing*?" Drusni demanded. "You weren't helping them—you were *stopping* them."

"I know," Raimey said, shying away from her touch.

And not just because of the pain. He had betrayed her. He had betrayed everyone. All he wanted now was to turn and run, as fast as possible, as far away as possible.

To run, and hide, and then to die. There was nothing else left for him now.

"What happened?" she asked. There was no anger in her voice, or accusation either. Only bewilderment and fear and concern.

"I don't know," he said with a tired sigh. "All of a sudden, I couldn't control myself. All I can think of is that the humans must have put something in my brain to control me."

"But how could they do that?" Drusni asked. "The parts of your brain and spinal chord that were once human were replaced by your Qanskan body a long time ago."

Raimey stared at her in astonishment. "How did you know about that?"

She hunched her fins. "I've learned a lot about you in the past one and a half dayherds, Manta," she said quietly. "After you . . . left . . . I made it part of my life to talk to everyone who knew about you. I even got Counselor Latranesto to come up to Level Four and talk with me."

She stroked his fin gently. "I never realized just what you went through to be a part of our lives. Will you forgive me for whatever I may have done to hurt you?"

Raimey took a deep breath, the last core of painful hardness in his heart melting away. "You don't have anything to apologize for," he told her. "All of it was my overreaction. When you told me about you and Pranlo—I'm sorry, Drusni. I didn't mean to hurt you. I just—"

"It's all right," she said softly. "You're my friend, Manta. You always have been. You always will be."

———

Faraday let out a quiet sigh. Not until that moment did he realize just how heavily the rift between Raimey and Drusni had been weighing on him for the past eighteen months. "At least that's resolved," he murmured.

"I'm deeply touched," Liadof growled. "Mr. Beach, why isn't he moving?"

"I thought we could at least let them have a couple of minutes together," Beach said hesitantly.

"Did I *authorize* a couple of minutes of togetherness?" Liadof snapped. "Or did I give you a direct order to the contrary?"

"A few minutes isn't going to make any difference, Arbiter," Faraday put in. The thought of yanking Raimey away from such a personal moment and throwing him back into the fight . . .

"And the Protectors aren't making any progress against the cage," Milligan added. "There's plenty of time."

"Well, isn't this precious," Liadof said contemptuously, looking around the room. "Closet romantics, the whole lot of you."

Faraday felt his face flush with warmth. "This isn't a matter of romanticism—"

"But we're not here to smile and cry with Raimey and his girlfriend," Liadof cut him off. "We're here to free humanity from this Solar System. Anyone who can't remember that is free to return to his quarters. Is that clear?"

No one spoke. "Good," she said. "Now. Any new damage to the cage, Mr. Milligan?"

"None registering," Milligan reported sullenly.

"What about the spy probe?" she asked. "Is it in position to observe yet?"

"Mostly," he confirmed, peering at another bank of displays. "It's still a little far, but we can keep an eye on Raimey with it."

"Then switch Omega's sensors to long-range mode," Liadof instructed him. "See if you can spot any sign of the Counselors and Leaders."

She turned to Beach. "And *you*, Mr. Beach, get Raimey moving."

Raimey's first warning was the sudden light-headedness and the glazing over of his vision. "Oh, no," he breathed. "It's happening again. I can feel it starting."

"You can't let them do this to you," Drusni insisted. "You have to stop them."

"How?" Raimey pleaded. "How can I fight it when I don't even know how they're doing it?"

"Well, how *could* they be doing it?" Drusni said. "You know how your people do things. Is it some kind of thing like that?" She flipped her tails up toward the probe and cage.

Something electronic? "I suppose so," Raimey said doubtfully. "I mean, it has to be *something* like that. But you're right; my whole brain has changed since I got here. Unless it was specially designed to work with Qanskan biochemistry."

"I don't know what those words mean," Drusni said. "But there must be a way to stop it."

"No," Raimey said. He could hear his voice trembling now. "Putting wires and microequipment into someone's brain is a complicated business. If they went to that much trouble, they'd have made sure I couldn't break out of it."

"I can't accept that," Drusni said firmly. "Please, Manta. Please. You have to find a way."

And then, as if coming from the clouds above, Raimey heard a voice. A vaguely familiar voice, speaking in soft tonals as if fearful of being overheard.

"It's all in your mind, Raimey. It's all in your mind."

"It is all part of your thoughts, Raimey," the translation came over the Contact Room speaker. "It is all part of your thoughts."

"What the *hell*?" Liadof barked, leaping to her feet. "Who said that? Who *said that*?"

No one answered. No one even moved. "Hands in the air," she ordered, striding up to the curved control board, her eyes darting back and forth between the techs. "I said *hands in the air*, away from your boards. *Now!*"

"Arbiter, what's the matter with you?" Faraday cut in, scrambling to his feet. "Those were Qanskan tonals."

"And whoever it was called him *Raimey*, Colonel," she snarled back. "None of the Qanska ever call him that. Someone *here* sent him that message, translated through the computer."

Faraday winced. He'd hoped she wouldn't pick up on that. "I can't see what difference it can possibly make—"

"Dr. Sprenkle," Liadof said, her voice suddenly glacially calm. "Your microphone switch is on."

Sprenkle didn't say a word. His hands still held up in the air, he stood up and turned to face her. "Guard," Liadof said, her voice still quiet as she beckoned to one of the Sanctum cops. "Take him to the station brig. The charge is treason."

"What?" Faraday demanded. "You can't be serious."

"Ms. McCollum clearly acted under your orders, Colonel," Liadof said as the cop stepped forward, pulling a set of wristcuffs from one of his belt pouches. "Dr. Sprenkle just as clearly did not. The charge is treason."

"I protest," Faraday said sharply as the cop pulled Sprenkle's arms behind his back and secured them. "This is illegal, and I will not stand for it."

"You do whatever you want," Liadof bit out. "The charge stands. Take him away."

Silently, the two men headed for the door. As he passed Faraday, Sprenkle's eyes flicked sideways, just for an instant, to meet his. Faraday opened his mouth, wondering what he was going to say—

Sprenkle's eyes flicked away again. Still in silence, he and the cop left the room.

"Now," Liadof said, her quiet voice filling the stunned

emptiness like a mass of subzero air. "Mr. Beach, if you please. Get him moving."

Beach took a deep breath. "Yes, Arbiter," he said. "Right away."

EIGHTEEN

"*It's all in your mind, Raimey. It's all in your mind.*"

"It's all in your mind?" Drusni echoed, sounding bewildered. "What does that mean?"

"I don't know," Raimey said slowly, thinking furiously. That had been Sprenkle's voice, he recognized now. And from the flurry of angry conversation he could vaguely hear in the background, it seemed that someone up on Prime wasn't at all happy with the psychologist for saying it.

Which meant it was some kind of clue. Possibly even a clue to this control they had over him.

But what?

He growled under his breath, wishing to the Deep that Sprenkle hadn't tried to be so coy with his hint. He'd probably hoped whoever was in charge would miss the significance of it. But from the shouting that had followed, clearly that had been a waste of effort.

But just as clearly, he'd expected Raimey to get the message. *It's all in your mind. It's all in your . . .*

And then, suddenly, Raimey felt his aching muscles stiffen. Of course. *It's all in your mind*—the favorite catchphrase of his Psychological Advertising Techniques 101 professor. The professor who had instructed them about the use of subliminals, keywords, semantic triggers, and cultural progressions in the world of advertising.

"You were right," he told Drusni. "It's not any kind of gadget they put into my brain. It's been put into my mind."

"I don't understand," Drusni said, flicking her tails in confusion. "What's the difference?"

"My physical brain isn't the same one I had when I came here," Raimey said stumbling over the words in his haste. He could feel the sense of light-headedness starting to fade in on him. Whoever was playing puppet with him seemed to have won the argument, and the strings were starting to tighten again. "But they knew my mind and personality would remain even after all the cells had changed," he went on. "So what they did was implant some kind of subliminal commands and triggers in my subconscious mind. Now they're using them to take control of my body."

"But it's your own mind," Drusni protested. "Why can't you make them stop?"

Raimey sighed. "Because no matter what I look like on the outside, at the center I'm still human," he told her. "My thoughts, my emotions—all of them are human. And it's through that emotional matrix that they're controlling me."

Drusni didn't reply. Probably didn't understand a word of what he'd said. Raimey could feel his muscles starting to twitch now: The control words being sent and received, if he remembered Professor Negandhi's lectures correctly. A few more ninepulses, and he would again be charging up to try to fight off the Protectors again.

"All right," Drusni said suddenly. "You say it's because you're not Qanskan enough that these words have strength over you. All right. What would it take to make you more Qanskan?"

"What do you mean?" Raimey asked, frowning.

"We need to make you a true and complete Qanska," she repeated. "Or at least enough of one that their tricks won't work anymore. What can we do?"

"Nothing," he said quietly. "It's too late. I might as well let the humans take me up there and get it over with."

"No," Drusni said fiercely. "I won't accept that. You're my friend, Manta. I'm not going to just give you up. Not to them."

Raimey's heart was starting to ache again, the way it had hurt for all the ninedays since her rejection of him so long ago. But this time the ache had a strange and bittersweet richness to it instead of the hollow emptiness that had haunted him for so long. "Thank you," he said softly, reaching over to stroke her fin with his. "I guess in my determination to have you for my bond-mate, I forgot how good it was to simply have you for a friend."

His fin twitched away from her of its own accord. "It's started," he said tightly. "This is it. If they can't stop me any other way . . . would you say good-bye to Pranlo for me? And tell him I'm sorry?"

"No," Drusni said, her voice suddenly grim and determined. "Not yet."

"What?" Raimey asked, frowning. His fins spread wide, his tails started to beat the air, and he found himself swimming up again toward the cage above.

"I said not yet," Drusni repeated. She caught up with him, turning her distended belly toward his. "We're not giving up yet." She maneuvered closer, pressing her belly against his—

And with a horrified shock, Raimey realized what she had in mind. "Drusni!" he gasped. "What are you doing?"

"You said your emotions were human," she said, her voice shaking with fear and desperation and dark resolve. "All right. Maybe there's a way to give you a big enough run of Qanskan emotion to push those other emotions away."

"No," Raimey pleaded. She was maneuvering into position now; and he, with his useless body, could do nothing to stop her. "This is wrong, Drusni. It's *wrong*. Please— it's not worth it. Please. Don't worry, I won't be able to stop the Protectors anyway."

"I'm not worried about you stopping the Protectors," she said. "They'll do what they have to. So will I."

"It's not worth it," Raimey said again, his whole body shaking as a twin wave of anticipation and dread washed over him. He'd wanted this so badly . . . but not like this. Clouds above, Deep below, not like *this*. "All you're going to do is hurt yourself."

"Or maybe I can save a friend." She took a deep, shuddering breath. "Here we go. . . ."

And as their bodies joined, the wave of emotion became an overwhelming hurricane, whipping through Raimey's heart and mind and soul with an ecstasy that was as alien as it was powerful. It was like everything he'd ever wanted, all swirled together in a kaleidoscope of bright colors and tingling tastes and ringing sounds. Impossible to describe or explain; possible only to experience. He wanted to laugh, to sing, to shout.

And to cry.

"I'm sorry, but I don't have the faintest idea what's going on," Beach said, waving his hands helplessly as he looked back and forth between his displays. "All I know is that none of these tonals he's babbling are translating."

"Is she still holding on to him?" Liadof asked.

"Looks like it," Milligan said. "Hard to see, though—they're stirring the air something fierce."

"She's trying to keep him away from the cage," Liadof decided. "Well, let her try. Mr. Beach, move him straight down, then circle him back up again toward Omega."

"Yes, ma'am," Beach sighed, tapping keys on the McCarthy board. "I'll try."

"What do you mean, you'll try?" Liadof demanded sharply. "You'll do it. Or you'll end up like Dr. Sprenkle and Ms. McCollum."

"All I'm saying is that it may not be possible," Beach said. "He's supposed to be heading for the cage already, only he isn't. But I can try it again."

For a long minute the only sound in the room was the dull rhythmic thudding of the Protectors as they slammed themselves into the side of the Omega probe. "The keywords have been sent, and the order's been given," Beach said at last. "Tom? Any movement?"

"Nope," Milligan said, shaking his head. "And Drusni

isn't exactly pinning him to the mat, either. He could get away from her if he really wanted to."

"That's it, then," Faraday said, trying to keep the pleased relief out of his voice. The Qanska were still trapped in Liadof's cage, but at least Raimey was finally free of her control. In a battle like this, you took your victories where you could get them. "He's broken it."

"Damn," Liadof muttered under her breath. "Those key-words were supposed to be stronger than that. I wonder how the hell he did it."

She shrugged. "Well, no great loss. He simply gets to slink off instead of being beaten to death by the others. I trust Dr. Sprenkle will find that adequate reward for his act of treason."

"Yes," Faraday murmured, keeping his eyes on the displays. "I'm sure he will."

He could feel her eyes studying him. Then, peripherally, he saw her shift her attention back to the drama taking place far below. "But the game goes on," she continued. "Mr. Milligan, move the spy probe closer to Omega. I want a better look at what the Protectors are doing to the cage."

With one last surge of ecstasy, it was over. Drusni's grip on him loosened, and the wind whipped between them again as they fell slowly apart.

And as the windstorm of emotion began to fade from Manta's mind, a black cloud of shame and guilt rolled in to take its place.

Because Drusni's idea had worked. It had worked perhaps too well. By mating with her—by merging his body and soul and mind with her for those powerful few minutes—he had truly become one flesh with her.

And in the process, somewhere deep at the core of his being, that merging had become permanent. Part of whatever it was that made him human had been replaced by something that was purely Qanskan.

And with that change had come the knowledge of the terrible evil he had just committed.

He had mated with a female who was not his rightful bond-mate. Worse, a female who was the bond-mate of his best friend.

He looked over at Drusni. She was drifting on the wind as if dazed or in some deep and dark despair, her fins hunched as if she too felt the evil of what she had done.

He wanted to go to her, to comfort her, to tell her that it would be all right. But he couldn't. He couldn't face her. Not now. Not after what he'd done. There was no way he could ask for forgiveness. No way she could ever forgive him.

He turned away, his heart throbbing with pain and self-loathing. He should never have come back. To have seen her again, to have regained her as a friend . . . and now, to have it end like this. No, he should never have come back.

He would leave now. And he would never see her again.

He turned around again for one last furtive look at her. And as he did so, a sound from above penetrated his cloud of guilt and shame. The sound of Protectors slamming themselves into the humans' cage . . .

And suddenly, the black cloud swirling around Manta's heart began to light up with the lightning flashes of anger. This was *their* fault. Not Drusni's; not even his. *Theirs*. And if he couldn't ask forgiveness from Drusni, the humans could certainly expect none from the Qanska.

The humans shouldn't have come back. Not like this. And Manta meant to bite that lesson straight through their skin.

Flexing his fins, he started upward toward the dark object floating above him. The Protectors were still ramming themselves against the side, he saw, with no indication that they were making much headway. No surprise there. Thanks to Manta and their studies of him, the humans knew a great deal about Qanskan physiology and capabilities. They would have carefully designed their cowardly weapon to withstand Qanskan attacks.

But Manta was a tool-using creature. And the ultimate tool for this job was quite close at hand.

He could hear Drusni calling to him as he swam upward, the quiet agony in her voice adding to the pain whistling through his heart. Perhaps she thought her sacrifice had been for nothing, that he was still under the control of the evil beings above them.

If so, she would learn the truth soon enough. The same time the humans did.

The bottom of the cage loomed directly above him, the rows of jagged spikes pointed down like the teeth of a giant mouth awaiting its prey. Easing back on his speed, he rose toward them; and just as he reached the tips, he rolled over onto his back and let himself float the rest of the way upward.

Manta's skin had grown thick and tough over the long ninedays of his adulthood, and the spikes barely scratched the outer layer. That would hardly do. Flipping over, he dived down again for a few powerful strokes, then turned back and swam upward again toward the cage, this time making sure he was moving faster. Again, he rolled onto his back as he approached, presenting his belly to the spikes.

And gasped as he hit and the sharp points dug into his skin. He wiggled once; and with a multiple flowering of bright yellow, the blood began to pop out of his new wounds.

Wincing, he eased himself down off the spikes. The tiny droplets of yellow blew away from his belly as the wind caught them, forming little perforated trails across the sky. Flipping his head around into the wind, keeping well clear of the spikes this time, he headed away beneath the cage.

"What does he think he's doing?" Liadof said contemptuously, shaking her head. "Did he really think the spikes would be fragile enough for him to break?"

"Maybe he's just confused," Faraday suggested, his heart

suddenly pounding in his chest. Was Raimey thinking along the same line he was? If so, there might still be a chance to turn this grand scheme of Liadof's into the fiasco it deserved to be.

Provided, of course, that Liadof herself didn't catch on until it was too late. Surreptitiously, he tapped his myrtle-wood ring for luck. "After all, with most animals the belly is the weakest part," he added, hoping she wouldn't get suspicious at this sudden surge of helpfulness.

"I think it's that way with Qanska, too," Milligan spoke up, his voice just slightly off. So he'd figured it out, too. "I'm not sure, though. Too bad we can't consult Ms. McCollum."

"You could get her back in here," Faraday suggested, getting into the spirit of things. "Maybe she'll have some ideas."

Liadof snorted. "You never give up, do you, Colonel?"

Faraday gazed at the display. "No, Arbiter," he said softly. "I don't."

Manta cleared the last row of spikes and turned upward along the side of the cage, rolling over to put his back to the wind. Far above him, the Protectors were continuing their ramming attack, and he saw two or three of them look warily in his direction as he cleared the underside of the cage. Standing ready to fend him off, no doubt, if he tried to interfere with them again.

No danger there. Manta intended to stay as far away from them as he reasonably could.

With the wind at his back, the thin multiple trails of blood drifting from his wounds began to spatter into the mesh of the cage as he swam upward alongside it. Picking a likely-looking spot along the lower part of the side, he brought his fins to a stop, letting the wind press his belly firmly against the cold metal. He wiggled a couple of times, resting against the side of the cage, taking the opportunity to peer more closely inside.

The humans had done pretty well for themselves, he saw. There were ten children in the cage, ranging from one-size Babies to a couple of four-size Youths. Three female Breeders were inside, too, swimming back and forth among the terrified children, trying to calm and comfort them. Manta wondered if they'd all voluntarily gone in with their young, like the one Breeder he'd seen, or if the humans' aim was simply bad enough that they'd caught a couple by mistake.

But that didn't matter. What was important was that there were three adults in there who could hopefully listen to directions with steady fins and get the children moving when it was time.

And then, from somewhere downwind, Manta heard a distant warning call. Not the terrified pleading that had drawn him here, which was still being shouted by the Breeders and children who had escaped the humans' clutches. This one was an old and very familiar call.

Vuuka!

He took a careful breath. *And now*, he quoted the old human phrase to himself, *it's show time*.

"What's he doing?" Liadof asked, her voice uneasy. "Damn it, Colonel, what's he *doing*?"

"What do you mean?" Faraday asked, feigning puzzlement as he tried to keep the excitement out of his voice. Raimey had the answer—he was sure of it now. Just a few more minutes . . . "Looks like he's trying to see into the cage."

"He doesn't have to shove himself right up against the mesh to look inside," Liadof countered darkly. "What's he thinking, that the metal will help stanch the blood?"

"You're asking the wrong person," Faraday said. "As Mr. Milligan pointed out, you've sent away our Qanskan physiology expert."

Liadof didn't bother to respond. "Mr. Beach, there's

some new bellowing going on in the background," she growled instead. "What are they saying?"

"They're warning of approaching Vuuka," Beach reported.

Liadof hissed gently between her teeth. "They're zeroing in on Raimey's blood. He should have known that would happen."

"Probably," Faraday agreed.

"And yet he's still just sitting there," Liadof went on, the first hint of uncertainty creeping into her voice. "Why isn't he trying to get away? Doesn't he realize he's the one they'll be coming after?"

"I don't know," Faraday couldn't resist saying. "You've sent our psychologist away, too."

"Vuuka coming into view," Milligan announced. "Looks like . . . six, seven . . . looks like nine of them. Couple of big ones—ten meters each. The rest are reasonably small, in the three- to six-meter range."

"Well, at least that solves the problem of the Protectors batting their brains against the cage," Liadof muttered. "They're certainly not going to have time for any more of that nonsense now."

Faraday smiled tightly to himself. No, the Protectors wouldn't be hitting the cage anymore. They wouldn't have to.

And for all her arrogance, Liadof wouldn't even see it coming. She had shown already she didn't understand Qanskan physiology, or Raimey's personality and psychology.

Now she was showing she didn't even remember history.

The warning calls were getting louder and nearer. Above Manta, the Protectors were beginning to respond, the rhythm of their attack faltering as the majority swam off to confront the incoming predators. Briefly, Manta wondered if they'd noticed that it was his blood that was drawing them, then put the thought out of his mind. If this worked, he hoped there wouldn't be any repercussions for his actions. At least, not this particular action.

If it didn't work, he would probably be dead soon anyway.

He could see the Vuuka now, approaching rapidly from the far side of the cage. A good-sized group, eight or nine of them, swimming in along his blood trail. They had probably spotted the children inside the cage, and he wondered if their blood-fogged brains had noticed the metal mesh lying between them and that particular group of prey.

The lead predator, one of the biggest of the group, apparently hadn't. He slammed nose-first into the cage at full bore, bouncing back with the most surprised look Manta had ever seen on a Vuuka. He didn't get much chance to recover; an instant later, he was rammed from above by a pair of Protectors.

The rest of the Vuuka quickly got the message. Veering off the blood trail, they swept around to both sides of the cage, swinging wide around the mesh. Probably hunting for the source of the blood, Manta knew, but also undoubtedly ready to take on anything else edible that fell across their path. The rest of the Protectors had dropped behind them, trailing at a cautious distance but ready to move in if it became necessary.

Manta watched them as they came, trying to keep an eye on both directions at once. Fortunately, most of the children were long gone from the area, leaving no one but the Protectors and a few Breeders watching from a nervous distance.

Plus, of course, Manta himself. The tears the humans' spikes had made in his belly should be nearly healed by now, but there would still be dried blood caked to his skin. If it started flaking off, it would draw the predators straight to him.

And with this many of them, there wouldn't be a lot of maneuvering room for him to work with. Especially given that none of the Protectors would likely be interested in helping him.

The lead Vuuka in each of the two groups had disappeared from sight now, blocked from Manta's view by the curvature of the mesh to his immediate right and left. Which meant that, for the few seconds it would take them to come around the front and back of the cage, Manta was likewise out of their sight.

Which meant it was time to go. Pushing back off the mesh, he expanded his buoyancy sacs and begin to drift slowly up the side of the cage. *By movement and blood do Vuuka hunt*, Counselor Latranesto had told him that first day of his life. Manta could only hope that he himself wouldn't be showing enough of either to attract them.

Both groups of predators had emerged from their respective sides of the cage now, all of them bearing straight toward him. *Steady*, Manta ordered himself firmly, fighting against the urge to push his fins against the air and swim away as fast as he could while he still had a head start. The lead Vuuka on the right was speeding up, his flukes pumping faster as he sensed himself closing in on the source of the blood trail he'd been following. He opened his jaws wide—

And with a triumphant roar, dug his sharp teeth into the mesh where Manta had been pressed a few ninepulses earlier.

The spot where he had left a patch of bright yellow Qanskan blood.

Liadof stiffened in her chair, her finger stabbing toward the main display. "What in the *world*—? What are they doing? Helping the Qanska?"

"Yes, but not on purpose," Faraday told her. "They're attacking the spot where Raimey left his blood, that's all. Or had you forgotten the historic voyage of Chippawa and Faraday?"

She twisted her head to stare at him. "What are you talking about?"

Faraday looked back at the display, a flood of personal

memories flashing through his brain. The rest of the Vuuka
had joined in with the first one now, all of them tearing at
the metal mesh with an insane ferocity. "I'm talking about
my trip into the depths of the Jovian atmosphere," he told
Liadof. "Don't you remember? A Qanskan Baby—Counselor Latranesto, in fact—cut himself on our *Skydiver*'s
tether as he swam past. In the process he left some of his
blood on the metal; and within seconds, a Vuuka was chewing happily away. Made damn fast work of it, too."

He gestured at the display. "And from the looks of it,
this particular bunch isn't going to have much trouble with
your cage, either."

"Not if I can help it," Liadof snarled. "Mr. Boschwitz,
get Omega moving. Any direction, full speed."

"Acknowledged, Arbiter," the voice on the speaker said.

She hissed between her teeth. "So the Vuuka can chew,"
she said acidly. "Fine. Let's see if they can also swim."

It was working. By the clouds above, it was actually working.

Slowly, not daring to move too quickly, Manta rippled
his fins and began easing himself around into a head-down
position. He couldn't afford to attract attention, not with
the Vuuka still so close. But despite the risk, he was determined to get a look at the snarling clatter of teeth on
metal he could hear going on beneath him.

It was an awesome sight to behold. Awesome and frightening both. The Vuuka were going at it as if some sort of
mass feeding frenzy had completely taken them over.

What was even stranger, they were showing no signs of
slowing down. Manta's plan had been for them to each take
a bite or two from the cage, realize their mistake, and move
on, leaving the mesh hopefully weakened enough for the
Protectors to batter their way through.

But that wasn't what was happening. Surely even with
the taste of blood slowing their brains they could tell that

this wasn't Qanskan skin and muscle and bone they were biting at. Couldn't they?

Or was it perhaps something more subtle? Could the metal actually be tastier than fresh Qanska?

Bizarre, but possible. Manta remembered one of his physiology discussions with McCollum in which the subject of blood composition had briefly come up. The memory of the conversation was a little vague, but he seemed to remember her mentioning that Qanskan blood had a high metal content, several times that of the human counterpart, and with a better variety of metal types as well. Strange though it seemed, it could be that the Vuuka knew perfectly well what they were doing, and were actually enjoying their meal.

Manta smiled grimly to himself. This was, he decided, going to kill two Sivra with one tail slash. Not only would it free the trapped Qanska, but it would also give them a weapon they could use if the humans ever tried to pull such a stunt again.

It was difficult to see what was happening in the middle of the flurry of bodies, but he knew the Vuuka had to be getting close to eating their way through the mesh. The timing here was going to be critical: It would be a sad victory indeed if the predators succeeded in breaking through the humans' cage only to then devour the children Manta had gone to all this dangerous effort to free.

The Protectors were clearly thinking along the same lines. They had gathered together a cautious distance from the manic Vuuka, talking in low voices among themselves and twitching uncertainly back and forth as they pondered the question of when to move in for the attack.

Or maybe they were waiting for Manta, with his closer vantage point, to give them a signal. Rippling his fins to hold his position, Manta focused his attention on the mesh. If the Vuuka would just keep at it until there was a hole big enough for the Breeders inside to slip out through . . .

And then, from above him, Manta heard a noise that

froze the air in his lungs. The propellers of the probe above the cage were starting up.

The propellers that he knew could move the cage faster than a Qanska could swim. And if faster than a Qanska, faster than a Vuuka, as well?

He twisted around again to look up, heedless of the risk this time. The giant turboprop propellers were visibly spinning within their protective cowlings.

No, Manta pleaded silently, staring at the engines and trying frantically to come up with a way to stop them.

Because once the humans got the probe and cage moving, there would be no way to stop them. They could outdistance any pursuit, Qanskan or Vuukan, and keep it up until the wind had driven away all traces of Manta's blood. And when they finally brought it to a halt, there would be no one at its new resting place who would know how to pull the trick Manta had used in order to finish breaking it open.

The humans would have won. They would get the stardrive they wanted, or they would continue to trap Qanskan children until they did.

The probe and cage were starting to lumber across the wind now. Manta drove upward, his eyes searching the sleekly curved metal surfaces desperately for a weakness. But there wasn't one.

Unless . . .

His eyes fell on the mesh screen covering the intake side of the turboprop cowling. The mesh there was considerably finer than the one that made up the cage. Could a Qanska, swimming at top speed, ram his way through the mesh and into the propeller itself?

The thought was terrifying. In his imagination, he could see himself hitting the blades; could feel the tearing of skin and muscle and bone, a disintegration of his body far worse than even a pack of Sivra could manage.

But at least it would be fast. Faster than living the rest of a Qanskan lifetime with that last, broken image of Drusni haunting his vision wherever he looked.

The probe was picking up speed. Driving hard, he swam forward, trying to get around in front of the nearest engine's intake. He deserved to die anyway. This way, at least, his death could have a purpose.

Maybe that would be how Drusni would remember him. Maybe she could be that forgiving.

But he doubted it.

NINETEEN

The whine of Omega's turboprops was starting to fill the Contact Room as the engines revved their way toward full speed. "But what about your demands?" Faraday asked, frustration churning his stomach. If the probe got away now, all of the Qanskans' effort not to mention Raimey's—would be for nothing.

And this insane standoff would continue.

"What about them?" Liadof countered. "The Leaders know what we want."

"But they won't know where to deliver their answer," Faraday argued. Out of the corner of his eye, he saw that the inertial indicators at the bottom of the display were flashing. Omega was starting to move.

But Faraday wasn't really watching the indicators. His full attention was on the image coming from the spy probe. Darting up alongside the cage like a minnow swimming past a crab pot, Raimey was charging upward toward the operational part of the Omega probe. Swimming with a determination Faraday had seldom if ever seen in him.

And it didn't take a genius to figure out what he was doing. He was heading for Omega's engines, clearly hoping to prevent the hostages from being whisked away.

And there was only one way Faraday could imagine he might accomplish that.

Don't do it, Faraday pleaded silently with the image. It would cost Raimey his life; and it wouldn't stop Omega from getting away anyway. With one engine gone it would be more sluggish, but it could still outpace any Qanskan attackers in the long run. Surely Raimey could see that. Had he gotten so worked up by the Vuuka attack that he couldn't think straight?

Perhaps he had. Omega was picking up speed, and so was Raimey.

Liadof had noticed him, too. "What's he doing?" she muttered from Faraday's side.

"Trying to stop the probe," Faraday told her, hoping that his reading of Raimey's plan was wrong. But no. Raimey had already passed the trailing communications and control antennae, and at the rate Omega was accelerating he would never make it to the group at the bow end before the probe got away from him. And there was no other exposed equipment anywhere that Faraday could see.

Which left only the propellers. And the supreme sacrifice.

"He's going for the engines," Liadof said suddenly, her voice a mixture of disbelief and indignation. "Is there any way he can hurt them? Colonel?"

"Not without hurting himself," Faraday said bitterly. Out of another corner of his eye, he noticed Milligan fiddling with his sensor controls. "But if he doesn't mind dying for his people, and if he can get through the forward baffle screen—"

"Damn it," Liadof bit out. "Mr. Boschwitz—get Omega up to full speed. *Now*."

"Yes, Arbiter," Boschwitz's voice confirmed. "I'm running the engines through their prescribed ramp-up; it'll just be—"

"I said *now*!" Liadof cut him off. "Full power *now*!"

"But—acknowledged, Arbiter," Boschwitz interrupted himself. "Full power now." The engine noise jolted suddenly up in pitch and intensity—

And then, to Faraday's astonishment, it just as suddenly dropped off completely.

Liadof literally leaped out of her chair. "Boschwitz!" she shouted. "You bungling little—" She choked back the rest of the curse. "Get them going again. Now!"

"I'm trying," Boschwitz said, his voice cringing "They're not responding. Any of them."

"He warned you there was a proper ramp-up procedure," Faraday reminded her. "They've probably overheated or safety-locked or something."

"Shut up," Liadof snapped. "Mr. Boschwitz?"

"Still not responding," the controller said tightly. "Colonel Faraday's right—the diagnostic's indicating some kind of safety interlock."

"Then override it," Liadof ordered, striding forward to stand behind McCollum's vacant chair and peering at the diagnostic displays. "Everything can be overridden."

"Yes, ma'am, but I need to know the problem first," Boschwitz explained. "The overrides are specific to the particular interlock—"

"I don't care how you do it," Liadof shouted. "Rip them all out if you have to. But *get that probe moving!*"

"Too late," Milligan murmured, pointing up at the main display. "They're through."

Faraday looked at the view from the spy probe. Milligan was right. The Vuuka had chewed a hole completely through the mesh, still jostling against each other as they gnawed away at the edges. The hole was still pretty small, but already the youngest of the Qanskan children trapped inside should be able to squeeze through.

"Yes, well, they're not through enough," Liadof said tartly, an odd note creeping into her voice. It was an edge that in a lesser personality might be the first beginnings of panic. "Mr. Boschwitz, you have thirty seconds to get Omega moving. If you don't, I'll have you arrested on a charge of treason."

"Don't be absurd," Faraday said, keeping his voice low. "You can't blame him for this."

"I can blame anyone I want," Liadof said shortly. "I'm an Arbiter of the Five Hundred. This is my project; and it will *not* fail."

She turned bitter eyes toward Faraday. "Or else."

———

Above him, the huge driving engines suddenly stopped.

Manta slowed the rippling of his fins, letting himself coast to a confused stop. Was he misreading the sounds here?

No. The engines had stopped, the probe itself coasting to a halt.

What in the Deep were the humans up to now?

He didn't have the haziest idea. But it didn't matter. This was their opportunity to get the children and Breeders out, and he intended to take it.

He rolled over and looked down. From his distance and angle it was hard to tell, but it looked like the Vuuka had succeeded in eating through the metal cage. If the humans would be considerate enough to leave their engines off just a little longer . . .

A movement to the side caught his eye. A group of perhaps twenty Protectors had gathered a short distance away and were starting to drift toward the thrashing Vuuka. "Wait," Manta called, hoping the Vuuka were too busy to pay attention to him. "Not yet."

"Don't worry," a gruff voice came from his right. "They know what they're doing."

Manta turned, to find a Protector floating beside him. "What?"

"I said they know what they're doing," the other repeated, his eyes on the feeding frenzy below. "They'll wait until the opening is large enough for all inside to escape before they drive the Vuuka away."

"Good," Manta said, frowning. Maybe it was just that the Protector was concentrating so hard on the events below; but somehow, Manta had the distinct impression he was deliberately not looking at him. "Who are you, anyway?"

"The question is who are *you*?" the Protector countered, still not raising his eyes. "You, Manta, child of the humans."

So that was it. Someone had recognized him, or else they'd heard Drusni call him by name.

And he was in for it now.

"I am indeed a child of the humans," Manta said, keeping his voice low. "But my childhood is over. Now, I'm a Breeder of the Qanska."

"Are you?" the Protector retorted. "Does a Breeder of the Qanska help the humans capture our children?"

"The humans had me under their control," Manta told him. "They made me try to stop you from freeing the children. But that's over now."

"Perhaps," the Protector said darkly. "Or perhaps they have let you go merely so that they can use you to another purpose."

"A purpose that involved letting me ruin their plan?" Manta asked, flipping his tails pointedly at the dark shape and huge engines above them. "This device cost them a great deal of time and effort to construct; and as you may have noticed, I was the one who lured the Vuuka who are busily destroying it. There's no reason they wouldn't have stopped me from doing that if they still had the power to do so."

"Perhaps there *was* no reason," the Protector said. "Perhaps it was simply the random whistling of the wind. Or are humans not subject to the winds?"

"Trust me, they would have," Manta assured him. "Humans have a reason for everything they do."

"Do they really?" the Protector demanded. "And what was their reason for you to shatter the honor and life of a bonded female by mating with her?"

In the past few ninepulses Manta had almost managed to forget about that. Now, it came rushing back like the edge of a twistwind. "It wasn't like that," he said through suddenly aching throats. "It was . . . I can't completely explain what happened."

For a long moment the Protector remained silent. "You don't need to discuss it with me," he said at last. "I'd rather you not, in fact. But be assured, you *will* discuss it soon

You've committed a crime of violence and disgrace, and the Counselors and the Leaders and the Wise will be required to pass judgment."

"Yes," Manta said quietly. "I understand."

"But until then—" the Protector flipped his tails "—it's time for action."

Manta looked. The group of Protectors who'd been standing by to the side weren't standing by anymore. They were in full charge, driving their way toward the Vuuka at the cage.

"The opening must be large enough," the other Protector said, rippling himself into motion. "Wait here. We'll drive off the Vuuka."

"I'm coming with you," Manta said, pushing off the wind into his wake.

"No," the Protector snapped, half turning around. "You're a Breeder, and you've violated the law enough times today already. Now *wait here*."

Manta sighed and let his fins come to a halt. "Very well," he said quietly. "I obey."

"Damn it all," Liadof ground out between her teeth, her thin hands balled into thin fists in her frustration. "They're getting away. Boschwitz, they're getting *away*."

"I'm sorry, Arbiter," Boschwitz's voice came back, the words edged with his own frustration. "I can't get this damn thing to clear. The error messages keep shifting back and forth, like we've got two or three separate faults, all of them intermittent."

Liadof spat out a set of jawbreaker syllables; some blistering Russian curse, no doubt. Not that Faraday could really blame her. With their attention fixed on the cage, the Vuuka had been caught completely by surprise by the massed Qanskan charge. Even worse, at least from the Arbiter's point of view, chewing on the hard metal that way had apparently been exhausting to even Vuukan jaw muscles. Disorganized and too tired to fight back, the predators had quickly scattered before the attack.

The three Breeders inside the cage had been ready. Even as the last two Vuuka were being butted away by the Protectors, the first of the Qanskan children had been sent swimming out through the hole, his fins flapping with nervous haste as he passed bare meters away from one of his deadliest enemies. A Protector had intercepted him and ushered him away to safety, clearing the path for the next child in line to make her break for freedom.

The last of the children were out of the cage now, and the first Breeder had begun the more cautious maneuvering necessary to ease her larger bulk through the hole.

And Faraday could finally breathe a silent sigh of relief. Liadof's scheme had seriously damaged relations with the Qanska, and it was going to take some fancy talk and footwork on someone's part to heal that breach.

But not nearly as much as it would have taken if that same someone had had to do all his talking while a group of Qanska were being held hostage somewhere in the wilds of the Jovian atmosphere.

And all because the normally perverse demon of equipment glitches had chosen for once to smile on them. A simple interlock fault, plus a lot of ingenuity on Raimey's part, and Liadof was going to have to back out with her tail between her legs. *For want of a nail*, the old line echoed through his mind—

"Mr. Milligan," Liadof said suddenly. "What are those red lights on your board?"

"Excuse me?" Milligan said, frowning down at his board.

"Lift your hands," Liadof ordered, taking a step toward him. "Keep them away from the controls."

"I don't understand," Milligan said, his hands reluctantly coming up.

"I think you do," Liadof said icily, bending over for a closer look. "Mr. Boschwitz, what does 'proximity sensor lockdown' mean?"

"What?" Boschwitz asked. "Where?"

"All over Mr. Milligan's board," Liadof said. "What does it mean?"

Boschwitz hissed into the speaker. "It means we've found the problem," he said darkly. "One of the standard safety interlocks is that if a proximity sensor shows you up against something solid, you can't move that direction without an override. By overloading the whole batch of them, he's tweaked it so that they're *all* showing something solid. You can't go anywhere; ergo, the engines shut down to standby."

"Why didn't you override it?"

"Because the glitch kept changing," Boschwitz growled. "He must have been alternating between different sensor-group overloads to keep me from ever catching up with the right one. Keep his hands away from his board and I can get Omega moving."

Liadof looked up at the display. "It's too late," she said, her voice ominously quiet. "Go ahead and do the overrides and bring Omega back up to reel-in position. No hurry."

"Yes, Arbiter."

Liadof gazed down at Milligan. "Mr. Milligan. Do you have anything to say?"

Milligan folded his arms across his chest. "Not really."

She nodded as if that was the answer she'd been expecting. Shifting her gaze to the doorway, she hooked a finger in invitation to the remaining Sanctum cop. "Escort Mr. Milligan to the brig. And while you're at it, you can take Colonel Faraday back to his quarters. The show's over."

She looked at Faraday. "For now," she added.

Silently, Milligan stood up and walked toward the approaching guard. For a moment Liadof watched him go, her eyes betraying nothing of what was going on inside her. The cop reached Milligan and began to cuff him; and as he did so, Liadof turned around to face the sole remaining tech seated at the curved control board. "Or shall we go ahead and make it a clean sweep, Mr. Beach?" she invited.

Beach's lips compressing briefly. "I'd rather not, Arbiter," he said firmly. "I like my job. I'll stay."

She studied his profile briefly, then nodded. "Very well, Mr. Beach. Carry on."

She turned back to Faraday. "This isn't over yet, Colonel. But we'll speak about that later."

"I'm sure we will," Faraday said, standing up calmly as the Sanctum cop motioned him to his feet. *When push comes to crunch*, he'd asked Sprenkle after that fateful meeting in his quarters a week and a half ago, *are they going to stand with me?*

He had his answer now. They would. And they had.

Or at least most of them had.

Beach had returned his attention to his board, giving Faraday a view of a studiously calm profile. Still, three of the four had stood with him. That was a number he could be proud of. If he ever found a way out of this mess, he promised himself, he would make sure they were rewarded for their loyalty.

If.

The last of the trapped Breeders made it through the hole in the mesh; and only then did the big engines above Manta finally roar to life. *Wonderful timing*, he thought sardonically. Though he doubted it was the original timing the humans had had in mind.

Getting his fins moving, he swam away from it, keeping a careful eye on the front end of the cage. Humans liked to keep their options open, he knew, and that cage could still hold a captured Protector or two.

But apparently they'd had enough. Instead of heading level or downward, as it would have if they were going to hunt more Qanska, the probe angled upward toward the distant clouds above.

It was over. And the Qanska had won.

Manta rolled over on his back and watched it leave, fatigue lying heavy on his fins as the emotion and tension of the battle began to drain out of him. Yes, the Qanska had won. But for him, at least, the victory was going to be mixed at best. That Protector had been right; he was going to have to answer to the Counselors and the Leaders and the Wise for everything that had happened today.

Both his own actions, and very likely those of the humans. As far as they were concerned, after all, he would always be Manta, child of the humans.

Should he try to talk with them? Use the subvocalization trick and ask them what in gritty wind they had been doing?

He flipped his tails decisively. No. They could have talked to him at any point along the way, either before they sent their probe or at any time since. If they hadn't been interested in his opinion then, they were unlikely to be interested in it now.

He smiled grimly to himself. He very much hoped that they had noticed his contribution to the Qanskan victory. Let them bask in the knowledge of what ignoring him had cost them.

The probe had receded to a tiny speck in the sky when he heard the distant scream of fear.

He rolled back over, a flash of resentment whistling through him as he forced tired muscles back into action. What now? Had more Vuuka sensed the commotion and come over to see what was going on?

Well, whatever it was, it wasn't his concern. He was just a Breeder, after all, as everyone on Jupiter was fond of telling him. This was the Protectors' job. Let them handle it. The cry for help came again—

And Manta jerked like he'd been hit by lightning.

It was *Drusni*'s voice.

The fatigue in his muscles vanished as if it had been dropped into the Great Yellow Storm, replaced by a terrified strength. *Female Breeders nearing birth can give off cues of receptiveness*, Latranesto had told him. *But mating at that time can kill the unborn young.*

And in humans, Manta knew, a miscarriage usually involved a certain loss of blood. . . .

He threw himself across the wind, the aching terror in his heart driving a terrible strength into his muscles. *No*, he pleaded with the universe. *Please. Not Drusni.*

And then, in the distance, he saw her, locked in a writhing struggle with two Vuuka only slightly smaller than she was. Fighting for her life.

And spraying all around was the bright yellow of Qanskan blood.

Something nudged against into his side. Manta twitched over, his rage boiling suddenly to the surface. Half curling, he slapped his tails as hard as he could at his attacker—

"Stay back," the Protector beside him ordered, grunting as Manta's tail slash caught him across his back just behind the ear. "You hear me? Stay back."

"To the Deep with you," Manta snarled, uncurling and lunging forward again.

"I said *stop*," the Protector barked, speeding up himself and catching up with Manta. He gave him another nudge for emphasis, a harder one this time. "We'll handle this."

Manta ignored him. Jaws clenched, he kept going—

And was nearly knocked upside down by the turbulence as four big Protectors suddenly shot past him, swimming toward Drusni and her attackers.

The Protector beside Manta took advantage of his momentary confusion to push himself into Manta's path. "It's under control," he growled. "You'd just be in the way."

"There'll be more of them," Manta warned, gasping for air. "All that blood—"

"We'll take care of it," the Protector insisted. "Besides, the Counselors and the Leaders and the Wise want to see you. Now."

Manta looked behind him. The four Protectors were nearly to Drusni and the Vuuka now. For better or worse, it was out of his strength. "All right," he murmured, his throats aching. "Lead the way."

TWENTY

Latranesto hadn't changed much in the past couple of dayherds, Manta thought as the big Qanska hovered there between two of his fellow Counselors, looking strong and almost regal. He'd probably grown a little since their last meeting, and his markings were a bit more faded, and he seemed to be having more trouble than usual maintaining his position in the Level Four air.

And his skin was marred by a few more lumps where various predators had tried for a quick meal and failed. Even at the lower levels, apparently, Qanskan life was not calm and peaceful.

But his eyes were just as bright as ever as he gazed across at Manta. "Well, Manta," he said. His voice seemed more gravelly, too. "Once again, unpleasant events have brought us together."

"Yes," Manta agreed, striving to keep his own voice calm. "This is becoming a very bad habit."

"You will speak with respect to the Counselors of the Qanska," the Counselor to Latranesto's left said sharply. His markings, Manta noted, were very similar to Latranesto's.

In fact, all three Counselors looked remarkably alike, except that the one to Latranesto's right was a female. All of them siblings, perhaps?

"I beg the Counselors' pardon," Manta said. "But I'm concerned for my friend. Why won't anyone tell me what's happened to her?"

"Your *friend*?" the male Counselor demanded harshly.

"You mean the female whose weakness you took advantage of to obscenely mate with her? The female whose child died as a result, and is even now being mourned by his herd?"

"That same herd who nearly lost many of its other children as a result of your people's actions?" the female Counselor to Latranesto's right added, her voice as bitter as her colleague's. "*That* is the female, and *that* is the herd you now claim as friends?"

"The humans are not my people," Manta said, hearing the tension in his voice. "And as for the rest of it, I would have willingly given my life to prevent it from happening."

"Yet your life is still here," the male Counselor said pointedly. "The child's is not."

Manta flicked his tails. What could he say to that?

"Tell us about your actions this day," Latranesto said.

Manta focused on him. The big Counselor's eyes were steady on him, but he thought he could detect a hint of sympathy hidden deep in his expression.

Sympathy? Or something else?

"As you know, the humans have spoken to me many times in the past," he reminded them in a low voice. "But they gave me no warning of this attack. I arrived to find their machine pursuing and capturing the children of my former herd, and the herd of my friend Drusni. When I tried to stop them, they took control of my body and used me to interfere with the Protectors."

"How did they gain this control?" Latranesto asked.

"They used my human origins against me," Manta said, wincing at the memory. How could he have done such things to his people? "The way my thoughts and feelings are put together. And I was unable to free myself until Drusni . . . until she suggested that we . . ." He trailed off.

"Are you telling us that it was *Druskani* who initiated the mating?" the male Counselor demanded. "How dare you imply such a thing?"

"Especially with her absent and unable to refute your claims?" the other added with a contemptuous flip of her tails. "Such arrogance added to the crime itself—"

"Please," Latranesto cut her off. "Continue, Manta."

Manta took a deep breath. "The mating was wrong," he said. "I knew it then, and I know it now. But with my body controlled by the humans I was unable to prevent it from happening."

"How convenient," the male Counselor muttered.

"But afterwards," Manta went on doggedly, "after the . . . the emotions of the action had faded away, I finally found myself free of their control."

He straightened to his full length, or at least as best as he could while flapping hard to hold himself in position in the dense air. "And then I did what I could to stop them and free the children."

"And at the risk of your own life," Latranesto added. "There was, after all, no promise that the Vuuka you had attracted would not attack you instead of the humans' machine."

Manta eyed him. Was Latranesto actually on his side here? "I was fortunate," he said.

"You may have been fortunate," the male grunted. "But not all the Qanska were. Or did you expect that *all* the Vuuka you drew to that area would follow your blood trail?"

Manta winced. "Yes, I was told," he said quietly. "Four other children and a Breeder also died." He looked the male Counselor squarely in the eye. "And I *do* mourn them."

"Your feelings and emotions are not on trial here, Breeder Manta," the Counselor countered. "It is your actions that we must judge."

"Yet feelings and emotions are often the Breeders of the actions," Latranesto murmured. "And if his emotions are human, how can we expect his actions to conform to those of the Qanska?"

There it was again: Latranesto acting more like his advocate than his judge. "Yet I don't believe my emotions are human anymore," Manta said firmly. "I consider myself truly a Qanska."

"Do you?" the female Counselor asked, an odd intensity to her voice. "Your emotions are Qanskan, you say. But what about your thoughts? Have you also become a Qanska in thought as well as feeling?"

"I don't know," Manta said honestly. "I don't know which of my thoughts are human or which are Qanskan All I can point out is, again, that I risked my life to protect Qanskan children."

"Yet you have done such protecting before," Latranesto reminded him. "And you have said that the desire to protect others is a strong human trait. That would imply you are still human in both thoughts and desires."

Manta felt his throats tighten, feeling like he'd just hit a downdraft. He'd just concluded that Latranesto was on his side here; now, suddenly, the Counselor seemed to be trying to prove that Manta was still dangerously human.

"The protective urge is strong in some humans," he said. "But not all. Besides, isn't that same urge present in Qanskan Protectors, as well?"

"In Qanskan Protectors, yes," the female said. "But you're a Breeder."

"The evidence seems clear," Latranesto said. "I believe he does yet think like a human. Certainly his chosen method of protecting the children was not one any Qanska would have thought of."

He twitched his tails. "In my opinion, that will always be a part of him."

"Perhaps," the female said.

"No," the male said firmly. "I say he is Qanskan. Warped and perverse, but Qanskan nonetheless. And as such—"

"Peace," Latranesto cut him off. "The examination is ended."

He backed up a few lengths. The other two Counselors swiveled around toward him, and for a few ninepulses the three of them hovered snout to snout, murmuring together in low voices. Manta watched them, his tired fins feeling as heavy as if he were lugging a pair of Youths on each of them. Whatever they were going to do, he wished they would just get it over with.

Then maybe they would finally tell him what had happened to Drusni.

The Counselors finished their debate and swiveled back around to face him. "We have reached our decision," Latranesto declared, his voice sounding suddenly as tired as Manta felt. "Manta, child of the humans, in your actions this day you have committed a terrible crime against the Breeder Druskani, the Breeder Prantrulo, and their unborn child. Moreover, in committing this crime, you have dishonored all of the Qanska. These facts cannot be argued."

He paused, and Manta took a deep breath. Here it came.

"Yet in your actions you also protected the lives of many other Qanska," Latranesto continued. "Whether you are still a child of the humans, we cannot say with certainty. We can only balance your actions of this day against each other."

He paused again. The two other Counselors, Manta noted, seemed oddly still, despite their flapping fins.

"When those actions are balanced, it becomes clear that you cannot continue to move about freely," Latranesto said. "We have therefore chosen two Qanska to accompany you. You will stay with them and allow them to guide you wherever they so choose."

Manta suppressed a grimace. No punishment, but he wasn't getting off scot-free, either. More baby-sitters, two of them this time.

"This hearing is now ended," Latranesto said. "You may go, Breeder Manta."

"Thank you, Counselors of the Qanska," Manta said. "May I now be informed as to the condition of my friend Druskani?"

Latranesto rippled his tails in a gesture of sympathy. "Her fate is still uncertain," he said quietly. "The Nurturers are still treating her."

A cold lump settled into Manta's heart. At least she was alive. But the very fact that she was still being treated wasn't a good sign. "May I see her?" he asked.

"No," Latranesto said. "She has gone into seclusion, and is seeing no one."

"I see," Manta murmured. And if and when she was ready to see people again, he would bet his name wasn't going to be high on her list. Chances were, he would never have the chance to apologize.

Though even if such a chance ever came, he wouldn't know what to say anyway. Probably just as well that he would never see her again.

"You may go," Latranesto said again.

Manta flipped his tails once in acknowledgment and turned away. Letting his aching muscles relax, he began floating upward.

"And now," Latranesto added, "we will hear the charges against Protector Virtamco. Let him be brought before us."

Manta's fins spasmed painfully as he abruptly reversed direction. Protector *Virtamco*? Tigrallo's replacement, the one Manta had run away from after Drusni had turned him down? *That* Protector Virtamco?

It was him, all right. Directly below, Manta could see Virtamco's familiar color pattern swimming toward the three Counselors, his back unnaturally stiff, another Protector at his side. "Wait a ninepulse," he called, trying to push himself downward toward them. "What charges?"

"He allowed you to escape from his guidance and care," a male voice came from behind him.

Manta rolled over to look. Two Qanska, a Protector and a Nurturer, were swimming toward him. "He let me escape?" he asked stupidly.

"He was chosen by the Counselors and the Leaders and the Wise to accompany you," the Protector said. "He failed in that task. He must therefore face judgment."

"But it wasn't his fault," Manta protested, still pushing against his own buoyancy. Running away had been his idea, not Virtamco's. He had to get down there and make them understand that.

It was no use. With the bigger Protector now on trial,

the whole court was sinking downward toward the more comfortable—at least for the Counselors—air density of Level Five. Already they were beyond a Breeder's reach, and heading still deeper.

With a sigh, he gave up the effort. "What are they going to do to him?" he asked as he started drifting upward again.

"That's what the trial's supposed to determine, isn't it?" the Protector told him acidly.

"Come on, Manta," the Nurturer urged more quietly, giving him a gentle nudge. "This level can't be very comfortable for you. Let's go."

"Where are we going?" Manta asked. Not that he really cared. If Drusni didn't want to see him, it didn't much matter where he went.

"The Counselors think you need to see more of our world," the Protector said. "So that's what we're going to show you."

Liadof had warned that she would be seeing him again soon, Faraday remembered, just before she'd thrown him and Milligan out of the Contact Room. Faraday had taken the threat seriously, and had spent the walk back to his quarters organizing his thoughts and the arguments he would make in his defense.

But as he sat in his quarters, and the minutes dragged into hours, he began to wonder if she had somehow forgotten her threat. The hours stretched in turn into days, and he began to wonder if she could possibly even have become incapable of carrying it out.

Finally, on the fourth day, he had a visitor.

But it wasn't Liadof.

"Hello, Colonel," Hesse said, ducking his head in a slightly nervous-looking nod as the Sanctum cop outside ushered him in and closed the door behind him. "I hope I'm not intruding."

"Not at all," Faraday said, getting up from the desk chair

where he'd been working and gesturing to it. "Please: sit down."

Hesse hesitated, glancing around the room. "Well . . ."

"Please," Faraday said again, crossing to the bed and sitting on the edge.

"Thank you," Hesse said. Gingerly, Faraday thought, he swiveled the chair around to face the bed and sat down. "I should first apologize for not coming to see you sooner. I meant to, but there were . . . certain difficulties."

"I can imagine," Faraday agreed. "Frankly, I'm surprised you were able to get in to see me at all."

Hesse waved a deprecating hand. "Arbiter Liadof is from the Five Hundred; I'm from the Five Hundred. Professional courtesy, you know."

"Really?" Faraday said, lifting his eyebrows.

"What's that supposed to mean?" Hesse asked cautiously, squirming slightly in his chair.

"It means you look like you're sitting on a fire ant nest," Faraday said bluntly. "Let me guess. Liadof doesn't know you're here at all, does she?"

Hesse swallowed. "Well . . . to be honest . . . but actually, it doesn't matter."

"That's clear," Faraday said dryly. "You want to explain it in English now?"

Hesse took a deep breath. "Okay," he said, letting the breath out in a whoosh. "Okay. Bottom line is that the Omega Probe fiasco has put the Five Hundred into a complete uproar. The whole thing was Arbiter Liadof's personal baby, and now it's sort of spit up in everyone's face."

Faraday chuckled. "And the Five Hundred are somewhat perturbed?"

"That's putting it mildly," Hesse said, relaxing a little. "She's spent most of the past few days in her private communications room here on the station, working like crazy to shore up her support."

"Against whom?" Faraday asked. "Pressure from some other faction?"

"Pressure from at least two other factions, actually,"

Hesse said. "Things still haven't completely settled down, but it looks like her group will manage to hold on to their position, but with their strength seriously diminished."

"I see," Faraday said. "You'll forgive me if I don't leap for joy, Mr. Hesse, but I've heard all this before. You get whispered rumors that change is in the air, but somehow nothing ever really comes of it. Sort of like a forecast of a cold front in the middle of a Central North American summer."

"I understand," Hesse said. "But this time, it happens to be true. It's practically guaranteed that they're going to have to make some concessions or compromises if they want to hold on to their power."

"Well, personally, I'm not going to hold my breath," Faraday said. "But okay, let's assume for the moment that it actually happens. What's it going to mean as far as Jupiter and the Qanska are concerned?"

Hesse's lips compressed briefly. "Arbiter Liadof believed that her—well, let's call it what it was. That her extortion plan was the quickest way to get hold of a Qanskan stardrive. She managed to convince the rest of the Five Hundred, which was how she got approval for Omega in the first place. Now, there's going to have to be some serious rethinking."

"What kind of rethinking?" Faraday pressed. "That could just mean redesigning Omega to be Vuuka-proof and sending it back down."

"And that might be the direction Liadof will be pushing," Hesse agreed. "But the other factions are going to have their own ideas, too. Hopefully, one or more of them will be acceptable to those of us who know the Qanska best."

"That would be nice for a change," Faraday said, eying the other closely. "Let's back up a step. Where and on what are you standing in all this alleged chaos?"

"Oddly enough, I'm standing square in the middle of it," Hesse said, his lip twitching in what might have been an ironic smile. "I've been invited by one of the factions to represent their interests here."

Faraday blinked. "You? Forgive me, but . . . *you*?"

"I agree, actually," Hesse admitted candidly. "But who else have they got? It would take weeks for them to choose someone else, bring him up to date on Changeling, and then get him out here. In the meantime, Liadof would have essentially a free hand."

"I suppose that makes sense," Faraday conceded. "Congratulations on the promotion. Now, where am *I* standing?"

"Well, actually, that depends on you," Hesse said, starting to look nervous again. "I've been directed to ask what it would take to obtain your cooperation and support."

Faraday had imagined a lot of scenarios erupting around him as a result of the Omega Probe disaster. Being invited to join a palace coup hadn't been one of them. "Interesting offer," he said. "Though I'm constrained to point out that my influence around here is not exactly at a high point right now."

"You might be surprised," Hesse said. "You're still a hero, you know, with a name that's known and respected all across the System. That name might be enough to tip the balance of power if things got tight enough."

He smiled faintly. "Plus, of course, you have a certain level of expertise on Jupiter and the Qanska in general."

"None of which will be of any use without a good team backing me up," Faraday said. "What's happened to the three Alpha Shift people Liadof had arrested?"

Hesse shifted uncomfortably in his seat. "They're due to be shipped back to Earth on the next transport," he said. "Liadof's ready to load a bunch of charges on each of them, up to and including treason for Milligan and Sprenkle. Cooperating with the enemy under fire, I think the statute is she's using."

"Get the charges dropped."

Hesse's eyes went momentarily wide. "Colonel, I can't do that."

"I thought you represented a powerful faction of the Five Hundred," Faraday said. "Fine. Let's see just how powerful they are."

"You're asking them to directly challenge Liadof's group," Hesse hissed as if afraid of being overheard. "I already told you they're not ready to do that yet."

"You also told me the Five Hundred are currently embroiled in a great and wonderful spirit of compromise and concession," Faraday reminded him. "See how far that spirit will stretch."

"I don't think it'll stretch *that* far," Hesse said. "I mean, after all, Liadof blames Alpha Shift for her failure, and she's determined to make an object lesson out of them."

"In that case, your group should point out that object lessons can cut both directions," Faraday said. "If they get put on trial, all the facts of the case are going to come out. *All* of them; including the fact that the Qanska have a stardrive."

Hesse frowned. "What's the problem with that? No one in the Five Hundred was planning to hide it from the rest of the System."

"The problem is that you don't have it yet," Faraday told him. "And the way things are going, you're not going to have it any time soon, either. Trust me; you announce something like this to the general public, and you'd better be on the verge of trotting out a working model."

Hesse winced. "I hadn't thought about that," he said slowly. "You're right, that might be a lever we can use against her."

"You could also remind her that all three are pretty small fish," Faraday added. "She can afford to throw them back."

"I suppose it's worth a shot, anyway," Hesse said reluctantly. "All right. Anything else you want?"

"That *I* want?"

"As the price for your support," Hesse said. "You must want *something*. Right?"

"You've been in politics too long, Mr. Hesse," Faraday said, hearing an edge of disgust in his voice. "Not everyone in this universe acts solely on the basis of what they think they can get out of it."

Hesse reddened. "I'm sorry, Colonel," he said. "I just assumed . . ."

"Tell me your faction's views on the Qanska," Faraday said. "What are your goals regarding their lives and safety, and our relations with them?"

Hesse pursed his lips. "To tell you the truth, I really don't know," he admitted. "I'll ask, though."

"Do that," Faraday said. "Then we'll see what kind of support I can give them." He looked around the cramped room. "Assuming that I continue to have a position to support anyone from, of course."

"I wouldn't worry about that," Hesse assured him. "If Liadof's faction didn't have the nerve to toss you aside before Omega, they certainly can't risk doing so now. As I said, you have the name and the prestige."

He stood up, a kind of jerky motion that made him look like he was on strings. "Anyway, I'd better get going."

"One more question," Faraday said. "What happened with Manta?"

Hesse blinked. "Oh. Right. Nothing much, actually. He had to go on some sort of trial to account for his actions. But after some discussion they let him off."

"How big a trial was it?" Faraday asked. "Who was there?"

"I didn't ask," Hesse said. "I can if you want me to."

"This is all coming from Mr. Beach, I presume?"

Hesse hesitated, then nodded. "Yes, but please don't mention that to anyone else," he said. "He's still more or less in Liadof's good graces, and it wouldn't do to have her know he's been talking outside the Contact Room."

"I understand," Faraday said. "And you say Manta was allowed to leave?"

"Yes, but not alone," Hesse said. "This time they gave him *two* baby-sitters: one male, one female. I guess they don't want to lose track of him again. Last we knew, they were headed south."

" 'Last we knew?' " Faraday asked, frowning. "Aren't we still watching him?"

Hesse shook his head. "The spy probe's low on fuel," he said. "Liadof decided we'd do better to leave it near the herd and keep an eye on them instead."

"Especially since Manta isn't likely to be useful to her anymore?" Faraday suggested acidly.

"Something like that," Hesse conceded. "Sorry."

With an effort, Faraday refrained from cursing. "What about Drusni? Is she all right?"

Hesse shrugged helplessly. "As far as we know, she's still alive and undergoing treatment. But she's gone into seclusion, outside the spy probe's range."

"Figures," Faraday muttered. "Do me a favor, will you? Let me know the minute you find out anything about her."

"Sure," Hesse promised. "And I'll get in touch with my supporters right away and see if we can get those treason charges dropped."

"*And* find out what their plans are for the Qanska," Faraday reminded him.

"Right."" Hesse stepped to the door and rapped twice. "I'll let you know as soon as I hear something."

The door slid open. "Thank you," Faraday said. "I'll see you later."

Hesse nodded. "Good-bye, Colonel."

The door slid shut behind him. Faraday listened for a moment as his footsteps retreated down the corridor. Then, shifting position, he stretched out on the bunk. Lacing his fingers behind his head, he stared up at the plain gray ceiling.

So it had started. He'd known it would eventually, given the sheer scope of the Omega Probe disaster. Liadof was undoubtedly fighting for her career here; and she struck him as being one hell of a fighter.

He *was* rather surprised to find Hesse involved. But in retrospect that made sense, too.

But at least things were in motion. All he could do now was wait, and watch for a chance to snatch something good out of the political chaos. For himself, and for McCollum, Sprenkle, and Milligan.

And, if he was very lucky, maybe even for Manta.

TWENTY-ONE

Ahead, in the gathering gloom, Manta could see a long, thick cloud of dark blue drifting on the wind. "How about here?" he suggested. "This looks like a good place to stop for the sundark."

"You must be joking," the big Protector beside him snorted. "You know how many predators are probably hanging around a run of *breekis* that size?"

"Especially Sivra," the Nurturer added. "Three or four different packs can sometimes hide in a run that big, just waiting for an unwary Qanska to come close."

"So let's not be unwary," Manta argued. "I'm hungry."

"You're always hungry," the Protector said with a sniff. "We'll find some place a little safer to eat."

"Of course I'm always hungry," Manta muttered under his breath. "That's because you never want to stop to eat."

"What was that?" the Protector challenged.

Manta grimaced. "Nothing."

Giving the *breekis* a wide berth, they continued on. And for probably the ninetieth time in the past two ninedays, Manta decided he hated this.

Hated this; and hated *them*.

Their names, which they'd finally and grudgingly given him, were Gryntaro and Wirkani. They were apparently not a bonded couple, but putting together bits and pieces of their conversation Manta had concluded that they had nevertheless been swimming together for quite a long time. From the look of Gryntaro's lumpy body, it was clear he'd gotten into a lot of fights with both Vuuka and Sivra. From the smooth lines of Wirkani's, it was also clear she'd been equally successful in avoiding them.

"Here we go," Wirkani said, flipping her tails to the right. "See? A nice little run of *ranshay*, just waiting for us."

"I see it," Manta said, making a face as he looked at the brown smudge drifting in the wind. It was *ranshay*, all right, which meant they wouldn't go to sleep hungry. But without any of the silvery-blue *jeptris* to spice it up, it was going to be a disappointing meal.

"You might be a little more grateful," Gryntaro rumbled as he angled toward the run.

"Sure thing," Manta muttered. "Watch me being grateful."

"Come on, Manta," Wirkani said encouragingly. "Don't mind Gryntaro. There's plenty for all of us."

Manta sighed. Gryntaro was the epitome of the rough-and-tumble, no-nonsense type of Qanska, the sort who would be instantly and unanimously put in charge if the Counselors and Leaders and Wise ever decided to organize an army and take on the Vuuka in a straight-up battle.

He also had all the compassion of Pakra leavings, and if he had even a breath of humor between his fin tips Manta had yet to spot it. The sort of Qanska you'd want beside you in trouble, but probably wouldn't invite to go off eating with you.

Wirkani, in contrast, was almost a complete opposite. She was unfailingly cheerful, to the point where she practically drove Manta insane sometimes, and had a tendency to mother him that was rather embarrassing.

And yet, where Gryntaro's gruffness seemed genuine, Wirkani's pleasantness felt somehow artificial or forced. Almost as if she was play-acting for his benefit.

Or maybe for Gryntaro's. Maybe she really didn't like him any more than Manta did.

In which case, why swim with him at all? Because Latranesto and his Counselor buddies had told her to?

He sniffed under his breath as he caught up a mouthful of *ranshay*. Back at his trial, he'd concluded he was being let off easy. Now, stuck with these two, he wasn't so sure anymore.

Something moving to the side caught his eye. He looked up—

"What?" Gryntaro asked sharply, looking up too.

"Oh, it's just a Brolka," Wirkani said soothingly. "Nothing to be afraid of."

"I know what it is," Manta growled, watching as the miniature Qanska snatched a few bites from the other side of the *ranshay* run and then darted off. It was the first one of the creatures he'd seen since he and his new companions had left the Centerline.

And the sight of it reminded him that he never had figured out what exactly they were.

Well, no time like the present. "Or rather, I *don't* know," he amended. "What are those things, anyway?"

"They're Brolka, of course," Gryntaro said, glaring at him. "Don't play silly games."

"I'm not playing games," Manta insisted. "I never even heard of Brolka until twenty or thirty ninedays ago. Where do they come from?"

"Where do you think?" Gryntaro retorted. "From Qanska, of course."

Manta stared at him. "From *Qanska*?"

"Like Babies," Wirkani said. "You *do* know where Babies come from, don't you?"

"Of course," Manta said, a creepy sensation flowing through him as he looked back and forth between the two of them. This couldn't possibly be right. "Are you telling me," he asked carefully, "that Brolka are Qanskan *Babies*?"

Wirkani actually gasped. "Don't be ridiculous," Gryntaro bit out, sounding even gruffer than usual. "They're food animals for the Vuuka and Sivra. Do you think we would give up Babies to be food animals?"

"But you just said they come from Qanska," Manta protested, thoroughly confused now. "If they come from Qanska, why aren't they Qanska?"

"Because they're smaller and heavier than Qanska," Wirkani said, her normal cheerfulness starting to sound a little strained. "They don't talk, they don't grow more than about four-size long, and they don't understand us. They're just food animals."

"Maybe you're one of them," Gryntaro added sarcastically. "If you don't understand something this simple—"

"Wait a ninepulse," Manta interrupted, struggling to figure this out. "So Brolka are born from Qanska. Are they born the same time as Qanska, or at different times?"

"The same time," Wirkani said, frowning at him. "A group is born, all at once, usually with one Qanska and four to six Brolka."

"And they all come from Qanska?" Manta asked. "Or can the Brolka then breed together?"

"What, you think we've got enough female Breeders to make this many Brolka?" Gryntaro scoffed. "I thought you humans were supposed to know something about people and animals."

"Now, now, Gryntaro," Wirkani admonished him. "No, Manta, the Brolka breed together just fine. Even better, actually. They can have as many as eight or nine at a time. You really *don't* know all this?"

"No one ever told me," Manta murmured, feeling about as windswept as he'd ever been in his life. So that was it. Typical Qanska births came as a litter, with the mix including one sentient Qanskan Baby and a whole mess of nonsentient food-animal runts. The Baby joined the herd, and the Brolka just . . . swam away?

It was breathtakingly weird, and borderline obscene on top of it. But the more he thought about it, the more he had to admit there was a certain logic to it. True, it cost a lot of biological effort for a Breeder to create a bunch of animals while she was also creating a Baby. But at the same time, the more animals there were swimming around, the less likely the new child would find itself at the business end of a set of Vuukan teeth. Provided there were enough food plants floating around to sustain the larger population, the arrangement would definitely be to the Qanskan good.

At least, that was how it had seemed to work in the northern regions, back when he was swimming with Beltrenini and her friends. He remembered noting at the time that he hadn't had nearly as much trouble with predators as he'd had as a child, or even on his travels away from Centerline.

Which left only one question. If it was such a universally good plan, why weren't the Qanska in the Centerline region doing it?

Because they clearly weren't. He'd witnessed a fair number of births while he was swimming with the herd, and he'd heard about a lot more that he hadn't personally seen. And he'd certainly endured his fair share of the story circles where the leaders of the herd had pedantically listed the requirements and obligations and expectations in a young Qanska's life.

And in none of it had he seen, heard of, or heard about Brolka.

"They didn't tell you?" Gryntaro asked sardonically as he scooped up another mouthful. "Or were you just not paying attention?"

"Don't worry about it," Wirkani added encouragingly. "I'm sure there are things around each of us every day that we don't notice. Learning is what makes life exciting."

"Or maybe I *was* listening, but this was something they didn't talk about," Manta shot back. "Because there aren't any Brolka in Centerline, and I wasn't supposed to know about them. You think?"

Gryntaro gruffed something and turned away. "It's not quite the way you make it sound, Manta," Wirkani said, sounding a little embarrassed. "If it's not talked about, it's because civilized Qanska don't do things that way anymore. We prefer to have our children alone, without any of these other . . . complications. It's simpler, cleaner, and much less dangerous for the Breeder mother."

"I can understand that," Manta said, keeping his voice neutral. A nice theory, and he didn't believe it for a minute. As a business major he hadn't had much time for science

courses; but those he *had* taken had made it clear that biological cycles and procedures rarely came down to a matter of personal choice. Certainly not the ones having to do
with reproduction. Maybe the Centerline folk had convinced themselves it was more civilized, but there had to
be something else behind it.

But what?

Impatiently, he shook the thought away. Once, he would
have brought this information to the humans' attention, and
he and McCollum would have spent a few ninedays nosing
the possibilities and ramifications back and forth.

But now, as far as he was concerned, McCollum, her
database, and all the rest of the humans could go to the
Deep. The mysteries of life on Jupiter were none of his
concern anymore. All he cared about now was his own
survival.

He was chewing on yet another bite of *ranshay*, and gazing out into the distance to the north, when he saw the
flicker of movement.

He caught his breath, freezing into immobility as his eyes
tried to pierce the gathering darkness. It was back: the same
person or thing that had been stalking them ever since
they'd left Centerline.

It never came close enough for him to get a good look
at it, but it was never very far away. At first he'd thought
it was a hungry but shy Vuuka, looking for an opportunity
to split one of them away from the others and get a quick
meal. But subsequent glimpses had shown the stalker was
the wrong shape for that. It was definitely a Qanska, and
from the size probably a Breeder or small Protector.

And even though he'd never seen it clearly enough to
identify the markings, he had long since concluded there
was only one Qanska who could possibly be interested in
stalking him this way.

Pranlo.

He shivered. Pranlo. The former friend whose bond-mate
he'd attacked. Possibly even killed.

The former friend whose child he definitely *had* killed.

Which wasn't at all how it had been, of course. But it was how everyone else saw it. He doubted Pranlo would see it any differently than the rest of the world.

He looked over at Gryntaro. The Protector was eating stolidly away, rhythmically munching his *ranshay* calmly and only occasionally glancing around to watch for predators. If he had noticed their shadow, he wasn't showing any sign of it.

Should he tell him? Put him on his guard that there was trouble lurking in the eddies behind them?

He grimaced. No. If Pranlo was looking for revenge, let him go ahead and take it. It wouldn't bring back his dead child, but if it would make him feel better Manta was willing to pay the cost.

"You finished?" Wirkani asked.

Manta looked over at her. A tendril of *ranshay* was hanging out of the corner of her mouth, and as he watched the wind plucked it away. "Why?" he asked. "I thought we were staying here for the sundark."

"What, with this much light left?" Gryntaro said, flipping his tail at the near-perfect darkness around them. "Don't be silly. We can get a little farther before we stop."

"If you're finished eating, that is," Wirkani added.

Manta looked back toward where he'd seen Pranlo. But it was way too dark to see anything there now. Maybe Gryntaro and Wirkani *had* seen him, and this was their way of trying to lose him without worrying Manta.

But it didn't matter. He was ready to die anyway. If not this sundark, then whenever.

And one way or another, he had certainly lost his appetite. "Sure," he said. "Let's go."

The distant sunlight was in the eastern sky, and Wirkani was already awake when Manta dragged himself out of the swirl of unpleasant dreams he'd wrestled with all sundark. "Good sunlight, Manta," she greeted him cheerfully, her fin tips undulating as she held herself beside him. "Did you sleep well?"

"It wasn't too bad," Manta said, looking around. "Where's Gryntaro?"

"He thought he heard some predators moving around before light," she said, rolling over and doing some flip-stretches. "He went to take a quick look around."

Manta grimaced. Predators? Or Pranlo? "So where exactly are we going?"

"What do you mean?" Wirkani asked, rolling back over to face him.

"You told me the Counselors wanted me to see more of our world," Manta reminded her. "But we seem to be heading pretty much straight south."

"Where else should we be going?" she asked. "You already know what life is like along Centerline."

"North and south are where things are different," Gryntaro said gruffly from behind him.

Manta twitched violently; he hadn't heard the Protector's approach. "You sure are the jumpy one," Gryntaro commented, swimming around Manta to Wirkani's side. "We ready to go?"

"Sure," Manta said, looking around. There was no sign of anyone else nearby, either Pranlo or predators.

What there *was*, though, was a whole new group of colors floating along in the winds. "What's that?" he asked, flipping his tails toward them.

"Which one?" Wirkani asked. "The green-speckled-brown, or the purple-and-yellow?"

"Both," Manta said. "I've never seen either of them before."

"The green-and-brown one is *fomprur*," Wirkani told him. "The other is *preester*."

"The *preester*'s better eating," Gryntaro added, flipping his fins and starting toward the flow of colors. "Let's do it and get out of here. We've still got a long way to go."

"Okay," Manta murmured, falling into the flow behind him. So there it was: the first appearance of Brolka yesterday coinciding with the equally sudden appearance of new varieties of foodstuffs. He'd gotten the feeling during his northern journey that that was how it worked, but back then he hadn't been paying close enough attention to be sure. This time, he was.

So what did that mean? He remembered speculating that it would only make sense for Breeders to have combined litters of Qanska and Brolka if there was enough food to go around. Did this mean that guess had been correct?

He snorted under his breath. Probably not. This was an ecology problem, after all, not a business one. He could try to think of it in terms of supply and demand if he wanted to, but that couldn't possibly be the entire story.

But then, why should he care about any deeper meanings anyway? As long as he had the system figured out well enough to survive, esoteric questions like this could go to the Deep.

They reached the floating food and dug in. The *preester* was indeed the better tasting of the two, he quickly decided, though the *fomprur* wasn't all that far behind. Not that it would have mattered how the stuff tasted. The previous sundark's abbreviated meal had caught up with his stomach, and he sloshed into the two runs with a will and an appetite.

Gryntaro and Wirkani were both waiting with varying degrees of patience by the time he'd finally eaten his fill. "About time," Gryntaro grumbled. "I thought you were going to be at it all day."

"What's the hurry?" Manta asked as he scooped up one last mouthful.

"The hurry is that we don't get to go back to civilization until—"

"Which one did you like best?" Wirkani interrupted smoothly. "The *preester* or the *fomprur*?"

"Oh, the *preester*, definitely," Manta said, frowning at her. "You can't go back to civilization until what?"

"Until we finish your tour, of course," she said cheerfully. "I trust you're paying attention to everything we've been showing you?"

"Of course," Manta said.

"Good," Wirkani said. "It's important that you learn everything about our world."

"So can we go?" Gryntaro said. Flipping his tails, he turned to the south and swam off.

"Sure," Manta murmured. Only they hadn't really been showing him anything, he thought with a frown as he and Wirkani headed off in the Protector's wake. They'd been willing to answer his questions, but neither of them had taken any kind of initiative as far as instruction was concerned.

So what had Gryntaro *really* been about to say?

He had no idea. But it was something Wirkani clearly hadn't wanted said.

He sighed. Something else to worry about. Like he didn't have enough of that already.

Gryntaro was really beating the air up there, starting to pull slowly away from the others. With a grimace, Manta hurried to catch up, keeping an eye out for predators, new foodstuffs, and anything else that might be new and unfamiliar.

And, of course, for Pranlo.

TWENTY-TWO

They continued on without serious incident for another six ninedays. Always they headed straight south, veering only occasionally for food or to avoid predators, keeping the prevailing westerly winds steady on their right.

At first Manta had found the restless roar in his right ear to be annoying. After that he'd wondered whether the wind pressure might permanently damage his hearing, leaving him more vulnerable to predators sneaking up from that side. Now, this far into the trip, he'd gotten to where he hardly even noticed it.

They stayed mostly on Level Four, far beneath the Qanskan herds Manta could sometimes hear floating above them in the upper levels. Once in a while they spotted some Protectors and Nurturers, or a pair or group of Counselors. As with food runs, those were occasions where Gryntaro would veer off their southward course, shifting direction to avoid all contact or communication with the other Qanska. Manta never did figure out whether Gryntaro was afraid of delaying his tour with idle chatter, or whether he simply didn't want to deal with the "uncivilized" beings who lived this far off Centerline.

The Brolka became more numerous as they continued south, too. And while their presence lowered the incidence of predator attacks, it didn't eliminate them entirely. At least four Vuuka took a close look at the three travelers along the way, though only one of them was rash enough to actually give it a try. And one day, right at sundark, they were jumped by a small herd of Sivra-sized predators of a type Manta had never seen before. On both occasions the presence of an experienced Protector made the difference between serious trouble and relatively minor nuisance, though in the latter case Manta did end up with two new lumps on his fins and body as souvenirs of the battle.

Again, there was no warning from the humans that either of the attacks were coming. Apparently, the humans had written him off entirely.

Along with the obvious differences in plant and animal life, he also noticed that the sunlight was showing subtle changes as they continued on. Though the light was always diffuse this deep beneath Jupiter's cloud layers, Manta began to notice the angle of the rays shifting northward and their intensity fading as the three of them traveled farther and farther south. He tried to remember whether Jupiter had the kind of rotational angle that would leave one of the poles in continual darkness for part of its solar revolution, but if that aspect had been included in his Earthside training it had slipped his mind completely.

Still, the south pole had to be a hundred million sizes from the equator, a good two dayherds' journey at the steady pace they were making. Surely Gryntaro wasn't planning on taking them *that* far.

But even as the sunlight diminished, Manta also noticed that, paradoxically, the air around them seemed to be getting warmer. He'd thought he'd noticed that same effect during his northward trip, but at the time had put it down to the presence of Beltrenini and her friends, who tended to crowd closer to him than those Qanska he'd grown up among. Later, after he'd left them and was heading back home to Centerline, he'd assumed his more rapid swimming was simply warming him up.

But neither of those was the case now. Yet it was still getting warmer.

More radiation from the planetary core, perhaps? That was certainly one possibility. He knew from his conversations with McCollum that Qanskan eyes and bodies were highly efficient at utilizing the full range of the electromagnetic spectrum to see with or be warmed by, gathering everything from high frequency radio waves all the way to hard gamma radiation. He also remembered that Jupiter's rapid rotation gave it a serious equatorial bulge, which meant that as they traveled toward the poles they were at the same time moving gradually inward toward the center of the planet.

But it didn't seem like that should be enough to account for such a noticeable temperature rise. Could there be some other factor involved, then? Something artificial, perhaps, that was giving off either extra radiation or direct heat?

Like maybe a stardrive?

It was a startling thought. To even think that Latranesto and the other Counselors would casually send him off to see their most priceless secret seemed ludicrous.

But at the same time, he could also see it making perfect sense from their point of view. The Counselors and the Leaders and the Wise had presumably been told of the demand the humans had broadcast from their child trap. Even though this particular attack had been repulsed, they understood humans well enough to know that this wouldn't be the end of it. Maybe they had decided that the best course of action would be to quietly turn the device over to the humans for them to study, in the hope that they would keep their word to return it afterward.

And he couldn't forget that their last line of questioning at his trial had centered around whether he was still human. He had denied it, but it had been clear that Latranesto, at least, hadn't been convinced.

He lashed his tails in frustration. It was subtly insulting, actually, given that he'd already told them he wasn't working for the humans anymore. But more importantly, it was a bad way to do business. At the very least, Latranesto and the others should try to negotiate something for their stardrive instead of simply giving it away. Some kind of guarantee, though how that would work in practice Manta couldn't guess. And of course, giving in to extortion was never a good idea.

More than once he thought about trying to discuss the issue with Gryntaro and Wirkani. But each time he suppressed the urge to broach the subject. Clearly, Latranesto had taken pains to keep all this a secret from him, and they might not take kindly to the announcement that he'd figured it out.

Still, the very fact that he now knew what was going on sent a welcome breath of new life into the monotony of the journey. He began to pay attention to everything around him: observing the animals and plant life, studying each passing Qanska to see if it looked like it might be on guard duty, and generally watching for signs that they were getting close.

Which meant that, when the abrupt and violent end of the journey came, he was looking in exactly the wrong direction.

"How much farther are we going?" Manta asked as the three of them settled down to eat. The meal today was a new one on him: a rather spicy orange-colored plant Wirkani had identified as *cloftis*.

"What, you mean today?" Gryntaro asked, glowering as he nibbled disdainfully at one corner of the run. He had proclaimed his distaste for *cloftis* at their first sighting of the orange flow and urged that they continue on until they found something more palatable. But Wirkani had been hungry, and had insisted, and here they were. "I suppose that depends on how long we spend with this waste of air space."

"It won't be much longer," Wirkani said soothingly. "Tell me, what do you think of the *cloftis*?"

"It's not bad," Manta said, taking another bite. Wirkani seemed inordinately concerned lately with his opinion of the various new plants they were running into out here. Was she that obsessed with food, or was that simply her favorite way of changing the subject?

"It's one of my favorites," she said, taking another

mouthful. "Though of course there's no accounting for taste," she added, flipping her tails in a slightly condescending way toward Gryntaro.

"So you've been out here often?" Manta asked, probing gently. "I mean, this stuff doesn't seem to grow in Centerline."

"We've done the trip a few times," Gryntaro said, his voice suddenly and strangely cautious.

"The Counselors and the Leaders and the Wise have sent us to both the northern and southern regions on several occasions," Wirkani added more casually. "I prefer the southern, myself. The food's better."

"And of course it's warmer?" Manta suggested.

Gryntaro sent him an odd look. "Warmer?"

"Yes, warmer," Manta repeated, looking back and forth between them. He'd been expecting the comment to spark some kind of reaction, but all he could see on either of them was puzzlement. "Isn't it warmer here than in the northern regions?"

"Not that I ever noticed," Wirkani said.

"Me, neither," Gryntaro seconded.

"But it *is* warmer than in Centerline," Manta persisted. He wasn't imagining it, was he? "Right?"

"If you say so," Gryntaro said impatiently. "Look, this is getting ridiculous. Wirkani?"

"I suppose so," she said, an odd note of reluctance in her voice. "Yes, I agree."

Manta grimaced. So much for that theory. Either the stardrive wasn't responsible for the extra warmth, or the two of them were terrific actors.

Or else he *was* imagining all of it.

"Good," Gryntaro said. "You finished eating yet, Breeder?"

"Sure," Manta told him. "Let's go."

"Now, don't say that just because Gryntaro's impatient," Wirkani cautioned. "If you haven't eaten your fill, say so right now."

"No, it's okay," Manta said.

"Because you may not be eating anything more for a while," she said. "I want to make sure you're all right."

"I'm fine," Manta assured her, frowning. First questions about his taste in food, and now questions about whether he was getting enough to eat. His own mother hadn't been this solicitous. "Really. I've had plenty."

"All right," she said, her voice sounding oddly tense. Flipping her fins, she swam up and over him. Manta took one last nibble of the *cloftis*—

And gasped as, with a *whoosh* of collapsing buoyancy sacs, Wirkani dropped hard straight down on top of him.

"Hey!" he yelped, fighting not to choke as that last mouthful tried to stick in the wrong throat. "What are you doing?"

"I'm sorry, Manta," she said, her voice muffled as her body pressed down, pushing the two of them deeper into the atmosphere. "I really am."

"Come on, this isn't funny," Manta protested, wiggling back and forth and trying to get free of her, his mind flashing back to that first time Beltrenini had pulled this same stunt.

But where Beltrenini had been cheerful and casual about the whole thing, there was an edge of grim determination in Wirkani's voice that was swirling up a whirlwind of fear inside him. He wiggled harder—

"Stop squirming," Gryntaro rumbled, shoving a fin against Manta's side to hold him in place. He was sinking alongside them, helping to keep Manta in position in the hollow between Wirkani's body and fin. "You'll just make it harder on yourself."

"Make what harder?" Manta demanded. This was no Beltrenini-style food run—that much was for sure. But what in the Deep *was* it? "Come on, please. What's going on?"

But there was no answer. Only the pressure of Wirkani's body on top of his, and the stiffness of Gryntaro's fin.

They passed the lower part of Level Four and sank into Level Five. Manta continued to squirm, but the deeper they went the less effective his wiggling seemed to become.

A new plan was called for; and with a conscious effort, he forced his muscles to relax. Whatever insane plan Gryntaro and Wirkani had scooped together for him, he would do better to conserve his strength and watch for a chance to fight back. At their twelve-sizes long to his own sevensize, at least they didn't outweigh and out-size him as much as Beltrenini had.

And of course, they couldn't go as deep as the Counselor and her friends could, either. Level Five was about the limit for a Protector and Nurturer, which wasn't that much farther than a Breeder like Manta could manage. That meant that his own buoyancy wouldn't hold him as tightly in place here as it had with Beltrenini.

So, given all that, what in the Deep did they think they were going to accomplish here?

"You have him?" Gryntaro called.

"I have him," Wirkani's muffled voice confirmed. "Do it quickly, all right?"

"Sure."

Leaving Manta's side, Gryntaro swam away, curving around in a wide circle. Keeping an eye on him, Manta gave his fins one more tentative wiggle.

But Wirkani had been right. Her weight and his buoyancy were holding him pretty solidly against her.

Still, if he could distract the two of them, just for a pulse or two . . .

Gryntaro finished his circle and came to a halt facing Manta. "Manta, child of the humans, you have been examined by a triad of Counselors of the Qanska," he intoned, his gruff voice suddenly darkly official. "Under the direction and guidance of the Counselors and the Leaders and the Wise, they have passed sentence upon you."

"What are you talking about?" Manta protested, a horrible feeling starting to churn in his stomach. "What sentence?"

"It has therefore been decreed that you are to be sent into exile from Centerline Qanskan civilization," Gryntaro continued in that same voice. "You will never again be permitted—"

"Wait a ninepulse," Manta cut him off. "Please, wait. Counselor Latranesto never said anything about punishment. You were there—you heard him. He said I could go."

"Don't be a fool," Gryntaro growled. "Did you really think you would escape justice for the terrible crimes you committed against Breeder Druskani, Breeder Prantrulo, and their unborn child?"

"But I explained all that," Manta said, desperation edging into his voice. Exile? "It wasn't my fault. It really wasn't."

"The sentence has been passed," Gryntaro said, ignoring him. "It will now be carried out." Flipping the ends of his fins, he started moving forward again. Drifting around toward Manta's left, he opened his jaws—

"Wait a pulse," Manta said, shrinking back from the sight of those teeth. "Please. What are you going to do? I mean, you said exile, right? What are you going to do?"

"Gryntaro," Wirkani's muffled voice came.

"What?" the Protector asked.

"He really does have a right to know," she said. "Go ahead and tell him."

Reluctantly, Manta thought, Gryntaro stopped. "You've been exiled from Centerline," he said. "We have to make sure you won't try to come back. Therefore—" he flicked his tails over his back toward the side of Manta's head. "—I'm going to bite out your left ear."

A jolt of terror and disbelief shocked through Manta. "*What*?" he gasped.

"You'll still be able to function well enough to survive," Gryntaro continued, his voice almost obscenely calm. "But you'll find that the pressure of the winds in the open cavity will make it painful for you to swim northward for very long. Far too painful for you to ever undertake the journey back to Centerline."

"I'll stay with you long enough to make sure you're healing properly," Wirkani added. "It *will* mostly heal."

"I'll be removing the ear itself, plus all the parts of it

that lie beneath the skin," Gryntaro said. "There will be pain, and for that I apologize. But I know what I'm doing, and I'll be as quick and clean as possible."

Manta was having trouble breathing. "You don't have to do this," he pleaded, his teeth chattering uncontrollably. "I won't come back. I promise."

"It'll be easier if you hold still," Gryntaro said, beginning to drift forward again. "If you squirm, I'll only wind up biting off more than I have to." He opened his mouth, his breath warm on the side of Manta's head.

From the depths beneath them, something flashed suddenly into view. Manta caught just a glimpse of rapid movement as the jaws opened wide beside him—

And with a grunt of pain, Gryntaro jerked and doubled over as a blur of color slammed up hard into his belly, catching him squarely in the lungs. The Protector rolled half over onto his side, fin tips twitching as he gasped for breath.

Manta gaped in astonishment. But before he could do anything more than that, the blur slid deftly past Gryntaro's bulk and continued upward. There was the whistling hiss of something slashing across Wukail's skin, and her shrill scream of pain joined in with Gryntaro's deeper wheezing. The Nurturer tilted to the side—

And with a hard twist the opposite direction, Manta rolled out from underneath her, popping out and bouncing upward like a baby being ejected from its mother's womb. Stretching out his buoyancy sacs, he headed as fast as he could for the upper levels.

Above him, his rescuer was similarly moving upward, and Manta could see those lumpy and distended fins rippling as he added a horizontal component to his upward movement. Manta tried to do likewise, but his muscles were still trembling too much from residual panic for him to get them moving. He continued to rise, watching as the other slowly began to leave him behind.

Abruptly, the rescuer seemed to notice the widening gap. With a smooth twist of his body and tails, he abandoned his forward motion and curved back around toward Manta.

"Well, come on," he called. "You want to stick around here all sundark?"

A very familiar voice; and for the second time that terrible day, Manta felt his throats tighten in surprise and uncertainty and fear.

It was Pranlo.

They swam the rest of the day together in silence, pushing themselves to the limit as they tried to put as much distance as possible between them and Manta's erstwhile companions. Keeping quiet seemed only prudent; and for his part, Manta didn't have any extra lung power to spare for conversation anyway.

He could only hope Pranlo's silence was for the same reasons.

They swam until sundark, and a little ways beyond it. Only then, finally, did Pranlo signal a halt.

"Whew!" he said, breathing hard as the two of them coasted to a stop in the buffeting winds. "I haven't had a swim like that in dayherds. Nice to know I can still do it. How about you? You okay?"

"I'm a little winded," Manta admitted, feeling nervous and awkward and fearful as he faced the other. "My fins are probably going to hurt in the sunlight."

"Hopefully not as much as those new friends of yours are going to hurt," Pranlo said, his voice sounding rather grimly satisfied. Maybe he was feeling awkward, too. "I was trying to catch that Nurturer's eye with my tails as I went past. Don't know if I got her or not."

"You definitely got Gryntaro square in the lungs," Manta said, trying hard to pretend this was just a casual conversation between two friends. "I tried that trick on a couple of Vuuka once. Works pretty good."

"Wish I could have seen their expressions," Pranlo said, moving in for a closer look at Manta's left ear. "He didn't get you, did he?"

"No, you were just in time," Manta assured him, wishing

he could read the other's face. There seemed to be more background light here than he remembered from a typical Centerline sundark, but it wasn't nearly enough for him to figure out what Pranlo might be thinking.

Odd that he hadn't noticed the brighter sundarks before during this trip. But then, the way Gryntaro had pushed them, he was usually fast asleep by this time of sundark.

"Yeah, it looks fine," Pranlo confirmed, drifting back again. "Good thing, too. I'd hate to have followed you all this way and then wound up being a couple of pulses too late. Drusni would never have let me hear the end of it."

Manta's heart twisted painfully inside him. Drusni. "Is she . . . I mean . . . ?"

"She's fine," Pranlo said. "She was still weak when I left, but the Nurturers assured me she was out of danger. She's probably mostly healed by now."

"At least physically," Manta murmured. "Pranlo . . . I . . ."

"It's all right," Pranlo said softly. "Drusni told me what happened."

Manta winced. "All of it?"

"All of it," the other said. "Like I said, it's all right."

Manta turned away from him. Even in the dim light, he couldn't stand to look his friend in the eye. "It's not all right," he said, the words hurting his throats. "What I did was . . . I can't even find the right words for it."

He flipped his tails restlessly. "I've been thinking about it ever since it happened," he went on, wondering if Pranlo was understanding any of this. "All my life, anything bad that happened to me was never my fault. At least, not as far as I was concerned. It was always someone else's fault, or even the whole universe's fault. Never mine."

"But this one *wasn't* your fault," Pranlo pointed out.

"Ironic, isn't it?" Manta said, grimacing. "For once in my life, I really *didn't* have anything to do with it; and so, of course, *this* is the one I feel worse about than all the rest of my screw-ups put together."

He sighed "And this is the one I can't ever make right."

"Not to mention the one you were going to be punished for," Pranlo pointed out.

Manta shivered, thinking about what had almost happened to him.

What still *would* happen if they ever caught up with him again.

Pranlo was apparently thinking the same thing. "We'll have to be careful, of course," he said. "They'll be on the watch for us as soon as those two get back to Centerline and whistle up the alarm."

"They'll be watching for me, anyway," Manta said. "With luck, you went by too fast for them to be able to identify you."

"Probably," Pranlo said dryly. "But if they catch us together, they shouldn't have any trouble figuring it out."

"We'll just have to make sure they don't, then," Manta said, suddenly making up his mind. "Do you want me to leave now? Or should I wait until sunlight in case we get jumped by predators—"

"Whoa, whoa," Pranlo interrupted. "Wait a pulse. What's this leaving stuff? We're going back to Centerline together, aren't we?"

"We most certainly are not," Manta said firmly. "Like you said, if they catch you with me, you've had it. Besides, I've been exiled. I can't go back."

Pranlo flipped his tails in contempt. "To the Deep with that," he said, just as firmly. "Hey, swimming circles around authority is one of the things you and I do best, remember? We can keep you hidden, even in Centerline. Besides, Drusni wants to see you, and I sure don't want to bring her way out here."

Manta's heart twisted a little more. "Drusni doesn't want to see me," he said. "Not after what I . . ."

"She knows what you did," Pranlo reminded him. "She also knows something you seem to have forgotten: that it was her idea in the first place. *And* that it saved the lives of a whole bunch of children."

"Yeah, right," Manta said bitterly. "And all it cost was

her dignity, her self-esteem, and her child. Yeah, that was sure worth it."

"She knew the risks at the time," Pranlo said quietly. "And she was ready to pay whatever it cost."

"But her own *baby?*"

"We had two other children swimming in that herd, you know," Pranlo said tartly. "A Midling and a Youth. They might have been grabbed on that machine's next pass."

"So she did it for her children?" Manta asked.

"Partly," Pranlo said. "And partly to help the children who'd already been caught."

He flipped his tails. "But the biggest reason she did it was for you."

Manta felt his muscles tense. "For me?"

"You were as much a captive of the humans as the children were," Pranlo said. "She knew that. I really think that for that alone she would have paid the price, even if there hadn't been any children involved. She was willing to do whatever it took to set you free."

"No," Manta said, tails twitching in agitation. "That can't be."

"Okay, fine," Pranlo said calmly. "So which one of us are you calling a liar? Her, or me?"

Manta clenched his jaws. "I'm not calling anyone a liar," he said. "I'm suggesting you're bending the truth to be kind. Trying to make me think that she doesn't . . . that she doesn't hate me."

"*Hate* you?" Pranlo gave a little snort. "Listen, you big striped idiot. Who do you think sent me out here to keep an eye on you in the first place? My mother?"

Manta swiveled around to stare at him, not daring to believe it. "You mean she really doesn't . . . ?"

"We're friends, Manta," Pranlo said quietly. "All three of us. Always have been; always will be. It'll take a lot more than getting caught up in some Pakra-scorned human scheme to change that."

Manta swallowed hard. "The Three Musketta, huh?"

"Exactly." Pranlo yawned. "And right now, at least one

of the Musketta needs to get some sleep. How about you?"

"Definitely," Manta said. "One last question, though. How did you manage that trick where you came up from underneath Gryntaro to ram him in the lungs?"

"What do you mean, how did I manage it?" Pranlo said, suddenly sounding very sleepy. "I just swam underneath him, then stretched my buoyancy sacs. It seemed like the direction he would least expect an attack from."

"Yes, but how did you *do* it?" Manta persisted. "We're Breeders, and Breeders aren't supposed to be able to get below Level Four."

Pranlo yawned. "Kind of a mystery, isn't it? I saw what they were going to do, figured out what I had to do to stop them, and then just swam my little fins off doing it. I guess I was just inspired."

Manta made a face. "Willing to do whatever it took to set me free?"

"Something like that," Pranlo said. "Like one bond-mate, like the other, as the saying goes. Or maybe there's something about Drusni that just sort of rubs off on everyone she meets."

"Yes," Manta murmured. "There certainly is."

"Still, you know me," Pranlo added; and in the darkness, Manta could imagine him grinning. "Tweaking authority figures is a hobby of mine anyway."

"Ah," Manta said. "So in other words, you weren't so much interested in saving my skin as you were in having some fun?"

"I don't think I'd put it *quite* that way," Pranlo said blandly. "But hey, like I always say, saving a friend's ear and having fun is better than just saving a friend's ear."

"Interesting behavioral guideline," Manta commented.

"It's a little limited in application, but I like it," Pranlo said. "See you in the sunlight, Manta. Sleep well."

Manta took a deep breath, exhaled it in a quiet, almost peaceful sigh. "Sure," he said.

And for the first time since that horrible incident with Drusni, maybe he actually would.

TWENTY-THREE

"As seems to be traditional in these cases," Hesse said as he settled into Faraday's desk chair, "I've got some good news, and some bad news."

"I think the fact that you're here at all probably qualifies as good news," Faraday commented. "It's been almost a month since you last dropped by, you know. I'd just about concluded that Liadof had gotten you shipped back to Earth with the rest of Alpha Shift."

"Actually, the disposition of Alpha Shift is the good news," Hesse said. "After some long and rather serious conversations, my backers in the Five Hundred have convinced Arbiter Liadof to keep them here on Prime for the time being."

"Good," Faraday said. "But they're still under arrest?"

"Well, sort of," Hesse said, his forehead creasing a little. "I know they've been moved out of the brig back to their quarters. I think it's the same kind of house arrest that you're under."

"Have they been formally charged?"

"I don't know," Hesse said. "I don't think so."

"Then how are they being held?" Faraday persisted. "There's a statutory limit as to how long you can hold a prisoner without a formal charge and arraignment."

"Yes, I know," Hesse said. "I think Liadof's gotten around that by putting them on confined suspension of duty, or some such."

"Never heard of it," Faraday rumbled. "Sounds phony."

"Probably is," Hesse agreed. "But you have to look at

the bright side. As long as they're not charged, we've got the chance to return their lives and careers to them without anything at all showing up on their official records."

"Meanwhile, they're on forced solitude," Faraday countered. "And without a trial, they'll also never have the chance to clear their names."

"I just said they wouldn't have any marks on their records," Hesse reminded him.

Faraday snorted. "You ever hear of a rumor mill that cared a damn about official records?"

"No, I guess not," Hesse conceded. "I'm sorry, but this was the best I could do."

Faraday waved a hand in resignation, let it fall back into his lap. "If it's the best you could do, then it was the best you could do," he said. "I suppose it could be worse. You said that was the good news?"

"Yes," Hesse said, grimacing. "The bad news is that the faction I represent has lost some of its support in the Five Hundred. That means Liadof and her side have pulled back from the brink, and are reasonably firmly in power again."

Faraday shook his head. "I told you," he said, the words tasting bitter. "Another midsummer cold front. So what's her next move?"

Hesse hesitated. "I'm not really sure," he said. "There are hints and rumors, but she's playing this one very close to the table. What I *do* know is that she's been having discussions with some of the top Sol/Guard generals. And not just about the Mars protests, either."

An icy chill rolled up along Faraday's back. "She's not considering general martial law, is she?"

"I'm sure she wouldn't do that," Hesse said hastily. "At least, I don't *think* she would," he amended more slowly. "On the other hand . . . no. No, that's crazy."

"Your people on Earth better keep an eye on it," Faraday warned, the cold feeling diminishing but not going away. Just how far was this woman willing to go, anyway?

"I'm sure they are," Hesse promised. "But just to be on

the safe side, I'll remind them about it this afternoon when I call."

"Good," Faraday said. "I'd hate to wake up some morning and find out the whole System had been betrayed. Especially by people who have been so loud in the past about how much they revere it."

Something like a shadow passed across Hesse's face. "Yeah," he said quietly. "I know what you mean."

"So," Faraday said. "The rest of Alpha Shift locked in their rooms, Liadof in power, and Sol/Guard being dragged into deep political conversations. Anything else?"

Hesse shook his head, seeming to shake off some odd mood at the same time. "No, that's about it. I'm sorry the news couldn't have been better."

"I understand," Faraday said. "I know these political maneuverings can take time. How is Mr. Beach?"

"Mr. Beach?" Hesse echoed, blinking. "He's fine, as far as I know."

"Is he still with Alpha Shift?"

"I think so," Hesse said. "There's been some shuffling around to fill all the gaps, but I think he's still running Alpha's communications."

"You say 'all the gaps,' " Faraday pointed out. "More than just the three from Alpha Shift?"

"Quite a few more," Hesse conceded. "It seems some of the members of Beta and Gamma Shifts took exception to you being 'removed from active participation,' I think is how Liadof put it. Five of the eight expressed their displeasure firmly enough that they were kicked out into house arrest, too."

"Good for them," Faraday said, smiling tightly. So out of the twelve original Contact Room personnel, only Beach and three others were still working for Liadof. She must be spitting twist fasteners over this one. "I'll bet that put some lumps in her gravy."

"She wasn't fit to be near for two days," Hesse said candidly. "But she's brought in some of her own people since then, and they seem to be coming up to speed reasonably well."

"Maybe, but I'll bet they're not ramping up as well as she thinks they are," Faraday pointed out. "You don't pick up the subtleties of Qanskan language and sociology overnight."

"True," Hesse said. "Though the computer's getting pretty good at sorting out the language stuff, at least."

"What about Manta? Any news?"

"None," Hesse said. "The spy probe's still following the herd, and Mr. Raimey hasn't shown up there since his trial. There *has* been a fair amount of conversation among the Qanska about the Omega Probe, but it's mostly a rehash of what happened. If any word has come up from the lower levels regarding the Leaders' reaction or intentions, we haven't heard about it."

Faraday nodded. "And nothing about Pranlo or Drusni either, I suppose?"

"No," Hesse said. "Near as we can tell, Drusni's still off recovering in seclusion. No one's seen Pranlo swimming with the herd lately, so we assume he's with her."

"What about their children?"

"The other Breeders and Protectors are watching them." Hesse's lip twitched. "I don't know if it's significant, but I should probably also tell you that Liadof's been making an effort lately to identify exactly which of the children are theirs."

Faraday felt his eyes narrow. "What for?"

"I'm not sure," Hesse said. "But I know she's decided that Drusni is partially to blame for Omega's failure."

"You think she's planning some sort of revenge?"

Hesse shifted uncomfortably in his seat. "Not revenge, exactly," he said slowly. "I don't think revenge is ever her primary goal in anything. But she's certainly got an agenda, and I think she'd plow through pretty much anyone to achieve it."

"As we've already seen," Faraday agreed darkly.

"We have?" Hesse asked, frowning.

"Sure," Faraday said. "McCollum, Sprenkle, Milligan, and the other techs. And me."

Hesse's face cleared. "Oh. Right. I thought you were talking about what she's probably been doing in the Five Hundred, and I wondered how you could possibly know what's been going on back there."

"Yes, I imagine there will be a lot of careers made and broken over this," Faraday said, nodding. "Was there anything else?"

"Nothing I can think of," Hesse said, standing up. "I'll see what we can find out about what Liadof is up to, and get a reading on the current balance of power in the Five Hundred. Oh, and I'll also confirm that all the techs are actually under house arrest and not in the brig."

"Thank you," Faraday said. "I'd appreciate it if you would do what you can to make sure they're as comfortable as possible."

"I'll do that," Hesse promised.

"And see what you can find out about Manta," Faraday added. "I don't like us losing track of him this way."

Hesse shrugged. "Me, neither," he said. "On the other hand, his subvocalization setup should still be functional. If he ever wants to talk to us, he knows how to do it."

"Only if we've got a probe close enough to relay the signal," Faraday reminded him.

"Oh," Hesse said with a grimace. "Right. Well . . . maybe we can put a few more high-atmosphere probes into service."

"You do that," Faraday said. "And while you're at it, try nudging your backers to insist to Liadof that we locate him."

"I'll try," Hesse said doubtfully. "But frankly, I don't think anybody much cares about him anymore. Events have passed him by, and I don't think he's likely to be much more of a player in any of this."

Faraday smiled tightly. "Never assume, Mr. Hesse," he said. "Never assume."

The run of dark-purple *kachtis* floated serenely along, holding stubbornly together in large clumps against the moderate winds of Level Two. Manta floated alongside one of the larger clumps, the sight and smell of it evoking childhood memories. Peaceful memories, for the most part, in stark contrast to the nervousness ripping like a hungry Vuuka through his soul.

Drusni was coming.

Why Pranlo had chosen this spot for their meeting Manta didn't know. Probably because the *kachtis* made for a good rendezvous point, a place where he could wait for a day or two if necessary and yet the others would still be able to locate him.

Of course, the other side of that was that a run this rich would normally be swarming with children, their parents, and their Protectors. Why this one wasn't was anyone else's guess.

Or maybe not. Manta had already spotted three Vuuka swimming slowly around in the distance. Clearly, the predators had also figured out that this run would be a good spot to pick up a quick meal, and had therefore staked it out.

So far they had shown remarkable patience, continuing their circling without making any attempt to come closer. But Manta knew that sooner or later they would decide there were no children coming and that they might as well try their luck with a Breeder.

And that point might arrive when Drusni did. If she still looked even marginally impaired, they would probably be on her in a pulse.

He set his jaw firmly. Let them try. If they made as much as a single move toward her, he would personally beat the fins off each and every one of them. Taking slow, deep breaths, he tried to relax.

"Manta?"

And then, suddenly, there she was, swimming a little

stiffly toward him at Pranlo's side. Manta threw one last cautioning look at the Vuuka, and swam forward to meet them. Wondering what in the world he was going to say to her.

But the painful awkwardness he feared never even got started. Drusni saw to that. "Manta, it's so good to see you," she said warmly as they came together. "Pranlo told me a little of what happened. Are you all right?"

"I'm fine," Manta assured her. "Thanks to Pranlo, anyway." He reached a fin toward her; hesitated—

She must have noticed his sudden uncertainty. Stretching out with her own fin, she gave his a gentle stroke. "I'm glad he was there when you needed him," she said. "You were certainly there when we needed you."

"Was I?" Manta murmured, the fear and guilt rising in his throats like the taste of blood.

She touched his fin again. "Yes," she repeated, more firmly this time. "You saved all of us. *All* of us."

Cautiously, afraid to do so but unable to look away, Manta gazed into her eyes. And slowly he realized something he'd somehow missed during the tension and turmoil of their last frantic meeting.

The Drusni he'd grown up with no longer existed. Somehow, while he wasn't paying attention, the clumsy, exuberant, fragile, giddy Youth he'd known had matured into a quieter, stronger, more confident Breeder.

Strong enough to handle the terrible experience he'd inflicted on her. Confident enough to know she could repair any damage that experience might do to her relationships with those she loved.

And honest enough, he realized suddenly, not to lie to him merely out of fear for his feelings. If she said she could handle what had happened, he could trust that she could.

He took a deep breath, feeling the weight of guilt and fear beginning to drain from his heart. Yes, he would always carry a measure of pain over what had happened. But never again would it be the kind of debilitating horror that would hover like a line of Vuuka between them. Whatever needed to be worked through, they would work through it together.

The way friends should.

"Pranlo tells me you're doing better, too," he said. "What can I do to help?"

She smiled, some of that younger, grinning Youth peeking through. "You could try to stay out of trouble for a while," she suggested. "It seems like you're always going down to Level Four for long conversations with some Counselor or another. It's getting to be a really bad habit."

"Actually, so far it's always been Counselor Latranesto," Manta said, striving to match her tone. "I think maybe he's been assigned to me permanently."

"Wow," Pranlo said solemnly. "First your own private Protector, now your own private Counselor. We're mixing with greatness here, Drusni."

"Absolutely," she agreed, laughing. A mature laugh, but again with some of the youthful giggling beneath the surface.

"And don't either of you forget it," Manta said, mock-severely. "So let's have a little respect—"

He broke off. Directly ahead, swimming into view around the far end of the *kachtis* run, were three Protectors.

Moving slowly in their direction.

"Take it easy," Pranlo said quietly, drifting up beside Manta where he would block the Protectors' view of his markings. "It's not like we're on Level One or something. We're allowed to be here."

"But they're coming toward us," Manta pointed out tensely.

"Relax," Pranlo insisted. "Come on—they can't possibly be looking for you yet. They're probably just checking out the *kachtis* run for some nearby herd."

"But we should still leave," Drusni said, nudging up beside Manta. "Nice and easy . . ."

Casually, trying not to make it look too obvious, they began to swim away, sinking slowly down toward Level Three as they went. Pranlo and Drusni stayed between

Manta and the Protectors, taking a bite out of the edge and underside of the run every so often to make it look as if the three of them had just finished a meal.

They had cleared the end of the *kachtis*, and Manta was starting to breathe again, when four more Protectors suddenly dropped in on top of them from inside the run.

The Protectors escorted them down to Level Four, a route Manta had grown painfully familiar with. At the end of the journey, to his complete lack of surprise, Latranesto was waiting.

What *was* surprising was the fact that the Counselor was all alone.

They settled in front of him, and for a ninepulse Latranesto eyed them in silence. Then, with a flip of his tails, he gestured to the four Protectors. "Leave us," he ordered.

Silently, they obeyed. Latranesto watched until they were out of sight. Then, he turned his full stare onto Manta. "Well, Manta," he rumbled. "What exactly are we going to do with you?"

"What happened with the human machine wasn't his fault." Drusni spoke up defiantly before Manta could find an answer. "If the Counselors and the Leaders and the Wise had listened to all the testimony—"

"Peace, Breeder Druskani," Latranesto cut her off, his eyes flashing briefly in her direction. "The Counselors and the Leaders and the Wise *have* listened to all the testimony of that incident. *And* we have considered many facts and thoughts and concerns that you are unfamiliar with. You will therefore remain silent, and you will listen."

Drusni flicked her tails, but obediently closed her mouth. "There's no reason for them to be here, Counselor Latranesto," Manta said, putting all the quiet persuasion into his voice that he could manage. "I'm the one who's been condemned. They're not guilty of any crime."

"Aren't they?" Latranesto countered pointedly. "Interfering in a legal judgment? Helping a Qanska escape proper punishment? Attacking a Protector and a Nurturer of the Qanska—?"

"Wait a pulse," Pranlo cut in, sounding thoroughly puzzled. "How could you know about that? They couldn't have swum *that* much faster than we did."

"There was no need," Latranesto told him. "There is a way of speaking that is available only to the Wise who swim through Level Eight. They can thump their bellies with their fins, making sounds that travel a great distance. Those who reach that age and size are taught a code through which they can send any message they wish, to anyone else on Level Eight."

"But Protectors and Nurturers can't reach Level Eight," Pranlo said, sounding even more puzzled.

"They don't have to," Manta told him. So the Qanska had their own version of a jungle-drum telegraph system. One more handy little tidbit the humans didn't know about. "They can reach a Counselor on Level Four, who can reach a Leader on Five, who can reach one of the Wise on Six or Seven. He then drops to Level Eight and sends the message, which is relayed as many times as necessary and then sent back up the levels to Counselor Latranesto."

"You understand such things," Latranesto commented approvingly. "And you understand them quickly. That is most gratifying."

"I understand some things, anyway," Manta said. "What I don't see, though, is what's so special about Level Eight. And why haven't I ever heard this thumping before? Surely the sound doesn't travel *only* on Level Eight."

"But it does," Latranesto said. "Only those of the Wise who are on Level Eight at the time will hear it."

Manta flipped his tails, conceding the point. It was something esoteric about the physics of that level, no doubt. Possibly something having to do with the radiation or magnetic fields down there. With his business major background, he probably wouldn't be able to figure it out even if Latranesto laid all the facts out for him.

Even if Latranesto *knew* all the facts, which he probably

didn't. "I'll take your word for it," he said. "We'll have a longer conversation about it someday."

"Yes," Latranesto murmured. "And not only do you understand many things, but you question and gnaw at those you do not. Such curiosity is one of the chief traits of you and your human brothers."

Manta set his jaw. "The humans aren't my brothers," he declared firmly. "Not anymore. Whatever claims they might have had on my loyalty and service were lost forever when they launched that unprovoked attack on Qanskan children."

He straightened himself out to his full length. "I'm a Qanska, Counselor Latranesto. Now, and forever."

The defiant words faded into the silence of the whistling wind. "Perhaps," Latranesto said at last. If he was impressed by Manta's ringing declaration, it didn't show in his voice or expression. "Many of the Counselors and the Leaders and the Wise agree. Many others do not."

"Then they're wrong," Drusni said. "I know, better than anyone."

Latranesto's tails twitched. "Perhaps," he said. "Or perhaps your eyes are dimmed by friendship and hope."

"Eyes are never dimmed by friendship, Counselor Latranesto," Manta said quietly. "Friendship, love, and loyalty are what enable the eyes and heart to see better."

"Many others do not agree," Latranesto said again. "That was the reason this grand idea was abandoned and you were condemned to exile. Some believe you will always be human in heart and mind, and will forever serve as their agent."

"And I've told you that I won't," Manta repeated. "I wish I knew a way I could prove it to you."

"Do you?" Latranesto countered. "Do you really?"

Manta felt his breath catch in his throats. There had been something in the way the Counselor had said that. . . .
"Yes," he said. "Tell me how."

For another ninepulse Latranesto hesitated. Then, his eyes drifted off into the distance. "Allow me to remember in your presence," he said. "Do you know what first attracted the Qanska to your people, Manta?"

Manta grimaced. "I thought it was you running into Chippawa and Faraday's tether line."

"No," Latranesto said, his tails undulating slowly in deep memory. "It was afterwards, after the Leaders and the Wise had examined them and sent them back to Level One. Our plan was for one of the Protectors to break the skin of the Counselor who carried them, drawing some of her blood. The Vuuka who responded would, we hoped, tear away the rest of the skin that covered their machine and permit them to escape."

Manta thought back over the history of that voyage. "It worked, too," he said.

"Yes," Latranesto said. "And if that had been all that happened, we might never have opened a conversation with your people.

"But it wasn't all. What caught our attention was that the humans inside had already created a plan of their own. It was a method that used a power we had never seen before."

"Fire," Manta murmured.

"That was the word," Latranesto confirmed. "The machine had already shown your people were a race who had methods and abilities far beyond ours."

His eyes suddenly focused on Manta again. "What the plan and the fire showed was that you were a race of problem-solvers."

Manta felt something prickling across his skin. *Problem-solvers?* "Are you telling me," he asked carefully, "that you have a problem?"

"A very serious problem, Breeder Manta," Latranesto said solemnly. "One which the Counselors and the Leaders and the Wise have decided must not be revealed to you."

"I see," Manta murmured. "But you're going to tell me anyway?"

Latranesto twitched his tails. "I am placing my own life between your teeth," he said, his voice heavy with reluctance. "You see, you swim between two opposing winds, Breeder Manta. There are those of the Counselors and the Leaders and the Wise who believe you have become truly Qanskan, and have lost all your human abilities. They believe you can't help us. In the other wind are those who believe that you are still human, and that you therefore remain a threat to the Qanska. They believe you *won't* help us. Both sides thus agree that you must never know the true reason you were asked to come into our world."

"And what about you?" Manta asked. "What do *you* believe?"

"I believe that you are a unique creature," Latranesto said. "That your loyalties have become Qanskan, but at the same time your mind and abilities remain human."

He lashed his tails again. "And I am prepared to risk my own life on that belief. For if it is revealed that I told you, your same punishment will also fall upon me. Or perhaps something worse."

"I understand," Manta said, a bad feeling beginning to wrap itself around his throats. What in the world could be happening here that would be this serious? "I'll do everything I can to help."

"What's the problem?" Pranlo asked.

Latranesto sent him a startled look, as if his swim through the past had made him forget that he and Manta weren't alone. For a pulse Manta thought he might order the other two away; but with a twitch of his tail, he merely turned back to Manta. Perhaps he realized he'd already said too much. "It's our world, Breeder Manta," he said, waving his fins to encompass the air around them. "Our entire world."

"What's wrong with it?" Manta asked.

Latranesto seemed to sigh. "It's dying."

TWENTY-FOUR

Drusni gave a little gasp. "Dying?" Pranlo demanded. "What do you mean?"

"I mean that the ancient pattern has returned," Latranesto said solemnly. "The pattern that has followed us to every new world we've ever found."

Manta's heartpulse sped up with reflexive excitement. *Every new world* . . . "Then it *is* true," he said. "You *did* come from somewhere else, as the humans believe. How long have you been here?"

"Not very long," Latranesto said. "Perhaps twenty-two Qanskan lifetimes. One hundred and seventy suncycles, as the world counts the passage of time."

"A hundred and seventy suncycles," Manta murmured, savoring the irony of it. A hundred and seventy Jovian years. Two thousand years, in Earth measurement.

Yet Faraday's argument for a Qanskan stardrive had been based on the fact that none of Earth's probes had ever spotted a Qanska until his own fateful *Skydiver* expedition. The humans had reached the correct conclusion, but for a completely wrong reason. "That's a pretty good stretch," he said.

"Perhaps as the humans count time," Latranesto said. "Within the span of Qanskan history, it's not much more than a nineday."

Manta thought back to the long and sometimes boring story circle sessions, where the history of the Qanska had been passed on to the new children in the herd. If their life here was just a nineday, the storytellers had clearly hit only the high points. "Tell me about this ancient pattern," he said. "How does it work?"

"It begins when the Wise arrive at their new world," Latranesto said. "They begin to populate, as do all who have come alongside them. And for perhaps the first twenty lifetimes all goes as it should."

He lashed his tails restlessly. "But then the life pattern begins to change. Food plants disappear from the Centerline, as do some of the smaller animals. Small predators, cousins of the Sivra, die or go away. One day, the Brolka vanish from the birth pattern."

Manta flicked his own tails, remembering the differences in flora and fauna he'd observed in the northern and southern regions. "And it always starts in Centerline? In every world you've come to?"

Latranesto hesitated. "I don't know how it's been on other worlds," he admitted. "But in this place, and at this time, it has certainly happened that way."

"There are still Brolka being born in the outer regions," Manta pointed out. "I've seen them."

"So have I," Latranesto said. "But that gives no comfort. Once the pattern has started, we know of no way to stop it. The balance fails, and the fading of life continues. Eventually, many suncycles from now, the ancient pattern will encompass the entire world."

"And then?" Drusni asked quietly.

"Then all who are still alive on that dayherd will slowly die," Latranesto said sadly. "All except those who are able to make the journey to another world. But though they may leave, the ancient pattern will follow them."

"And this has been going on for how long?" Manta asked.

"As long as the story circle of the Qanska can remember," Latranesto said. "A very long time."

"I see," Manta said quietly. In his mind's eye he could see a long line of Qanska stretching into the misty past, and another stretching forward into the future. All of them trying to escape the leisurely curse haunting their race.

All of them failing.

"What else do you know about it?" he asked.

"I can list for you the details of the pattern, and the order in which the plant and animal vanishings occur," Latranesto told him. "We know them all too well. But what it all means, or why it happens, I can't tell you."

He flicked his tails at Manta. "You are a problem-solver, Manta, born of a race of problem-solvers. I plead with you on behalf of the Qanskan people. Can you find an answer to this problem?"

"Wow," Pranlo said under his breath. "Nothing like starting out snout to teeth with the biggest Vuuka swimming. You couldn't give him a simpler problem to warm up with?"

"This is why he's here, Breeder Prantrulo," Latranesto said, sounding annoyed at the other's levity. "The only reason. After the first human machine escaped, and for nearly a suncycle afterward, the Counselors and the Leaders and the Wise argued and discussed the possibility of asking the humans for help."

"Why didn't you?" Manta asked.

"Because we didn't trust them with the knowledge of our weakness," Latranesto said. "And, I might add, the events of a few ninedays ago seem to have justified that decision."

Manta grimaced. "No argument there."

"What we needed was someone who could understand our people," Latranesto went on. "We had combined once before with an alien species, so we knew it could be done. The Counselors and the Leaders and the Wise therefore decided to invite a human to join us, in the hope that he would learn to care enough for us to be willing to help."

"I see," Manta said, trying to decide how he felt about this sudden revelation. So there had been no altruism involved; no pure scientific curiosity, no simple desire for cultural exchange. Right from the very start this had been a grand scheme by the Qanska to use him.

But then, he could hardly blame them. Besides which, it wasn't any different in principle than the game the humans had been playing. "All right," he said. "This kind of problem is a little out of my area of expertise, but I'll give it a try."

"You must do more than just try," Latranesto insisted. "You must succeed. And you must succeed quickly."

"What's the rush?" Manta asked, frowning. "I thought you said we had hundreds of suncycles before things got serious."

"We and our world have time, yes," Latranesto agreed, his voice suddenly ominous. "But you yourself do not. You've refused the judgment of the Counselors and the Leaders and the Wise, and you've defied and attacked the Protector and Nurturer assigned to carry out that judgment. Unless you redeem yourself by finding a solution to the ancient pattern, there will be no way for me to protect you from the consequences of those actions."

Manta winced. He should have seen this one coming. "So I'm on my own."

"We're both on our own," Latranesto corrected tightly. "I've stretched my fins to the limit on your behalf, Manta. My own future faces the same Vuukan jaws that yours does."

Manta lashed his tails in a heavy nod. "I understand," he said. "I'll do my best."

Latranesto seemed about to say something, but then merely flicked his tails. "Of course," he said. "That's all I can ask or expect. Do you wish the details of the vanishings?"

Manta hesitated. "Not right now," he said. "I know the general pattern. That should be enough to get started on. If I need more details, I can always get them from you later."

Which, if not technically a lie, wasn't exactly the whole truth, either. The details could very well be vitally important; but only to someone who actually knew what in the Deep he was doing. Given Manta's own awesome lack of knowledge about ecological science, if he couldn't get the drift of this thing from the generalities, all the specifics in the world weren't going to do him a single bite of good.

"Very well," Latranesto said. "If you decide you need more information, just come back here. I'll stay in this area for the next eighteen ninedays."

"Understood," Manta said. "How should I contact you? Will I need to find a Protector to take you a message?"

"Absolutely not," Latranesto insisted. "You must stay away from everyone, especially Protectors. No, I'll come up to Level Four a short time before sundark every day in case you've returned."

"That should work," Manta agreed. "Next question: what about Pranlo and Drusni? Are they in the same trouble you and I are?"

Latranesto grunted something under his breath as he turned to look at the other two Breeders, holding position quietly off to the side. "The message from Gryntaro and Wirkani did not identify them," he said. "It was only because I knew your history that I suspected Breeder Prantrulo was the one involved in your escape. That's why I had my Protectors watching Breeder Druskani."

"Ah," Manta said. "I'd wondered how you found us so fast."

"If you go now, the two of you can leave in peace," Latranesto told them. "But beware. If you're caught in Manta's presence again, there will be consequences for you both."

He flicked his tails. "And as with him, there will be nothing I can do to protect you."

"We understand," Pranlo said. "Thank you."

"And don't worry," Drusni added. "If there's a solution to this problem, Manta will find it."

With an effort, Manta held his tongue. He didn't have even a ninth of Drusni's confidence in his problem-solving abilities. But there was no point in deflating her buoyancy.

"Then go," Latranesto said gravely. "The next time we meet, may you bring me good news."

"That would be nice for a change, wouldn't it?" Manta admitted. "Ever since I got here, it seems I've been a straight run of trouble for you."

"Yet you will fulfill the hopes of those who brought you here," Latranesto said quietly. "I, too, have that trust."

Manta took a deep breath. "I'll do my best," he promised again. "Farewell."

He swiveled to face Pranlo and Drusni. "And thank you," he said. "For everything. I'll be back as soon as I can." Not daring to wait for their response, he flipped around and swam away.

Pranlo had been right, he told himself grimly as he turned his right ear into the wind and headed south. A devastating curse that had defied the best Qanskan thinkers throughout their long history; and *this* was the problem they were expecting him to solve? This wasn't just the biggest Vuuka swimming; this was all the Vuuka on Jupiter lined up in a row, waiting to take a crack at him.

He had no idea how to begin. None whatsoever. Clouds above and the Deep below, he'd studied business in school. *Business.* Profit and loss, inflow and outflow, pluses and minuses, sales and bargaining and corporate design. About the only things he knew about ecological disasters were the costs involved in preventing them and how to structure the financial losses that ensued if they happened anyway.

The humans up there on the station might be able to take a crack at it. Faraday and the others had access to information and expertise he couldn't hope to come up with down here. Maybe he should give them a call and see if they would be willing to chew it over.

He flipped his tails viciously. No. Not until he had some idea what the trouble was. Any beings who would swim so crookedly as to try to hold children for ransom could just as easily sell the Qanska a useless bill of goods. Without some idea of where the source of the problem lay, the Qanska would have no way of knowing if the humans were being honest with them or not.

Which unfortunately circled him right back to his original question. How in the Deep was he supposed to begin?

He was still turning the problem over in his mind, trying to get a tooth-hold on it, when he suddenly noticed that

Pranlo and Drusni were swimming quietly alongside him.

"What are you two doing here?" he asked, frowning as he coasted to a halt.

"What does it look like we're doing?" Pranlo answered. "We're coming with you. So you think the answer lies in the southern regions?"

"Wait a pulse; wait just a Vuuka-mangled pulse," Manta growled. "Let's get something straight right now. You two are in the clear. You can go back to Centerline and your children and pick up your lives where they were before all this other mess happened. So go do it."

Drusni looked over at Pranlo. "He doesn't learn very fast, does he?" she commented.

"You do have to wonder sometimes," Pranlo agreed. "*I* remember us saying something about friendship. You?"

"Me, too," Drusni said, flipping her tails in a nod. "Maybe he just wasn't listening."

"Come on, this is no time to be funny," Manta snapped. "It was *you* two who weren't listening. If they catch you with me, you're going to be with me permanently. All of us with our ears bitten off, exiled to who knows where. What happens to you then? What happens to your *children* then?"

"We'd be in trouble," Drusni agreed, her voice steady. "But that's not going to happen, because you're going to come up with the answer Latranesto wants."

"And what if I don't?" Manta shot back. "Because *I* sure as the Deep don't know if I can pull this off. I don't mind risking my own future; I don't even mind risking Latranesto's. But I don't want to risk yours."

"What about the future of the Qanska?" Pranlo asked quietly. "Are you willing to risk *that*?"

Manta felt his throats tighten. "I already said I was going to do my best."

"Good," Drusni said. "In that case, we're going with you. I don't know how it is with humans, but in my experience Qanska never really do their best alone. It always takes at least two, working together, for each one to achieve that."

"In this case, it takes three," Pranlo put in. "The Three Musketta swim again!"

Manta sighed, his heart aching inside him. "I know you're being serious," he said quietly. "Both of you. And I'll never be able to tell you how much it means to me. But I don't even know what use *I'm* going to be on this. I can't even begin to guess what kind of help you can be."

"Maybe all we'll do is listen," Drusni said. "A long time ago I told you that talking about a problem with friends was sometimes the best way to solve it."

"Yes, I remember," Manta said reluctantly. "But I doubt this is exactly what you had in mind."

Pranlo snorted. "Oh, come *on*, Manta. Show me a Qanska who gets to pick his problems, and that's the herd *I* want to swim with."

"Then it's settled," Drusni said firmly. "Right, Manta?"

Manta sighed again. "It looks like I'm outvoted," he said, giving up. "If you want to know the truth, I *would* appreciate the company."

"See?" Pranlo said. "Already you're making better decisions."

He flipped his tails and started off again across the wind. "Come on, let's go—we've got a job to do. The Three Musketta, on their finest adventure yet."

"Yeah," Manta murmured as he turned to follow. "Let's just hope it's not their last."

Early on in his house arrest, pacing restlessly around his increasingly cramped quarters, Faraday's frustration had conjured up images of himself as a prisoner in one of those seventeenth-century period vids he'd loved as a child. He pictured himself locked in the dungeon of some medieval fortress, with only a tiny window available to let in light and air.

Still, mental dramatics aside, he had to admit his position was hardly that desperate. His quarters weren't made of stone, they weren't dank and cold or even particularly uncomfortable, and he certainly hadn't been totally forgotten by the outside world. Hesse's nervously furtive visits proved that much.

And of course, his single window had a scope and power which his seventeenth-century counterpart could never have dreamed of.

The main newsnets, not surprisingly, weren't particularly useful. The public activities and pronouncements of the Five Hundred were duly reported, discussed, and analyzed, but nowhere was there even a hint of the turmoil and power struggles Hesse had said were going on behind the scenes.

But then, Faraday would hardly expect there to be. Secret power struggles were, by definition, secret. Fortunately, the public channels weren't his only resources. Patiently, methodically, he scoured through them, looking for some clue as to what Arbiter Liadof was up to.

And it was on one of the more obscure Sol/Guard data channels that he finally found it.

"I got your message," Hesse said as the ever-present Sanctum cop closed the door of Faraday's quarters behind him. "Is anything wrong?"

"That's the question of the hour," Faraday told him, getting up from his desk chair and gesturing the other to sit down. "The last time you were here you told me that Liadof had been talking with the top Sol/Guard generals, but that you didn't know what all that was about. Right?"

"Right," Hesse said cautiously, settling gingerly into the chair. "Don't tell me you've got it figured out."

"Not all of it, but I think I've found a piece of the puzzle," Faraday said. "Have you ever heard of the Nemesis Project?"

Hesse's eyes narrowed. "That's a multi-megaton nuclear arsenal sitting out in Mars orbit somewhere, right? Set up about fifty years ago as a defense against potential Earth-collision asteroids?"

"That's the one," Faraday nodded. "Or rather, that's the group. Now that we've got so many colonies scattered around, Nemesis isn't a single arsenal anymore but about a dozen stockpiles set up in strategic places around the System."

He leaned over Hesse's shoulder and tapped a spot on the display. "I was sifting through a listing of Sol/Guard daily status reports when I ran across this."

"Wait a second," Hesse said, frowning up at him. "How come you still have access to military infonets?"

"Because I'm still a military officer," Faraday reminded him mildly. "Why shouldn't I have access?"

"I just thought—" Hesse broke off. "No, of course you do. You've never been charged, so none of your clearances have ever been revoked."

"Exactly," Faraday said. "Playing games with the legal structure doesn't always work out exactly the way the player had in mind."

"Indeed." Hesse gestured to the display. "So what exactly am I looking at?"

"The current status report on Nemesis Six," Faraday said, tapping the display again. "Sol/Guard General John Achmadi in command. Formerly of leading Jovian orbit."

Hesse gave him a sideways look. "'Formerly'?"

"Formerly," Faraday confirmed. "My reading of astrogation data is a little rusty; but as near as I can figure, Nemesis Six is on its way here."

"You've got to be kidding," Hesse said, staring at the display. His voice sounded sandbagged. "It's coming *here*?"

"Sure looks like it." Faraday lifted his eyebrows slightly. "The question is, what does Arbiter Liadof want with a nuclear weapons platform?"

There was an odd tension around Hesse's eyes as he gazed at the display. "My God," he murmured. "Well . . . you tell me. What do *you* think she could be up to?"

"Well, I doubt she's declaring war on Jupiter Prime," Faraday said dryly. "Aside from that, I haven't got a clue. I take it your reaction means your people haven't heard anything about this?"

Hesse lifted his hands helplessly. "If they have, they

haven't said anything to me," he said, starting to sound on balance again. The shock of the revelation must be passing. "I'll get a message to them right away. The implications . . ." He shook his head.

"Run even deeper than you probably realize," Faraday said. "Are you by any chance familiar with military procedure concerning the transfer of Sol/Guard equipment or personnel?"

Hesse looked up at him, an odd expression on his face. "No. Why?"

"I didn't think you would be," Faraday said. "And I'd bet oceanfront real estate that Arbiter Liadof isn't, either."

He gestured to the display. "General Achmadi is coming here. Presumably to Jupiter Prime; presumably to turn over something or someone under his command to Project Changeling."

"Under authorization from Sol/Guard."

"And after discussing the matter with Liadof and the Five Hundred," Faraday agreed. "That part's all well and good. And I presume that when she talked with Sol/Guard about this, she did so as an agent of the project. Anyone connected with Changeling—you, me, even Mr. Beach—can represent us in making arrangements like that. *But*."

He let the word hover in the air a moment. "*But*, under Sol/Guard regulations, Achmadi can *only* turn whatever it is over to the head of the project."

Something flashed across Hesse's face. "Which is you," he said.

Faraday smiled tightly. "Exactly. Liadof may have taken practical control of Changeling, but my name is still the one at the top of the mission statement."

"That's right," Hesse breathed. "Because she hasn't dared petition the Five Hundred to replace you."

"As you've said, I've got the name and the prestige," Faraday reminded him. "Which puts her square in the middle of a box with only two ways out. One, she has to go ahead and take that risk, which ought to play right into the

hands of your group. Or two, she's going to have to come
to me when Achmadi arrives."

"Yes, I see," Hesse murmured, his fingertips drumming
thoughtfully on the edge of the desk. "This may very well
be the opportunity we've been waiting for."

He stood up abruptly. "I'll get in touch with my backers
right away," he promised. "Let's see what they can come
up with."

"Do that," Faraday urged. "At the very least they need
to be told that Nemesis Six is on the move."

"Right," Hesse said. "What else should I tell them?"

"You could give them the likely timetable," Faraday suggested. "Nemesis platforms aren't designed for speed, and
Six was pretty far in front of Jupiter to begin with De
pending on how much of a hurry Liadof's in, I'd guess
we've got another three to four weeks before Achmadi gets
here."

"Good," Hesse said grimly. "That's about the speed the
Five Hundred seems to move at anyway."

He stepped to the door. "I'll be back before Achmadi
arrives," he promised. "One way or another, I think this is
about to come to a head."

"Indeed," Faraday said quietly. "Good luck."

Hesse rapped on the door. The guard opened it, Hesse
stepped through, and the door closed again behind him.

Slowly, Faraday sat back down at the desk. Yes, it was
coming to a head, all right. The big question now was
whether all of the players in this little game would react
the way he was expecting them to.

Only time would tell. Three to four weeks worth of time.

Hissing softly between his teeth, he went back to his
search of the military databases.

And wondered what in hell Liadof wanted with a nuclear
weapons platform.

TWENTY-FIVE

The Brolka spooked as Manta eased up alongside it, scattering *fomprur* in all directions with its fins as it darted away. It jerked again as Pranlo suddenly appeared in front of it, twisting into a right-angle turn to duck away from him. Straight toward Drusni; but even as she lunged forward to intercept, the Brolka made another twisting turn that ending up with it pointed toward open air. Another splash of *fomprur*, and it was off and running.

Manta muttered a curse under his breath. So much for *that* approach.

"Nimble little guys, aren't they?" Pranlo commented, watching the Brolka disappearing in the distance as he swam up beside Manta. "You sure we need to catch one of them?"

"I'm not sure of anything," Manta growled, feeling disgusted with the whole thing. "I just thought it might be useful to see one up close."

"What for?" Drusni asked as she coasted up to join them. "I mean, I'm sure it's for something useful," she added hastily. "I just don't understand exactly what."

"Don't worry about hurting my feelings," Manta assured her with a sigh. "I don't even know if any of this is useful anymore. As far as I can tell, all we've been doing for the last nineday is treading wind and chewing air."

"Then why exactly are we doing it?" she asked reasonably.

"Because I'm out of ideas," Manta confessed.

"That was fast," Pranlo murmured. "A whole nineday, and we're giving up already?"

Manta flipped his tails helplessly. "I warned you," he reminded them, a cloud of depression starting to blow across his feelings. What in the world had he been thinking, agreeing to tackle this problem? "I told you this wasn't my area of expertise."

"Well, area of expertise or not, we're not giving up," Drusni insisted. "I still have faith in you."

"So does Latranesto," Manta muttered.

"Yes, but I have more," Drusni said. "Because I know you better than he does. And because I've seen you in action."

Manta winced. "With the probe?"

"That too," she said calmly. "But I was thinking more about that time we spotted that Sivra pack riding on a Vuuka."

Manta flicked his tails. "I don't remember being particularly clever with that one."

"You weren't exactly stupid, though," Drusni said. "You recognized the danger, even though Sivra normally couldn't get up to Level One. And you quickly took strokes to solve it: You sent me for the Protectors, and you kept attacking the Sivra so they couldn't get a solid grip on the Breeder they were attacking."

She touched his fin. "But mostly I was thinking about the fact that you didn't give up and quit until the Protectors arrived. And you're not going to give up now."

Manta shrugged his fins. "I'm not so sure."

"I am," Drusni said firmly. "You don't give up, and you're smarter than you think. That's a good combination. So just relax and let it happen, okay?"

Manta grimaced. Relax. With his life, Pranlo's and Drusni's lives, and the future of the entire Qanskan people balanced across his back. Relax.

"Let's try going over what we already know," Pranlo suggested. "Maybe you'll see something you hadn't noticed before."

Manta flipped his tails. Sure, why not? "Fine," he said. "Okay. The plants and animals start dying out, certain ones first, a list of which is available if we think it'll do us any good."

"And it starts in Centerline," Drusni added.

"Right," Pranlo said. "Now, what's different about Centerline?"

"It's not as warm as the southern regions," Drusni offered. "Did we decide it's darker at sundark, too?"

"Yes," Manta confirmed. "I made some observations back near Centerline while I was waiting for Pranlo to bring you to see me."

"Right," Pranlo said. "And you said that was because . . . ?"

"Because of extra radiation in the outer regions," Manta said. "I don't know why that would be, though I seem to remember that the magnetic field gets stronger as you head toward the poles. That could have something to do with it."

"Whatever all that means," Pranlo said. "You sure you're not just making up all these words to impress us?"

"*You're* not the ones I have to impress," Manta reminded him dryly.

"Right," Pranlo said, just as dryly. Then he sobered. "You know, though, that might be something to consider if it comes down to that."

"If what comes down to what?" Manta asked, frowning.

"If we can't come up with a solution, maybe you should just make something up that sounds impressive even if it doesn't mean anything," Pranlo said. "At least that would get Latranesto and the other Counselors off your back."

"Pranlo!" Drusni said, sounding shocked. "That's *lying*. How can you even suggest such a thing?"

"Well, why not?" Pranlo countered. "Manta didn't ask to have this oversized Vuuka dropped on him. Besides, you heard Latranesto—it'll be hundreds of suncycles before things start getting really bad. Why shouldn't Manta get to live out the rest of his life in peace?"

"Because it's dishonest," Drusni said.

"Sure, but this bunch of Counselors will never know," Pranlo shot back. "They might not know even if he *does* fix the problem. It might take until we're all dead for anyone to notice things getting better."

"I don't care," Drusni said.

"Okay, okay, that's enough," Manta cut in. "This isn't worth arguing about. I appreciate your concern for my life and happiness, Pranlo, but I'm not going to lie to the Counselors. If I can't figure out how to fix this thing, I'll say so."

"So there," Drusni said with a sniff.

"And if you want to know the truth, I'm surprised you'd even suggest such a thing," Manta added. "Don't you want to grow up to be one of the Wise and get to go live on Level Eight?"

"Right," Drusni seconded. "*I* plan to live there someday. Aren't you coming with me?"

Pranlo flipped his fins. "Personally, I'm not going to worry about it," he said. "I figure some Vuuka's going to get me long before that."

"*Pranlo!*" Drusni scolded. "What a thing to say!"

"And speaking of Vuuka," Pranlo said casually, "that's another thing about Centerline. There are more predator attacks back there, Vuuka and Sivra both."

It took Manta a pulse to get his mind back on the original subject. "Maybe," he said. "Though that doesn't necessarily mean there are more predators. The Brolka in the outer regions draw off a lot of the attacks. But that leads us to something else we know: that the bulk of the Qanska live in Centerline. Anything else?"

"There's less interesting food there," Drusni commented, snagging a tendril of silvery-blue *jeptris* as it floated past her. "This stuff is a *lot* better."

"And that has to be the key, somehow," Manta said, eying the tendril. "The lack of plant variety in Centerline."

"So what do you think it means?" Drusni asked as she took a bite.

"I wish I knew," Manta said, still staring at the *jeptris*

as it dangled from the corner of her mouth. It had been dayherds since he'd really looked at Jovian plants, he realized suddenly. Probably not since those first heady days as a Baby, in fact. Ever since then, he'd basically followed the usual Qanskan pattern of identifying the various food plants strictly by color and then gobbling up the ones they wanted.

Which meant that he'd never really looked at these outer-region plants at all . . .

Drusni must have seen something in his expression. "You have something?" she asked.

"I don't know," Manta said. "On Earth, I know, this kind of problem usually mean there's been overgrazing. People or animals have eaten some variety of plant down to almost nothing, which then upsets some other ecological balance."

"Well, if it was a matter of overeating, the *chinster* and *prupsis* would be long gone," Pranlo pointed out. "At least from Level One. I loved that stuff when I was a Midling."

"Me, too," Drusni agreed, taking another bite. "I sure wouldn't have passed them up for *this* stuff, at least back then. What did you call it again?"

"*Jeptris*," Manta told her. "And you're right; it *is* a little too spicy for most children to appreciate."

"Tastes change as you get older," Pranlo said. "So you're saying it must have been the adults who—what was that word again? Ate too much of it?"

"Overgrazed," Manta supplied.

"Right. Who overgrazed the *jeptris*?"

"I guess that makes sense," Manta said slowly. "Except then what happened to the *jeptris* on Level One? There aren't all that many adults allowed up there."

"Maybe it doesn't grow on Level One," Drusni said.

"Beltrenini said it did," Manta told her. "Hold on a pulse, will you? Don't eat that last bite."

"What, you want it?" Drusni asked as he maneuvered closer to her.

"No, I just want to look at it," he said, coming to a halt practically snout to snout with her. The *jeptris* was a delicate thing, he saw. Thin filaments of silver were twisted together with other filaments of light blue, the whole thing looking rather like a French braid with tiny leaves at the intersection points. Woven into the middle of the pattern, spaced at precise intervals between the leaves, were what looked like cone-shaped berries.

And that single look was all it took. "This *is chinster*," he told the others.

"What are you talking about?" Pranlo protested. "*Chinster* is light purple, all of it. This stuff is silvery blue."

"I know that," Manta said. "But it's *chinster*, all right. Or else a really good spinoff."

"A really good what?" Drusni asked.

"A spinoff," Manta said. "That's like a new product that's derived from a larger but mostly unrelated product—"

"Whoa, whoa," Pranlo cut him off. "Can you give that to us in tonals?"

"Sorry," Manta apologized. For a pulse there he'd drifted back into business school mode. "What I'm saying is that *jeptris* and *chinster* seem to be very much the same sort of plant. They've got the same form, same structure—even the shape of the berries is the same. The only differences I can see are in the color and taste. It's as if one of them is nothing more than a different version of the other."

"All right," Drusni said cautiously. "Maybe. But how does something like that happen? A plant is a plant, just like a Qanska is a Qanska and a Vuuka is a Vuuka. How does it change into something else?"

"I don't know," Manta admitted, his first rush of excitement fading away. It had to be a mutation of some kind. Didn't it?

But how could a mutation that was massive enough to change color and taste not also change the plant's appearance? Shouldn't it at least make it look a *little* different?

He was still floating snout to snout with Drusni. Silently, he backed away from her, turning his tails to his friends.

What was he doing here, anyway? He was just a humble

business major, on a world that had never even heard of the concept. Spinoffs he understood; profit and loss he understood. Inflow and outflow, structure and management and takeovers and economics. Those he understood.

But not this scientific stuff. Not any of it.

Problem-solver. Like the Deep he was. Business problems, maybe. Spinoffs, profit and loss, inflow and outflow—

His wind of thought hit an abrupt calm. Spinoffs. Inflow and outflow . . .

And Level Eight. Inflow and outflow and Level Eight . . .

"Manta?" Drusni murmured tentatively.

And suddenly, there it was, staring him in the face. The answer to all of it.

Maybe.

He spun back around to face them, a sudden surge of energy flowing straight out to his fin tips. "I've got it," he said.

"What?" Pranlo and Drusni said in unison.

"I know what's going on," Manta said. "I don't know all the details; not yet. But I know what's happening. And I know why.".

"Well, don't keep us in suspense," Pranlo said. "What is it?"

"I should have listened to myself from the beginning," Manta said. "Inflow and outflow. Basic business concepts."

He smiled tightly. "And Level Eight," he added. "Where all good little Qanska hope to go when they grow up to be the Wise. Come on."

He flipped over and headed north. "Wait a pulse," Pranlo called after him. "Where are we going?"

"Back to Centerline to see Latranesto," Manta called back. "If I'm right, we're going to need the humans' help to figure out what exactly to do to fix the problem."

"What does Latranesto have to do with the humans?" Drusni asked as she and Pranlo caught up and settled into a pacing swim beside him.

"He doesn't," Manta said. "But I know humans, and they

don't ever give anything away for free. I'm going to need something I can trade with them."

"And you think they're going to want a lumpy Counselor?" Pranlo asked, sounding confused.

Manta flicked his tails. Latranesto, he suspected, was not going to like this. Not a single bit. "No," he said. "Not exactly."

"Well, it's confirmed," Hesse said, dropping with jerky awkwardness into Faraday's desk chair. "Nemesis Six is definitely on the move, and it's definitely coming here."

"How long before it arrives?" Faraday asked. "We've still got two to three weeks, right?"

"Two weeks and four days," Hesse said, drumming his fingers silently on the edge of the desk. "Assuming it stays with its current schedule."

"So we've still got time," Faraday concluded. "There's no need to panic just yet."

"Panic?" Hesse suddenly seemed to notice what his fingers were doing. "Right," he apologized, bringing them to an abrupt halt. "Sorry. I'm just . . . this whole thing's got me spinning three ways from clockwise. What in the System is she up to?"

"You tell me," Faraday said. "I'm not very up-to-date on what's been happening around here lately."

"But that's just it: I don't know," Hesse said. "I've been over Six's equipment list twice. If there's any special sensor or search gear aboard, I can't find it."

"What about the crew?" Faraday asked. "Anyone aboard with special expertise?"

"Not that I can find in any of the crew profiles," Hesse said. "Near as I can tell, the whole Nemesis project is basically a sort of high-class, low-profile grunt duty. You go out and sit in the middle of nowhere waiting for a call that never comes."

"Or at least a call that hasn't come *yet*," Faraday reminded him soberly. "If and when a rogue comet comes by with Earth in its crosshairs, we'll be damn glad we've got those stockpiles sitting ready to go."

"Maybe," Hesse said, not sounding convinced. "But anyway, you sit out there for a few months and then get rotated back to civilization. Doesn't seem like the kind of place you'd stick someone with special talents or training."

"How about the political aspect?" Faraday suggested. "Anyone's son or daughter or nephew on Nemesis Six who she might be hoping to influence?"

"I suppose that's possible," Hesse said doubtfully. "I don't have a complete listing of all the System's high and mighty to run a comparison against. But if that was what she wanted, why bring the whole platform here? Why not just send a transport?"

"Good question," Faraday conceded. "So what does that leave us? The weapons themselves?"

Hesse grimaced. "Frankly, that's all I can see."

Faraday nodded. He'd suspected they would arrive at this conclusion sooner or later. But all the other possibilities had at least had to be looked at. "So what could she want with a pair of half-gigaton nukes?"

"Only one thing I can think of," Hesse said. His fingers, Faraday noted, had started their silent drumming again. Clearly, he was having a really hard time with this. "And I don't like it at all."

"So tell me," Faraday prompted.

Hesse seemed to brace himself. "You remember we talked once about the way Liadof handled defeat?"

"Yes, I remember," Faraday said.

"Maybe I was wrong," Hesse said. "I mean, about what I said then about revenge never being her primary goal. Or maybe she thinks she's found a way to meet her agenda *and* get revenge at the same time."

Faraday frowned. "You're not actually suggesting she's planning to use Nemesis weapons against Jupiter Prime, are you?"

"Not Prime, no," Hesse said grimly. "I think she's going to use them against the Qanska."

Faraday pursed his lips. So there it was, at last. Exactly as he'd anticipated. "There is, of course, no way in hell we can let that happen," he told Hesse. "The Omega extortion attempt was bad enough. Using nuclear weapons against the Qanska would be a deliberate act of war."

"I know," Hesse said soberly. "And it gets worse. From the way she keeps insisting we keep track of the herd where Mr. Raimey grew up—"

He swallowed. "Well, I'm afraid that's the one she's going to go after."

Faraday nodded. Again, as anticipated. "Which, not coincidentally, is also the herd where Pranlo and Drusni are swimming."

"Or at least where their children are," Hesse said. "Pranlo and Drusni themselves haven't been seen there for several weeks. But Liadof might even like that better. Kill the children; leave the parents alive to suffer their loss."

"Charming," Faraday murmured. "There's one other point. If Liadof blames Drusni for Omega's failure, she undoubtedly blames Manta for the rest of it. If and when he reappears, where is he likely to go but his old herd, to swim along with his old friends?"

"Oh, hell," Hesse muttered. "I hadn't even thought about that. But you're right, that probably *is* where he'd go."

"He *hasn't* reappeared, has he?"

"Not yet," Hesse said. "No one in the herd's been talking about him, either. At least, not with anything new."

"And the subvocalizer isn't picking up anything?"

"Not since Omega. Wherever he is, he's out of range."

Faraday pursed his lips. "All right," he said. "I guess the time has come. What do your backers need from me in order to stop her?"

Hesse's eyes widened briefly. Maybe he'd expected to have to do more convincing. "Well, basically, we need your public support," he said, stumbling slightly over the words. He really *was* nervous about all this. "A live newsnet conference, maybe, where you can officially come out against Liadof and her faction."

"Too risky," Faraday said, shaking his head. "Too many ways Liadof could cut the transmission before I even got going. Especially way out here."

"How about a recording, then?" Hesse suggested. "We could make a permchip of your statement and then transport it off Prime where she couldn't control the transmission."

"That's even worse," Faraday told him. "A permchip could be intercepted, and we'd never even know it until it was too late."

He cocked an eyebrow at Hesse. "Besides, it occurs to me that this is a bit premature. I don't even know for sure if these supporters of yours will even back me up."

"Oh, they will," Hesse assured him. "They've made that very clear."

"They may have made it clear to *you*," Faraday countered. "They haven't said word one to me. I can't afford to stick my neck out without a reasonable assurance that it won't get chopped off."

He smiled tightly. "Or at least, that it won't get chopped off alone," he amended. 'We must all hang together—' "

" 'Or we shall all hang separately,' " Hesse finished for him. "Benjamin Franklin; yes."

"And as true today as it was back then," Faraday said. "Looks to me like the ball's back on your side of the net."

"Yes, of course," Hesse said, getting to his feet. "All right, I'll talk to them and see what kind of guarantees they can come up with."

"Good," Faraday said. "And remind them to make it fast. We've got less than three weeks before Nemesis Six gets here."

"I will," Hesse promised. He hesitated, just noticeably, then nodded. "Good-bye, Colonel," he said, stepping to the door and knocking. "I'll get back to you as soon as I can."

Faraday nodded in return. The guard opened the door, and Hesse was gone.

With a tired sigh, Faraday turned back to his desk. So there it was: Liadof's opening shot in this insane private war of hers. A war, if she got her way, that would leave her in an even stronger position than she enjoyed right now.

And with consequences to the Qanska that would be impossible to predict. To the Qanska, and to Manta.

Or whatever it was Manta had become.

He sat down in front of his computer. For better or worse, the die was now cast. The players were taking up their positions on the chessboard, and the game was about to begin in earnest.

And in the quiet battle about to take place, a pawn could easily see as much action as a queen or a knight or a bishop.

Maybe even the pawn named Colonel Jakob Faraday.

TWENTY-SIX

E ven taking into account the drift of the winds, Latranesto had ranged somewhat farther afield than Manta
had expected him to go. Hunting for food, probably, or else
avoiding predators.

Still, with three of them available to cover the likely
search area, it only took a couple of days of false starts
before they finally made the sundark rendezvous.

"You're back sooner than I'd expected," Latranesto commented as he and Drusni swam up to where Manta and
Pranlo were waiting. "Have you come to hear the details
of the vanishings?"

"That won't be necessary," Manta said. "I know what
the problem is."

Even in the fading light, he could see the shocked reaction that rippled across the Counselor's fins. "Already?"
he asked incredulously.

"Already," Manta assured him, trying to sound more
confident than he felt. All the way back to Centerline he'd
been thinking over his theory; and while he was personally
convinced he was right, it still *was* only a theory.

"Unbelievable," Latranesto declared, his fin tips rippling
again with nervous excitement. "Well, don't hide the end
of this story. Tell me."

"I will," Manta promised. "But there's another matter we
need to discuss first. Tell me about your journey here, and
the device you use to travel between worlds."

The undulating fin tips suddenly stopped dead in the air.

"You ask for that which the humans also demanded of us," Latranesto said, his voice wary. "Why?"

"Because if I'm right about this, we'll need the humans' help in solving our problem," Manta explained, keeping his voice even and reasonable. "For that, I'll need something to bargain with."

"But you will not simply give it to them?" Latranesto asked, his voice dark with suspicion.

"Absolutely not," Manta promised. "Part of my human training was in the technique of bargaining with others in exactly this way. I intend to use all of that ability on behalf of the Qanska."

"And what if the humans take first, but then do not give?"

"Trust me," Manta said grimly. "I'll make sure we get what we need before they get what they want."

"Trust," Latranesto murmured. "To trust a human."

"No," Pranlo put in softly. "To trust Manta."

For a ninepulse there was only the whistling of the winds around them. Latranesto gazed into the gathering darkness, his tails lashing back and forth in indecision. Manta kept silent, uncomfortably aware that the whole thing could fall apart right here and now. If Latranesto wasn't even willing to tell him where the stardrive was hidden, he would certainly be unwilling to let the humans borrow it for examination.

And without such a commitment from the Qanska, there was no way Manta was going to persuade Faraday and the humans to help them out.

With a final flick of his tails, the Counselor exhaled in a rolling sigh. "Very well," he said. "The way to other worlds is in the air below Level Eight. Through what is called the Deep."

"I understand," Manta said. So the stardrive was buried deep in the atmosphere. That made sense. "How do you get to it?"

"You swim, of course," Latranesto retorted. "What did you expect?"

"Sorry," Manta apologized. "I guess I just assumed that Level Eight was as deep as a Qanska could go. I thought you had to call the machine or something so that it would come up to meet you."

Latranesto frowned. "What machine?"

"Your stardrive, of course," Manta said, frowning back. "I thought that was what we were talking about."

"You asked how we travel between worlds," Latranesto said. "That's what I'm telling you. I said nothing about any machine."

"But—" Manta floundered. "That's what you have to use for this kind of traveling. Isn't it?"

"There is no machine, Manta," Latranesto said quietly. "That's why we can never give the humans what they demand. There is no machine, but only a place. A place within the darkness and pain and fear of the Deep."

Manta's skin was starting to crawl. What Latranesto was suggesting . . . "What sort of place is it?" he asked carefully. "I mean, where exactly is it? And how is it different from other places on Jupiter?"

"It is a place encompassing in and of itself," Latranesto said, his voice shifting into the sing-song pattern of Qanskan story-circle legends. One more story, Manta knew, that no doubt had been carefully deleted from his own herd's lessons. "There is pressure—great pressure—and an eerie light. There is a frightening confusion of twisting winds and multiple directions that defy the strong and overwhelm the weak. Only those of the Wise with the strength of will and the spirit of determination can reach it."

"I never heard anything about this," Drusni murmured quietly.

"They made sure our herd's storytellers kept quiet about it," Manta explained. "Though you'll notice they couldn't suppress it completely. Expressions like 'to the Deep with it,' for instance."

"I always thought that just meant 'let it die,' " Pranlo commented soberly.

"*I* thought it meant 'to hell with it,' " Manta said, tasting the irony. So in other words, what he'd always taken to be the Qanskan concept of hell was in actual fact their pathway into the heavens.

"But why hide it from us?" Drusni asked, sounding puzzled.

"Not from you," Manta told her. "From me. And of course from the humans they figured would be listening in."

He turned back to Latranesto. "Which means you knew right from the start that this was what they wanted."

"We didn't *know*," Latranesto hedged. "But we did suspect."

"But that's my point," Drusni persisted. "It wasn't something the humans could steal from us, so why not let them know the truth?"

"Because if the humans had found out they couldn't obtain a stardrive here, they'd have lost interest in the Qanska in a pulse," Manta said sourly.

He looked at Latranesto. "And if they did that, who would solve the problem of your dying world?"

"You are offended and insulted, Manta," Latranesto said. "I understand."

Manta smiled. "Actually, I'm neither," he assured the Counselor. "I mostly find it pleasantly ironic. Both our races, playing the same game against each other without knowing it. It's really kind of amusing."

"Maybe to *you*," Latranesto growled. Apparently, he didn't like being considered amusing "But amusement ends where the life of our world begins."

"As it also does with the humans," Manta conceded, thinking back to what Faraday had said about the social pressures building up within the System's population. "I apologize, to both of you."

"Anyway, please go on, Counselor Latranesto," Pranlo said. "What happens when one of the Wise gets to this place? What does he have to do then?"

"If he has the strength of mind to reach the Deep, there

is nothing more he must do," Latranesto said. "The Deep itself will carry him to another world."

"Which other world does he go to?" Manta asked. "Are there any choices or decisions?"

"No," Latranesto said. "As I said, there is nothing more he must do. Wherever he is going, the Deep chooses for him."

"I see," Manta murmured. So there it was. Some strange combination of pressure, radiation, and convoluted magnetic fields deep within the atmosphere was somehow able to create a portal between Jupiter and similar gas giant worlds.

Maybe between all of them, in fact. There could conceivably be a vast network of hyperspace portals buried deep within the atmospheres of every gas giant in the galaxy.

A network accessible only to beings who had never even seen the stars.

"Wait a pulse," Pranlo said slowly. "If only the Wise can go through the Deep like that, why are there Vuuka and Sivra here? Where did *they* come from?"

"The Wise brought them, of course," Latranesto said. "Along with all the seeds of the food plants which we eat."

"They *brought* the predators with them?" Drusni echoed. "Why in the world would they do *that*?"

"They had no choice," Latranesto said mildly. "Look at your companions. Look at yourself, for that matter. What do you see?"

Manta frowned at the others, and in the fading light saw them looking back at him with equal confusion. What was Latranesto getting at?

And then, suddenly, he had it. "The skin lumps," he breathed, flicking his tails at the bulges dotting Pranlo's fins and body. "All those predators that have tried to take a bite out of you and gotten covered up."

He looked at Latranesto in confusion. "But they're *dead*. Aren't they?"

"Are they?" Latranesto asked. "Are they truly dead, or are they merely in a very deep sleep?"

"Good point," Manta conceded. "I don't know."

Latranesto flipped his tails in a shrug. "Neither do I. Nei ther do any of the Qanska. All we know is that when the Wise reach the next world, their outer skin is torn away and all those buried within are revived."

"A remarkable capacity for regeneration," Manta murmured.

"What was that?" Drusni asked.

"I was just remembering one of the first things I ever heard about the Qanska," he told her. "That you have the ability to recover and rebuild your bodies after an attack. Maybe the Vuuka and Sivra have something of the same ability."

"Or perhaps it is a unique property of the journey itself," Latranesto suggested. "There are a great many things about the journey that we don't know."

He flicked his tails. "We're not a problem-solving race."

The light of the sun was gone now, Manta noticed, with only the diffuse glow coming from deep inside the planet still there for them to see by. "So now you know the truth," the Counselor said after a ninepulse. "What will you do next?"

"Well, the first thing to do is get some sleep," Manta said.

"Sleep?" Drusni asked. "I thought we were in a hurry to get this whole thing up and swimming."

"A reasonable hurry, yes," Manta agreed. "But it's hardly desperate. It's sundark, we're all tired, and I need some time to digest what Counselor Latranesto has told me. Besides, we have to go find the nearest human probe before we can talk to them."

"I thought you could speak with them at any time," Drusni said.

"I don't know if I can or not anymore," Manta said. "Besides, that method works in English. I'm not sure how well I know that language anymore. Simpler to find a probe."

"There's one near the herd where Druskani and Prantrulo's children swim," Latranesto said. "It's less than a nineday away."

"Sounds good," Manta said. "We'll leave at sunlight."

He gazed out into the swirling winds. "And on the way," he added, "I'll tell you what I think the problem is, and why we'll need the humans' help to solve it."

Latranesto sank downward toward the lower levels, where his natural buoyancy balance would let him sleep more comfortably. Drusni and Pranlo locked fins and drifted off to sleep together on the wind.

Leaving Manta alone in the darkness. Trying to figure out what in the Deep he was going to do.

Because as of right now, the bargaining plan he'd tentatively worked had gone straight down the Great Yellow Storm. How could he bargain in good faith with a stardrive that didn't exist?

Especially for a stardrive the humans could probably never even get to?

But one way or another they had to get the humans' help. The more he thought over his theory, the more he was convinced that the Qanska could never fix this by themselves. They needed the humans; and the humans wouldn't give that help without something in return.

Unless he conned them out of it.

The thought made his fins squirm. He could certainly argue that the humans had it coming to them. They'd sent him here under false pretenses, lying to him and the Qanska both as to their intentions.

Not to mention that grand kidnapping/extortion attempt. That alone was a huge debt they owed the Qanska.

But at the same time, the Counselors and the Leaders and the Wise hadn't exactly been forthright about their goals for this project, either. How much did that take off the humans' debt? What was the right equation to use, or the proper credit/debit balance?

No. There was no equation to use here, no balancing of ethical scales. Whatever the humans had done to him and the other Qanska, lying to them would be wrong. He would not allow himself to sink to that level.

And with that decision made, the rest of it fell simply and quietly into line. He could still bargain with Faraday; but he would make it clear from the beginning that he would be bargaining only for the *secret* of the stardrive, not the stardrive itself. If the humans balked at that, then they would just remain forever in ignorance.

But they wouldn't. Manta had once been human, after all. He knew them better than that.

Taking a deep breath, he relaxed his fins and let the wind take him. Tomorrow was going to be a busy day. He'd better get some sleep.

TWENTY-SEVEN

"Colonel Faraday?" The muffled voice called, the words half buried in the staccato of nervous-woodpecker tapping on his door. "Colonel Faraday!"

"Hold on," Faraday said, throwing off the blankets and blinking his eyes at his clock. It was just after four in the morning; and unless he was still dreaming, that was Hesse's voice out there in the corridor.

"Colonel Faraday?"

He wasn't still dreaming. Pulling on his slacks, Faraday grabbed a shirt and stepped to the door. Liadof's men still had a passcard to his room, but he'd learned how to gimmick the door at night to give himself a little privacy. Draping the shirt over one shoulder, he flipped on the light and pulled off the access panel to the opening mechanism. A couple of wires put back where they belonged, and the door was functional again. Pulling on his shirt, he keyed the release.

Hesse had the slightly disheveled look of a man who's just thrown on his own clothing, and there was something tensely wild around his eyes. "Sorry to wake you, sir," he said as he stepped inside. His voice, now that Faraday could hear it more clearly, was as agitated as his eyes. "We've got a situation here."

"What are you talking about?" Faraday asked cautiously, the skin on the back of his neck beginning to tingle. Something was very wrong here; Nemesis Six wasn't due at Prime for at least another week and a half. There shouldn't be any crises happening now. "What's happened?"

"I don't know," Hesse said, his breath coming in ragged gasps as if he'd run the whole way from his quarters. "All I know is that Liadof's been called urgently to the Contact Room, and there's word she's about to call you there, too."

Glancing back at the closed door behind him, he reached into his inner jacket pocket and slid out a folded sheet of paper. "I wanted to get this to you before that happens," he continued, holding it out toward Faraday, "It's the guarantee from my backers that you wanted. Here; you have to sign it."

"Put it on the desk," Faraday instructed him, sitting back down on the bed and snaring his shoes. "Open it up and lay it out; I'll read it while I finish dressing."

"Do it fast," Hesse warned, fumbling the paper open and smoothing it out on the desktop. "They could be here any minute."

Faraday stepped past him and sat down at the desk. It was official document paper, he saw: rip-proof, fire-proof, tamper-proof. This was serious business, all right. Leaning over to pull on his shoes, he began to read. *The undersigned does hereby declare and state that he stands in alliance with the Citizens for Liberty*—

"The Citizens for Liberty?" he asked, frowning up at Hesse. "Isn't that the group that's been protesting the Mars crackdown?"

"That's the one," Hesse confirmed, glancing back at the door again. "My backers have been sponsoring them as sort of unofficial public-relations arm. They're using the CFL to help stir up public sentiment against governmental excesses."

"I hope that's not their only outlet," Faraday grunted. "The CFL sounds awfully strident sometimes."

"No, they're just one of several groups," Hesse said. "It's a standard wide-spectrum PR approach. The CFL reaches the people who are the most angry at the crackdown, while other groups concentrate on connecting with the moderates and undecideds. The CFL is just the one that's getting the most press at the moment."

"Ah," Faraday said, looking back down at the paper as he started fastening his shirt.—*with the Citizens for Liberty against the blatantly illegal actions of Arbiter Katrina Liadof and the Five Hundred . . .*

He finished with his shirt and rested his left elbow on the edge of the paper, cupping his chin in his hand as he skimmed down the rest of the document. "Doesn't look unreasonable," he commented when he had finished. "Only I thought your backers were supposed to be supporting *me*. This looks more like a guarantee of *me* supporting *them*."

"Well, of course it has to work both directions," Hesse pointed out. "They can hardly give you a blank check for support without acknowledgment that you're on their side, too. That's why the word *alliance* is used. That makes the whole thing mutual."

"I suppose that makes sense," Faraday agreed. "I might have felt more comfortable if they'd looped me in with one of the less radical groups, though."

"The idea isn't for any of us to be comfortable," Hesse said tartly. "What we need is for people to be angry about this, angry enough that there's real public pressure on the Five Hundred to back away from what Liadof's side is doing. From *everything* they're doing, from the Martian crackdown on down. That's the only way you're going to be able to protect Drusni's children and the other Qanska from getting nukes thrown down their throats. We've got to throw her out, and we've got to get her out *now*. There's no time to let you ramp up from concerned to annoyed to righteously indignant and finally to angry."

"I suppose not," Faraday conceded.

"So sign and let's get on with it." Hesse looked at the door again. "And make it quick," he added. "I think I hear someone coming."

He was right; Faraday could hear the approaching footsteps, too. Picking up a pen, he rested his hand on the edge of the desk and scrawled briefly across the line at the bottom. "There," he said, tossing the pen aside and standing up. "Better tuck it away out of sight. I'll get my jacket."

His timing was perfect. Even as he stepped away from the desk, there was a fresh pounding at his door. "Colonel?" a deep voice demanded.

"Come on, take it," Faraday hissed.

Lunging to the desk, Hesse scooped up the paper, hastily folded it back together, and stuffed it away inside his jacket.

Just in time. Behind him, the door slid open and one of Liadof's Sanctum cops strode in. "Colonel, you're wanted at the Contact Room," he announced. His eyes seemed to suddenly notice that Faraday was fully dressed. "Which I take it you already know," he added, throwing a brief and unreadable look at Hesse. "Come with me."

The corridors were mostly empty and quiet as Faraday followed the cop to the Contact Room, Hesse trailing behind them. The security officer at the entrance had obviously been briefed; he passed all three of them through with only a perfunctory glance at their IDs.

Liadof was waiting for them, standing in front of the command chair, her posture unnaturally stiff. "Colonel Faraday," she said formally. "I apologize for awakening you at this hour."

"No apology necessary, Arbiter Liadof," Faraday said just as formally as he glanced around the room. Despite the late hour, he noted, Beach was in his usual spot at the communications station. Either he'd been moved here to Gamma Shift, or else Liadof had roused him out of bed, too. The other three men seated at the wraparound control panel were complete strangers to him. "What seems to be the problem?"

He looked back at Liadof in time to see her lips compress briefly. "It's not really a problem," she said. "We've just heard from Mr. Raimey."

She flicked a glance in Beach's direction. "And there seems to be a certain confusion as to what exactly he's trying to say."

Faraday frowned. "The computer can't make it out?"

"The computer's translation is ambiguous," Liadof said. "Mr. Beach seems to think it's not ambiguous at all. As the other local expert on Qanskan tonals, I thought it might be interesting to get your take on it, as well."

"I'll do my best," Faraday said, trying hard to read her face. What new game was she playing now? "You have a copy?"

"Mr. Beach?" Liadof invited. "Play him the raw, pre–grammar-adjusted message."

Beach touched a switch, and the room filled with the rumbling sound of Qanskan tonals. *My name is Manta-born-of-humans with the World In-between Machine-of-the-clouds-above attempting to converse*, the words rolled from the speaker. *I will with Colonel Faraday about the secret of the Qanskan path between worlds to speak only.*

The message began to repeat; and Faraday felt his breath catch in his throat. *The Qanskan path between worlds.* "He says, 'This is Manta, child of the humans, trying to talk to the Jupiter Prime space station,' " he translated, trying to keep his voice steady. So Manta had done it. He'd found the Qanskan stardrive. " 'I want to speak with Colonel Faraday only about the secret of the Qanskan stardrive.' "

"Yes, that's basically the way the computer translated it," Liadof agreed. "The sticking point is what exactly the word 'only' means here."

Faraday blinked. *Only?* "Have you asked Manta about it?"

"We've tried," Liadof said. "He hasn't responded to our transmissions. So tell me, Colonel: what does 'only' mean here?"

Faraday frowned, listening to the message again as it ran through another repeat. To him, it seemed perfectly straightforward: Manta wasn't going to give them the actual stardrive, but would only discuss the secret technology involved with it.

Yet from what Liadof had said, it sounded like Beach was arguing for some other interpretation.

Granted, Beach was more versed in tonals than Faraday himself was. But not that much more. What could he be hearing in Manta's message that Faraday wasn't getting?

Out of the corner of his eye, he could see Beach turned halfway around at his station. Beach, who had refused to stand with the rest of his Alpha Shift teammates when push had come to crunch. Beach, who had instead preferred to keep his head down, stay in Liadof's good graces, and keep his career intact.

Beach, now looking back over his shoulder at Faraday. An odd intensity in his eyes; an equally odd stiffness in his back . . .

And then, suddenly, Faraday got it.

He smiled to himself, that last nagging thorn in his side finally fading away. McCollum, Sprenkle, Milligan—each of them had taken advantage of an opportunity to help him and Manta when the chance had come their way McCollum had slipped Faraday a sketch of the Omega Probe; Sprenkle had given Manta the hint that broke Liadof's implanted McCarthy control over him; Milligan had fiddled his sensors to give the Manta the time he needed to free the Qanskan hostages. Only Beach had refused to rock his own boat, putting himself and his career above anything so petty and expendable as loyalty.

Or so Faraday had thought. So, probably, had the rest of Alpha Shift. So, certainly, had Liadof, or she wouldn't have kept him on duty.

They'd all been wrong. Beach hadn't defied Liadof for the simple reason that the proper opportunity to do so hadn't yet come along for him.

Now it had . . . and as he looked at the stiffness in Beach's posture, Faraday finally realized what he was up to.

"It's perfectly obvious, Arbiter," he told Liadof calmly. "Manta's saying he'll discuss the stardrive; but that he'll only discuss it with me."

The lines in Liadof's face deepened. "Really," she said suspiciously. "How very convenient."

Faraday shrugged. "You asked my opinion," he reminded her. "But Mr. Beach is the real expert. What does *he* say?"

Liadof looked over at the other. Beach, Faraday noted,

had quietly turned back around to face his board. But he could also see that much of the tension was gone from the big man's back. He'd taken a big gamble, as big as any of his Alpha Shift teammates had. If Faraday hadn't caught on in time and backed up his interpretation, Beach would quickly have joined the others in Liadof's doghouse.

But he had. And faced with that unity, Faraday couldn't see that Liadof had any choice left but to capitulate.

Neither, apparently, did she. "Very well, Colonel," she said with clear reluctance. "You're hereby reinstated to full duty with Project Changeling. Mr. Beach, see if Mr. Raimey's ready to talk to us yet."

"A clarification first, Arbiter," Faraday said. "Are you simply allowing me to return to duty? Or are you reinstating me to the position specified in the project's mission statement?"

"You're back in full command, Colonel," she growled. "All right? Is that what you wanted to hear?"

"Yes, it is," Faraday said. "Thank you."

"You're welcome," Liadof said. "Now, call Mr. Raimey."

"In a moment," Faraday said, turning toward the pair of Sanctum cops standing guard inside the doorway. His people had stood by him when it counted. It was time he returned the favor. "You two," he ordered. "Go bring Mr. Milligan, Dr. Sprenkle, and Ms. McCollum here."

"Colonel—" Liadof began.

"And you three—" Faraday added, ignoring Liadof and gesturing to the techs at the control board "—are dismissed. Thank you for your service; you may return to your quarters."

"None of you move," Liadof cut in tartly. "Colonel, what do you think you're doing?"

"What does it look like I'm doing?" Faraday asked mildly. "I'm taking command of Project Changeling. Command authority always extends to personnel assignments."

For a moment Liadof's eyes flicked across his face, studying it. Faraday held her gaze evenly, bracing for the inevitable firestorm. But she merely shrugged. "I see," she said. "Very well, then. As you wish."

"Thank you," Faraday said. He gestured again to the cops; silently, they left the room.

"But don't think this is over," Liadof added as the three techs also filed from the room, leaving Beach sitting alone at the board. "It isn't."

Faraday hesitated, wondering if he should wait a little longer. But no. It was time to have this out. "Actually, Arbiter, it is," he said bluntly. "You see, I'm no longer just a lone, vulnerable man standing in your way. I've now acquired the backing and support of a sizable faction of the Five Hundred. You can't push me around anymore, or twist this project to your own personal whims. I have authority again, and I don't intend to give that up."

"I see," Liadof said, sitting down in the command chair. "Mr. Beach, would you step outside?"

"Colonel?" Beach asked, looking at Faraday.

"Go ahead," Faraday told him.

Silently, as had the others before him, Beach left the room. Liadof touched a switch on her control panel, and the door slid shut. "So, Colonel," Liadof said, settling herself comfortably. "You have support from the Five Hundred, do you?"

"Yes, I do," Faraday assured her. "Signed, sealed, and guaranteed. And if you'll pardon my immodesty, with my name on the roster beside theirs, we'll have public opinion on our side in no time. Rest assured, we're going to put a stop to your private war of vengeance against the Qanska."

"Really," Liadof said. "And how has all this been accomplished while you've been locked in your quarters?" She lifted a hand. "No, wait. Let me guess. You've just become a member in good standing of the Citizens for Liberty. Earth branch, no doubt."

Faraday's eyes narrowed. "I'm sorry?" he said carefully.

"The Citizens for Liberty," Liadof repeated, a grim satisfaction in her voice. "An organization which has been linked with protests and terrorist activities all across the

System. An organization which no one in the Five Hundred would be caught dead being associated with. An organization which three hours ago was declared outlaw."

She lifted her eyebrows slightly. "And an organization whose members automatically commit treason simply by the act of joining."

She smiled tightly. "Congratulations, Colonel Faraday," she said. "In signing that paper, you've just notarized your own death warrant."

TWENTY-EIGHT

Slowly, Faraday turned to look at Hesse. The other was staring at the floor near his feet, his mouth tight and pained. "I thought you said she never did anything for revenge."

"You don't understand, Colonel," Hesse said. His voice was low, his eyes unwilling or unable to lift to meet Faraday's. "I did it for you."

"Of course," Faraday said. "For me."

"He's right," Liadof said. "I have nothing against you personally, Colonel, though I doubt that works the other direction. But as you said, you have a name and prestige that could have been dangerous, both to me and to Project Changeling as a whole. You had to somehow be neutralized."

"Of course," Faraday said again. "Putting me on trial for treason should do the job nicely."

"No," Hesse insisted, looking up at Faraday for the first time. "That's not what's going to happen."

"Why not?" Faraday shot back. "Because a high-profile trial would give ammunition to her opponents in the Five Hundred?"

"My faction has no opponents, Colonel," Liadof said. "At least, none that pose a serious threat. All that talk of dissension was simply part of the web I had Mr. Hesse spin for your benefit."

"Maybe it was a lie when he was spinning it," Faraday countered. "But it could become reality faster than you think. Or do you really believe the Five Hundred will simply sit quietly by while you launch nuclear weapons against the Qanska?"

Liadof snorted. "Don't be absurd. I have no intention of using weapons against the Qanska, nuclear or otherwise."

Faraday grimaced. "So that was just another lie. How much time and energy have you been putting into my destruction, anyway?"

"Don't flatter yourself, Colonel," Liadof said. "My priorities are the same as those of Project Changeling: to locate and obtain the Qanskan stardrive. Everything else is a distant second place. Including you."

"And no one wants your destruction anyway," Hesse added earnestly. "All we want is your cooperation."

"I thought all you wanted was my silence." Faraday cocked an eyebrow as another thought suddenly occurred to him. "Unless, of course, Nemesis Six really *is* on its way here."

"Very good, Colonel," Liadof said approvingly. "Yes, General Achmadi will be here sometime next week, and at that point I'll need your authorization to take possession of his nuclear weapons."

Faraday felt his throat tighten. "I thought you said you weren't going to attack the Qanska."

"I'm not," she said. "We're going to explode them one at a time in isolated areas in the northern and southern Jovian polar regions, where no Qanska live. By analyzing the sonic shock waves and their echoes, we're hoping we can get a clue as to the stardrive's location."

Faraday nodded. So that was the plan. A pure, reasonable scientific experiment, with nothing that could be used politically against her. Especially given that the Five Hundred had undoubtedly already approved it.

All of which Hesse would have known from the beginning.

"So that's it," he said quietly. "I haven't got any allies, I haven't got any illegal or unethical deeds I can hang you with, and by the time you've finished plastering this document all over the newsnets I won't even have a reputation."

He looked back at Hesse. "What was that you said? That you did it for me?"

"Don't be so hard on the boy," Liadof chided before Hesse could answer. "I already told you that you had to be neutralized, one way or another."

"And the more humiliating the method, the better?"

Liadof shook her head. "You're still missing the point. In a perfect world, that CFL document will never see the light of day. All it is is insurance against you trying to fight me."

"Ah," Faraday said bitterly. "Of course. Extortion with the Qanska; blackmail with me. At least your methods are consistent."

"Would you rather I have simply destroyed you outright?" Liadof demanded. "That *was* my other option, you know. To bring you up on charges over what you and your teammates did to the Omega Probe and have you fired."

"You'd have lost," Faraday said stiffly.

Liadof snorted. "Hardly," she said. "Not with my faction orchestrating the whole affair. They would have been our questions, our judges, and our results."

"What about public opinion?" Faraday asked. "Or were you going to orchestrate that, too?"

"Of course," Liadof said with a casual wave of her hand. "You're a popular enough figure, but let's face it: Interest in Changeling has faded too far for anyone to work up much emotion over you."

She considered. "And of course, all the publicity around the trial would have been under our control, too. No, Colonel. For all practical purposes, you'd have been dead. And McCollum, Milligan, and Sprenkle would have gone down along with you. Is that really how you would have wanted it?"

Faraday didn't answer. "You don't have to answer," Liadof said. "Now, instead, once Changeling has served its purpose you'll be free to retire, collect your pension, and live out your life as the quiet old hero. And your Alpha Shift teammates will still have their careers."

"I see," Faraday murmured, looking at Hesse again. "I appreciate your efforts to protect me, Mr. Hesse. I'm just sorry that in these past few years together you never learned that there are things I consider more valuable than my reputation."

"If you'd prefer to go down fighting, we can still do that," Liadof offered, some annoyance starting to filter through the civilized veneer of her voice. "I can arrange for you to crash in political flames if that would salve your conscience or your pride."

She gestured at the control board. "But right now, we have business to attend to. Mr. Raimey is waiting."

She keyed the switch beside her, and behind them the door slid open. "And unless I'm mistaken, so are the rest of your people. Everyone; come in."

They filed in, Beach leading the way, with McCollum, Sprenkle, and Milligan behind him. The latter three seemed rather dazed, with Milligan still blinking sleep from his eyes. "What's going on, Colonel?" McCollum asked cautiously.

"We're back in business," Faraday told her. "Manta's contacted us and wants to talk. Everyone get to your stations; procedure is by the book."

Sprenkle and Milligan exchanged uncertain glances, but no one spoke as they fanned out to their sections of the board. Stepping up behind Beach, Faraday wondered briefly just how much of the situation he'd been able to explain to the others before Liadof had called them all in.

And wondered how much of it they'd believed.

"All right, Mr. Beach," he said when everyone was settled. "Let's see what Manta has to say."

"Yes, sir." Beach touched a series of switches and gestured toward the mike protruding from his station. "You're on, Colonel."

"Good morning, Manta," Faraday called. "This is Colonel Faraday. Welcome back."

There was a brief pause, and then the room again began to rumble to the sound of Qanskan tonals. "Thank you, Colonel," the computer translated. "I wasn't aware you'd missed me."

"Some of us have," Faraday assured him, keeping half an ear on the tonals to make sure the computer was doing an accurate translation. "I'm afraid I can't say that about everyone, unfortunately. There have been some personnel changes at the top of the project. I presume you understand."

There was a pause, and in the silence he heard Liadof mutter something under her breath. The tonals began rumbling—"I wondered about that," the translation came. "It didn't seem like something you would do."

"Definitely not," Faraday said. "And on behalf of the Five Hundred and all of humanity, I apologize. It will never happen again."

"Easy, Colonel," Liadof warned quietly. "You don't speak for the Five Hundred."

"Manta?" Faraday called. "Did you hear me?"

"I heard you," Manta said. "And I'll hold you to that. I'm here to offer you a trade."

"I'm listening," Faraday said, feeling his heartbeat pick up its pace. "I understand you're willing to give us the secret of the Qanskan stardrive?"

"I am," Manta said. "In exchange for help with a problem the Qanska are having. Is McCollum available?"

"She's right here," Faraday confirmed. "Does the problem concern Qanskan physiology?"

"Partially," Manta said. "Or at least, that's the part of the puzzle I'm still not sure of."

"Well, let's hear it," Faraday said. "We'll do whatever we can to help."

"Just a moment," Liadof said, stepping up beside him. "We are of course willing to help, Mr. Raimey. But first we'd like to hear about the stardrive."

"Not yet," Manta said. "We'll deal with this problem first."

"No," Liadof said flatly. "You aren't in a position to bargain, Mr. Raimey."

"On the contrary," Manta said. "I think I'm in an excellent position to bargain. Colonel Faraday, who is this person?"

"Her name is Katrina Liadof," Faraday said. "She's a member of the Five Hundred."

"I see," Manta said; and though the computer translation didn't show it, Faraday could hear a definite hardening of Manta's attitude in the tonals. "Is she the one responsible for attacking my people?"

"*Your* people?" Liadof asked pointedly. "*We* are your people, Mr. Raimey."

"Not anymore," Manta said. "Colonel Faraday, I will not speak in this person's presence. Please ask her to leave."

Faraday turned to Liadof. "Don't even *think* it," she warned, her eyes flashing at him. "I'm not going anywhere."

Faraday touched Beach's shoulder. "Mike off," he murmured.

"Mike off," Beach confirmed.

"I'm not leaving," Liadof repeated.

"Then you sacrifice the stardrive," Faraday said bluntly. "What was that you said earlier?—Everything else is a distant second place? Or didn't that list include *your* pride?"

"He's bluffing," Liadof insisted. "You heard him. They have a problem, and they need our help. He can't afford not to give us what we want."

"Don't count on it," Faraday said. "You've seen how clever Manta can be. He might be able to come up with a solution on his own, and then we'd be out in the cold. Now's the time to make a deal, while he still thinks he needs us."

Liadof's eyes flicked over to Hesse, as if confirming that he and the damning document he carried were still there. Then, without a word, she stood up from the chair and stomped to the exit.

But instead of leaving, she merely stopped beside the

door and turned around. Crossing her arms across her chest, she stared defiantly at Faraday.

And that, Faraday decided reluctantly, was probably the best he was going to get. Stepping to the command station she'd just vacated, he sat down and turned on the chair's microphone. "Arbiter Liadof has left the conversation, Manta," he said, choosing his words carefully. "Now, how can we help you?"

"I'll start with a question for McCollum," Manta said. "Do you know anything about bits of growing message?"

McCollum looked blankly at Faraday as she turned on her microphone. "About *what*?"

"Let me think," Manta said. There was a pause. . . . "Qanskan . . . DNA," he said haltingly in English.

"Ah," McCollum said. "Yes, I know a little. Nothing very detailed."

"I don't need details," Manta said, switching back to tonals. "Question: Are there tiny flips in the groups-of-bits-of-growing-message?"

McCollum shook her head. "I'm not getting this, Manta."

"I think he's talking about genes," Beach suggested. "It's not in the Qanskan dictionary, so he has to improvise."

"That part I got," McCollum said. "But what are these tiny flips he's talking about? *Wait* a second. Manta, are you talking about gene triggers? Genes that turn different sections of the code on and off, depending on growth stage or hormonal stimulus or environmental conditions?"

Manta seemed to think it over. "Yes," he said at last. "Do those exist?"

"I don't know," McCollum said. "I'd need to get some Qanskan genes to run tests on. But I know that most Earth species have them."

"Earth comparisons aren't good enough," Manta said. "I need to know about Qanska."

"How about Vuukan genes?" Sprenkle suggested. "Would that help?"

"You have some?" McCollum asked.

"The Omega Probe cage came up slathered with Vuukan

blood and bits of torn tissue," he told her. "We've been—" he threw a look at Faraday "—a little off-duty since then, but someone must have saved a sample or two."

"In which case, they would also have analyzed it," McCollum agreed, her fingers tapping across her keyboard. "Let's see . . . okay, here we go. Let's see . . ."

She went silent, running a fingertip down one of her displays as she skimmed the report. "Mr. Milligan, what's the situation down there?" Faraday asked quietly. "Is Manta alone?"

"No, it looks like something of a delegation," Milligan reported, studying his sensor displays. "From the markings, we've got Manta, Pranlo and Drusni, *and* Counselor Latranesto."

So this was indeed an official conversation. Good. If they could get this hammered into place before Liadof found something else to object to—

"Got it," McCollum announced suddenly. "Boy, were you on target, Manta. There are a whole raft of them in here."

"Can you repeat that, please?" Manta said. "Some of those words didn't translate well."

Faraday frowned. The equipment buried in Manta's artificial spine should still be working, feeding him the human side of the conversation directly. Had it somehow failed?

Or had Manta simply forgotten how to understand English?

"There are quite a few trigger genes," McCollum told him. "Enough that you could actually get several different animals from this one single code, depending on which genes have been turned on and off. Like dog or cat variants; maybe even more."

"I understand," Manta said. "Is there any way for you to tell what the prompting factor might be?"

"Let me look," McCollum said, punching keys again. "Indications are that it's radiation of some kind. I'm not sure which part of the spectrum."

"It's not microwave or infrared," Milligan offered, studying his repeater display of her monitor as she skimmed down the listing. "The energy transition levels required are way too high for that. Must be soft X-rays, maybe even something higher."

"No, wait a second," McCollum said, her finger pausing on one of the lines. "Here's one low enough to be infrared-driven. Site 1557."

"Hang on," Milligan said, locating the spot. "You're right. Nuts. Well . . ."

"Could it be all the different light-parts that are involved?" Manta asked. "The whole herd of light-parts taken together?"

Across at his station, Sprenkle caught Faraday's eye. "He's leading the witness," he murmured. "That's significant."

Faraday nodded. And the precise significance of it wasn't hard to guess. "You seem to already know what's going on, Manta," he suggested. "Why don't you save us a lot of time and just tell us?"

There was a short pause. Then, a little hesitantly, the tonals began rumbling again. "Many types of plants and animals are disappearing from Centerline," the translation came. "Yet most of them are only brothers of those still here."

"Brothers?" Milligan asked under his breath.

"Variants," Beach told him.

"It's my belief that all the light-parts from Jupiter's center have decreased," Manta continued. "Without it, the tiny flips cannot function, and so the brothers stop being born."

"Interesting," Sprenkle murmured. "Mutation as a daily way of life."

"Strictly speaking, it's not mutation," McCollum corrected. "The genetic material is already there and in place, just waiting to be used. All the radiation is doing is turning different parts of the code on and off."

"Right," Milligan agreed. "Sites one through one million get turned on, you get a Vuuka. Sites one million through two million get turned on instead, and you get . . . something else, I guess."

"It's a novel approach to species diversity, anyway," Faraday commented thoughtfully. "The lowered radiation level should be easy enough to confirm from up here, if it's really happening. You say it's only affecting the Centerline regions, Manta?"

"Yes," Manta said.

"Mm," Faraday murmured. "You have any idea what might have caused it?"

There was another pause. "He knows, all right," Sprenkle murmured. "But he's afraid to tell us."

Faraday nodded. Afraid to show weakness, to put himself and the Qanska in a more vulnerable bargaining position. After the Omega Probe disaster, he couldn't really blame him. "If it'll help, Manta," he said, "you have my personal word that we'll do everything we can to help you and your people. Whether we get the stardrive or not."

At the edge of his peripheral vision, he saw Hesse stir. "A comment, Mr. Hesse?" he invited.

"I don't think Arbiter Liadof would be very happy if she heard you making promises like that," Hesse said carefully, jerking his head back toward where Liadof was standing. "Don't forget the, uh, the situation."

Faraday looked over at Liadof. Hesse was right; she didn't look very happy at all. "I remember the situation quite well, thank you," Faraday said, to both of them. "My promise still stands. Manta? We're listening."

"There's a region of the atmosphere called Level Eight," Manta said. "It's an area that can only be reached by those who have grown old enough and large enough to be called the Wise. There are no predators or scavengers in Level Eight, and a Qanska can live there as long as he can swim and find food."

"Sounds like the Garden of Eden," Beach commented.

"To the Qanska, it is," Manta agreed. "But like Eden, it carries within it the seeds of its own destruction. As I said, there are no predators or scavengers to bother the Qanska there. What then happens to one of the Wise when he dies?"

The techs looked uncertainly at each other. "Ms. Mc-Collum?" Faraday invited. "You're the resident expert."

"Thanks, Colonel," McCollum said dryly. "Well, the first thing that happens is that they stop breathing and swimming. Their muscles relax, which collapses their buoyancy sacs—"

"They sink," Sprenkle said suddenly. "They sink deeper into the atmosphere."

"And their bodies block the radiation," Beach said. "Sure."

"Manta, is that it?" Faraday asked. "Is that what's happening?"

"But there can't be that many bodies down there," Milligan objected. "I mean, they've only been on Jupiter for twenty or thirty years."

"Not true," Manta said. "I'm told it's been two thousand human suncycles since the first of the Wise arrived."

Milligan whistled softly. "They did a good job of hiding, didn't they?"

"Or we just did a lousy job of looking," McCollum countered. "Colonel, we'd have to do a numerical analysis; but if they've been on Jupiter that long, there could very well be enough dead bodies down there to block the radiation. Enough to mess up these gene triggers, anyway."

"Especially since most of them congregate in the equatorial regions to begin with," Sprenkle pointed out. "The vast majority of the bodies will end up floating in that same narrow band."

"Seems reasonable," Faraday agreed. "Manta, do you have any idea how deep this blocking layer is?"

"No," Manta said. "Counselor Latranesto has spoken with some of the Wise, and they've sent word all across Jupiter along the special speaking layer of Level Eight. So far, no one seems to know."

"Probably can't get down there until you're dead," McCollum said. "You can only collapse those buoyancy sacs so far on your own."

"A living Qanska would need a scuba diver's weight set," Sprenkle added. "Even then, the pressure might kill him."

"You understand our dilemma," Manta said. "If we can't reach that region, there's no possibility of solving the problem ourselves."

Faraday grimaced. He should have ordered Liadof out of the room, kicked her out by force if necessary. Now, it was too late. She'd heard Manta's confession, and knew the Five Hundred were in the driver's seat on this. "I'm sure we can do something to help," he said. "Mr. Milligan, pull up the specs on the various probes we've got on the station. I want to know which ones can go the deepest."

"Right," Milligan said, turning to his keyboard. "We might have to do some redesigning, though."

"We'll do whatever we have to," Faraday said firmly. "Manta, have you had any ideas as to how we might be able to break up this logjam, assuming we can get to it?"

"I was thinking of the probe that was used against our children," Manta said. "If we can move enough of the bodies out of the way, the radiation will be free to come through again."

"Sounds like a pretty slow process," Faraday said doubtfully. "Besides, won't they just rearrange themselves to fill in the gap?"

"And where do we put the ones we pull out?" Sprenkle added. "Haul them all the way to the polar regions?"

Faraday looked suddenly across at Hesse, gazing quietly at the displays. *The polar regions?*

"They wouldn't have to be taken that far," Manta said. "Just somewhere away from Centerline."

"There may be a faster approach," Faraday said, watching Hesse closely. So far the younger man didn't seem to have picked up on Faraday's line of thought. Had Liadof? "Possibly a way to clear away some of the bodies *and* stimulate these trigger genes at the same time."

And then, suddenly, Hesse got it. He twisted his head toward Faraday, his eyes wide. "You mean . . . the nukes?"

"Nukes?" Sprenkle echoed, as four heads turned in unison to look at Hesse.

"What nukes?" Milligan demanded.

Glancing around, Faraday saw Liadof starting across the room toward him, her face a dark shade of red. He waved her back, baring his teeth in warning. If Manta found out he'd lied about her being out of the room, they could kiss these negotiations good-bye.

For a wonder, she got the message. Her hands balled into fists, but she reluctantly nodded.

But instead of returning to the door, she stepped over to Hesse. Wrapping one hand around his neck, she began murmuring into his ear.

"We have a pair of half-gig weapons on the way here," Faraday explained to the others, fighting to keep his mind on his train of thought as he watched Liadof and Hesse whispering together. "Arbiter Liadof planned to set them off in the polar regions in order to create a global pattern of sonic shock waves that would show where the Qanskan stardrive is located. I think I can persuade her that she can put them to better use breaking up your logjam."

He paused for effect. "Provided, of course, that there's no longer any reason for us to have to go hunting for the stardrive."

"And if I may add, Mr. Raimey, we've fulfilled our part of the bargain," Hesse spoke up. "Or at least we know how to do so. It's your turn to give *us* something."

Manta seemed to take a long time to think that one over. "I cannot give you a stardrive to study," he said at last. "But after you have broken the barrier and we can see that full life has returned to Centerline, we will take you to the path between worlds."

"How do we know you'll keep your promise?" Hesse asked. "What guarantees do you offer?"

"What guarantees do you want?" Manta countered.

Liadof whispered in Hesse's ear again. Hesse jerked, staring at her in disbelief. Liadof gestured imperiously toward the displays; with a grimace, Hesse nodded. "We want to hold some hostages," he said, the words coming out like pulled teeth. "Specifically, your friends Pranlo and Drusni." He took a deep breath. "And their children."

"No!" Faraday snapped, jumping to his feet. "Not a chance."

Liadof gestured again. "That's our price," Hesse said with a sigh. "If you want our help—"

"Excuse us, Manta," Faraday cut him off, teeth clenched together. "We need to have a conversation up here. And you probably need to find some food and then get some sleep. Can you return to the probe at sunlight?"

"Yes," Manta said, the tonals deepening in tone. "We will speak again at that time."

"Thank you," Faraday said. "We'll hopefully have this straightened out by then."

"I trust so," Manta said. "Farewell."

"All mikes off," Faraday ordered, flipping off his own microphone. He waited until the techs had complied, then turned to Liadof. "Arbiter, with all due respect, what the hell do you think you're doing?"

"Carrying out Changeling's mission statement, of course," she said icily. "Unlike you, who would simply give the Qanska everything they want and ask nothing in return."

Faraday looked at Sprenkle. "Dr. Sprenkle, an opinion. What's the state of Manta's mental health?"

"His basic personality seems mostly the same as when he left us," Sprenkle said. "However, while the foundation hasn't changed, there's definitely been a great deal of growth and maturation. More, frankly, than I would have expected even a few months ago." He hesitated. "He also seems to have picked up some of the Qanskan sense of honor."

"I see," Faraday said. "Bottom line: If we carry out our side of a bargain, will he carry out his?"

"Absolutely," Sprenkle said. "What he mostly needs right now is to reestablish some trust in us. Both for his own sake, and that of his standing among the other Qan-ska."

Faraday turned back to Liadof. "So that's it," he said firmly. "We need to show some good faith."

He lifted his chin defiantly. "And we're going to do so, whether you like it or not. I've given Manta my word."

He'd thought Liadof's eyes were as hard as they ever got. He'd been mistaken. "I think, Colonel," she said softly, "that it's time for us to have another little chat."

"I agree," Faraday said, just as softly. He looked around the board. "Stay on top of the situation, everyone. Everything's to be done by the book."

"Yes, sir," Beach answered for all of them.

Faraday nodded and turned back to Liadof. "Please; after you."

They swam until the human probe was just a glint in the distance before any of them dared speak again. "Manta, I won't do it," Drusni said, her voice trembling. "I won't let them take my children."

"You won't have to," Manta told her grimly, lashing his tails in frustration and uncertainty. What in the Deep was going on up there? Faraday was the human who'd talked him into coming here in the first place, the one who'd stood by him through all the confusion and pain of those early ninedays. Could he really have become so cruel?

He lashed his tails again. No. He could hardly remember the human language anymore, relying instead on the tonals the humans' translator sent through the probe. But the receiver they'd planted in his brain was still working; and he could still make out the differences between human voices. It had been Faraday who had spoken up against the other human's demand for hostages.

For that matter, it had been Faraday who'd insisted on cutting the conversation short. Did he have a plan to stop these other humans?

"What if they won't help us otherwise?" Latranesto

asked darkly. "We've now told them of our weakness; and on top of that, you've basically told them we don't have the machine they want. We have nothing left to hold them to their promise."

"Not true," Manta said. "We may not have a machine; but we *do* have the pathway they want. Besides that, we have Faraday's promise that they will help us."

Latranesto snorted. "The promise of a human. Do you really believe we can trust that?"

"I trust his intentions," Manta said. "Unfortunately, he may no longer have the power to carry out the promises he makes. If this human Liadof is really part of the Five Hundred, she holds more power than Faraday."

"Are these Five Hundred evil?" Pranlo asked.

"Not necessarily," Manta said. "But they have great power, and they've become accustomed to wielding it. Among humans, that's a dangerous thing."

"Then if they're against us, there is no hope," Latranesto said.

"No," Manta said, looking back at the probe. "There's still Faraday. We'll just have to hope he can persuade the Five Hundred to cooperate with us."

"And if he can't?" Drusni asked.

"I trust that he can," Manta said. "If he can't . . . well, we'll just have to find something else to bargain with. If we can."

"We'll find something," Pranlo said. "You have confidence in Faraday; I have confidence in you."

He flipped his tails. "And while we discuss it, I'm hungry. Let's go find something to eat."

TWENTY-NINE

They found a small discussion room down the corridor that—not surprisingly, given the hour—was unoccupied. Liadof stomped her way inside, with Faraday right behind her. Hesse, grim and silent, followed a distant third.

"Sit down, Colonel," Liadof ordered as she dropped into the chair at the head of the table. "Mr. Hesse, close the door."

"You're not taking hostages, Arbiter," Faraday said as he sat down at the opposite end of the table. "Absolutely not."

"I'm impressed by your high moral standards, Colonel," Liadof bit out. "I'm equally impressed by the shortness of your memory. Have you forgotten our earlier conversation?"

"No," Faraday said tartly. "Have *you* forgotten your own high-ground position? I thought getting the stardrive was your first and only priority."

"There is no stardrive," Liadof said sourly. "You heard him: 'I cannot give you a stardrive to study.' What else can that mean but that they haven't got anything?"

" 'But after you have broken the barrier, we will take you to the path between worlds,' " Faraday finished the quote. "What's the difference between that and actual hardware?"

"The difference is that if there's no physical stardrive, then there's nothing we can use," Liadof said. "Some esoteric stargate or wormhole buried deep inside Jupiter may be handy for them, but it's useless to us."

Faraday shook his head. "No. I'm not convinced this is anything but a semantics problem. That statement could just as easily mean that there *is* a stardrive, but that they're simply not going to let us study it."

"In which case, there's still no point in continuing this process, is there?" Liadof retorted. "Mr. Hesse, sit down. You're making me nervous."

Silently, Hesse stepped over from where he'd been fidgeting by the door. Choosing a chair equidistant from the two antagonists, he sat down.

"I didn't mean they would *never* let us study it," Faraday said patiently. "But they clearly want their problem taken care of first."

"Fine," Liadof said. "And I'm willing to meet them halfway. But if it *does* exist, I want to at least get a look at it before we proceed any further."

Faraday shook his head. "We need to show good faith," he said. "You heard what Dr. Sprenkle said. If we do that, we can trust Manta to come through on his part of the bargain."

"Can we?" Liadof demanded. "Dr. Sprenkle's opinions notwithstanding, the fact is that we really don't know how Mr. Raimey thinks anymore. If he decides to stiff us, we go home empty-handed."

Faraday leaned back in his seat. "And *that's* what you're really afraid of, isn't it?" he said. "The fear of looking foolish; of not being able to deliver the hand-wrapped birthday present your faction promised the Five Hundred when they took power."

"My personal political standing is not the issue, Colonel," Liadof said evenly. "And, just for your information, that standing is also not in any danger."

"Then what does it cost you to be magnanimous?" Faraday urged. "Fix the problem for them. Be a hero on Jupiter, and at the same time buy yourself some goodwill throughout the System. All it'll cost will be a couple of nuclear warheads that no one's using anyway."

"And you'll also be demonstrating great foresight,"

Hesse murmured. "After all, you're the one who asked for the weapons in the first place."

"That's right," Faraday said, pouncing on the idea. If he could just persuade Liadof that helping Manta was in her best interests . . . "In fact, if you'd like, we could even backdate the radiation studies we're going to do so that you could claim to have noticed the decrease in equatorial output a couple of months ago. You suspected the problem, deduced a solution, and commissioned more study."

"Interesting idea," Liadof said. "Unfortunately, I've already told the Five Hundred and Sol/Guard that the weapons were for a sonic study."

"You could say you weren't yet absolutely sure of the facts," Hesse suggested. "Rather than start rumors, you used the sonic study idea to get the weapons transferred here. If the radiation thing turned out to be a false alarm, you could still use them for the sonic study."

"Very clever," Liadof agreed. "Both of you."

Her face settled into its deep lines. "And all *that* would cost would be letting you assist me in a lie, which would give you a lever you could use against me for the rest of my life." She shook her head. "Nice try, Colonel."

Faraday sighed. "Arbiter, what's it going to take to get through to you? I'm not interested in power, or levers, or your destruction. All I want is to open up the universe to humanity, and to do it in a way that lets me sleep at night. Is that too much to ask?"

"You'll have to ask your friend Mr. Raimey about that," Liadof said brusquely, getting to her feet. "He's the one standing in your way. Excuse me, but I have to get a report ready to send to the Five Hundred."

Faraday took a deep breath. "Then you're going to have a fight on your hands," he warned her. "I'm going to use those nukes to fix Manta's logjam problem. And if you get in my way, I *will* take you down."

Liadof paused halfway to the door. "Are you insane?" she asked, the skin around her eyes crinkling as she stared at him. "You have no authority here."

"On the contrary," Faraday said. "I'm in complete charge of Project Changeling. You said so yourself less than an hour ago."

"And I can just as easily take that authority back," she said, sounding vaguely bewildered. "You know, I don't think I've ever seen power go to someone's head quite so fast."

Faraday shook his head. "No. Half an hour ago you could have done that, and there would have been nothing I could have done to stop you. But not now. By now, Mr. Beach will have sent the full transcript of our conversation with Manta back to Earth."

"Nonsense," Liadof retorted. "I didn't hear you give any such orders."

"Sure you did," Faraday said. "When they all came in, remember? 'Procedure is by the book,' I told them. I don't know how you did things when you were in charge, but *my* book always included automatic forwarding of all Jovian conversations."

A touch of uncertainty edged into Liadof's glare. "Mr. Hesse, go see what's going on back there," she ordered. "And put a stop to it."

"Don't bother," Faraday advised as Hesse stood up. "By now, the transcript is shooting toward Earth at the speed of light. In half an hour the Five Hundred will know we've been offered the way out of the Solar System in exchange for help with the Qanskan logjam problem. Half an hour after that, the public will know all about it, too."

"Only if the Five Hundred want them to know," Liadof countered.

"Maybe not," Faraday said. "We also have access to the newsnets from here on the station."

"You can't put classified material on the newsnets," Liadof snapped. "That's a direct violation of Sol/Guard regulations."

"Ah, but I'm the one in charge here," Faraday reminded her. "As long as we're not talking official military or government secrets, *I'm* the one who gets to decide what's classified and what's not."

"The Qanskan stardrive *is* a governmental secret," Liadof snapped.

"Not officially," Faraday said calmly. "As far as I know, its existence has never even been acknowledged, let alone classified."

He lifted his hands. "Face it, Arbiter. An hour from now my name and that of Project Changeling will be back at the top of the conversational stack."

Liadof smiled coldly. "And you think I didn't recognize that possibility when Mr. Raimey first contacted us? Come, Colonel, give me at least a little credit for brains. Why else do you think I sent Mr. Hesse scrambling to make sure you signed that paper before I let you back in?"

"Because you didn't think a man who'd convicted himself of treason could afford to stand against you?" Faraday suggested.

"Because even if such a man were brash enough to try, his signature on that paper would quickly destroy whatever public popularity he might have," she said. "But if you choose to commit social suicide on the newsnets, by all means do so. *I* certainly don't need you anymore."

"Oh?" Faraday asked. "What about Manta? He won't talk to anyone but me, you know."

"I don't need him anymore, either," she said. "I'm sure Counselor Latranesto will be more than willing to take his place as bargainer for the Qanska. If they have anything left to bargain with. Come along, Mr. Hesse." She turned back toward the door—

"All right, then," Faraday said. "I guess there's nothing more to be said. We'll take this to the public and let them decide."

He gestured to Hesse. "In which case, you probably ought to retrieve your Judas document from Mr. Hesse."

"Indeed," Liadof agreed, turning back. "Mr. Hesse?"

"Yes, Arbiter." A pained expression on his face, Hesse reached into his pocket and pulled out the folded paper.

"And," Faraday added softly, "you might also want to take a look at the signature."

For a moment Liadof froze, her hand stretched halfway toward the paper in Hesse's hand. Then, like a pouncing rattlesnake, the hand darted out to snatch it from his grip. She pulled it open, her eyes dropping to the line at the bottom—

Her head twisted back up toward Faraday. "What the hell is *this*?" she bit out.

"It says 'Charlie the Carp,'" Faraday said helpfully. "He's that animated spokesman for the Association of Fish Hatcheries—"

"I know who he is," Liadof snapped. She turned her glare on Hesse. "Hesse?"

Hesse's mouth was hanging partway open in disbelief. "Arbiter, I swear—"

"Don't blame Mr. Hesse," Faraday told her. "The fact of the matter is, I've been on to your little game from the very beginning."

"Really," Liadof said icily, her eyes still on Hesse. "I wonder how."

"Don't blame him for that, either," Faraday said. "He played his part just fine." He cocked an eyebrow. "The problem was with the script you gave him to read."

"What do you mean?" she demanded. "What problem?"

"Problems like telling me Mr. Beach was giving him the inside scoop on what was happening on the project, but then describing Manta's new caretakers as a male and female," Faraday said. "Mr. Beach would never have referred to them that way; he'd have called them a Protector and Nurturer, which was what they were. Then there was the whole idea of an opposing faction in the Five Hundred who wanted me to join them. That one was just a little too convenient."

"I wondered about that," Liadof muttered.

"Yes," Faraday said. "And finally, the crowning touch: the fact that after several weeks he was *still* their only representative here. They could surely have brought in someone with more experience by that time. *If* they really existed."

"I see," Liadof said, her voice sounding like she was trying to grind the words into powder between her teeth. "So you signed a phony name. It's still your signature."

Faraday shrugged. "I held the pen rather awkwardly. It might or might not be close enough."

"Your fingerprints are on the paper."

"I never picked it up."

"Your sweat, then," she persisted. "DNA analysis."

"I never even touched it," Faraday told her. "I held it down with shirtsleeved elbow Sol/Guard issue shirt, by the way—there are millions of them around the System. And I rested my hand on the edge of the desk, not the paper. There's absolutely nothing there to link me to that document."

Liadof's breath, Faraday noted, was coming rather heavily. "And you think this was all I had against you?" she asked, waving the paper.

"Maybe not," Faraday said. "But without that paper, you don't have enough to beat me. Not now. If you choose to fight, you're going to lose."

He paused. "The alternative is to settle this quietly, right here and now," he added. "And it's still not too late for you to get the credit and glory for getting humanity out of the Solar System."

Her eyes narrowed as she studied him. "Are you telling me," she said slowly, "that you don't want it yourself?"

"Not at all," Faraday confirmed. "I've already told you what I want."

"Really." She smiled tightly. "Not even if all that credit and glory translates to more political power in my pocket? Power which I could easily turn around and use against you?"

Faraday gestured toward Hesse. "Mr. Hesse told me you

never seek revenge for its own sake," he said. "I'm willing to take the chance."

Slowly, almost unwillingly, Liadof stepped back to her chair. "All right, Colonel," she said, laying the paper down on the table. "I'm listening."

THIRTY

"We're almost to the end of Level Seven," Milligan reported, alternating his attention between three different monitors. "Pressure's scaling as predicted; no problems."

"What about the tether?" Faraday asked, his thoughts flashing back to that resonance humming noise his *Skydiver*'s tether had picked up on that fateful ride. "Is it handling the winds okay?"

"The wind is definitely picking up," Milligan said. "But so far the tether seems to be handling it just fine."

"What about the tether ship?" Faraday asked.

"They report everything running green," McCollum said, pressing the earphone tightly against the side of her head. "We're getting an annoying wind-hiss, though."

"Tell them to get used to it," Faraday advised. "It'll probably get worse before it gets better."

"Right." McCollum began speaking softly into her mike.

"Coming up on Level Eight," Milligan said.

"A shame we didn't think to get a monitor down to you, Manta," Sprenkle called. "You'd have been able to see what your Garden of Eden looks like."

The Contact Room rumbled with tonals. "That's all right," the translation came. "I fully intend to live long enough to see it in person. Besides, your vision is so much poorer than ours. I doubt your machine would give me much of a look."

Sprenkle smiled. "Touché."

Beside Faraday, Liadof stirred. "Which brings up another

question," she said. "What makes you think *we're* going to be able to see anything that deep, either? Those cameras only go down to deep ultraviolet."

"Yes, but they also go the other direction into the infrared," Faraday reminded her. "If there really is a mass of dead bodies down there, they should be absorbing high-energy radiation from Jupiter's core and reemitting it at lower frequencies. At least some of that should come out as infrared."

"I hope so," Liadof said. "Otherwise, this whole exercise will be a complete waste of time and—"

"Turbulence!" Milligan barked. "Massive turbulence, hitting the probe."

"How bad?" Faraday snapped, jumping up from his chair and stepping behind Milligan. The inertial readings, he noted uneasily, were going crazy.

"Bad enough," Milligan said grimly. "The thing's being knocked around like a Ping-Pong ball."

"Manta, do you copy?" Faraday called. "We've hit a layer of turbulence. Do your people know anything about that?"

"I don't know," Manta said. "I've never heard anyone speak of it."

"How about Latranesto?" Beach suggested. "He might know something."

"He went down to Level Six to watch the probe's descent," Manta said. "I'll ask him when he gets back up here."

"Assuming we still have a probe by then," Liadof ground out.

"It'll make it," Milligan assured her. "As long as the tether doesn't break, the probe should hold together."

"Tether ship status?" Faraday asked.

"They're getting bounced a little, but they're holding position," McCollum reported. "The winch mechanism seems to be holding up all right."

"Tell them to keep a close eye on it," Faraday ordered.

"I just hope there aren't too many more of these layers down here."

"I think we'll find there's at least one more," Beach said. "Probably at the bottom of Level Eight."

"What makes you say that?" Faraday asked, frowning.

"Remember what Manta said back when he first resurfaced?" Beach reminded him. "He mentioned a special speaking layer of Level Eight."

"Of course," Milligan said suddenly. "Put a turbulence layer on either side of Level Eight, and you've got yourself a huge sonic waveguide. Just like a fiber optic cable, only for sound instead of light: The message bounces back and forth between the layers as it propagates down the mostly calm area in the middle."

"Which is how the Wise can call all around the planet but no one above them can listen in," McCollum said, nodding. "I've been wondering about that."

"Clever," Sprenkle remarked. "And it makes perfect sense that the Wise would keep that fact as secret as possible. All social power structures depend to one degree or another on good communication."

"If you don't mind, Dr. Sprenkle, let's save the sociology lecture for later," Liadof said tartly. "We have something a little more urgent on our plate right now."

"Urgent, perhaps, but nothing we can do anything about," Faraday pointed out. "At this point the probe's pretty much on its own."

"Unless we haul it out of there," Liadof retorted. "Is there something wrong with simply getting it out of there before it tears itself apart?"

"Actually, there's not much point in doing that," Sprenkle said. "From the wind pattern readings, I'd say it's already well past the halfway mark."

"And it's holding together?" Faraday asked.

"We're still getting transmissions along the tether," Milligan said with a shrug.

"There," Sprenkle said, pointing to one of the displays. "Look—it's through."

He was right, Faraday saw: The inertial indicators were settling down. "Confirmed," Milligan said. "We're back to steady westerlies again."

He looked over his shoulder at Faraday. "Do you want me to hold it here while the diagnostics check it over?"

"No, keep it moving," Faraday said. "The diagnostics can run just as well on the fly as they can stationary. Let's just hope the lower layer isn't as bad as this one."

"And hope it's the last," Liadof added. "I don't suppose you know anything about that, either, Mr. Raimey?"

Manta's tonals began rumbling through the speakers. "I don't know anything about what lies below Level Eight," the translation came.

"Of course not," Liadof said, half under her breath. "You don't know anything useful, do you?"

There was just the slightest pause. "I'm sorry my knowledge is not up to your standards," Manta said. "Colonel Faraday, can you tell me when you'll be sending the weapon down?"

"Give us a break, Manta," Faraday protested. "We don't even know how deep it's going to have to go yet."

"You said you already knew."

"We know how deep we *think* it should be," Faraday corrected. "But that's based on a whole collection of different density and structural assumptions."

"That's why we're sending the probe," Liadof added. "Why, are you in a hurry or something ?"

"My people have a problem," Manta reminded her, his voice hardening. "We'd like it to be solved."

"And that's all there is to it?" Liadof pressed.

"I don't understand the question," Manta said.

"Then let me put it another way," Liadof said. "It occurs to me that there are only two general places where this alleged stargate of yours can be located: Either it's somewhere above the cadaver logjam, or it's somewhere below it. Does that make sense, Mr. Raimey?"

"I suppose," Manta said hesitantly. "I don't really know."

"Now, logically, it can't be below it, because apparently

even dead Qanska can't go any deeper than that," Liadof continued. "Therefore, it must be above it."

She threw a hard look at Faraday. "And if it's above it, then our probe should be hitting it very soon now. Wouldn't you say, Colonel?"

All four techs had turned around to look at her. "What exactly are you suggesting, Arbiter?" Faraday asked carefully.

"I'm suggesting one of two things," Liadof said, her voice hard and cold. "Either the whole stargate story is a complete boxful of lies; or else we're about to find it ourselves, right here on our own."

She lifted her eyebrows. "In either case, one way or the other, I don't see that we need the Qanska anymore."

Faraday stared her in disbelief. She couldn't be serious. To pull something like this *now*? "I trust you're not suggesting we back out of our agreement," he said. "I've given my word. *You've* given *your* word."

"Based on a story that may not be true," Liadof countered. "Mr. Raimey was a business major. He knows the value of a contract made under false pretenses."

She raised her voice a little. "What about it, Mr. Raimey? Do you and the Qanska expect a service to be offered in return for lies?"

"It's not a lie," Manta insisted. "The pathway exists. I just don't know where."

Something pinged. "Hitting the next turbulence layer," Milligan announced, turning back to his board.

"Sorry, but I don't believe that anymore," Liadof said. "And you can tell Counselor Latranesto I said so. Unless the probe hits this supposed region of pressure and winds and multiple directions—whatever the hell *that* means— then we're just going to conclude that it doesn't exist."

Sprenkle cleared his throat. "That hardly seems fair—"

"Shut up," Liadof cut him off. "Mr. Milligan, anything odd showing up in your readings?"

"It's a little hard to tell right now," Milligan ground out. "Once the turbulence ends, I'll take a look."

"Make it a good one," Liadof ordered. "And a fast one. If this is all a lie, I want that probe brought back up before it takes any more damage."

"Just a moment," Manta called. "Counselor Latranesto has returned."

The speaker went silent. "Mr. Beach?" Liadof asked. "What's happening?"

"They've both moved off a ways from the probe," Beach replied. "Probably wanted to talk in private."

"Arbiter, you can't be serious," Faraday said, keeping his voice low. "We had a deal."

"So we did," Liadof acknowledged. "But you know as well as I do how often deals shift and change. Especially with changing circumstances."

She turned steady eyes on him. "You made me look bad in that conference room, Colonel," she said, her voice so quiet he could barely hear her. "You pushed me into a corner, with no way out except to give you what you wanted. A very effective technique, you have to admit."

She looked back at the displays. "Now, it's my turn."

Faraday stared at her, feeling like he'd been slapped across the mouth with a live electrical wire. "Is *that* what this is about?" he demanded. "Your pride?"

"Call it what you want," she said, turning back to the displays. "Mr. Beach?"

"They're coming back," Beach reported.

"Good," Liadof said. "Mr. Milligan, are we through the turbulence yet?"

"Just coming out of it," Milligan muttered.

"Excellent," she said. "I'm waiting, Mr. Raimey. Convince me all of you are worth my trouble."

A deeper and highly agitated-sounding set of tonals began rumbling through the speaker. "This is Counselor Latranesto," the translation came. "You cannot do this. Not now."

"I'm sorry, Counselor," Liadof said. "But I don't deal with liars."

"I'm not a liar," Latranesto insisted. "It's simply that you won't find the pathway here along Centerline."

"I'm afraid I don't believe you," Liadof said flatly. "Ms. McCollum, signal the tether ship to prepare to reel in the probe. We're finished here."

"Wait," Latranesto all but pleaded. "You believed me before. Why won't you believe me now?"

"Because I've had time to do some thinking," Liadof said. "Most of your people congregate along Centerline. Logically, the only reason for them to do that is if that's where they came out of this so-called pathway of yours. Therefore, if it's not on Centerline, it doesn't exist."

"Of course we came out along Centerline," Latranesto said. "That's how it always is, according to the stories. But that doesn't mean that's where the pathway begins."

"Then where is it?" Liadof asked softly. "Prove it's not a lie."

There was a desperate, wordless rumble. "The pathway begins in the farthest north," Latranesto said. "Where all directions meet."

"You mean at the north pole?" Faraday asked.

"More likely magnetic north," Liadof said. "The Qanska use Jupiter's magnetic field to help navigate, don't they, Ms. McCollum?"

McCollum sighed. "Yes."

"Very good," Liadof said. All the firmness and indignation had vanished from her voice without a trace, leaving something almost genteel in its place. "Thank you, Counselor Latranesto."

"So what happens now?" Faraday demanded, the bitter taste of defeat in his mouth. So Liadof had won. At the last second, she'd kicked all their carefully negotiated agreements aside and forced the Qanska to give in to her.

"What happens now?" Liadof echoed, lifting her eyebrows at him. "We continue the mission, of course. Ms. McCollum, tell the ship to get the probe moving again."

"Which direction?" McCollum asked, frowning back at her.

"Down, of course," Liadof said, as if it was obvious.

"Let's find out where this logjam is we have to break up."

Faraday blinked. "Excuse me?"

"What part of it don't you understand?" Liadof asked, clearly enjoying his confusion. "We made a deal with the Qanska. We're going to carry that deal through."

"But you just—"

"I'm an Arbiter of the Five Hundred," she reminded him evenly. "My job is to make deals, and to negotiate, and to find common ground. But mostly, it's to make sure Earth gets what it wants."

"And now you've got it," Faraday said. "So . . . ?"

"You really don't understand, do you?" Liadof gestured toward the displays. "I have no problem with keeping deals, Colonel, or for delivering payment promised for value received."

She smiled tightly. "I just want to have my half of the deal delivered first."

"I see," Faraday said. "So you pushed the Qanska into a corner of your own. You made a promise, then threatened to withhold it."

"The System gets what it wants; the Qanska get what they want," Liadof said calmly. "By definition, everyone is happy. I frankly don't see what your problem is."

Faraday gazed at her, torn between disgust and pity. "No," he said. "I don't suppose you do."

She snorted. "Carry on, Colonel. Let's get this taken care of." Turning, she left the room.

The techs were looking back at him again. Or maybe they were staring after Liadof; Faraday wasn't sure which. "Manta?" he called. "Did you hear all that?"

"Yes," Manta said, his voice cautious. "I'm not sure I understand it, though."

"It means the trouble at this end is over," Faraday said. "Arbiter Liadof's managed to satisfy her wounded professional pride, and the deal's back in place."

"You're sure about that?"

"It was never really in doubt," Faraday told him firmly. "One way or another, I would have made it work."

"Of course," Manta murmured. "When will you be sending the weapon? Soon?"

In a hurry to get it done, no doubt, just in case Liadof took a fancy to renege again. Faraday couldn't really blame him. "As soon as possible," Faraday assured him. "We need to confirm the location of the logjam and make sure the weapon is armored enough to handle the pressure. They're already working on that last part. If the probe makes it down there all right, I'd guess we'll be ready to move in a week or two. Possibly sooner."

"Partly it depends on how fast you can clear the Qanska out of that area," Milligan added. "Even living with radiation all the time the way you do, I can't imagine a blast like this being very healthy for you."

"Though you never know," McCollum added. "It may create all sorts of interesting metabolic stimuli. We might get a surge of these alternate forms in the next Qanskan generation."

"Yes," Manta said, almost as if talking to himself. "The pressure will be the most difficult part, I suppose."

Apparently Manta's thoughts were still back on the question of the weapon's deployment. "Probably," Faraday agreed. "But that turbulence will be a kicker, too. I see now why only the Wise ever make it to Level Eight, and why predators never make it at all. You'd need a lot of strength to get through that top layer."

"Strength is important," Manta agreed, almost absently. "But it's mostly a matter of size alone. With enough extra weight, even a Breeder could probably get through."

"You'd better not tell anyone else that," Sprenkle warned dryly. "The Wise probably wouldn't like it if their private retirement community was suddenly turned into a weekend resort."

"Don't worry, I won't say anything," Manta said. "You'll be lowering the weapon on a tether, I presume?"

"That's the plan," Faraday said, frowning. There was something suddenly odd about Manta's voice, something he couldn't quite place. "Given the turbulence, I doubt a free-swimming system would ever make it where we wanted it to go."

"Yes," Manta murmured. "Continue, then. You'll keep us informed?"

"Of course," Faraday said, frowning a little harder. He didn't have to have Sprenkle's degree in psychology to know that something had just happened inside Manta's mind. Something important.

The question was, what?

He had no idea. But as he glanced around at the techs, he noticed that Beach, too, seemed to be frowning oddly at his control board. Either Beach had had the same epiphany, or else he had some private trouble of his own.

"More turbulence," Milligan called. "Seems to be milder this time."

"You know, I'll bet the logjam winds up being between two of these layers," McCollum suggested. "That would be a good way to hold all the bodies in place."

"Get the computer scrubbing the images from the probe," Faraday ordered, stepping back to his chair. They had work to do; and for the moment, at least, Manta's state of mind would have to wait.

So would Beach's, for that matter. Sitting down again, Faraday made a mental note to talk to the tech about it later.

They found the layer of floating bodies right where theory had predicted it would be. And, to McCollum's highly verbal satisfaction, they found it sandwiched between two mild turbulence layers.

It also wasn't the compact, layered clump that Faraday had envisioned, but something looser and more spread out. Less like a mass graveyard, he decided at that first glimpse, than simply a group of superhuge Qanska swimming in close order together. A few slightly smaller animals could be seen here and there in the gaps, both Qanska and a few large predators who had managed to elude the scavenging

Pakra after their deaths and make it through Level Eight. There was also a fair sprinkling of stray bones apparently left over from Pakra meals.

But whether logjam or fighter air-show formation, the effect was just as Manta had guessed. Above the layer of bodies, the radiation readings were predominantly in the low-energy end of the electromagnetic spectrum: mostly infrared, with small percentages edging into the short-wave radio and visible regions. Below the layer, once the tether ship crew managed to tease the probe between the floating bodies, were the heavy concentrations of ultraviolet, X-ray, and gamma radiation required to turn on and off most of the Qanskan trigger genes.

The tether ship crew got the probe reeled back in and returned it to the station. There Faraday and the others studied the records from the onboard sensors, and held what seemed like endless discussions with Latranesto and Manta and the techs building the pressure casing for the nuclear weapon. Some of the discussions became heated, with the techs saying the pressure and maneuverability requirements couldn't possibly be met, and Faraday insisting that by God they would be.

And finally, after all was said and done and said again, the date was set.

"Manta?"

Manta rolled over, peering into the gloom of Centerline sundark. Drusni was floating up behind him, her fin tips brushing gently against the wind. "Hi, Drusni," he said. "You're awake early."

"So are you," she pointed out. "I noticed you twitching a little while ago. You all right?"

"Sure," he said, trying to sound like he meant it.

He might have saved himself the effort. "You haven't slept at all, have you?" she asked quietly.

He grimaced. "No," he conceded. "I've tried. But I can't."

"You should have wakened me," she said. "I would have kept you company."

Manta flipped his tails. "I didn't want to do that," he said. "No point in all of us being tired today."

She moved closer to him. "What's wrong? Is it something about the machine the humans are going to be lowering this sunlight? Are you worried that it won't fix the problem? Or that they might change their minds and not send it at all?"

Manta hesitated. How could he answer that? What could he say? There was so much he wanted to tell her; so much he wanted to hear from her, and discuss with her, or just float silently and comfortably alongside her.

So much he knew now they would never have the time or opportunity for.

But he couldn't tell her even that much. If he let slip the slightest hint of what was about to happen, he would only frighten her.

No. Better for all concerned if he just went quietly, alone, into that long sundark.

"I really don't know what's going to happen," he said, choosing the safest part of the truth. "Faraday says they've gotten the pressure and control problems solved and are going to go through with it. But Faraday isn't the only Leader anymore. And we already know the kind of games this Liadof human likes to play with agreements."

Drusni reached out to stroke his fin. "They'll come through," she assured him. "You were once one of them, you know. If they're not interested in doing it for us, surely they'll do it for you."

Manta snorted gently. "Sure," he said. "You, uh, you and Pranlo going to be helping with that last sweep of Level One?"

"I think so," she said, maneuvering around to get a closer look at his expression in the dim light. "You're going to be with us, aren't you?"

"No," Manta said, trying to keep his voice casual. "The humans want me to follow the machine down to the bottom of Level Four. Make sure it doesn't draw some wandering Vuuka's attention."

"As long as there isn't any blood on it, I can't see why the Vuuka would care," Drusni said, frowning. "But if you do that, are you going to be able to get away in time?"

"Oh, sure," Manta said "It'll still have to go all the way down, way past Level Eight. Plenty of time."

"Uh-huh," Drusni said, still frowning. She wasn't buying this, Manta realized with a sinking feeling. "You know, maybe Pranlo or I should stay and go along with you. I'm sure Latranesto has enough people to check Level One."

"No, that's all right," Manta said quickly. "It's more important that you make sure all the children are out of range of the blast. Besides, there really isn't anything you can do to help me."

"Yes, but—"

"No buts," Manta said firmly. "I don't need your help. You go with Pranlo and make sure everything's clear above."

For a long ninepulse she floated silently beside him. Then, gently, she reached out and stroked his fin again. "Okay," she said. "But you be careful."

"Sure," Manta said. "Anyway. It must be almost sunlight. I might as well head up and get ready."

"Okay," she said. "Unless you want to talk a little longer."

He looked at her, her face and body shimmering in the dim light; and suddenly, completely unbidden, a stray memory flickered to life in the back of his mind. That human woman—Brianna? Was that her name?—the last human woman he'd ever loved.

Or at least, the last woman he'd thought he loved. Because now, with the perspective of age, and with the end of his life swimming swiftly toward him, he suddenly saw her with fresh eyes. What he'd thought back then was a quick and easy spontaneity had been in reality a lack of forethought and planning. Her version of wit, while funny enough, had relied on jokes and cruelty at other people's expense.

And the unjudgmental acceptance of everything and everyone that he'd so admired had been nothing more than the sign of a lazy, undiscerning, shallow character.

How could he have ever been attracted to such a woman? How could he even have tolerated her presence in the same room with him?

There was only one answer; a painful, embarrassing answer. The young Matthew Raimey, the human he had once been, had been just as shallow and self-centered and foolish as she was.

It was odd, he thought distantly, how you didn't even notice the changes taking place in yourself.

"Manta?"

He focused on Drusni, the memory of Brianna fading thankfully into the mists. Drusni, who had willingly paid a horrible price to protect her people, and had then shrugged it off in an attempt to salve Manta's own conscience.

"I asked if you wanted to talk some more," she repeated.

He sighed. Yes, he wanted to talk longer. He wanted to talk with her until sunlight turned to sundark, and nineday turned to nineday into nineday. He wanted to talk with her, and to laugh with her, and to be with her, until they were both too old to swim through Level Eight and slipped peacefully into death.

But they would never have that time now. And without it, there was no point in trying to squeeze anything more out of a few more ninepulses. "No, that's okay," he told her, flipping his tails. "I'd better get going." He hesitated. "Good-bye, Drusni. And . . . be sure to say good-bye to Pranlo for me."

With a final flip of his tails, he stretched out his buoyancy sacs and headed up. "Manta?" Drusni called after him. "Wait a pulse."

He ignored her, pushing hard against the air with his fins to put as much distance as he could between them. He had, he knew, begun his life on Jupiter as a royal pain in the tails to everyone around him. Lately, he'd tried to turn that around, to serve his friends and his people as best he could. Trying to make up for all the pain and frustration and anger he'd caused. Trying to return something good to them for this gift of life he'd been given.

Had he succeeded in bringing the scales back into balance? He didn't know For that matter, he didn't know if they ever truly could be balanced. How could anyone sweep away an unkind word, or a vicious thought, or an unfair rumor?

Or the death of a loved one's unborn child?

No, there was no balance possible. All he could do was serve them all as best he could, and hope that the past could somehow be put aside.

And now, here at the end, he had one last act of service to perform. One last gift to offer his people.

He continued upward, heading for the spot where the humans would soon be lowering their weapon. Away to the east, the sunlight was beginning to filter into the darkness.

THIRTY-ONE

"Tether ship reporting in," McCollum announced. "They're ready to start lowering the package."

"Tell them to stand by," Faraday said. "Mr. Milligan, you getting anything on any of the probes?"

"Everything seems clear," Milligan said. "Looks like we're good to go."

"Good," Faraday said, glancing one last time over the status displays. All did, indeed, seem to be ready. "Ms. McCollum, order the tether ship to proceed."

"Yes, sir," McCollum said. She repeated the order into her microphone, then leaned over her displays. "Tether ship has begun lowering the package," she reported after a minute. "Time to top of Level One, approximately five minutes."

Faraday nodded, and a taut silence descended on the room. The tether ship crew was the most experienced one on the station, with probably a hundred similar maneuvers under their belts. They knew what they were doing.

On the other hand, they'd never done it with a live half-gigaton nuclear weapon before. This would not be a good time for random mistakes to start creeping in.

"Payload's entering the upper atmosphere," Milligan reported. "No bouncing or instabilities yet."

"Wind is holding within acceptable limits," Sprenkle added. "We've got a storm developing a few kilometers to the northwest, but the projected track shows it staying well clear."

Faraday began to breathe again. Apart from the turbulence layers lurking down around Level Eight, this was the part everyone had worried about the most. Even under the best of conditions, the relatively sudden transition from vacuum to high-speed atmosphere could be a tricky one to handle. With the weight and bulk of the pressure shielding they'd had to build around the nuke, this was not the best of conditions.

"I'm getting something on Probe Four," Milligan said suddenly. "One Qanska, moving up fast toward the package."

"Who is it?" Faraday asked. "Anyone we know?"

"It's Manta," Beach murmured under his breath.

"It is?" Faraday said, frowning at him. With all the frantic activity of the past week and a half, it suddenly occurred to him that he'd never gotten around to asking Beach about the odd expression he'd seen on him back during that pivotal confrontation between Liadof and Counselor Latranesto. "How do you know?"

"It's Manta, all right," Milligan confirmed before Beach could reply. "What in the world is he doing here?"

"Maybe he's helping make sure the area's clear," McCollum suggested.

"Or he's here for some other reason," Faraday said, still looking at Beach. That same odd expression was back. "Mr. Beach, do you know something we don't?"

Beach shook his head. "Not really," he said. "It's just a . . . a feeling, I guess. Something Manta said, back when Arbiter Liadof was trying to bludgeon the stargate's location out of Counselor Latranesto."

"What was it?" Faraday asked.

"That's the problem: I don't know," Beach said. "Maybe it wasn't something he said, exactly, but the *way* he was talking. Something in his voice, or the way he was using the tonals."

"Yes," Sprenkle spoke up slowly. "Now that you mention it, I remember noticing something in his voice, too."

"Well, what was it?" Faraday asked again. "Come on; between the two of you, you know as much about the way

Manta talks and thinks as any ten other people in the System. Was he mad at Liadof for what she was doing? Mad at the rest of us for letting her do it?"

"I don't think it was anger," Sprenkle said. "Not exactly."

"I agree," Beach said. "It was—" He groped for words.

"Keep working on it," Faraday said tightly. "Mr. Milligan, what's he doing? Is he bothering the weapon?"

"Not at all," Milligan said. "He just seems to be riding down along with it."

"Where is it now?"

"Near the top of Level Two," Milligan said. "And unless we do something, we're going to be losing sight of it pretty soon, too. You want me to drop Four to keep an eye on it?"

Faraday hesitated, studying the locator display. "Nothing new on Seven's status, I take it?"

"Nope," Milligan said. "The thing's still doing lazy circles down on Level Three. Whatever went wrong with its rudder and control system is still wrong."

Faraday made a face. Murphy's Law in action. The one day they needed every single probe was naturally the day one of them would choose to go out of commission. Already their probes were spread too thin across the region, scattered strategically around to help Latranesto and the other Qanska make sure no one accidentally wandered into the blast zone. With Probe Seven making useless donuts in the air, leaving Probe Four where it was would mean the nuke would be out of their sight until it got near Probe Twelve, way down on Level Five. "And Manta's staying with the package?"

"Like he was glued there," Milligan said. "Maybe he's just giving it an escort."

Faraday pursed his lips. Still, what could happen to the weapon between Levels One and Five? "You'd better leave Four where it is," he decided. "It's the only one we've got that can cover that part of Level One. If Pranlo suddenly finds there's someone missing from the gathering point, we may need it available to do a fast search."

"Right," Milligan said. "Package is falling out of view . . . there goes Manta with it."

Faraday nodded. "Any headway, Mr. Beach?"

"It had to do with Liadof," Beach said. "You were right about that. But it wasn't just anger. It was something deeper. Like his world view had just gotten altered or something."

"And you're getting all this just from the tonals?"

Beach waved a hand helplessly. "I know it sounds crazy," he admitted. "But I know Qanskan tonals, and I know Manta. I know what I heard; I just can't put it into words."

Faraday grimaced. "This isn't getting us anywhere," he said. "Dr. Sprenkle, get on the computer and pull up the record of that conversation. We need something more than vague recollections of what Manta might have been feeling about whatever was sort of being said."

"I remember something," McCollum said suddenly. "We were talking about how the blast itself might stimulate the trigger genes and bring about a surge of alternate life forms. But I remember thinking that he wasn't really listening."

"Right," Beach said, snapping his fingers. "He was still back on how we were going to deploy the nuke. He wanted to know if we were going to use a tether on it."

"And he made some other comment," McCollum said. "Something I remember really wondering about."

"Do you remember what it was?" Faraday asked.

She shook her head. "Just that it was something really odd. I'm sorry."

Faraday hissed between his teeth. But then, he wasn't doing any better at pulling out the memories, either. The last week had been just too hectic. "Dr. Sprenkle, find me that record," he ordered. "I want to know what the hell Manta's got planned."

———

Beside him, the massive human weapon lowered itself ponderously along on its relatively thin tether line. Even through all the shielding and pressure protection, Manta imagined he could see the faint glow of its internal radiation leaking out. All around him, the world was brightening as the sun made its all too rapid passage across the sky.

And above him, the humans' spy probe was fading into the mists of Level One.

It was almost time.

He found himself staring at the weapon as it sank through the air beside him. The very thought of what he was planning was turning his stomach into an agonized knot.

But it had to be done. Already the human Liadof had shown the kind of negotiator she was; and Manta had studied humans like that in his business classes. Humans like Liadof never let a deal remain fixed. They would push and prod and argue and threaten and renege until they had everything they wanted.

And there was more Liadof wanted from the Qanska. Manta couldn't imagine what that might be, but it was sure as sundark that there was *something*. People like Liadof always wanted more. And the time she would most likely choose to spring her next demand would be right as the answer to their desperate problem was already in sight.

In other words, right about now.

Only the Qanska didn't have anything else to give her. And so she would push and prod and argue and threaten and renege . . . and when she didn't get whatever it was she thought they were holding back, she would reel the weapon back in and take it away from them.

It was up to Manta to make sure that didn't happen.

Up above, the watchful probe had completely vanished now. He and the weapon were out of the humans' sight.

Time to go.

He dived away from the glowing weapon casing, heading at a sharp angle downward toward Level Three. The tether was going to be the only really tricky part, but he'd had two and a half ninedays to come up with a plan.

He would find out now just how good a problem-solver he really was.

The probe he'd sabotaged was still where he'd left it, circling in the winds, its propellers spinning bravely but uselessly away. He approached it cautiously, making sure to keep out of view of its cameras. Timing it just right, he darted in and locked his teeth solidly around one of its stabilizer fins. Turning around, wondering what the humans would make of the abrupt change in the probe's view, he turned and headed back.

The weapon had made better progress than he'd expected during his absence, and he arrived at his projected interception point to find only the tether stretching downward toward the Deep. Flipping over, fighting against the strange tendency of the probe to turn sideways as he did, he started down the tether.

He caught up with the weapon near the bottom of Level Three. The connection between the tether and the pressure casing, he'd already decided, was probably his best bet. Gripping the probe in his mouth as tightly as he could, he began swinging its back end carefully against the casing, feeling like a diamond cutter working on an immensely valuable gem. This was the trickiest part of the whole plan, he knew, where a single careless mistake would ruin everything.

But he'd planned it carefully; and after only three impacts he saw that he'd succeeded. The protective cowling on one of the propellers had been crumpled back just far enough to expose an edge of the spinning blades without damaging the propeller itself.

And he was ready. *For you, human Liadof*, he thought toward the clouds above, and swung the spinning propeller into the side of the tether.

The alarm from Milligan's control panel cut through the Control Room like a trapped banshee. "Collision!" Milligan snapped. "Something's hit the tether!"

"Hit, nothing," McCollum corrected, jabbing a finger at the reading on one of the displays. "It's had a whole slice taken out of it."

"Abort deployment!" Faraday ordered, taking a long stride to Milligan's side. What the hell was happening? "Tether ship, you hear me? Stop it *now*."

"No!" Milligan insisted. "Colonel, we can't. Look at the tensile strength readings. You try to bring it up now, or even stop it, and the whole tether could snap."

Faraday ground his teeth helplessly as he looked at the readings. But Milligan was right. "Countermand that, tether ship," he said. "Keep it moving down, as smooth and steady as possible. Mr. Milligan, get Probe Four down there."

"On its way."

Faraday looked at Four's video display as the probe drove downward through the atmosphere. So far nothing but swirling air and the long black tether line . . .

And then, right at the edge of the display, there it was. The nuke, the now half-cut tether line—

And Manta, the rogue Probe Seven gripped in his mouth like a dolphin holding a prize salmon.

Using one of the probe's propellers to cut away at the tether line.

"Manta, stop!" he shouted. "Manta? *Damn* it. Milligan, get that probe into hearing range."

"He can hear you," McCollum said with a sigh. "He's just not listening."

"Get it down there anyway." Faraday gritted his teeth. With almost half the tether cut away, the nuke was being held up by little more now than a wing and a prayer. Any extra jostling, and they would lose it completely. "Sprenkle, what's the wind situation?"

"Holding steady," Sprenkle said. "And for whatever it's worth, I've got that conversation now. I think I've found the part we were all thinking of."

Faraday nodded grimly. "Go."

There was a soft click, and the computer's translation of Manta's voice came on the speaker. "Strength is important," the voice said thoughtfully. "But it's mostly only a matter of size. With enough extra weight, even a Breeder could probably get through."

"That was. it," McCollum said quietly. " 'With enough weight, even a Breeder could get through.' We'd been talking about Level Eight and the Wise. Why mention Breeders at all?"

"Unless he was thinking about himself," Sprenkle murmured.

"Wait a second," Milligan said slowly. "Are you saying he's thinking about taking the nuke down *himself*?"

"Not thinking about it," Beach corrected, his voice dark. "By cutting the tether that way, he's pretty much committed himself to it. It'll never make it through the turbulence layers now. Not without some protection."

"But how does he think he's going to carry it?" Milligan demanded. "He can't just—oh, hell."

"You got it," McCollum said, her voice dark with dread. "He'll carry it the only way a Qanska can carry something that big."

"But why?" Milligan demanded, sounding bewildered. "Why is he doing this?"

"Because of Liadof," Faraday said. Now, too late, the whole thing was obvious. "Liadof, and the underhanded way she threatened to back out of the agreement so as to squeeze out the stargate's location. Manta's making sure she can't do it again."

On Probe Four's display, Manta had shifted his grip on the probe in his mouth, working it around so that the propeller end lay over the intersection of his body and his right fin. From looking like a prize salmon, the thought flicked through Faraday's mind, to becoming a giant back scratcher. "And there's no way for you to shut down the propellers?" he asked Milligan, just to make sure.

Milligan shook his head. "I've been trying for the last two minutes," he said. "He must have taken out the control lines when he wrecked the rudder. They'll keep spinning till they run out of fuel."

Faraday nodded heavily. "Then there's nothing we can do."

On the display, Manta jerked suddenly; and with a splash of bright yellow blood, the exposed propeller dug into the skin on his back. "He's ready," McCollum murmured. "All he has to do now—"

She broke off as, without warning, a dark shape cut suddenly across the view from Probe Four's camera.

And as they watched, dropped straight toward Manta.

Manta winced in pain as the propeller blades sliced into his skin. An unpleasant but very necessary part of his plan. By making sure that Liadof couldn't suddenly pull the weapon back above the clouds, he had at the same time also doomed it to failure. With its tether damaged, it would never make it through the turbulence below without snapping the rest of the line, including the core signal wire necessary for setting it off.

Which meant that the only way for the mission to succeed would be if the weapon could be guided through to its target as a protected part of a Qanskan body.

He let go of the probe; and as it spun away, droplets of blood flying off its propeller, he thought back to the Qanskan Wise who had done the same thing for Chippawa and Faraday in their *Skydiver* over two suncycles ago. He had covered them with his own skin to protect them from the pressure and turbulence before returning them to the upper levels.

What had happened to that Wise afterward? Had he returned to Level Eight safely? Or had the huge bleeding wound left by the *Skydiver*'s departure drawn too many Vuuka for him to fight off? With a flush of shame, Manta realized he'd never asked about that. For that matter, he'd never even bothered to learn the Qanska's name.

Maybe generations to come would better remember Manta's name. Then again, maybe they wouldn't. Feeling the blood trickling along his fin, he maneuvered himself beneath the descending weapon—

And with a suddenness that made him gasp, something large and heavy slammed into his back.

He reacted instantly, twisting over and shoving back with his fins as hard as he could, trying to force his attacker away. But the other apparently knew that trick. He stayed right with Manta, pressing even harder against his back and the open wound there. Manta slashed his tails up, trying to startle or distract the other—

"Ow!" Pranlo's voice grunted in his ear. "Take it easy, will you?"

Sheer surprise froze Manta's muscles. "*Pranlo?* What are you doing here?"

"At this particular pulse, trying to keep your blood from spreading all the way to Level Six," Pranlo said shortly. "Hold *still*, will you?"

"That's not what I meant," Manta growled. "Come on, get off. I've got a job to do."

Pranlo didn't budge. "What, you mean the job of getting yourself killed?" he asked. "Sorry, but we're not letting you do that."

Manta winced. *We?* "Drusni's here, too?"

"Of course I am," Drusni answered, swimming around into Manta's line of sight. "Manta, how could you even *think* of doing something like this?"

Manta sighed. "I have to," he told her, his heart aching as he looked at her. "If I don't, the machine will never make it where it needs to go. And our world will continue to die."

"But it doesn't have to be you, does it?" Drusni asked, her voice pleading. "Why does it have to be you?"

"Because I'm the one who's here," Manta said. "Please, Drusni; Pranlo. This was hard enough before, when no one knew about it. All you're doing is making it worse. Please just leave and let me do it."

"No," Pranlo said firmly. "If it has to be done, then it

has to be done. But Drusni's right. You're not the one who's going to do it."

A sudden suspicion sliced into Manta like a pack of Sivra. Was Pranlo suggesting—? "No," he insisted. "You're not going to do this."

"No, he's not," a new voice rumbled from the side. "I am."

Drusni gave a startled little gasp, twisting around to look. Manta jerked with surprise of his own, rotating under Pranlo's weight to turn toward the voice. Another Qanska was swimming toward them, a big Protector.

And from his markings . . .

"Who are you?" Drusni demanded, her voice quavering.

"Oh, come now," the Protector said mildly. "I know it's been a long time, Breeder Druskani; but don't tell me you don't remember me?"

"It has indeed been a long time," Manta murmured. "Hello, Protector Virtamco."

"I greet you in turn, Breeder Manta," Virtamco said gravely. "I've come to do what has to be done."

"And I wouldn't argue with him if I were you, Manta," Pranlo advised. "I've already tried, and he's bigger than both of us."

"I don't care how big he is," Manta growled. What in the Deep was going on here, anyway? Was the whole world lining up to pile across his back? "What gives you the right to take this job?"

"You know, Manta, for a smart Qanska you can be really dumb sometimes," Pranlo said. "Or do you think you're the only one on Jupiter with feelings?"

Manta frowned. "I don't understand."

"I failed you," Virtamco said; and even through the pre-occupation of his own fear and annoyance, Manta found himself wincing at the shame in the Protector's voice. "I was assigned by the Counselors and the Leaders and the Wise to protect you. Not only did I not fulfill that duty, but it was my words and my attitude that drove you from Centerline. I sent you alone into the outer regions."

He lashed his tails. "So I've come here today to ask your forgiveness, and to do whatever I can to make it right."

Manta grimaced. He'd hated Virtamco at the time for what he'd said then. Hated him for a long time, in fact.

Now, from the perspective of age, those harsh words hardly even seemed worth mentioning.

They certainly weren't worth dying for.

"I don't put any blame on you for that," he told Virtamco. "I was . . . well, let's all admit that I wasn't very pleasant to be around back then. And on top of that, it must have sounded like the height of arrogance for me to be asking you . . . what it was I asked."

He flipped his tails. "What I'm trying to say is that I don't consider you having done anything that requires my forgiveness. But if *you* think so, then you certainly have it."

Virtamco rippled his fins. "Thank you," he said quietly. "But one may not simply accept forgiveness without also offering restitution. I'm ready for that part."

"But this is crazy," Manta objected. "Didn't you already receive punishment from the Counselors over that? *That* should be all the restitution you need to make."

"Except that there was no punishment," Virtamco told him. "The Counselors merely reminded me of my failure, and again gave me the task of protecting you."

"So why are you just showing up now?" Manta shot back. It was cruel, he knew, but he had to snap Virtamco out of his ridiculous guilty mood and get this conversation over with. The weapon was still sinking through the air, and he could feel his buoyancy sacs collapsing as he and the others drifted downward alongside it. A little more delay, and it would be too deep for him to get to.

Or had that been their plan all along?

"What makes you think he hasn't been around?" Pranlo countered. "Just because you haven't seen him?"

"Well, I could start by asking where he was when Gryntaro was getting ready to bite off my ear," Manta said pointedly.

Pranlo snorted. "Oh, come *on*. How do you think I got deep enough to go shooting up and bounce him off you?"

Manta stared at Virtamco. "But . . ."

"The Counselors had ordered you exiled," Virtamco said. "But I could see that Counselor Latranesto was unhappy with that requirement of the law. When I met Prantrulo, he didn't find it difficult to persuade me to assist him."

Manta sighed. "Look, Virtamco, I understand your feelings," he said. "But you can't let guilt control your actions. Especially guilt over something that wasn't really that bad."

"You don't understand, Manta," Virtamco said. "I came to ask your forgiveness, and I'm relieved and gratified that you've granted it to me. But that's not the only reason why I'm going to take the human machine to its place."

"The point is that we can't afford to lose you, Manta," Pranlo said. "Not just Drusni and me, because you're our friend, but all the Qanskan people. We need you."

"This won't be the end of our problems," Virtamco reminded him. "There will be more; and you, alone of all of us, have the gift of finding solutions."

"You wouldn't just abandon us, would you?" Pranlo added. "Surely you're not that selfish."

Manta took a deep breath, his tails twitching, his heart locked in indecision. "But I can't just ask someone to go die in my place," he said helplessly.

"Then we will take the decision from you," Virtamco said evenly. "Prantrulo?"

"I'm ready," Pranlo said.

Abruptly, the movement startling in its quickness, Virtamco flipped his tails and shoved himself toward them. Reflexively, Manta ducked—

And as the Protector's back swept past him, Pranlo opened his mouth wide, his teeth ripping across the skin.

"No!" Manta gasped, lunging uselessly forward as the yellow blood spattered across his face.

"Let me be," Virtamco said. Flipping around again, he slid smoothly beneath the descending weapon, letting it settle onto the fresh wound on his back. "I'll take it from here."

"This isn't right," Manta said again, his stomach twisting in guilt. "I should be the one doing this, not you."

"No," Virtamco said again. "Part of my task has always been to instruct you in the ways of the Qanska. I often failed in that task; but now, here, I offer my final lesson. You've already proven yourself willing to serve others, even to the point of giving of your life for them. That is indeed the height of wisdom, and honor, and courage."

He smiled. "But equally wise and honorable is to have the courage to allow others to serve you. Even many of the Wisc never learn that lesson, or else have too much pride to allow it."

He flicked his tails in salute. "Farewell, Manta, child of the Qanska. I give you to your friends, and to your people."

Slowly, Manta let his fins come to a halt. Virtamco continued to sink downward; and as he watched, Manta could see the Protector's skin beginning to grow protectively up around the weapon.

Quietly, Pranlo and Drusni floated up beside him. Together, they watched until Virtamco was lost to view in the mists. "Come on, Manta," Pranlo said, touching his fin. "Time to go."

The Contact Room had been silent for a long time, each of them with their own private thoughts, when McCollum finally stirred. "Tether ship reports the weapon is in position," she said quietly.

"Thank you," Faraday said. "Are all Qanska clear of the area?"

"All probes show clear," Milligan said.

"And Latranesto has also confirmed everyone's out of range," Beach added.

"And Manta?" Faraday asked.

Sprenkle lifted his eyebrows. "He's clear, too," he said. "With the rest of his people."

Faraday nodded. *Manta, child of the Qanska.* Virtamco had been right, he realized. Matthew Raimey, self-centered human being, no longer existed. In his place was now Manta, child of the Qanska, mature beyond his years.

And if this worked as they all hoped, the greatest Protector his people had ever known.

Project Changeling had started in desperation and greed. It was ending in peace and a minor miracle.

Not bad for a few years' work.

"Activate the weapon, Mr. Milligan," he said, leaning back in his chair. "Let's do it."

H ey, Manta! Wait up, will you?"

Manta rolled ponderously over onto his side, hearing the echoes of distant childhood in the deep voice rumbling from behind him. It was Drusni, of course, making her own ponderous way down toward him "Hi, Drusni," he greeted her. "Is there trouble?"

"Not really," Drusni said, settling in beside him. "Pranlo sent a message down from the rear. We're starting to string out again."

"Right," Manta said, slowing his pace. In his eagerness to move ahead with this, he sometimes forgot that not all of those going with them had his same speed and stamina.

Or maybe just his same weight. Even among the Wise, he was considered pretty hefty. "How about you?" he asked. "You holding up okay?"

"I'm doing fine," she assured him. "I was thinking a while back that this is just like old times again. You, me, and Pranlo, sneaking off from the herd on some grand adventure. The Three Musketta, together again."

"Together forever," Manta said, rolling over again to look at the hundreds of other Wise filling the sky behind him. "Though I don't know if this exactly qualifies as leaving the herd behind."

"Oh, well, I was thinking of the herd as being the rest of the Qanska back there in Centerline," Drusni explained, flipping her tails toward the south. "The ones who are just too content with life here to strike out and try something new. *That's* the herd. This is more like we're sneaking off with a few friends."

She tapped his fin. "And speaking of friends, have you decided yet which of the females you're going to mate with when we reach the new world and get stripped back·down to Breeders again?"

"Don't be silly," Manta said, gravely serious. "You know you're the only female I could ever truly love."

"Of course," she replied, equally serious. "I know that. But you have to think of the new world. You can't leave it to Pranlo and me to populate it all by ourselves, you know."

She flipped her tails. "Besides, some of those females strike me as the kind who'll be pretty pushy when they can frisk around again. I wouldn't want any of them getting the idea that I was standing between them and you."

Manta smiled. "Actually, there are a couple I'm considering," he told her. "Though I get the feeling Beltrenini thinks she deserves to be at the front of the line."

"And?" Drusni prompted. "Is she?"

"I don't know," Manta said reflectively. "After all that time she and I spent together in the northern regions, I might have trouble thinking of her as anything but a mother figure."

Drusni snorted. "Right. Trust me; when she's a Breeder again, you'll forget all that."

"Really," Manta murmured. "Imagine being able to re-member way back to being a Breeder."

"Hey," Drusni said, slapping his fin in mock annoyance. "In case you've forgotten, I'm exactly the same age *you* are."

"Nonsense," Manta said huffily. "You're a whole nine-day older."

"Am not," Drusni insisted. "Half a nineday at the most."

Manta smiled. "You know, I think you and Beltrenini are going to get along just fine together. Frightening though that thought might be."

"I hope so," Drusni said. "I like her a lot. And I think she'll make a great bond-mate for you."

"And besides, she's one of the pushy ones you were worried about?"

"You never heard that from me," Drusni said firmly. "And that just leaves one question."

"Which is?"

She flipped her tails. "Is it permissible to have *Four* Musketta at the same time?"

Manta smiled. "Absolutely."

"Good," Drusni said. "Then I'm ready. What was that phrase again? To the Deep, what?"

" 'To the Deep, ho,' " Manta told her.

"Right," Drusni said. "To Manta's Deep. Ho!"

With a surge of her fins, she pushed out in front of him. Manta smiled again, increasing his own speed to catch up with her. Echoes and memories of the past, indeed.

But as he gazed at Drusni, he knew that it was the present, not the past, that held the greater contentment and joy.

And it was the future that promised an infinitely greater adventure. For all of them.

Yes, indeed. Manta's Deep, ho!

"Magnetic fluctuations getting stronger," the young woman at the sensor station reported, her voice crisp and official. "We should be getting close, Commander."

"Acknowledged," the young man in the command chair replied, equally crisply. He was considerably older than the woman, of course, and undoubtedly well trained. But to Faraday, he still looked far too young to be in command of humanity's first colony ship to the stars.

But then, to Faraday, *everyone* aboard the *Matthew Raimey* looked far too young.

Well, almost everyone.

"They sure do teach parade and polish these days, don't they?" the man seated beside him murmured, the servos in his gravity suit humming softly as he shook his head. "I always worry that that much professional form is a way of painting over basic incompetence."

"Careful, Arbiter Hesse," Faraday admonished him. "You're far too young to become that cynical."

Hesse snorted. "Maybe to *you* I'm young," he countered. "To everyone else aboard, you and I are the Grand Old Spits of this trip. And you know it."

"Hey, I *could* have been the Grand Old Spit, singular," Faraday reminded him. "No one made you come along on this. You could have stayed on Earth with all that power and glory and comfort and been happy."

"You have a very warped view of happiness if you think it consists of sitting around with the rest of the Five Hundred discussing crop allocations," Hesse said dryly. "Besides, this is really nothing more than the final act of Project Changeling. How could I *not* be here? Any more than you could?"

"Nonsense," Faraday said. "I'm here solely because the Five Hundred find me awkward to have around anymore. How did you put it back then? Humanity needs a frontier for the restless and ambitious, and where the troublemakers can be dumped?"

"I think that last one was yours," Hesse pointed out. "Are you suggesting you're a troublemaker?"

"I'm certainly politically inconvenient," Faraday said. "Old heroes who refuse to fade into the sunset are like that."

He looked around the control room. "Fortunately for us, most of the rest of this particular crowd fall into the 'adventurous' category."

"Though that'll certainly change," Hesse murmured. "If this works, I imagine the Five Hundred will be commissioning a whole series of these ships. The malcontents will get their turn, never fear."

Faraday nodded. If it worked. But no one back on Earth would ever really know that, would they? All they could ever know would be whether or not the *Raimey* vanished into the Deep with Manta's group of Qanskan colonists.

They wouldn't know if the huge colony ship made it out the other end, to whatever gas giant planet this particular Deep connected to. They wouldn't know if the *Raimey* would have the power to make it up out of the planet's gravity well and into that other, distant solar system.

And they wouldn't know whether or not there would be a planet in the system that could be made into a new home for the three thousand colonists crammed together inside the *Raimey*'s pressure hull.

But then, no one aboard the ship knew those things, either. They weren't just adventurers, Faraday decided. They were the ultimate gamblers, staking everything on a single roll of the dice.

Absently, he stroked a fingertip across his myrtlewood ring. And speaking of gambling . . .

"You know, Albrecht, there's one thing I've never quite had the nerve to ask," he commented. "And just in case this doesn't work, it might be nice to know."

"Sure," Hesse said. "Ask away."

"Way back when Liadof was planning to destroy me to keep me from interfering with her plans for Changeling, she sent you to my quarters with that treasonous document for me to sign," Faraday said. "You remember?"

"Like it was yesterday," Hesse said, smiling. "I'll never forget the look on her face when she saw that 'Charlie the Carp' you'd written on the signature line."

"Me, neither," Faraday said. "And that's the question. You'd carried that paper all the way from my quarters to the Contact Room, walking along behind me. After that you had it sitting in your pocket, over in a corner, while the rest of us hashed things over with Manta and the other Qanska."

He lifted his eyebrows. "Tell me the truth. Didn't you *ever* just take it out to see whether I'd signed it properly?"

Hesse's wrinkled face was the image of perfect innocence. "General Faraday, I'm surprised at you," he said reprovingly. "I was under Arbiter Liadof's authority at that time, constrained by law to support her in every way possible. If I'd realized she'd stepped out onto an unsupported limb that way, don't you think I would have said *something* to keep her from moving still farther along it?"

He waved a servo-enhanced hand. "I mean, even with your future and the fate of the Qanska hanging in the balance, my legal obligations were perfectly clear."

"Of course," Faraday murmured. "Forgive me for even asking."

"I should think so," Hesse said. "Well, I think I'm going to the mess hall for a cup of tea. Lieutenant Seibei's optimism notwithstanding, I think it'll be a while yet before we hit the Deep. Would you care to join me?"

"Not right now," Faraday told him. "I was thinking of taking a quick nap."

There was a distant creaking of seams. "Be my guest," Hesse said, throwing a suspicious glance at the ceiling. "Though how you can sleep comfortably knowing what's out there is beyond me."

"Just a matter of practice," Faraday assured him. "I've been here before, you know."

"Right." With a hum of servos, Hesse got to his feet. "I'll see you later. Happy dreams."

"Thank you," Faraday said. "Happy tea."

Hesse waddled his way to the door and left. Shifting his attention to the bank of displays, Faraday gazed at the awesome view of the hundreds of Qanskan Wise blazing the trail ahead of them. Qanska who were leaving Jupiter, not because they had to, but because they wanted to.

It would work, he knew. It would all work. This many eager gamblers couldn't possibly be wrong.

And with the soft sounds of the beeping instruments and the muffled rumbling of the wind outside tugging soothingly at his ears, he drifted off to sleep.

ABOUT THE AUTHOR

TIMOTHY ZAHN is the author of more than a dozen original science fiction novels, including the very popular *Cobra* and *Blackcollar* series. His recent novels include *Angelmass* and *The Icarus Hunt*. He has had many short works published in the major SF magazines, including "Cascade Point," which won the Hugo Award for best novella in 1984. He is also the author of the best-selling *Star Wars: Heir to the Empire*, among other works. He lives in the Pacific Northwest.